THE True Meaning OF SMEK DAY

by Adam Rex

DISNEY • HYPERION BOOKS

NEW YORK

First Disney • Hyperion paperback edition, 2009

5 7 9 10 8 6

Printed in the United States of America

This book is set in 11-point Akzidenz Grotesk.

Library of Congress Cataloging-in-Publication Data on file.

ISBN 978-0-7868-4901-7

Visit www.hyperionbooksforchildren.com

V475-2873-0 14266

SUSTAINABLE FORESTRY INITIATIVE

Certified Chain of Custody
Promoting Sustainable Forestry

www.sfiprogram.org
SFI-01054

The SFI label applies to the text stock

For Steve Malk
And for Ms. Jennifer Lopez

Mom & me, Spring 2011

ASSIGNMENT: Write an essay titled
THE TRUE MEANING OF SMEKDAY.
What is the Smekday holiday? How has it
changed in the year since the aliens left? You
may use your own personal experiences from the
alien invasion to make your points. Feel free
to draw pictures or include photographs.

All essays will be sent to the National Time
Capsule Committee in Washington, D.C. The
committee will choose one winning essay to be
buried with the National Time Capsule, which
will be uncovered one hundred years from now.

Essays must be at least five pages long.

Gratuity Tucci
Daniel Landry Middle School
8th Grade

THE TRUE MEANING OF SMEKDAY

It was Moving Day.

Should that be capitalized? I never would have capitalized it before, but now Moving Day is a national holiday and everything, so I think it should be.

Capitalized.

Anyway.

It was Moving Day, and everybody was crazy. You remember. It was chaos; people running around with armfuls of heirloom china and photo albums, carrying food and water, carrying their dogs and kids because they forgot that their dogs and kids could carry themselves. Crazy.

I remember one lady with a mirror, and I thought, Why save a mirror? And then I watched her run down the street with it in both hands, arms outstretched like she was chasing vampires. I saw a group of white guys dressed as Indians who were setting fires and dropping tea bags down manhole covers. There was a man holding a chessboard high over his head like a waiter, looking all around him on the pavement, shouting, "Has anyone seen a black bishop?" over and over. I remember Apocalypse Hal was on the corner by the Laundromat. Hal was a neighborhood street preacher who worked at the fish and crab place next door. He wore a sandwich board sign of Bible verses and shouted angry things at passersby like "The end times are near" and "Seafood sampler $5.99." Now his sign just read "TOLD YOU SO," and he looked more anxious than angry.

"I was right," he said as I passed.

"About the fish or the apocalypse?" I asked. He followed beside me.

"Both. That should count for something, shouldn't it? That I was right?"

"I don't know."

"I didn't think it would be aliens," he mumbled. "I thought it would be angels with flaming swords. Something like that. Hey! Maybe they *are* angels! You find some pretty weird descriptions of them in the Good Book. There's this one angel in Revelation with three heads and wheels."

"I think they're just aliens, Hal," I said. "Sorry."

Apocalypse Hal stopped, but I kept walking. After a few seconds he called after me.

Hal (before the invasion)

"Hey! Girl! D'you need help carrying stuff? Where's your pretty mom?"

"I'm going to meet her right now!" I shouted. I didn't look back.

"Haven't seen her in a while!"

"'Sokay! Meeting her!" I said. It was a lie.

I was all alone because Mom had already been called up to the spaceships by signals from the mole on her neck. It was just me and my cat, and I have to tell you, I wasn't feeling too friendly toward the cat. I'd carried her for a while, but she squirmed like a bag of fish, so I set her down. When I walked she followed me, flinching whenever someone ran by or honked a car horn, which was all the time. It was *step step jerk, step step jerk*, like she was doing the conga. Eventually I looked behind, then all around, and didn't see her anymore.

"Fine," I said. "See ya, Pig." And that was that. My cat's name is Pig. I probably should have mentioned that.

The weird thing about writing for people in the future is that you don't know how much you need to explain. Do people still keep pets in your time? Do you still have cats? I'm not asking if cats still exist—right now we have a lot more cats than we know what to do with. But I'm not really writing this for people *right now*.

I mean, if anyone besides my teacher ever sees these words, it'll be because I won the contest and this essay was buried in the time capsule with the photographs and news-papers, and it was dug up a hundred years later, and now you're reading it in, like, a five-legged chair while snacking on roast planet or whatever. And it seems like you should know everything about my time already, but then I think of how little I know about *1913*, so maybe I should clear up a few things. This story starts in June 2013, about six months after the alien Boov arrived. Which also makes it six months after the aliens completely took over, and about a week after they decided the entire human race would probably be happier if they all moved to some little out-of-the-way state where they could keep out of trouble. At the time I lived in Pennsylvania. Pennsylvania was on the eastern side of the United States. The United States was this big country where everybody wore funny T-shirts and ate too much.

I'd been living by myself after Mom left. I didn't want anyone to know. I had learned to drive our car short distances by nailing cans of corn to my church shoes so I could reach the pedals. I made a lot of mistakes at first, and if anyone was walking on the sidewalk at 49th and Pine after dark on March 3rd, 2013, I owe you an apology.

But eventually I got really good. Like, NASCAR good. So, while most people were reporting to the Boovish rocketpods for relocation to Florida, I figured I'd drive there myself, with no help from anyone. I got directions off the Internet, which wasn't as easy as it used to be, because the Boov had started shutting it down. But the route looked easy. The website said it would take three days, but most drivers weren't as good as I was, and they wouldn't be eating frosting and root beer so they could drive nonstop, either. I worked my way through knots of people, past a woman with a baby in a crystal punch bowl, past a man carrying rotting boxes that bled baseball cards all over the streets, and finally to the community tennis courts, where I'd left the car.

It was a little hatchback, the size and color of a refrigerator and only about twice as fast. But it didn't use much gas, and I didn't have much money. I'd drained our bank account, and there was less than I'd expected in the rainy-day fund that Mom had kept at the bottom of an underwear drawer in a panty hose egg labeled "DEAD SPIDERS." As if I hadn't always known it was there. As if I wouldn't have wanted to look at dead spiders.

I threw the camera bag and backpacks into the backseat, and suddenly got a dead weight in my stomach from the loneliness of it all. I turned my head this way and that, looking past the panicky people. Looking past a man wearing oven mitts and holding a pot roast, for God's sake, pardon my language. I don't know what or who I was looking for— certainly not the cat. But I called her anyway.

"Pig!" I yelled. "PIIIIIIIIIG!"

Shouting "Pig" outdoors usually attracts some attention, but no one paid me any that day. Actually, on my third "Pig," one guy ducked, but I'm still not sure what that was about.

Anyway, just as I was turning to get in the car, a fat gray cat came barreling across the street and leaped up onto the dashboard. She turned around and stretched her cheek out for a scratch.

"Oh," I said. "Okay. I guess you can come. But you'll have to do your business at rest stops."

Pig purred.

By this point, I was thinking it would be nice to have

Pig

some company, as I didn't expect to see anyone else for a couple days. I assumed the highways would be empty, you see, what with nearly everybody taking the rocketpods.

I was right and I was wrong.

Did you know that cats don't like riding in cars? They don't, or at least mine didn't. Before we started out, I reset the trip odometer, so I know that Pig spent the first twenty-two and a half miles staring out the rear windshield and hissing. She clung to the headrest of the passenger seat like a Halloween decoration, back arched and poofy.

"Calm down!" I shouted as I dodged abandoned cars on the highway. "I'm a *really good driver!*"

She stopped hissing and started growling, sort of. You know how cats growl. Like pigeons who smoke too much.

"I could have left you home, you traitor. You could have moved in with your *precious Boov.*"

I have no trouble looking at a cat and steering at the same time, but for some reason the car sort of hopped over a skin of tire tread in the road, and Pig squealed and shot off the headrest, looped around the backseat a couple of times, and darted over the gearshift, finally curling into a ball under the brake pedal.

"Uh-oh," I muttered. I pressed the brake gently, trying to coax her out. She hissed and took a swipe at the can of corn under my shoe.

I looked up at the road, dodged an empty motorcycle, then glanced back down at my feet.

"C'mon, Pig," I said reassuringly (while swerving to avoid a minivan). "Come on out . . . (oil tanker) . . . I'll give you a treat!" (Sports car. Why had everyone just left their cars?)

"Mrrr?" said Pig.

"Yeah! You want a treat? Treat? Treat?" I lilted over and over like a songbird.

Pig still hadn't moved, but I had a stretch of clear road. I was just keeping my eye on a big rig on the left, in the distance, and that's when I saw something move. It hung in the air over the trailer, lazily bobbing up and down. It was a mass of bubbles; soap bubbles; maybe. But some were the size of softballs, and others like basketballs, and they all stuck and interlaced together to make a star shape as big as a washing machine. Like this:

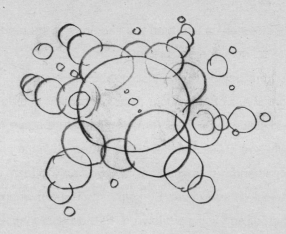

It didn't move with the breeze, it just dipped and rose slightly, as though tethered with invisible string to the big rig's smokestack. And as my eyes traced down the smokestack, I saw something else. Or some*one* else, standing on the road.

"There's a guy or something," I said, as much to myself as to Pig. The guy, or woman, or whatever, was wearing bright safety orange, easy to see, and maybe some kind of clear plastic helmet, and I thought, *Radiation suit?* and then we got close enough to see it was one of *them*. A Boov.

"Okay . . . okay," I whispered, and pulled the car as far to the right as I could without hitting the barricade.

The Boov noticed my approach and turned that weird body to face me. The sun was glinting off its helmet, but I think it raised its arm, palm out in a way that must be recognized across the galaxy as *stop*. Then again, it was hard to tell. They had such small arms.

I couldn't stop, but I could take my foot off the gas, so I

slowly lost speed as I hugged the shoulder of the road and said Hail Marys under my breath.

We were getting really close now, close enough to see that awful mess of legs under the Boov's body, and the broad, flat head inside the helmet. It made its gesture again, more forcefully, and it was definitely *stop*. I lifted my hand in return and smiled and waved and kept my eyes on the road. I didn't want to look at it anymore. So I almost missed it when the Boov's other arm whipped down to its side and snapped back up with something in its hand. All at once I recognized the thing from the TV, one of those horrible guns you saw a lot of when we'd still been trying to fight. Terrible guns that didn't even make a noise, or a light. They just pointed at you and then half your body was gone, just like that.

Well, one thing I *could* still do was hit the gas. I ducked and slammed on the pedal, and the car lurched forward, not nearly fast enough, scraping the highway barricade and sending up sparks like the Fourth of July.

The Boov shouted something I couldn't hear or understand. I tried to make a poor target of myself, swerving back and forth and looking up just in time to avoid hitting an SUV. I looked out at my right-side mirror and saw that it had been wrenched off by the barricade, so I looked at my rearview mirror and noticed that most of the SUV wasn't there anymore, a huge chunk scooped out as clean as ice cream, and so I tried to look at my left-side mirror, but it wasn't there anymore, either. I turned and saw the Boov fading into the distance, far away now. It wasn't chasing me.

"Oh boy, Pig," I said softly, and Pig crawled out from under the brake like it wasn't anything to her one way or the other.

A minute later I pulled to the side of the road and stopped, and looked around at the car. The Boov gun had disintegrated my mirror, and there was a hole in the left rear window where the beam had entered the car. I craned my neck and saw there was an even bigger hole in the rear windshield where it'd left. Each hole was as perfect as could be, like a biscuit cutter through dough.

"I hate them," I said. "I *hate* them. We were really lucky, Pig."

But Pig didn't hear. She was stretched out on the passenger seat, asleep.

Why did the Boov shoot? I didn't know—all I was doing was driving to Florida, like they wanted. But at mile forty-eight I found out why nobody else was on the road. There wasn't one.

We were curving around a bend when the car bucked over a pothole. My seat belt went taut as I jerked forward and back, pain twisting up my neck. Pig rolled off her seat, woke up briefly on the floor of the car, and fell back asleep where she was.

I swerved around chunks of asphalt and rounded

something that was less like a pothole and more like an empty swimming pool. Then another curve, and the road was gone. My little car dropped off a shelf of pavement into a crater of earth and tar, and I jiggled the steering wheel as I mashed my corn-can foot against the brake. We skidded and plowed through twisted metal curlicues that were once a barricade, then slid down the embankment, rolled over twice, and came to an abrupt stop in a MoPo parking lot.

The air around the car was orange with dust. I clutched the steering wheel like a life preserver. Pig was sprawled on her back in the crook where the windshield meets the dash. Our eyes met, and she gave me a short hiss.

So that was it. Nobody was taking their cars because the Boov had destroyed the highways. Of course they had.

I wearily unbuckled myself and fell out of the car. Pig followed and stretched and darted off after a bug.

I nearly puked. Can I say that in a school paper? That I puked? Because when I said "nearly," what I really meant was "repeatedly."

While I was bent over I noticed we'd blown a tire. I wasn't sure if there was a spare, but it didn't matter much one way or the other since I didn't know how to change it. All Mom had ever taught me about vehicle maintenance was the number of a tow truck to call if you stopped moving forward.

Well, it was a long shot, but I figured I might as well try to call *somebody*. I wasn't likely to get any answer, but we were too far from home to walk back now. I popped open the glove box and retrieved the emergency cell phone that only had one hour of talking time on it and was NOT A TOY. I flipped it open and pushed the power button, and it suddenly crackled to life. Strange voices gibbered back and forth on the other end.

"But I didn't even dial yet," I mumbled, and the voices stopped. "Hello?" I said.

The voices came again in bleats and pops, like a lamb stepping on bubble wrap. They grew louder, more agitated.

I quickly hit the power button again and flapped the phone shut. It was like something gross and alien in my hand now, so I pushed it back into the glove box and put a car manual on top of it.

Car manual, I thought. It might tell me how to change the tire. No. Later. It can wait.

I sat down. The sky was clear again, and blue. In the distance was a small town I didn't know. The tallest building was an old stone church, and this had a clean bite taken out of its bell tower. Nearby I could see broken telephone poles hanging like limp marionettes. I'd been sitting long enough.

"Maybe there's still some food in the MoPo store," I said brightly, looking for Pig.

For you time-capsule types, MoPo was something called a convenience store, as in, "The soda is conveniently located right next to the doughnuts and lottery tickets." People who

want to understand better how the human race was conquered so easily need to study those stores. Almost everything inside was filled with sugar, cheese, or weight-loss tips.

It was dark inside, but I'd expected that. Pig followed me
to the door, which opened with a jingle, and into the empty
store. The shelves were nearly bare, probably looted, except
for some moldy bread and yogurt health snacks called
NutriZone Extreme FitnessPlus Blaster Bars with Calcium.
There was also a bag and a few tins of cat food, which was
nice. I sat on the cold linoleum floor and ate one of the pink
health bars, and Pig had a tin of Sea Captain's Entree.

"I don't think we're going to make it to Florida," I said.

"Mao?"

"Florida. That's where we're going. Big state, full of
oranges."

Pig went back to her food, and I took another bite of
what I was beginning to think was just a big eraser.

"Maybe we can stay here. We're pretty far outside the city.
The Boov might not even notice."

"Mao."

"Sure we could. We could live in someone's house. Or a
hotel. And the town's probably full of canned food."

"Mao mao?"

"Fine. You're so smart, give me one reason why it wouldn't
work."

"Mao."

"Oh, you say that about everything."

Pig purred and settled down for a nap. I leaned back against an ATM and shut my eyes against the setting sun. I don't remember falling asleep, but it was dark outside when I woke with a loaf of bread under my head and heard the jingle of the front door.

I gasped for breath and scampered under a shelf. Too late I remembered Pig, who was nowhere to be seen. Something moved through the vacant store, its footsteps like a drumroll.

Go away, go away, I chanted in my head at what I was sure was a Boov. It skibbered past my row of shelves, and I got a look at its cluster of tiny elephant legs, clad in a light blue rubber suit. Boov. Probably sent to find me.

Then the drumroll stopped. A wet, nasally voice said, "Oh. Hello, kitten."

Pig.

"How did you come to be inside of the MoPo?"

I heard Pig purr loudly, the skunk. She was probably rubbing up against each one of its eight legs.

"Did someone . . . let you to inside, hm?"

My heart pounded. As if Pig might say, *Yeah, Gratuity did. Aisle five.*

"Perhaps you are being hungry," the Boov told Pig. "Would you enjoy to join me in a jar of cough syrup?"

The drumroll resumed. They were moving again. I poked

my neck out of the shelf in time to see them walk through a door marked EMPLOYEES ONLY.

I slid out and ran, unthinking, for the door. I pushed through with a shove and a tinkling sound and thought, Oh, yeah. The bell. A quick look behind me and I was off. I sped to the car, retrieved my bag, and made for a row of hedges that lined the parking lot. I was safely behind them and watching through a gap in the leaves just in time to see the Boov peek out of the MoPo. He, it, squeezed through the door and looked from side to side, scanning the lot for whatever had been dumb enough to forget the door jingled. Then he gave a start when he saw my car, and smiled back at Pig. I could see her though the door, her front paws up on the glass.

"Hello, hm?" the Boov shouted. He looked up toward the ruined highway and whistled through his nose.

I tried to make myself as small as possible, tried to stop my heart from pounding, or the blood from thrumming in my ears. The Boov pattered across the asphalt toward something new, something I hadn't noticed before.

In the corner of the lot was this crazy-looking thing, like a huge spool of thread with antlers. It was all plasticky and blue, and it was hanging in the air, about six inches above the ground.

"I would not to hurt you!" the Boov shouted again. "If you would enjoy to be my guest, there is enough cough syrup and teething biscuits for everyone!"

Bubble
thing

It, he, whatever, hopped his squat body atop the big spool, clamping down around the edges with his little elephant legs. His tiny frog arms reached up and gripped the antlers, and with a few flicks and twists, the blue plastic thing rose a foot in the air and sailed up the hill of shale and weeds to the highway.

"'Allo!" he shouted as he drifted away. "There is no to fear! The Boov are no longer eating you people!"

The Boov's weird little scooter disappeared over the ridge, and I darted out toward the store—for what? To get Pig? She probably preferred to stay with the Boov. But she was all I had, and the car wouldn't drive on a flat tire, and my only thought was to vanish into this little town and hope the Boov didn't try too hard to find me.

"Time to go, Pig," I said as I burst into the MoPo, my guts jangling like a nervous doorbell. She tried to slip out the door, after the alien, I guess, but I scooped her up.

"Stupid cat."

I pushed all the cat food and health bars into my bag and dashed out to the car. One last check to make certain I had everything, then I was gone. At the passenger door I remembered the cell phone, and wondered if I should take it, and it was about that time that I got a wicked idea.

Pig squirmed in my arms.

"Wrooowr'ftt," she said.

I laughed. "Don't worry. We're not going anywhere. We'll just march into the store and wait for your friend to come back."

Pig hissed quietly to herself.

Let me tell you how I thought this next part happened. I figured the Boov hovered around the old highway for a bit, *dum de dum*, thinking, *I sure for to am hoping I find Gratuity or whoever it am being, I eat her or I am to be turning her in or beaming her to Florida or something*, then the Boov maybe checked around the MoPo and probably in my car, and then he thought, *Ho hum, it am probably being just my imagination, there am no girl or whatever, me sure am stupid, sheep noise bubble wrap bubble wrap.*

Then the Boov parked his antler spool and went back

inside the MoPo, and wondered where Pig was, and when the door stopped jingling, he heard something. So he thought, *What am that?* and went to investigate. And as he neared the frozen food section, he could maybe tell it was the voices of other Boov, even though he was so stupid. And he saw there was a freezer door standing open that hadn't been open before, so he went right over to it and peeked in and made a sheep noise. Maybe at that moment he noticed all the freezer shelves on the floor next to my cell phone, but it didn't matter, because that was right when I kicked his alien butt inside and barred the door shut with a broom handle.

The Boov hopped up and down and turned to face me. I was happy to see he looked pretty startled, or frightened, and he pressed his thick face against the glass to get a good look at his captor. I did a little dance.

"What for are you did this?" he said. I think that's what he said. It was hard to hear through the glass. I wondered, suddenly, if he'd run out of air after a while. The thought made me uneasy, and I had to remind myself of the situation I was in.

"Good," I whispered. "I hope he does run out of air." I wished he could have been really cold in there, too, but there wasn't any electricity.

"What?" said the Boov faintly. "What said you?" His eyes darted from side to side like little fish. His frog fingers pawed at the glass.

"I said, you're getting what you deserve! You stole my mom, so I get to steal one of you!"

"What?"

"You stole my mom!"

"Mimom?"

"MY . . . MOM!"

The Boov seemed to think about this for a second, then his eyes lit.

"Ahh. '*My mom*'!" he said happily. "What is it about her, now?"

I shouted and kicked the glass.

"Aha." The Boov nodded as if I'd said something important. "Ah. So . . . can I come into the out now?"

"No!" I yelled. "You can not come into the out. You can never come into the out ever again!"

At this, the Boov looked genuinely surprised, and panicked.

"Then . . . then . . . I will have onto shoot with my gun!"

I jumped back, palms up. In all the excitement, I hadn't thought of that. My eyes darted to where his hips would be, if he'd had any. I frowned.

"You don't even have a gun!"

"Yes! YES!" he shouted, nodding furiously, as though I'd somehow proven his point. "NO GUN! So I will have to . . . have to . . ."

His whole body trembled.

"... SHOOT FORTH THE LASERS FROM MY EYE-BALLS!"

I fell into a row of shelves. That one was new to me.

"Shoot forth the lasers?"

"SHOOT FORTH THE LASERS!"

"You can do that?"

The Boov hesitated. His eyes quivered. After a few seconds he replied, "Yes."

I squinted. "Well, if you shoot your eye lasers, then I'll have no choice but to ... EXPLODE YOUR HEAD!"

"You humans can not to ex—"

"We can! We can too! We just don't much. It's considered rude."

The Boov thought about this for a moment.

"Then ... we are needing a ... truce. You are not to exploding heads, and I will to not do my DEVASTATING EYE LASERS."

"Okay," I agreed. "Truce."

"Truce."

A few moments passed in the utter quiet of the store.

"Soo ... can I come into the out n—"

"No!"

The Boov pointed over my head, tapping his fingertip against the glass.

"I can to fixing your car. I seen it is the broken."

I folded my arms. "What would a Boov know about fixing cars?"

He huffed. "I am Chief Maintenance Officer Boov. I can to fix everything! I can surely to fix primitive humanscar."

I didn't like that crack about my car, but it did need fixing.

"How do I know you'll do anything? You'll probably just call your friends and cart me off to Florida."

The Boov furrowed what might have been his forehead. "Do not you *want* to go to Florida? Is where your people is to be. *All* humans decide to move on to Florida."

"Hey! I don't think *we* got to decide anything," I said.

"Yes!" the Boov answered. "Florida!"

I sighed and paced the aisle. When I looked back at the freezer case, I saw the Boov had picked up my cell phone.

"I could talk to them," he said gravely. "I could call to them right now."

It was true. He could.

I slid the broom handle free of the door and opened it. The Boov lunged forward, and I instantly regretted everything, except then I realized he wasn't attacking me. It must have been a hug, because I can't think of any better word for it.

"See?" he said. "Boov and humanskind can be friend. I always say!"

I patted him gingerly.

It sounds crazy, I know that, but suddenly I was searching the little town for supplies while the Boov worked on my car. I don't think I have to say at this point that Pig stayed with him.

I hit five abandoned stores and found crackers, diet milk shakes, bottled water, really hard bagels, Honey Frosted Snox, tomato paste, dry pasta, a bucket of something called TUB! that came with its own spoon, and Lite Choconilla Froot Bites, which broke my usual rule against eating anything that was misspelled. The Boov had told me some things he liked, so I also carried a basket of breath mints, cornstarch, yeast, bouillon cubes, mint dental floss, and typing paper.

"Hey, Boov!" I shouted on my return. I could see him under the car, banging away. The car, I should mention, now sported three extra antennas. The holes in the windows were somehow not there anymore. There were tubes and hoses connecting certain parts of the car to certain other parts of the car, and a few of what I can only describe as fins. These appeared to be made from metal the Boov had salvaged from the convenience store. One of them showed a picture of a frozen drink and the word "Slushious."

There was an open toolbox, and the tools were every-where, all of them strange.

"This seems like an awful lot of trouble for one flat tire," I said.

The Boov stuck out his head.

"Flat tire?"

I stared back blankly for a second, then walked around to the other side. The tire was still flat.

"The car, it should to hover much better now!" he called happily.

"Hover?" I answered. "Hover *better*? It didn't hover at *all* before!"

"Hm," the Boov said, looking down. "So *this* is why the wheels are so dirty."

"Probably."

"Sooo, it did to roll?"

"Yes," I said crisply. "It rolled. On the ground."

The Boov thought about this for a long few seconds.

"But . . . how did it to roll with this flat tire?"

I dropped the basket and sat down. "It doesn't matter," I said.

"Well," the Boov replied. "It will to hover wicked good now. I used parts fromto my own vehicle."

He startled me at this point, the way he said "wicked." It was slang. Something I didn't expect him to use. And it wasn't even popular slang. Nobody said it anymore. Nobody but my mom, and sometimes me. I guess it made me think of Mom, and I guess it made me a little angry.

"Eat your dental floss, Boov," I said, and kicked him the basket. He seemed to think nothing of it, and did as I said, sucking up strings of floss like spaghetti.

"You do not to say it right," he said finally.

"Say what?"

"'Boov.' The way you says it, it is too short. You must to draw it out, like as a long breath. 'Bo-o-ov.'"

J. Lo examines the camera

After a moment I swallowed my anger and gave it a try.

"Booov."

"No. Bo-o-ov."

"Bo-o-o-o-ov."

The Boov frowned. "Now you sound like sheep."

I shook my head. "Fine. So what's your name? I'll call you that."

"Ah, no," the Boov replied. "For humansgirl to correctly be pronouncing my name, you would need two heads. But, as a human name, I have to chosen 'J.Lo.'"

I stifled a laugh. "J.Lo? Your Earth name is J.Lo?"

"Ah-ah," J.Lo corrected. "Not 'Earth.' 'Smekland.'"

"What do you mean, 'Smekland'?"

"That is the thing what we have named this planet. Smekland. As to tribute to our glorious leader, Captain Smek."

"Wait." I shook my head. "Whoa. You can't just rename the planet."

"Peoples who discover places gets to name it."

"But it's *called* Earth. It's *always* been called Earth."

J.Lo smiled condescendingly. I wanted to hit him.

"You humans live too much in the pasttime. We did land onto Smekland a long time ago."

"You landed last Christmas!"

"Ah-ah. Not 'Christmas.' 'Smekday.'"

"Smekday?"

"Smekday."

* * *

So anyway, that was how I learned the true meaning of Smekday. This Boov named J.Lo told me. The Boov didn't like us celebrating our holidays, so they replaced them all with new ones. Christmas was renamed after Captain Smek, their leader, who had discovered a New World for the Boov, which was Earth. I mean Smekland.

Whatever. The End.

Gratuity—

Interesting style overall, but I'm afraid you
didn't really fulfill the assignment. When the
judges from the National Time Capsule Committee
read our stories, they'll be looking for what
Smekday means to us, not to the aliens.
Remember: the capsule will be dug up a hundred
years from now, and the people of the future
won't know what it was like to live during the
invasion. If your essay wins the contest,
they'll be reading it to find that out.

Perhaps if you began before the Boov came?
There is still some time to rework your
composition before the contest entries need to
be sent. If you'd like to try again, I'll
consider it for extra credit.

Grade: C+

Gratuity Tucci
Daniel Landry Middle School
8th Grade

THE TRUE MEANING OF SMEKDAY

PART 2:

-or-

How I Learned to Stop Worrying and Love the Boov

Okay. Starting before the Boov came.

I guess I really need to begin almost two years ago. This was when my mom got the mole on her neck. This was when she was abducted.

I didn't see it happen, naturally. That's how it is with these things. Nobody ever gets abducted at a football game, or at church, or right after Kevin Frompky knocks all your books out of your hands between classes and everybody's looking and laughing and you have no choice but to sock him in the eye.

Or whatever.

No, people always get abducted while they're driving on empty highways late at night, or from their bedrooms while

they're sleeping, and they're returned before anyone knows they're gone. I know this; I've checked.

That's how it was for Mom. She burst into my room one morning, wild-eyed, hair a fright, and told me to look at her neck.

I blinked away sleep and stared where she pointed. I did this without question, because it had only been days since she'd woken me to say that Tom Jones was on the morning show, or that the paper had a "wicked good coupon" for dress shields.

"What am I looking at?" I said blearily.

"The mole," Mom said. "The *mole!*"

I looked. There was certainly a mole, brown and wrinkly, like a bubble on a pizza. It was right in the middle of the neck, on her backbone.

"'Sfantastic," I said, yawning. "Good mole."

the Mole

"You don't understand," Mom said, turning; and the look in her eye made me wake up a little. "It was put there! Last night!"

I blinked a couple of times.

"By the aliens!" she finished frantically.

I was so awake now. I looked closer. I poked it with my finger.

"I don't think you're supposed to touch it," Mom said quickly, and jerked away. "I feel really veryvery strongly that you shouldn't touch it."

There was something strange about Mom's voice just then. Something kind of flat and dull. "Okay," I said. "Sorry.

"So . . . what do you mean 'aliens'?"

Mom got up and walked around the room. Her voice sounded normal now, if not a little overwrought. She explained that they woke her up last night, two of them, and gave her a shot of something in the arm. She showed me, and there was definitely some kind of red dot on the inside of her right elbow. She knew they'd taken her outside, but she'd drifted off to sleep for a minute, and woke up in a large, shimmering room.

"Wait a minute," I said. "You fell asleep? How could you fall asleep in the middle of this?"

"I don't know," Mom answered, shaking her head. "I wasn't afraid, Turtlebear. I just wasn't. I was full of calm."

I had my own ideas about what she was full of, but I kept them to myself.

Mom went on to explain that the aliens, a lot of them now, had brought her aboard their ship to fold some laundry. They related, not with words but with complicated hand gestures, that they were really impressed with her laundry folding skills. She was guided to a table piled with bright, rubbery suits with tiny sleeves and too many legs. So she got to work. As she folded, she happened to notice another human, a Hispanic man, she said, far off at the other end of the room. They had him opening pickle jars. She thought she ought to say something, say hello, but there was so much folding to do, and then suddenly she felt a hot pain on the back of her neck, and she blacked out. When she woke it was morning.

"They put it on my neck. With some kind of mole gun," Mom said, nodding to herself.

"But . . . why?" I asked. "Why would a race of . . . of intelligent beings travel across the galaxy just to give people moles?"

Mom looked a little hurt. "*I* don't know. How should *I* know? But it wasn't there yesterday! You have to admit it wasn't there yesterday."

I looked at it, trying to remember. But who remembers a mole?

"Oh, Turtlebear, you believe me, don't you?"

Let me tell you what I didn't say. I didn't say it was all a bad dream. I didn't say she's been working too hard and eating too much cheese right before bed. I didn't tell her for the fiftieth time that I wished she didn't take those pills to help her sleep.

What I did say was I believed her, because that was how things worked in our house. When she'd return from the grocer's where she worked with a bundle of spoiled meat she'd saved from the Dumpster, I'd tell her it looked delicious. Then I'd throw it away. When I'd get home from school and find she'd blown our savings on an eight-hundred-dollar vacuum she'd bought from a door-to-door salesman, I'd tell her how great it was. Then I'd get on the phone and get our money back. I said I believed her about the aliens.

"Thank you, Turtlebear. Sweet girl," she said, hugging me tight. "I knew you would."

Maybe I should explain about the whole "Turtlebear" thing. It's a family nickname, apparently, going way back. My birth certificate says "Gratuity Tucci," but Mom's called me Turtlebear ever since she learned that "gratuity" didn't mean what she thought it did. My friends call me Tip.

I guess I'm telling you all this as a way of explaining about my mom. When people ask me about her, I say she's very pretty. When they ask if she's smart like me, I say she's very pretty.

"Sweet girl," Mom whispered, rocking back and forth. I hugged her back, my face inches from that mole.

There are companies that claim to make a greeting card for every occasion. If any of them are reading this, I couldn't find a "Sorry all your friends deserted you after your alien abduction" card when I needed one.

And poor Mom, she just couldn't keep her mouth shut. She told everyone at the grocery store about the whole thing. Even the laundry folding. *Especially* the laundry folding, like it was a really important detail. I wonder now if the aliens didn't do things like that on purpose, to make abductees sound more crazy.

I was kidnapped by aliens and they made me fold laundry.

I was abducted and the aliens made me clean their rain gutters.

You see what I mean?

So people stopped talking to her. Mom and the other ladies at the store usually went out together on Wednesdays for enormous margaritas served in ceramic sombreros. But one by one they made their excuses, and Mom suddenly had her Wednesdays free. One week she made me her spy, and I crept outside the Wall Street Taco Exchange and peeped through the windows. Sure enough, the grocery store ladies were there, swilling out of Mexican hats and laughing together. And I swear I could tell they were laughing about Mom.

"Were they there?" she asked when I returned to the car. "You didn't see them, right?"

I slumped in my seat. "Right," I said.

It was another Wednesday, actually, when I noticed that the mole had changed. I know it was a Wednesday because it was Brownies-and-Movies-Wherein-Guys-Take-Their-Shirts-Off Night, which had replaced Margarita Night when it became clear that the grocery ladies would either have evening dentist appointments or unexplained family emergencies every Wednesday from now until the End of the World.

The End of the World, of course, was only a few months away at this point. Even so that's still a lot of dentist appointments.

Anyway.

So the brownies were made, and the leading man had just removed his shirt to go swimming, and I was playing with Mom's hair when I saw it. The mole. It was easily twice as large, and a weird sort of purply color.

I held my breath. "When . . . did this happen?" I asked.

"Hmm?"

"When did it get . . . like this?"

Mom turned her head to look at me. "When did what get like what, Turtlebear?"

"Your mole. It's bigger," I said, and I pressed my fingertip into it.

Mom shot up from the floor, her face all tight and pinched.

"You shouldn't touch it," she said flatly. "It's not a toy."

I was a little offended. "I *know* it's not a toy. Of course it isn't. It's gross. Who would want a gross toy? Well, maybe boys would, but that's none of *my* business—"

"Just don't touch it," Mom snapped, and tore off into the kitchen. And this is when, as she was walking away, I saw the mole *glow.* Just for a second. It was bright red, like a Christmas light.

"Whoa!" I shouted after her. "Wait a minute!" I ran into the kitchen, and Mom turned to meet me.

"It's okay, baby," she said. "I'm not really mad, I just—"

"Shut up!" I said. "I have to tell you—"

"Don't you tell me to shut up. YOU shut up."

"Mom—"

"I don't like this behavior. You're acting very weird . . . ly. Weirdly. Is it weird or weirdly?"

"Mom, you have got to get that mole removed," I said.

"What? Why?" she said, looking confused. "What?"

"It's bigger than before, and it's changed color," I said. "Moles that change size and color, that's like, a sure sign of cancer."

Mom began vigorously shaking her head. "I'm not going to let some quack hack me to pieces," she said.

"But a second ago *I saw it glow*!"

There was a heavy silence in the kitchen. Mom looked at me like I had feet growing out of my head.

"Glowing moles are definitely cancerous," I added. I was pretty sure this was a lie, but I hate losing arguments.

Mom hesitated. Then she reached up to her spine and

touched the mole gingerly. She didn't like what she found, I guess, because her hand snapped back and she began to shake her head again, violently, like she had swimmer's ear. Like she was trying to shake a thought right out of her.

"I'm the grown-up, and you're the baby," she said finally, and left the kitchen. It was how a lot of our fights ended. Not this time.

"We can't just ignore this," I said slowly, sweetly. "We have to be brave and go to the doctor. Do you remember Dr. Phillips? You thought he was going to be scary, but everything turned out all—"

"Jesus, Gratuity, stop talking to me like that," said Mom, shooing me away. "This'll work itself out."

I huffed. "Oh, *yeah*. What, like everything else does around here? Yeah, everything else works out, and you never have to worry or think about it or do a thing. But you know why this is different? Because *I can't fix it this time!*"

"Oh, Gra—Turtlebear, don't—"

"I need you to cooperate because *I'm* not a doctor yet, and I can't take *your* mole to have it looked at without *you* attached to it, so I need you to just do as I say!"

Mom just stood there in a door frame for a really long time looking angry, then something like sad, then angry again.

"We'll talk in the morning!" she said, and slammed the door. Only, our doors were cheap and lightweight and about as good to slam as a wiffle ball is to hit.

41

"Mom . . ." I sighed. "Mom, you're—"

The door opened again, and she brushed past me to the other end of the hall.

"I knew it was your room," she mumbled.

The Shirtless Man Movie had clearly been ruined, so we both went to bed early. But I awoke three hours later on account of the twelve glasses of water I'd had before bed. After a few minutes I was seated at the computer.

I turned it on. I forgot that ours was one of those computers that makes a sound like a choir saying "Ahh" when you turn it on.

"Shh," I hissed, pressing my hands over the speakers. "Stupid computer."

I peeked out into the hall. Lights off, no sounds. I settled back into my chair and started the web browser, and went to Doc.Com, one of those medical websites. It loaded a cover story about whooping cough, and a banner ad that suggested I ask my doctor if Chubusil was right for me, and then finally the part where I could enter Mom's symptoms. I typed:

mole changes size color

After a moment, I added:

glows

and hit RETURN.

The search turned up something like 140 articles, with names like "Do I Have Cancer?" and "Oh, No!

Cancer?" and "Okay, So It's Cancer, Now What?"

Excited, I clicked on the best match and began to read. Maybe moles *do* glow, I thought. But the first item didn't mention it. Neither did the second. I read five articles before realizing my search had only turned up results for the words mole, changes, size, and color, except for one that mentioned getting a "healthy glow" in an essay about tanning salons. No mention of glowing moles.

You know that part in the story where the character thinks, *I bet I didn't really see a ghost after all. I bet it was just a sheet. Wearing chains. Floating through our pantry. Shrieking. I bet it was just my imagination.* You know how you always kind of hate characters who think that? You hate them, and you know you'd never be so stupid not to know a ghost when you saw one, especially when the title of your story is *The Shrieking Specter*, for God's sake, pardon my language.

This is that part of the story.

You see, the problem is, you don't *know* you're in a story. You think you're just some kid. And you don't want to believe in the mole, or the ghost, or whatever it is when it's your turn.

I decided then and there that the mole had not glowed. It was a trick of the light, or a hallucination, or smoke and mirrors, or any one of those things people say that are supposed to explain what happened but don't. Anyway, I stopped believing the mole glowed. I *had* to.

It didn't matter, because I still believed the thing had changed size and color, and that was scary enough. I shut down the computer and crept back down the hall. Pig followed, purring and making little figure eights around my legs. She probably thought she was getting an early breakfast, and when I didn't acknowledge her she meowed.

For a moment I thought I'd been caught when I heard Mom's voice from her bedroom. I froze in place, and her voice went on, one word, pause, one word, pause, like she was calling a bingo game. I couldn't help but be curious, so I padded slowly to her bedroom door. It was ajar, and I put an ear to the crack.

"Tractor," said Mom.

Tractor? I looked in.

"Gorilla," she continued, then, "Arancia . . . Domino . . . Emendare . . . Vision . . . Apparently . . . Mouse . . ."

She was lying on her back, talking in her sleep. In English and Italian. And dreaming about the weirdest roll call ever.

I listened a while longer, expecting her to stop, or to say something sensible. I don't know much Italian, but I knew enough to realize the Italian-to-English dictionary wasn't going to make any sense out of what I was hearing.

"Lasagna," said Mom.

"Good night," said I, and went back to bed.

The next day I made Mom an appointment to see a dermatologist. The appointment nurse said they could have a look at her in about a month, and I was sort of politely rude about this, and after a really vigorous conversation she moved it up to next week.

Next week. I'll get her there somehow, I thought as I put down the phone; and I couldn't have been happier, because I didn't know Mom would be gone in four days.

Let me just leap ahead those four days now, because there's really nothing to say about them. They were filled with meals and sleep and arguments with Mom, as though she weren't about to be taken, as though everything weren't about to change. We went shopping, we wrapped presents, went to Mass, put up the white plastic Christmas tree. If my life were a movie, you could expect that musical montage of scenes right now, the kind lazy directors use to show time passing. You know: there would be a bunch of funny, short clips of Mom and me at the store trying on different outfits, funny hats,

and now we're trying to make eggnog, but the lid comes off
the blender and the stuff splatters the walls and us, and we're

laughing, and now cut to us Christmas caroling outside someone's house, but, whoops! they're Jews, and all the while

"Jingle Bell Rock" or something is playing. And the next thing
you know, it's four days later. It was Christmas Eve, in fact,

but I don't want to dwell on that. This isn't a Christmas story. It's a Smekday story.

It was nighttime when it happened. I was in bed, but I wasn't sleeping. I was just lying awake, listening to the noise of cars and people speaking too loudly on the street, and thinking about something. Okay, I suppose I was probably thinking about what I was going to get for Christmas the next day, and it was hard not to. Though I guess Mom was *trying* to be quiet in the living room, it was plainly obvious that she was still up, stuffing my stocking with candy and CDs and things, or wrapping a present. After a while the noises drifted off, and I think I did, too. I hadn't been sleeping long, before I was startled awake by a big noise.

Sckruuuup

went the noise, from above, from up on the roof. And yes, for a moment I thought, Santa Claus? So sue me.

I got very *'Twas the Night Before Christmas* at this point as I stumbled to the window to see what had happened. That's when I got my first glimpse: a huge accordion hose, like a vacuum cleaner attachment, swinging down from the roof and sailing off into the darkness. I looked up quickly to see what it was attached to, but I saw only a huge dark shape high in the sky. In its wake, every car alarm in the neighborhood wailed, and every dog barked.

I heard Mom shout, *"Cannoli!"* from the living room.

Then, *"Earphones!"*

I ran out into the hall and stopped at the doorway.

"Eggbeater!"

Mom had fallen asleep stuffing my stocking. And she must have *really* fallen asleep, because she was still wearing the stocking up to her elbow. She was sitting on the floor, propped against the futon, bits of candy and ribbon spiraled around her.

"Chessboard!"

It probably goes without saying that she was chanting words like before. Only now she was shouting, red-faced, with her eyes shut tight.

"Granata!"

I crept, heart pounding, to her side, and got a good look at the mole. It was blinking, definitely blinking, purple and red and green, over and over and over.

"Somewhat!"

"Mom . . . ?" I said.

"Cookies!" she answered.

"Mom! Mom, wake up!"

"Annunciare!"

I shook her arm, the one without the stocking on it, but her eyes stayed closed.

"Mom!" I shouted.

"Mom!" Mom shouted. I think this was just a coincidence.

I don't really remember everything else she yelled. I didn't know I'd be asked to write it all down someday. Probably there were some nouns and verbs and things, there was definitely the name of a president but I don't remember which one, and the brand of shampoo she liked. But I remember the last word. I remember the last word she said.

"Zebra!"

Then it was over. The words stopped coming. Her eyes didn't open, but she sat quietly for a minute. I shook her again.

"Mom . . . Mom . . ."

She stood up. She stood up so quickly she pulled me with her. The mole was only purple now, no longer flashing. Just bright and steady, and I will hate the color purple for the rest of my life.

I let go, and she walked through the kitchen to the back door. I thought she'd run right into it, but she calmly slid off the chain and turned the bolt, then stepped through to the fire escape. I followed, wishing I was wearing shoes. It was freezing outside.

"Wh . . . where are we going?" I said, descending the stairs behind her. Once on the street, I kept an eye on the ground, stepping gingerly around broken glass and garbage. Mom didn't answer, but her purple mole stared down at me in an evil, purple way.

I don't know when I first noticed the humming. I think I'd been hearing it for a while, since before waking, even, but it was the sort of thing you could drown out, like cicadas in summer. But now as we walked, it grew louder. I knew without thinking that we were walking right toward it.

"C'mon, Mom, time to go home. It's C-Christmas Eve." I gritted my teeth to keep them from chattering.

"If you come home with me, I'll make you eggnog. I'll make you some *special* eggnog. With rum. Or . . . or vodka. With whatever's in the bottle with the pirate on it."

We were walking toward the Oak Hill Cemetery. It was a good cemetery, the kind with high stone walls and fat mausoleums. Obelisks and statues of sad angels. Normally, Mom would never have set foot in there.

And now, finally, I could see it. It was enormous, for one thing. Bigger than you'd expect, and then bigger still. It fell slowly through the air like a bubble. Like a bubble with tentacles. Like a snow globe the size of half a football field, with an underbelly covered in hoses. Suddenly it lit. Not with blinking lights like an airplane: it was like the globe was filled with a glowing gas, pale yellows and greens. And purples. And inside the globe were smaller globes, and layers of platforms and shapes, and on those . . . possibly . . . tiny figures moving.

But no: this isn't working. By describing the ship, I'm making it seem less than it was, and that's a sin.

It was terrible. And it was *wrong.* Just looking at it felt like losing. It was the great flying monstrous humming end of the world.

For days afterward, nothing seemed right. I didn't comb

my hair or brush my teeth. I never even opened my Christmas presents. Why bother? Now there were aliens. I wouldn't listen to music. It made me cry. All of it, it was too beautiful. And I'm not just talking about Beethoven or something. Old *NSYNC albums made me cry. The song the ice-cream truck played made me cry. I couldn't laugh, and hearing other people laugh made me angry. It was selfish and sick, like burning money. But I'm getting ahead of myself.

The ship landed. There was no landing gear. The six hoses just spread out like legs and held the ship's weight. Then it . . . *walked*. There's no other way to describe it. The whole great thing walked on hoselegs like a beetle toward us, picking its way through monuments and headstones.

I looked around for help, but there was no one else on the street.

"Mom! Wake up! Wake up wake up!" I screamed. She was standing still, and I ran to her side, clutched her leg. "Mom! I love you! I'm sorry! Let's go home!"

The ship raised a leg, and it flexed out like a worm toward us. And as it got close . . . I let go. I let go of my mom. I let go and hid behind a mausoleum. Because I was scared. And I know I deserve whatever you think of me for that.

The hoseleg pulled itself over Mom's head and half swallowed her, down to her waist. She didn't move, or make a sound. She still had my Christmas stocking on her arm. Then there was a noise like:

Foomp

and she sailed into the air; she sailed *away*, sucked like soda into that big humming head.

I don't know if I can write about everything afterward. It's going to sound like I'm trying to be dramatic, but it's not like that. It isn't for anyone else. You only fall because your legs stop working. And you don't fall to your knees, you fall on your ass into a patch of crabgrass like the Idiot of the Year. You scream for your mom because you really think it will bring her back. And when it doesn't, your skin feels too tight, and your lungs are full of cotton, and you couldn't call her again if you wanted to. And you don't get up, and you don't think up any clever plans, because you're only waiting to burst like a firecracker and die. It's the only thing to do.

That's all. There's more, but that's all I'm going to write about it. You asked me to write about the days before the invasion, so there's my answer, though it was sort of a personal question, and you maybe shouldn't have asked it. But that's all.

Anyway.

I wrote "ass" a couple paragraphs ago. Pardon my language.

So I sat in that graveyard for a while. I don't remember getting up and I don't remember going home, but there I was. I made myself a sandwich, and afterward I sat in a chair.

I forgot to breathe. I didn't know you could do that. From time to time it came to me that my chest was empty and my head light, so I gaped like a dying fish until I was full again. Then I stared and I thought about nothing. Nothing. That got boring, and I felt my stomach growl, and I thought, Wasn't there a sandwich? So I returned to the kitchen to find it still on the countertop, a cockroach sitting right in the center like a baseball pitcher.

And this is when I finally started to plan, but all of my plans were stupid. I think there's a part of the brain, probably somewhere in the back, that won't give up believing in magic. It was the part that made cavemen believe that drawing elks on stone would make for a good hunt the next day. And it's still chugging along, making you think you have lucky socks, or that your kids' birthdays will win the lottery. It made me think I could stop time in the cemetery with a wave of my hand, or summon Mom to my side with her name. Currently it was very busy, thinking over and over about how to go back in time, and what I should do when I got there.

The spaceships, by the way, didn't stay secret for long. They were all over the television, every channel, except for channel 56, which was still showing reruns of *The Jeffersons*.

There were news stories about the ships, and there were stories about how people were reacting to the ships. Some people were happy, and that made me nauseous. Folks every-where shot their guns up at the sky in celebration. Most people were panicking. Some were looting, because I guess they thought that with aliens invading they were really going to need new DVD players. I suppose nobody knew for sure then that the Boov were bad news, because they hadn't had their mothers vacuumed. I might have gone out and told them, but I was pretty sick. It seems you can't really go for a walk to the graveyard in the middle of a late December night with bare feet and no coat without spending the next few days sweating and shivering and kneeling in front of the toilet. I tried to reach 911, the FBI, the White House, anybody I could tell about Mom, but the phone lines were pretty much worthless. My guess is a lot of folks were calling their friends and family and saying,

"Have you heard about the aliens?"

And then their friend would say,

"What aliens?"

And the first guy would say,

"Turn on your TV!"

"What channel?"

"Any one but 56."

And as a result, I couldn't warn anybody. But they figured it out soon enough.

As it turned out, the ship that took Mom was one of the little ones. There were ships the size of Rhode Island in the skies over my city, New York, LA, Chicago, Dallas, not to mention London, Tel Aviv, Moscow, and about a hundred other

places. At first they just hung there like jellyfish. But then the jellyfish began taking bites out of things.

Nobody understood at first. I sure didn't. We didn't know then about the guns. The crazy Boov guns that don't make a flash or a sound. We only knew that, hey, the Statue of Liberty's head is missing. So's the dome of the Capitol, and the top of Big Ben. Oh, look, the Leaning Tower of Pisa is now the Totally Unremarkable Stump of Pisa. The Great Wall of China is the Great Speed Bump. The Boov ships had big guns. And the Boov themselves had a knack for knowing just what to shoot. They were pushing our buttons.

* * *

I have to talk about this. I can't get it out of my head. You future people, you probably don't remember the invasion at all. You weren't even born. But maybe something else really bad has happened since then. A hundred years is a long time.

When it happened, I'm sure you felt terrible. You were probably scared, and sad, and you wanted it to stop. That's how I felt during the invasion—that's probably how everyone feels. But were you excited, too? Just a little? Were you on the edge of your seat, wondering what would happen next?

And I wonder if you were a little proud. Proud to be living through something so important, something to tell your grand-children. Did you watch yourself watching the television, making certain that you looked brave, and stoic, and just sad enough?

I think other people felt like this. For so long afterward, on the TV and radio and on the street, everyone kept telling each other, "Everything has changed. The world will never be the same. The aliens changed everything."

And the thing is, of *course* they had. It should have gone without saying. But we went right on saying it, and after a while it sounded like a pat on the back. Everything had changed, but we had survived, so we *must* be strong. With each terrible newsbreak and emergency broadcast signal we thought, Now we have a story to tell.

I'm sorry—forget I brought it up. I have no idea what other people were thinking. It was just me. I'm awful.

When there was nothing new to report, the news channels took to showing the same footage over and over. The headless statues, the missing buildings, their absence so bizarre you swore you could still feel them there, like phantom limbs. And I have to remember that there were people, too, rubbed out as cleanly as the faces on Mount Rushmore. There were tourists in the Statue of Liberty when it happened. There were people on the Great Wall. They were gone, *erased*. I believe in heaven because of these people. I want to imagine them shuffling though the gates, blinking, confused, like travelers who fell asleep on the train. I want there to be a place where they're pulled aside by a kind stranger who says, "Okay, here's what happened."

But I'd be lying if I said I thought of them then. I couldn't concentrate on the loss of anyone, even Mom. My head was too numbed by the pictures. My brain was packed in pictures, stored away, waiting to be used again. I was probably impatient for something to happen.

All this intergalactic vandalism eventually drew out all the armies of the world, and we fought back. I can't really say much about that. Nobody handed *me* a gun and sent *me* off to fight. I was sort of busy anyway, trying to keep down fluids. But I watched it all on TV, like a movie. With the right sound effects, it could have been a comedy.

So it was like this: we brought out our tanks, our jets, our soldiers with guns. We brought out our Bradley Fighting Vehicles. I don't know what those are, but we had a lot of them. There were helicopters, aircraft carriers, and a thousand cold, deadly missiles peering out like monstrous eyes from their underground burrows. It might have looked impressive if not for the size of the Boov ships hanging just above the clouds like new moons. But then, in the end, it wasn't about whose guns were bigger. The Boov had a surprise.

This surprise quickly came to be called the Bees. They flew, most of them were about bumblebee size, and they buzzed as they passed. They were covered in tiny wires that looked like antennae, or legs. But they were silver, wingless, and had a strange mess of eyes in their fat heads. One of them would have looked cute on the end of a key chain.

fig. 3a–Bees

They swarmed down from the ships in dense clouds, then split off into groups according to some hidden plan. Some were as big as pickles, and some, if the TV news was to be believed, were too small to see.

Our soldiers fired up at them, stupidly. They might as well have been hunting hummingbirds. They tried to disperse them with concussive grenades. I *think* they tried this. I'm sorry, I'm trying to get this right, but it's really not my area. Teachers never ask me to write essays about jazz, or my shoe collection.

Anyway.

The important part is that the Bees didn't go after our people, they went after our things. They flew down the barrels of tanks. Down the muzzles of guns. They wormed into engines, squeezed through cracks to get at our computers, and were all over our satellite dishes like bees on a sunflower. I assume they did something to the Bradley Fighting Vehicles.

Then they all blew their lids. They used up every bit of energy they had all at once and popped like popcorn. They were white hot, and when they cooled they left behind a kernel of steaming metal slag. Every weapon, every computer, every communicator we needed to fight the aliens was suddenly gummed up with lumps of shapeless metal, like shiny turds. Pardon my language.

I like to think we would have picked up rocks, or sticks, or done *something* else at this point, but that was when the Boov finally decided to talk. They beamed out a message to all the TV and radio stations that still worked. It was a long message, and in pretty good English, but with that same pinched whine that J.Lo had. J.Lo the Boov, not J.Lo the singer/actress/perfume.

I'll spare you all the details of the broadcast. The important parts were:

A. The Boov had discovered this planet, so it was of course rightly theirs.

B. It was their Grand Destiny to colonize new worlds, they *needed* to, so there really wasn't anything they could do about that.

C. They were really sorry for any inconvenience, but were sure humans would assimilate peacefully into Boov society.

And D. If anyone had ideas to the contrary, they should know that there was now a Bee up the nostril of every president, prime minister, king, and queen on the planet.

So that was it. The human race was conquered by lunchtime. People everywhere shot their guns up at the sky in sadness.

That almost brings us back to where I started. Shortly after they conquered us, the Boov began to come down from the ships and move into our cities. Mostly people fled, and the Boov just walked right into modern-day ghost towns, all the while praising their glorious Captain Smek for providing so many pretty, empty houses in which to live. Some people resisted with whatever they had, but these efforts were put down. Maybe you've seen the famous video footage of a mom with three kids, defending her house with a baseball bat, swinging madly from her front steps as the uniformed bodies of the Boovworld home team strode slowly toward the infield.

Some people didn't leave town when the Boov came in, but this almost always ended badly. It ended badly for my upstairs neighbor.

I saw her out on the front stoop one afternoon with her arms full. She held a jewelry box and a stack of photo albums and her teacup Chihuahua, Billy Dee Williams.

"Ms. Wiley!" I shouted from my bedroom window. She halted and squinted up at me. "Do you need help with all that? Where are you going?"

Ms. Wiley stood beneath my window and set down her things. Billy Dee stumbled through the tall grass and ate a bug.

"'Lo, Gratuity. I'm leaving, I *guess*," she said.

"Leaving where?"

"Lived here twenty-five years," Ms. Wiley sighed. "You know that?"

"I know. Why are you leaving?"

"Not my apartment anymore. Belongs to them now, I suppose. One of them claimed it. One of them just came to my door and told me to get out and claimed it in the name of Captain Whoever-He-Is."

I tried to understand what she was saying. There was an alien in our building? Right now, right above me?

"I thought they were only settling in towns down the shore," I said. "It was on the news."

Ms. Wiley just shrugged her shoulders. She looked near tears.

"Your ma home?"

"No, she's . . . no."

"Tell her I'm sorry. I still had her big casserole dish, and I don't think she's getting it back now."

I told her it was okay, and asked if she needed a place to stay, but she was going to her sister's. There must have been scenes like this all over—the Boov just showed up on your doorstep, no warning, and kicked you out. Or maybe you'd find one already in your garage, eating things, and eventually he'd just make his way into the kitchen, or the bedrooms. And like a stray cat, he was there to stay.

Speaking of cats, it was around this time that the Great Housecat Betrayal came to pass. That's my own name for it; you can use it if you want to.

It wasn't exactly covered on what was left of human broadcasting, but word spread quickly. Cats *loved* the Boov. They left their human owners in droves, pouring out of windows and through tiny doors like it was the last day of school, rubbing up against the invaders, licking their legs.

Pig wasn't an outdoor cat, but she tried everything to get out. She always made a break for it when I left the apartment, but there were two more doors to get through before leaving my building, so she never got farther than the stairwell. When a Boov passed by on the street, Pig gazed out at him forlornly and put a paw up to the window, like some tragic heroine.

I almost just let her go a couple of times—but she was really more Mom's cat, and not mine to give away.

Anyway.

In a ridiculously short amount of time, the Boov determined that humans were unwilling to mix peacefully into their culture. They pointed out all the people who fled instead of welcoming their new neighbors, even those whose homes had been taken outright.

Captain Smek himself appeared on television for an official speech to humankind. (He didn't call us humankind, of course. He called us the Noble Savages of Earth. Apparently we were all still living on Earth at this point.)

"Noble Savages of Earth," he said. "Long time have we tried to live together in peace." (It had been five months.) "Long time have the Boov suffered under the hostileness and intolerableness of you people. With sad hearts I now concede that Boov and humans will never to exist as one."

I remember being really excited at this point. Could I possibly be hearing right? Were the Boov about to leave? I was so stupid.

"And so now I generously grant you Human Preserves— gifts of land that will be for humans forever, never to be taken away again, now."

I stared at the TV, mouth agape. "But we were here first," I said pathetically.

Pig purred.

The ceremony went on for some time. The Boov were signing a treaty with the different nations of the world. It all looked strange, and for more than the obvious reasons. Usually big political events are full of men in suits, but the Boov were joined now by totally ordinary-looking people. The woman who signed on behalf of the Czech Republic was carrying a baby. The man who signed for Morocco wore a Pepsi T-shirt. When it came time to sign with the United States, our country was represented by some white guy I'd never seen before. It certainly wasn't the president. Or the vice president. It wasn't the Speaker of the House or anybody else I'd ever noticed on television or elsewhere. It was just some sad, nervous-looking guy in jeans and a denim shirt. He stooped. He had a thick mustache and glasses. He was wearing a *tool belt*, for God's sake, pardon my language. We learned later it was just some random plumber. I think his name was Jeff. It didn't matter to the Boov.

So that's when we Americans were given Florida. One state for three hundred million people. There were going to be some serious lines for the bathrooms.

After this announcement, Moving Day was scheduled and rocketpods were sent. I decided to drive instead, and got shot at, and later went over an embankment because the high-ways had been destroyed. Pig and I hung out in a convenience store, and I hid from a Boov named J.Lo, but then I trapped him, and let him go when he promised to fix my car. Which now hovers instead of rolls. And has big hoses and fins.

Everybody on the same page? Great.

We packed up the hovercar, which I was now calling "Slushious," and settled into our seats. Somehow J.Lo had talked me into giving him a ride to Florida. His scooter, it seemed, was not for long trips, and he'd already gutted it to rebuild the car. He also argued, pretty persuasively, that I was a lot less likely to get shot by any more Boov if I had one of their own for an escort.

I almost balked when J.Lo sat up front, next to me. It was too friendly. But if he sat in the back it would have been like I was his driver, and anyway it was easier to keep an eye on him. Pig lay down on the Boov's headrest. I imagine she would have preferred his lap, but he kind of didn't have one.

"So," said the Boov, wiggling his legs, "what have I to call you?"

I thought a moment. He wasn't calling me Tip. Only friends called me Tip.

"Gratuity," I answered.

J.Lo stared. After exactly too long a pause he said, "Pretty," and looked away.

Whatever, I thought. I turned the key in the ignition, and the car growled to life like a sleepy polar bear. All those new hoses and things began shaking and flapping around. I was about to learn that, after J.Lo's modifications, the ignition switch was about the only thing that still did what it was supposed to do.

The gas pedal was now the brake pedal. The brake pedal opened the trunk. The steering wheel made the car float up and down. To go left or right you tuned the radio. That was just as well, we weren't going to be able to pick up any music anyway, but then I made the mistake of popping in a tape and our seats flipped backward.

We lay there for a minute, staring at the roof.

"I could hum," said J.Lo.

"Shut up," I suggested.

The parking brake shot the wiper fluid. The wiper knob opened the glove box. Pulling the air freshener honked the horn, and pressing the horn made the hood catch fire.

"Hold on! Hold on!" shouted J.Lo, running out the door. The hood yawned open and belched a fireball into the sky. J.Lo dove into his toolbox, threw what looked like an aspirin into the flames, and suddenly the car was covered in two feet of foam.

It took about a half hour to clean off the foam. It was cold and smelled like dessert topping.

"You know," I said as we prepared once again to leave, "I

don't know if this is going to work anyway. There isn't much gas left, and I don't know where we could still buy some. Come to think of it, I'm not sure my money is even *worth* anything anymore."

J.Lo smiled. "Ah. I to show something."

He crouched by the gas tank and snaked a length of hose inside it. Then he sucked on the end, which was gross, and soon a trickle of gasoline dripped out. He caught a few drops of it in this weird machine. It looked like a balance, with small glass vials on both sides and some kind of computery thing in the middle. Then he let the hose fall, and gas spilled out onto the chewed pavement.

"Hey! You're wasting it!"

"It does not to matter," said the Boov. "Look."

He fiddled with the computer, and the whole thing hummed. Then, as though its plug had been pulled, the little vial was emptied of its gasoline. I couldn't tell where it went.

"Nice trick," I said. "Now it's *all* gone."

J.Lo ignored me, and a second later the bottom of the other vial filled with gas from I didn't know where.

"Wait. What just happened?"

The Boov grinned. "I did to teleport the fuel fromto one place and the other."

"Teleport? *Teleport?* That's amazing! You guys can teleport things?"

J.Lo's smile fell a little. "Some things," he said.

"But . . ." I said, missing the point. "How does that help us? We still need more gas."

J.Lo's smile widened.

"Feedback loop," he said.

"Feedback loop?"

"Feedback loop."

We just stood there, looking at each other. A crow cawed in the distance.

"Are you gonna make me ask, or—"

"The computer, it changes up the gasoline into computer datas. A long code. We to transmit the code, the gasoline, but only a little bit. Not all."

"Not all," I repeated.

"But . . . herenow is the trick. The trick is, we are to *fooling the computer* into thinking we have to teleported it all."

"Uh-huh."

"But we have not."

"Sooooo . . ."

"So we are keeping most the gasoline on the one side, and to fooling that it is all on the other side, so the stupids computer duplicates the gasoline for to fill the cup. Like copying a file. Thento we are sending it back the others way, thens back another time, and back and back. Like so."

J.Lo fiddled again, and again there was the hum. What happened next looked like one of those time-lapse films where you watch a flower grow. Both of the vials buzzed and filled quickly with liquid. There was a hundred times more gas than when he'd started.

For a moment my brain wouldn't let me believe what I'd seen. But then, I was getting pretty used to seeing unbelievable things by this point, and I snapped out of it.

"You made gasoline," I said.

"Yes."

"You just . . . like . . . *cloned* some gasoline!"

"As you say."

"This is incredible!" I shouted. "You guys can teleport! You can clone things! You could, like, teleport to France and leave a clone of yourself behind to do your homework!"

The Boov frowned. "Everybodies always is wanting to make a clone for to doing their work. If *you* are not wanting to do your work, why would a clone of you want to do your work?"

"Okay, fine," I said. "But you can teleport. You can go anywhere! Why are we driving?"

J.Lo really scowled now. This seemed to be a touchy subject for him.

"Boov cannot to teleport. Humans and Boov cannot be teleported, can not to be cloned."

"But you just—"

"Impossible. Gasoline can to be teleported and cloned because it is all the sames, all mixed up. Complex creature like the Boov is not all the sames. Even simple creature likes the human is not alls the same."

"Hey—"

"The teleporter computer does not to have to know what order whichto arrange the new gasoline. Does not matter. But for Boov and humans, matters."

I was finally getting it. "You mean—"

"If Gratuity teleports, the computer cannot to keep track of all the molecules. Gratuity comes out a mixed-up puddle of Gratuity."

"Oh."

"Like a Gratuity milk shake, fromto the blender—"

"Okay, all right," I said, raising my hands. "I get it."

Again we fell into an uncomfortable silence. Then J.Lo sat down to make more gasoline, with Pig purring around his feet.

"Hey . . . did I . . . are you mad?" I asked, wondering immediately why I did. "What's wrong with you?"

J.Lo sighed. It made a crackly sound.

"The Boov have tried to fix this problem for long time. For . . ." He raised his eyes like he was doing math. "For an hundred of your years," he said finally.

"Jeez."

"As you say."

After a while we were on our way. The new controls for Slushious were hard to get used to, but I'm a quick study. J.Lo only gritted his teeth and clutched the door handle for about

the first fifteen miles, so afterward I had to throw in an occasional dip or wild turn to keep him guessing.

"I'm a really good driver," I said after a particularly daring
and unnecessary dive. J.Lo bleated something in Boovish that
I hoped was a prayer. Or a curse.

Later a stray dog crossed our path, and I hit the brake, or
rather the gas, a little too hard. J.Lo sailed forward and hit his
head on the dash with a wet slap.

"Seat belts," I said.

"Perhaps I could also to drive from time to time," said the
Boov.

"Nope. Sorry. Not your car."

J.Lo rubbed his head. A bruise had already formed,
swirling and changing color beneath his skin like a mood ring.

"I rebuilded it," he said. "Is like half mine."

I thought about this.

"Sure," I said, trying to sound reasonable, "but it wouldn't
be legal, you driving it. You don't have a license."

"Ah," he said, nodding. "Of course."

A long silence fell between us. It was like a whole extra
person in the car, this silence, watching me expectantly. I
started to imagine the silence was Billy Milsap, this kid from
my grade who always sat near me in every class. He never
said a word, never answered a question, and every time I
glanced at him he was already staring at me. No smile, not
even the good sense to look away when I caught him. The

silence in the car was an invisible Billy Milsap, hunched like a goblin in the backseat. Like any silence, it wasn't really silent at all, but had the same thick drone of Billy's mouth breathing. And the more time passed, the bigger it got. Also, incidentally, like Billy Milsap.

When the silence hung around through the whole state of Delaware, and Billy Milsap had grown so large he was spilling out the open windows, I couldn't take it anymore.

"I wish there was music," I said a little pointedly.

"I am sorry," said J.Lo.

I didn't really like it when he apologized.

"At least you guys didn't blow up *all* the roads," I said. There had been a long stretch of broken asphalt, but now the highway was smooth again.

"The Destruction Crews, they only are exploring roads—"

"*Exploding* roads. Not exploring."

"Yes. They only are *exploding* roads around the big humanscity. I did not understand whyfor they explode roads, on account I was not knowing about the humanscar that *roll*."

He said "roll" like it was something cute.

"What were you doing out there by the MoPo anyway?" I said. "All by yourself."

"There was there an antenna farm."

"An antenna farm? There's no such thing."

"A . . ." He searched for the right words. "A big field filled with the tall antenna towers. For to your radios. I was to sent to modify the towers, for Boov use."

We were passing through an abandoned city, past empty buildings like mausoleums.

"The job . . ," J.Lo continued, "it took too long. I missed my ride. So Gratuity nicely gives me the ride."

I didn't really like him complimenting me. And I got the impression he wasn't telling me everything about his work. But then I wasn't exactly sharing either.

"Maybe we could play some car games," I said.

"Car games?"

I tried to think of a game he might understand. I said, "I spy, with my little eye, something that starts with . . . G."

"Sausages," guessed J.Lo.

So we didn't play any car games.

Strange as it sounds, we actually started talking about old TV shows.

"What was the one," said J.Lo, "the one onto where the man wears a dress?"

I frowned. "You're going to have to give me more to go on," I said. "There's kind of a long tradition of men wearing dresses on television."

"Milton Berle!" J.Lo shouted, remembering. He laughed—I think it was laughing—for two whole minutes. I had no idea who he was talking about.

"Or the shows where to the men wear helmets and run at each other?"

"Sounds like football," I said. Or war footage, I thought.

"Yes. Also very funny."

"Have you watched all this TV since the Boov came here?" I asked.

"Oh, no. The Boov have to been getting the Smekland shows for long time. Many years. The signals travel through the space and we catch them on Boovworld. Do you know *Gunsmoked*? Or *I Am Loving Lucy*?"

"Sort of," I said.

"Did you to see the one where Lucy try to make the Ricky put her into the big show?"

He laughed again, like a trombone under water.

"Ah," he said finally. "Wicked funny."

There was that word again.

"Did you guys learn English from watching our television?"

"No," said J.Lo. "We had tutors. But you could to understand some of the shows, even without the humanswords."

"Oh."

"Do you know what is interesting?" the Boov asked. "Before we to came to Smekland, I thought it would to be funnier. And more exciting, also. All I knew was fromto the television signals, so I thought it was always tripping on footstools and car chasing. It is not quite liketo the television, is Smekland."

"No . . . " I said, "life isn't like TV. On TV, everything gets wrapped up quickly. On TV there are heroes who save the world from people like you."

I squeezed the wheel, stared at the long ribbon of yellow ahead of us. I'd sucked all the air out of the car. My stomach tightened a little as J.Lo glanced at me, then looked quickly away.

By the time we stopped for the night, Billy Milsap was as big as an ocean liner.

I chose a rest stop for our campsite. It was a little bit of human normalness that I could cling to. We could have stopped to sleep in a town, maybe even managed to get into a deserted motel. But then there would have been all of the gray empty streets and buildings surrounding me, and I didn't like the way they already looked like ruins, like monuments to some briefly rich but now-dead civilization. At a rest stop we could almost have been any two motorists pulling over after a long day on the road.

So we parked at the James K. Polk Rest Area.

"What did that sign to say?" asked J.Lo. It was the first thing he'd said in hours.

"'James K. Polk Rest Area,'" I said. "We're going to rest here."

J.Lo's eyes darted about as we hovered up to a squat lit- tle building. "Can we to *do* that? We are not James Kaypolk."

"I'm sure he won't mind."

It turned out to be a really good place to stop. Apparently, no one had thought to loot a rest area, and the vending machines were fully stocked with candy, gum, toaster pastries, Blue Razzberry Nums, orange crackers filled with cheese so yellow it was almost a light source, peanuts, L'il Tasties, Extreme Ranch Chips, Extreme BBQ Pork Rinds, Noda (the Soda Substitute), and mints. J.Lo was only interested in the mints, so I would have the rest to myself.

"How does the food to come into the out?"

I winced. "Well, normally you have to put some money into it. But I don't really have much."

"And I am broken."

"Broke."

"Broke."

J.Lo fetched his toolbox, which I was now convinced had *everything* in it, and produced something like a spray can, if spray cans were shaped like kidneys.

"Stand away," he said.

The kidney can exhaled a fine blue mist that smelled like coffee. J.Lo coated the Plexiglas front of the vending machine, and stepped back to admire his work.

"What now?" I asked.

"We to wait," said J.Lo as the Plexiglas began to steam.

I said that was fine. I had to use the restroom anyway.

"Yes," said J.Lo, following me to the ladies' room door. "I have also to do this thing."

"Whoa," I said, blocking the doorway. "You can't come in here. This is the girls' room."

Even as it came out of my mouth, I knew it sounded dumb. Dumb, I thought, and maybe even *wrong*.

"You . . . you are a boy, aren't you?" I asked. "I mean, don't take that the wrong way or anything—"

"J.Lo is a boy, yes."

I let that go. "So . . . you Boov have boys and girls . . . just like us?"

"Of course," said J.Lo. "Do not to be ridicumulous."

I smiled a wan little smile. "Sorry."

"The Boov are having *seven* magnificent genders. There is boy, girl, boygirl, girlboy, boyboy, boyboygirl, and boyboyboy-boy."

I had absolutely no response to this.

"I'm going to go to the restroom now," I said finally. "You use that one, over there."

J.Lo pattered off to the boys' room. He paused at the door, looking at the little man painted on it. A second later he produced some kind of pen from his toolbox, drew six more legs on the man, and went inside. I pulled the girls' room door shut behind me.

The bathroom was pitch black, except for a small slit of a window framing the pink moon outside. The air was stale and thick. It wrapped itself around me, and I wore it like a mummy. It was nice to be alone for a moment. But I didn't dwell on it; I was all business. I didn't stare for too long at my reflection in the mirror. I didn't cry or anything. I was okay. I was excited about getting to Florida. Beaches. Fun in the sun. Happy Mouse Kingdom was there. Mom had always loved Happy Mouse Kingdom.

After a while I washed my hands and splashed my face, then rejoined J.Lo outside.

He was standing in front of the vending machine, eating mints. The front had almost completely evaporated.

"I don't suppose you want any of the other stuff," I said, waving my hand at the junk feast awaiting me.

J.Lo answered through loud crunches. "No. Mints."

"You . . . can't just have mints. Not that it makes any difference to me—"

He swallowed. "I did also find delicious, fragrant cakes in the Boovs' room."

It would be months before I understood he'd eaten deodorizers out of the urinals.

I would have liked to sleep outside and look up at the sky. The sky looked really great when nearly the entire country was blacked out. Of course, now it looked dangerous, too. I wondered if it would ever be just the night sky again, and not a black sea, full of sharks.

Anyway, there were too many bugs to sleep outside. I got an anklet of red bites around each ankle, and the mosquitos just swarmed around J.Lo. We spent the night in Slushious: me in the backseat, J.Lo and Pig in the front. I may be one of the few people alive who has heard the sound of a Boov snoring. It will haunt me to my grave.

The next morning we did our business quickly and got back on the road. Do you know how you can be around a smell for a long time, but you have to leave it and come back to even notice it's there? When we were gliding back onto the interstate I noticed the smell.

Now, I have to admit that, at this point, I hadn't bathed in four days. There hadn't really been time. So I sniffed under my arms, but I was still very ladylike, thank you. I looked over at J.Lo. Pig was purring loudly at his feet, rubbing at his knees.

"Do you smell something?" I asked.

"I am smelling pine freshness," he replied, looking up at the cardboard tree hanging from the mirror.

"You don't smell something . . . kind of . . . fishy?"

J.Lo swung his legs in little circles. "I am not knowing this 'fishy.' How smells this—B-A-AAOOW!"

He nearly scared me right off the road.

"What? What is it?"

J.Lo frowned down at Pig. "The cat did to bite me!" he said.

"She bit you? Pig never bites."

Pig was still purring, still trying to rub against J.Lo's feet, which were now pulled up safely against his stumpy body.

"Well, she is to biting now! Now she is excellent biter!"

"Maybe you shouldn't have been swinging your legs around, then. What do you expect when you scare her like that."

But I knew that wasn't it. Suddenly everything made sense. I leaned to the right and drew a long breath through my nose. Fish.

"It's you!" I shouted happily. "You smell like fish!"

J.Lo was stunned.

"Noooo," he said finally. "I am not to smelling—"

"You do!" I insisted. "You smell just like fish. Stinky fish. No *wonder* cats like you guys so much! You're like a big piece of sushi."

J.Lo stared down at Pig. "Perhaps I am to needing a bath, then."

"You're forgiven, Pig," I said, laughing. "You couldn't help yourself."

"Please not to laugh," said J.Lo. "She bit wicked hard."

I stopped laughing. We drove in silence for a few minutes.

"Okay," I said. "What is it with that word? Wicked. Nobody says that anymore."

"Nobody?" asked J.Lo.

"Hardly anybody."

The Boov shrugged his frog arms, never taking his eyes off Pig.

"I do not to know. It was teached to me by the tutor. It is not a word?"

"It's a word," I said. How to explain? "It's just that . . . you're using it in a way that . . . isn't really common anymore. If it's all the same to you, I'd really like it if you didn't say it again."

J.Lo nodded. "It is all the same to me. I am not meaning to upset you, Turtlebear."

I must have slammed on the brakes, because the car squealed to a halt. I could feel my heartbeat in my toes.

"Get out!" I yelled.

"Wh—get into the out? Here? Wh—oh . . . okay."

Something about the look on my face sent J.Lo scrambling out the door, onto the edge of a grassy hill. Pig followed.

"Should I . . . Should I to—"

I slammed the door in his face.

I don't know how long I sat there, grinding the steering wheel with my hands, my insides like hot soup. I'm guessing thirty minutes. Or four hours. Somewhere between thirty minutes and four hours. J.Lo was still there, though, motionless beside the car.

I got out, slammed my door good and hard, and came around to face him.

"Where did you learn that word?"

The Boov twittered his fingers together.

"I . . . I was already to telling you I did learn it from the tu—"

"Not 'wicked,'" I shouted. "*Turtlebear!*"

"Is . . . is a perfectly good word."

"WHERE DID YOU LEARN IT?"

"Fromto th-the tutor. Is a term of affection."

I fell back against the car, all my breath squeezed right out of me.

"No . . ." I said. "It's *not*, okay? It isn't a word at all, except to me . . . and my mom."

I didn't like even mentioning Mom again. I didn't want the Boov to know his people had hurt me. But then he said something that turned me on my head.

"Oh! That is explaining! Gratuity's mom was probably J.Lo's tutor!"

After that, I was just a screaming tornado of fists. I battered the Boov with everything I had.

"What? Stop! No! Whyfor?" he shrieked.

I went back to the car, grabbed the Boov's toolbox, and began throwing its contents at him as he ran downhill.

"Oh, please," he said. "No . . . do not, we willto be needing that—"

I found one of those aspirin things and whipped it at his head. Suddenly he was a big, lumbering snowman trailing fat chunks of foam.

"Aaah! Help! Help now!"

I tackled him. The foam exploded all around us. I drew back to punch the Boov in the face. He uttered something in

Boovish and my knuckles cracked against his fishbowl helmet, which had just snapped into place.

"Ow! Stupid . . . Put that helmet back down!"

"No. Whyfor—"

"You stole my mom!" I said, rubbing my hand.

"Mimom?"

"My mom!"

We sat inches apart. I teetered on the edge of attacking him again.

"Oh, yes! Yes! Gratuity mom must havc to been one of the tutors! We invite many humans to help teach the Boov!"

I was hyperventilating. "The . . . the mole . . ." I said. "On her neck."

"Yes! A storage device! It holds up every word she say or think for long time. Then the Boov did call her back to remove this mole. Its information was to planted in all the Boov that was to live in Gratuity's area! Gratuitymom is very helpful!"

My eyes stung. I pawed at them with the heels of my hands.

"'Is'?" I said. "'*Is* very helpful'? Is she . . . She's still alive?" It hurt to ask. I just then realized that I'd thought she was dead.

"Of course she is alive!" said J.Lo. "What a question! She is alive and certainly to be waiting in Florida for her Gratuity!"

I couldn't decide between hugging him and kicking him in the head, so I just sat there. Purple spots swirled before my eyes, and I couldn't catch my breath. I felt like I was going to pass out. Then a few seconds later I went ahead and did it.

After the fight, it was more difficult to carry on as we had. I was just permanently steamed, a little at J.Lo, and a little at myself for feeling too exhausted or beaten down to even hate him properly. Given what I'd learned, I thought I was entitled to ditch the Boov somewhere and keep going on my own. But there he was, curled up in the passenger seat, tense, guarding against the human and the cat who would certainly start hitting or biting him at any moment.

    I eventually gave in and veered off the highway at a King Value Motor Lodge so we could break into a room and take showers. The motel grounds were empty, apart from a raccoon. Someone had taken out some sort of grudge against the ice machine. There were abandoned cars in the parking lot and a moped floating in the swimming pool. One of the vending machines was completely cleaned out. The second was tied with a chain to the back of a pickup truck, which, as far as I could tell, had dragged it for forty feet before running into a telephone pole. Then the machine had been smashed like a piñata and looted.

    Way off in the distance, a cluster of bubbles loomed in the sky. The smallest of them must have been bigger than a minivan, and they formed a shape like an octopus, or a

galaxy, trailing tendrils of singular bubbles in a disk around it. I felt like it was watching us as we approached the building.

J.Lo bent over in front of the doorknob to room fourteen. I was expecting some really interesting tool that melted the lock or turned it into butterflies, so I was disappointed when he just picked it with a hairpin.

The showerhead sputtered out something like gravy for ten minutes before the water ran clear. As J.Lo showered, I sat staring at the bathroom door, thinking, I could leave right now, I could leave without you. A little while later he emerged, and I took my turn.

We left the motel with armfuls of towels and little soaps, as was the custom.

* * *

WELCOME TO FLORIDA

said the huge metal sign. It was shaped like the state itself, and dotted with pictures of attractions and exports and things. It was in this way that I learned the state motto is "In God We Trust," which is just terribly original, and that the state beverage is orange juice, and that it's filled with old people and swamps. Way to go, Florida.

"What did that to say?" asked J.Lo as we hovered by.

"What," I said, "can't you read?" It wasn't the first time he'd asked this.

"It passed behind to us too fast."

I sighed. "It said, 'Welcome to Florida,' and then it said a lot of other things about beaches and oranges."

"Ah, yes. I am liking these oranges. Perhaps we could to be getting some—"

He was interrupted by a piercing wail behind us. I looked in the rearview mirror, which I dared not touch or the muffler would fall off, and saw a flashing light approaching.

"That's strange," I said. "That noise. It's a siren. It's like a strange siren." It seemed we had a cop following us. But I hadn't thought there *were* cops anymore.

"Why do you think—" I began to say, but J.Lo was scrambling into the backseat. He landed with a thump and pulled one of our blankets over his curled body. Pig followed him underneath.

"What's with you?" I shouted, with one eye on the view

behind us. It was night, and hard to see with that flashing light, but I could tell that there was no police cruiser or motor-cycle cop approaching. It was one of those gliding antler-spool scooter things, like the one J.Lo had left behind.

"Boovcop," I whispered. Then I grew angry. What if this Boov was a threat? Wasn't this exactly the sort of thing J.Lo was meant to be protecting me from?

"Get back up here!" I yelled at him as I slowed Slushious and cut the gas. In the mirror I could see both the scooter Boov coming around our left side and the blanketed lump of J.Lo trembling in the backseat.

"Stupid Boov!" I shouted, and then the scooter cop was right there. Right beside my window, knocking his little frog hand against the glass. I rolled down the window.

"What did you to say?" asked the Boovcop in a low, wet voice. He was dressed in gray-green rubber and a helmet with the flashing siren thing mounted on top. It was still turning and flashing, purple green, purple green, and making its weird noise, but softer now. He had these frilly epaulets, like the leader of a marching band. It was way too much shoulder decoration for someone with no real shoulders.

"What did I *say*?" I asked. "When?"

"Just now, before I did to knock on your window."

The Boov's eyes narrowed. Seconds passed. The siren whispered *ploobaloo?* over and over.

"It was French," I said.

"Say it again."

I hesitated. Did the Boov know French?

"Ah . . . stoopeeeda*bouf.*"

"What does it to mean?"

"It was a compliment. I was admiring your scooter."

I think I picked the right subject. I'd seen his scooter out of the corner of my eye, and it was a little fancier than J.Lo's had been. There was a lot of chrome and an entire aquarium full of turtles in the back. The Boovcop grinned and puffed himself up. And I mean that literally—his head actually got a little bigger.

"Yes, yes," he said, patting one of the antlers. "Thank you."

"Le mor*on*," I answered.

Soon the Boovcop's smile faded and he was all business again. "Why have you to come here so late? Alls other humans did to come three days ago."

"Yeah . . . I just thought, you know, that I could drive instead. Save you guys a seat on those rocketpods."

At my mention of driving, the Boov took a good look at Slushious. His throat crackled and whined.

"Humanscar . . . humanscar do not float."

"Well," I said, "that's not entirely—"

"Howfor does this float?" the Boov growled. His brow curled and pinched symmetrically, like an inkblot test that meant "angry." His head grew a little bigger. "Did someone *do* this to for you?"

I swear he dropped one arm to his side, and I was reminded of those guns. I didn't think before I answered.

"Yes."

In the rearview mirror I could see the big lump of blanket behind me begin to shake again.

Okay, so I'm not stupid. I had some impression at this point that J.Lo had not been totally up front with me. Maybe he was in some kind of trouble. Maybe he was even some kind of Boov criminal. Perhaps that was why he wanted a ride to Florida, so he could hide among the humans. The problem was that I didn't know, and I *couldn't* know what I was supposed to do. Would turning him in just get *me* in trouble? Would it be worse if I didn't?

"Who did do this forto you?" the Boov demanded. "Who did?"

"A Boov," I said slowly. "Some maintenance officer."

"Where?"

"Up north, in Pennsylvania. A couple days ago."

The Boov's face brightened. This seemed to interest him quite a bit.

"Was he working onto antennas? At an antenna farm?"

He *was*, of course, and now I really knew J.Lo was in some hot water. And it would have been the easiest thing in the world to jerk my thumb back at the jiggling woolly blob in the backseat and be done with it. But then I thought, looking squarely at the Boovcop's slowly inflating head, *You people* took something of mine. Something I want. So now I have something you want. I played it cool.

"He didn't say anything about a farm," I said. "His English wasn't so good. But he did say something about heading north. Into Canada."

"Ha!" shouted the Boov, and his head deflated with a soft whistle. "He will not to get far."

"Uh-huh. So . . . can I keep going? Into Florida?"

The Boov seemed more relaxed now, casually looking around the car.

"So you do not to know?" he said. "What has happened?"

"No," I answered, not liking the sound of the question. "What's happened?"

"You may to go," he said. "You are not the only latecoming person. Drive ontoward Orlando. Report onto the first Boov you see."

"Will they help me find my mom?"

"Mimom?"

"*My mom.* I need to—"

"Drive onto Orlando. Report onto first Boov," he said again; then his gaze froze on the backseat. On the blanket.

"Whyfor is that—"

"It's just my cat," I said quickly. "Pig! Treat!"

Pig made a little sound and crawled out from under the blanket.

90

The Boov frowned. "Your cat's name is 'Pig Treat'?"

"Um . . . Sure."

"You humans is so weird," he said, and he glided away.

"All right," I said, "start talking!" The Boovcop was safely behind us, and J.Lo was slowly crawling out from the blanket like a slug from a rock.

"Talking?" he said, wearing the blanket like a poncho. "Is there something for talking about?"

"The *whole point* of you coming along, the *only reason* I agreed to it, was because you were meant to play my escort if we met any other Boov. You were supposed to keep me safe! And now I find out you're in more trouble than *I* am."

J.Lo made a noise like *Maaa-aa-aa-aa-aa!* I figured this was him laughing.

"I is in no troubles!" he said as his eyes darted from window to window.

"So why'd you—"

"That Boov, it was . . . Carl. I just . . . was not wanting to see Carl just now. I owe Carl money."

"I heard as well as you did what he said—"

"*She* said," J.Lo corrected. "She."

"She?"

"She."

I shuddered. "*Fine.* I heard what *she* said about the antenna farm. They're looking for you. You can tell me why or you can be a jerk, but I know they're looking for you."

My last words faded away, and there was nothing but the hum of the car and the flapping of hoses. And under that, the bubbling sound of J.Lo's humid breath in the backseat. I looked out my window, but it was too dark to see anything. I would have liked to have seen the landscape, maybe to think about my visits here with Mom. Going to the beach, going to Happy Mouse Kingdom. I realized I might see Happy Mouse Kingdom again, if we made it to Orlando without being stopped. Without being stopped by any Boov, that is.

"Hey," I said as it hit me, "where are all the people?"

"Hm?"

"There's supposed to be, like, three hundred million people here. I thought there would be tents and shelters and people walking around everywhere."

J.Lo pressed his face against the glass. "Yes. Many humans. No Boov. Humans everywhere."

I had a terrible thought. I thought about the people in concentration camps in World War II, told by Nazi soldiers to take showers, and the showerheads that didn't work, and the poison gas that tumbled slowly through vents until every last one was dead. And then I thought about everyone two days ago, rushing to line up for those rocketpods.

"What . . . what did you do with them?" I said. My voice fluttered. I was almost too afraid to speak. "What did you do with them really?"

J.Lo crawled out from under his blanket. "I? I did not do nothing with the people. I am Chief Maintenance Officer Boov, not Humans Transport—"

"J.LO!" I shouted, my voice louder but raw. The car slowed and drifted onto the shoulder. I wasn't paying attention anymore. "Tell me the truth, J.Lo! Tell me the truth. Tell me."

J.Lo looked down at his hands and nodded, biting his lip. My stomach fell and my face went hot, but I was *not* going to cry, no matter what.

"I . . ." said J.Lo. "I . . . am not really chief maintenance officer. I am—"

"No! Nono . . ." I said. "I don't care about that now. What really happened to all the humans?"

J.Lo looked stunned. "Oh . . . *oh*. I do not know."

I searched his face. He really didn't know. He was a terrible liar.

"You thought they'd be here?" I asked.

"I thought this thing, yes."

We sat for a while in the still car, wondering where everyone was. I thought about what the Boovcop had said: *So you do not to know? What has happened?*

J.Lo edged up into the front seat again. Pig purred and actually curled up in *my* lap, if you can believe it.

"They are all right," J.Lo said. "They were probably taken unto some other place instead. You should not to expect such bad things of the Boov."

They've done such bad things already, I thought. But I didn't say it, because he wouldn't understand. History is written by the winners, so they say.

I noticed we were hovering in a ditch on the side of the highway. I gripped the wheel again.

"We're staying off the main roads until I know what's going on," I said. "I could be walking into some kind of trap. And *you* don't want to run into Carl again, I'm guessing."

J.Lo winced. "Her name is not Carl. I did not to know her at all."

I almost said *I know*, and then I almost nodded, but in the end I just sat there. I guided Slushious up an embankment, dropped her onto an access road, then began snaking my way through the city streets of what used to be Jacksonville.

Then I said, "So you're not the chief maintenance officer, huh?"

J.Lo waggled his head. "No. I was more what you would to call . . . ah . . . fixing person. . . ."

"Handyman?"

"A HandyBoov, yes," he said sadly. "I was at to the antenna farm to change the antennas for using by the Boov."

"You said that before," I reminded him.

"Yes . . . but I was not telling then that I made very big mistake with the antennas. I did not to do my job correctly. Now I must stay away fromto the Boov. Hide with the humans."

I might have told J.Lo that the humans probably wouldn't be any happier to have him than the Boov were, what with him stealing their planet and all, but the subject was driven from my mind by a building ahead of us.

Had it been a moonless night, I might not have seen it at all. It lay just beyond the pool of my headlights. I swiveled the car clockwise and aimed for the blue scrawled letters on the side of a Potato Potentate restaurant:

UMANS-HAY—
O-GAY OO-TAY THE INGDOM-KAY—
EET-MAY UNDER-WAY THE ASTLE-CAY
—BOOB

Boob?

"What does that to say?" asked J.Lo, leaning against the dash.

I stared at him for a moment, frowning.

J.Lo glanced at me, then cast his head quickly back to the wall.

"Is it . . . is it the English? So many little lines."

It was a secret message of some kind, of course, but from whom? It was hard to believe anyone would be so naive to think Pig Latin might fool a Boov. And it was even harder to believe that it did. Then I finally put it together.

"You can't read, can you?" I asked. "You can't read English."

J.Lo puckered his fingertips together, over and over.

"Mmmmm . . . no."

"You were never taught? You never"—I grimaced at what I was about to say—"learned from my mom?"

"Almost no one of us can read the humans words. Is very difficult. Nothing like the Boovwords."

"Why not?"

"Hm . . . most humans have . . . little flat pictures, and each of this little picture is meaning a part of a word. Liketo . . . building the word from different bricks."

It took a second before I understood what he was talking about.

"Letters," I said. "You're talking about letters. They build a word."

"Yes! Yes. We are not having these things. All Boov words are made of bubbles."

"Bubbles."

"Yes. They are bubbles in the air. How big are this bubbles, or how thick, or how joined unto each other; this is how we know which word is what."

I recalled the odd bubble formations I'd seen floating here and there. They were only writing. They were signs.

"So most of the Boov cannot to read the humans words. Is supposing to be a big secret."

Of course it is, I thought. If we knew, we could leave each other messages in Pig Latin, right out in the open.

"So why are you telling me," I asked, "if it's such a big secret?"

J.Lo shrugged. "What does these humans words say?" he asked again.

I looked at the message once more, hastily composed in spray paint; the favorite medium of anyone afraid of being caught.

"It says we need to go to Orlando," I said. "Which we're doing anyway."

"Oh, good," said J.Lo.

And that was that. There's a saying we use these days; maybe you future people don't say it anymore. When someone's easily tricked, we might say that it's "like taking candy from a baby." The saying doesn't mention that tricking the baby may be easy, but the candy tastes gross.

* * *

We were still about ten miles away from Happy Mouse Kingdom when I fell asleep. I don't know how long I slept; I was really tired. J.Lo was already snoring in the seat beside me, Pig curled up among his legs, but up to now I'd been pretty alert on account of a couple of close calls with patrolling Boov. I had only the parking lights on, and I'd managed to click them off before being seen by a scooter Boov on a side street. A few miles later I had to veer away from another, a big Boov with strange orange balls like shoes on the ends of his eight legs. I don't know if that one saw me or not, but he (she, it) was on foot and couldn't give chase.

I was beginning to relax again when I had to slam on the brakes to avoid hitting a parade of goats in tiny cars. Just as it occurred to me how weird that was, I blinked and the cars weren't there anymore.

"I'm going nuts," I whispered.

I sort of remembered reading somewhere that if you're cracking up, the best thing is to just close your eyes for a few seconds, so I did, and that's when I realized I wasn't driving at all. I was at school. I couldn't imagine why I thought I'd been driving; I was just a kid, after all. There was nobody else at my school, which was also Happy Mouse Kingdom. I'd forgotten, but it was. I knew I had to find my mom so I could tell her not to get the plastic surgery. She was having her face changed to look just like Happy Mouse, because she thought it would make me love her more. When I found her, she was standing next to the Snow Queen's Castle, and it was all right, she still looked like Mom. But no; it *was* too late. She *did* look like Happy Mouse. She *was* Happy Mouse, standing in the dark, as tall as the castle. When I opened my mouth to speak she put a fat, gloved finger to her grinning lips. Then with her other hand, she pointed straight down at the ground, and suddenly I tripped, and then I awoke to find we were about to drive through a Pricey's store window.

I stood up on the brake pedal (actually the gas pedal), and we rattled to a halt just inches from a row of naked mannequins. J.Lo snorted and shouted "Habish?" for whatever reason. Then he was awake, too.

"What . . . what happens?"

"Nothing," I said. "I was just . . . testing something."

"Ah," said J.Lo, nodding. "Did it work?"

"Yes. Perfectly."

"Good. I am thinking we should stop for sleep."

I nodded, and a few minutes later I found an underground parking garage in which to stay the night. I coasted down the ramps to the lowest level and parked against a wall. J.Lo and Pig settled into the backseat again, but I stayed perched in the front, thinking.

"Time for beds," J.Lo said. He was staring at me from the back.

"Ummm . . . I think I'm going to have a look around," I said. "On foot. I'll be back soon; I just want to see something."

There was a pause.

"I will come with Gratuity."

"No . . . no, that's fine. You sleep. I won't be long."

J.Lo's eyes grew. He kept looking at me, and I couldn't stop talking.

"It's just that . . . about a half mile from here is this place my . . . mom and I used to visit a lot. I'd like to go see it. Alone. Ha-ha." I laughed a little too loud. "Maybe she'll even *be* there!"

I hadn't really thought of that before now, but there were a lot of stranger places I could have found her.

"What is this place?" asked J.Lo. It was a perfectly reasonable question.

"Happy Mouse Kingdom," I said. "It's a . . . theme park, based on all these movies and cartoon characters. Happy

Mouse, of course, and Sailor Swan, and Mister Schwa . . ." He was still looking at me. "The Snow Queen . . ." I added. "Puncinello . . ."

"It is a themed park?"

"Yeah. Like . . . a big park with rides and people in funny costumes and really expensive food. But of course, the rides don't work now, and there aren't any people to put in the costumes," I said. "And there isn't any food."

I wanted to be careful not to make the place sound too attractive. I might have bad-mouthed it some more, except that I noticed J.Lo's eyeballs were sort of quivering at this point. The phrase "Devastating Eye Lasers" passed through my mind, but then he just started wailing.

"You are leaving me now, aren't you?"

I blinked. "Leaving? What, you mean *leaving* leaving? No, I—"

"You are! You are leaving me!"

"I promise, I'm—"

"YOU HATE ME!"

"Well, that's—"

"You are always have hating me and now you are to leaving me all alone—"

"Oh, c'mon, I wouldn't just leave . . . the car. Or the cat . . ."

His face looked like one of those tragedy theater masks, and he made a noise like,

"EEEEEEEEEEEEEEEEEEEEEEEEEEEEEEEEEEEEEEEEEE EEEEEEEEEEEEEEEEEEEEEEEEEEEEEEEEEEEEEEEEEE

EEEEEEEEEEEEEEEEEEEEEEEEEEEEEEEEEEEEEEEEEEEE
EEEEEEEEEEEEEEEEEEEEEEEEEEEEEEEEEEEEEEEEEEEE
EE—"

"Hey, look, keep it down, okay?"

J.Lo composed himself for a moment, but I noticed his eyes were starting to look wet. Which might have meant he was about to cry, but it bears mentioning that his face was also slowly turning yellow, so I don't know.

"Look, J.Lo," I said, "this is just something I have to do. My mom really loved Happy Mouse Kingdom, and . . . I miss my mom. She thought it was the most perfect place in the world. So clean and happy all the time, and . . . good."

J.Lo sniffed.

"I just want to go and make sure it's still there," I said, "and then I'll come back and go to sleep. I promise. I'm not up to anything. Or anything."

I found I had to look away when I told him this.

In the end he suddenly got very friendly and cooperative again, and agreed I should go. He dug through his toolbox and made me take this thing that looked like a miniature turkey baster.

"If you runs into troubles," he said, "like Boov patrols or somesuch, you squeeze this, and it to sends up noisy bubbles, and I rescue you!"

I said okay and took it. I showed him where the spare car key was, stuck with a magnet under the bumper, and then I walked to a flight of stairs that would take me up to the street. I made sure not to look back, but I didn't have to look to feel J.Lo's gaze clinging to me like a wet dog as I began to climb.

I could barely handle this Florida weather. Even at night I felt like a glazed ham. But I was comforted by the familiar landscape—the short trees piled thick with dark leaves, the tall, naked trees with green tufted heads. The tidy little pools and lakes that appeared over grassy hills with golf-course regularity.

It wasn't far to Happy Mouse Kingdom, and there were still signs everywhere. I passed seven billboards, and every one was for a theme park, or a resort, or a theme park/resort. They boasted about being the most magically fun, or wildest, or most penguin-filled. They claimed to have the biggest this or the most water-slidingest that. And I thought it would make sense if everyone ended up here. We could live out the rest of our fake lives amid the fake kingdoms and worlds, the lands and resorts and outlet malls. Wasn't this an outlet-mall America now? Just like the real one, only smaller and not as good.

A few blocks from the parking garage, I turned a corner to see a Boov walking in the same direction on the next street. He wore blue, like J.Lo, and was carrying a toolbox, and I almost called out to him to stop following me. I don't know what it was that told me suddenly to hide—something about the way this Boov moved, maybe. Maybe it was those orange ball things on the ends of his feet. But it wasn't J.Lo. I dropped like a stone behind a mailbox, landed right on my tailbone and bit my lip as the pain shot right up my back, all the while praying I hadn't been seen.

The Boov that wasn't J.Lo took something like a little rubber dome out of the toolbox. I don't know what he pressed or pulled or said or did, but suddenly a long, straight shaft sprouted from the top, and I thought, Oh, a retractable toilet plunger.

The Boov pointed the business end of the thing at a savings bank across the street. Then, without a sound, the bank began to disappear. He started at the bottom, so soon there was plenty of noise as the building toppled forward and crumbled to pieces. The Boov just continued working on the rubble, waving the plunger from side to side until there was nothing left but a bank-shaped hole in the world.

I really hoped he didn't feel the same way about mailboxes as he did about banks.

As I watched, the Boov skittered over to the now vacant lot and pulled something else from a loop on his uniform. It didn't look all that different from the turkey baster in my pocket, and with good reason. Bubbles percolated from its end, one at a time, some big and some small. He was like a conductor, and the bubbles danced at his command, joining together to form a tall, boxy shape, then a ring around the middle like a hula hoop. I wondered what it said. Then he scattered a handful of Ping-Pong balls over the lot, watered them, and covered each with a little jar. Satisfied, he toddled out of sight, and I heard the sound of an antler-spool scooter speeding away.

I got up from the sidewalk, rubbed my butt, and walked over to the closest jar. The ball inside had already sprouted like an onion, and transparent pencil-thin tubes slowly snaked skyward. I couldn't tell if it was food or architecture. Maybe it was an antenna farm.

Ten minutes later I reached the edge of the Kingdom. The parking lot was a graveyard, each empty plot marked off with white paint and a low, wide headstone. It stretched out a quarter mile, divided into sections named after cartoon characters. I walked through Rumpelstiltskin, Doofus, and Duke Elliphant on my way to the big bright old-fashioned train station that made up the front gates, and as I looked around the lot, I thought, It's clean. After everything, it's still clean.

Mom could never shut up about that. It was part of what made Happy Mouse Kingdom the Nicest Place on Earth. It was so clean, and everyone smiled, even when they were sweeping up trash or picking up half-eaten food. I'd made a game of trying to catch one of them looking unhappy, or just normal, but when I saw a teenager beaming like a beauty queen while she cleaned vomit off the side of the Big Rock Candy Mountain, I knew it wasn't a game I was going to win.

"This place is just perfect every time," Mom had said as we waited to pay our sixty dollars to get in. It was maybe the third time we'd been to Happy Mouse Kingdom together, and maybe the twelfth time I'd heard this speech. "And even after thousands of people walk through here today, even after all the ticker tape and the Invisible Hobo Parade, it'll be perfect tomorrow, too. You'll see."

I *would* see, too. We were buying a two-day pass. So while she was paying, just to prove her wrong, I carved a bad word into the paint on the base of the ticket booth. I used my house key, and I was careful not to be seen. Look, I know it was stupid, but I was just a kid, and I was going through this phase. Anyway, I was sure the swear word wouldn't be noticed, and I'd see it the next morning, and I'd be right and she'd be wrong.

There were a lot of people there that day, and they dropped a lot of things. There was a lot of ticker tape and balloons, and of course the twice-daily Invisible Hobo Parade. And the next day it certainly looked clean. I had to give them that. But they couldn't have thought of everything.

"Where are you going?" Mom asked as I broke away from her and ran to the ticket booth. "We already have our pass, we don't have to pay again."

"Just want to see something," I called back. She probably

didn't hear me, but it didn't matter. It would only take a second, then I'd have the rest of the day to gloat.

I pushed through lines of people and ignored their irritated looks and clucking tongues and knelt down at the base of the booth.

"No way," I whispered.

I had the wrong booth, that was the only explanation. I dashed one row down and tried again. There was nothing there.

And then I knew I'd been right the first time. It was the booth directly in line with the Duke Elliphant sign; I'd made certain of it the day before. I went back to look again.

"What's going on?" Mom said behind me. "Did you lose something?"

I stared in disbelief at the flawless ticket booth paint. You couldn't even tell they'd touched it up.

"Yeah," I said. "I guess so."

I mention all of this now to explain why, in the middle of the night in the Happy Mouse Kingdom parking lot, I walked to the empty ticket booth in line with Duke Elliphant and crouched down. It was just one of those things. It'd make a funny story to tell Mom when I found her.

Down at the base of the booth the word FART was scratched into the paint.

I leaned in closer. I squinted. I remembered the goats in

tiny cars I thought I'd seen earlier, so I traced the word with my fingertip. I felt the shallow trench my key had cut two years before, and tiny flakes of paint stuck to my skin.

"I *am* crazy," I told myself, and nodded. "Probably have been for a while." I poked the booth again and picked away the paint so you couldn't read the word anymore.

"There wasn't even any alien invasion, I bet. I'm just nuts. Most likely I'm strapped to a hospital bed right now, drooling and making animal noises."

It was a nice thought, but I didn't really believe it. I stood up and walked through a turnstile into the park. At some point I would find the rest of the human race, and eventually I'd track down someone who worked at Happy Mouse Kingdom, and they'd explain about the really interesting ticket booths that sometimes said FART and sometimes didn't. There wasn't anything else to do.

The inside of the park was not so clean. There was garbage all over the walkways, in the buildings and shops, plastic bags hanging like bagfruit from the skeletal trees. I caught sight of stray cats and at least one peacock. Broadway was the name of the main thoroughfare, lined with little stores that once offered Gifts from Other Lands. Now they were pretty much just full of rats.

At the end of Broadway I should have been able to see the Snow Queen's Castle, but I couldn't. Then I saw why. Most of it had been vanished by the Boov's guns. It was horrifying, somehow. It was like a person with no head. There was a little bit of tower here, half a drawbridge there, but the rest was sliced clean away. I thought of an old photo of my mom, taken when she was younger than me, waving from the draw-bridge of this castle and wearing one of those rubber mouse noses that everyone buys. I hoped she'd never have to see it like this.

And I wondered if this had any bearing on the message I'd seen:

HUMANS
GO TO THE KINGDOM
MEET UNDER THE CASTLE
—BOOB

That had been it, hadn't it? I'd taken a picture of the message but left it in the car. I supposed that even if the castle was gone I could still look *under* it. Was there a downstairs? I'd never noticed one before. I was staring ahead of me and thinking this when I saw what looked like a collie dog in front of a fire hydrant.

"Hey," I said. "Here, boy."

Now, the thing about Happy Mouse Kingdom, if you don't already know, is that some things are smaller than normal, and some things are bigger. You can see what looks like a huge Bavarian ski lodge or something, then get closer and realize it's only ten feet tall. They really screw with your sense of perspective. So that's why you can get pretty near a dog in front of a hydrant before you notice the hydrant is as big as a refrigerator and the dog is as big as a lion, and is shaped liked a lion, and is, actually, a lion.

"Oh," I said, stepping back. My mind raced. Part of it thought, Well, naturally, some of the animals must have escaped from the Wild World Animal Park, and part of it tried to remember if anyone in school ever told us what to do when faced with a lion; but no, of course they didn't, they were too busy teaching really useful things like the state capitals.

"The capital of Florida is Tallahassee," I told the lion as I backed slowly away. "The official beverage is orange juice."

The lion grunted and crouched low on his haunches. He stalked. The word for what he did was definitely "stalked." I'm certain that this word was coined just for lions; everyone else made a poor business of it.

"I probably don't taste good," I offered as I edged toward a shop corner. "You won't believe what I've been eating."

The lion's rear quivered impatiently. Then he suddenly stretched back like he was coiling his springs, and I took off running.

I ran like I never had. I drew air so hard it felt like pins in my chest. I weaved back and forth, around lampposts and in and out of alleys, hoping it might make a difference, hoping that lions weren't so good at hunting if their prey suddenly ducked behind a gift shop. I could hear his round paws pounding behind me, and the huff of his breath. And I realized that if I was looking for evidence that I'd lost my mind, I could do a lot worse than thinking I was being chased by a lion through the empty streets of Happy Mouse Kingdom.

I thought about what I had. I had some cheese crackers

in the pocket of my cargo pants. I had a camera and a pack of chocolate Ding-A-Lings in my camera bag. I had a turkey baster that made noisy bubbles when you squeezed it. I had my car keys, but unless I was going to scratch FART into the side of the lion, I didn't think they would help.

I leaped for the lowest branch of a tree and pulled myself up. Suddenly I felt a jerk, and the cat's claws were hooked through the strap of my bag, pulling me down.

I screamed and batted at the paw with my fist. Finally I saved the camera, and the bag's strap broke, and I left it to the lion as I hoisted myself higher, branch by branch.

The lion hunched over the camera bag, sniffing. He ate my Ding-A-Lings.

"Lions don't climb trees, right? That's leopards," I said between rapid breaths. I was full of butterflies. "Or panthers. Leopards or panthers."

The lion finished his snack and turned his attention to me again. He circled the tree, then stretched his tawny body up the trunk, sinking his claws deep into the bark.

"Lions don't climb trees!" I yelled.

I got a good look at his body now, his thick ribs nearly pushing through that bristly hide. I'm no lion expert, but his eyes looked sunken, and his legs were lanky and thin. He was old and he was starving.

"I'm sorry," I said. "I'm sorry you can't eat me."

The lion lay back down on the ground, never taking his

eyes off me. I didn't want to use the turkey baster. It would alert J.Lo to where I was, but it would alert every other Boov in town as well. I looked around. I was pretty sure I could crawl along one of the tree limbs and climb onto the roof of the Haunted House.

The lion whined.

"This is the best I can do," I said, tossing him my cheese crackers. "I saw a peacock near the sundial, if you like that sort of thing."

He sniffed at the crackers and ate them, wrapper and all. I shinnied along a branch, then another, and dropped onto the roof of the house. With a little maneuvering I made my way to an open window, pushed aside the skeleton leaning out of it, and went in.

It was dark, of course, and the air was thick and close. There wasn't a real room inside—just a catwalk. Looking downward through the elaborate stage set of the Haunted House was pointless. It could have been a bottomless pit, for all I could see. Here and there, a bit of moonlight slipped through a window or gap and bleached some of the darkness a dim blue.

I could only feel my way along the catwalk, searching for a way down. Strange shapes loomed out at me from every angle. In the dark every loop and coil of wire was a jungle vine or snake, and every theater light hung from above like a one-eyed bat. It might have been scary if I were the type who got scared. As it happened, I did feel sort of breathless and jumpy, but I think you have to expect that when you've just finished a lot of running and you haven't been eating well.

Anyway.

I found the way down by nearly falling off the edge. There was a sort of open tube running along one wall, formed from hoops and slats of metal. Inside the tube was a ladder.

Here's the thing: I thought the ladder would end when I got to the ground floor, so I wasn't paying much attention until it hit me that I'd been descending for a long time. Too long. I looked out around me and saw nothing. Really nothing. Like, you don't have any idea what nothing looks like, because there's always some light somewhere, leaking under a door or through a window crack. This was black like death.

This was honest-to-God-can't-see-your-hand-in-front-of-your-face dark. Pardon my language.

At one point I thought I'd come to the bottom. I reached out with my foot, but couldn't find the next step. Aha, I thought, the floor must be right below. So I stretched my leg out some more, and suddenly the section of ladder I clung to slid downward like the bottom of a fire escape. My stomach lurched, then lurched again as the ladder butted against something. There was the loud clang of metal on metal. And now I could feel another rung below. My ladder had only met up with another ladder, and I began to wonder if it would ever end.

The sensible thing would have been to turn back, to climb back up until I at least saw a window again. But I picked this time to remember part of the secret message:

MEET UNDER THE CASTLE

and it made me think, Is this what they meant? Am I underground?

It didn't seem so crazy if I thought about it hard enough. Maybe the Happy Mouse Kingdom people had underground tunnels so they could go from place to place without disturbing the guests. Maybe they even had a little subway under here, or something. Something that would lead to the Snow Queen's Castle.

So I kept going. The length of ladder that had so unexpectedly dropped now sprung back up as I let go. I descended another twenty, maybe thirty, steps before I ran out of rungs again. This time my foot found a hard, concrete floor, and I stepped away.

I reached out with both arms, swung them in slow, wide arcs, like I was trying to swim. I began to touch things around me. Strange things. Something that I hoped was a coiled hose. Something that I hoped was a sponge. I felt a stack of shelves, and these were filled with plastic bottles and maybe buckets, and one object that felt like the worst thing in the world but which turned out later to be a sandwich.

Then I felt the cage. It was all around. I was in some kind of chain-link cage, maybe six feet by ten, and I couldn't feel any opening. And I thought, Okay, that's it. They caught me. And it was a few panicky seconds before I reasoned that if the Boov wanted to capture someone, there was probably an easier way to do it than to hope they'd see a message in Pig Latin that would lure them like, a hundred miles to a theme park, where they'd be chased by a lion into a tree and onto a roof and then down a ladder into a cage that they could just climb back out of whenever they pleased. So I groped around a little more and eventually found the rack of flashlights.

The first couple I tried worked. I swished them around and saw I was in a supply cage, mostly full of cleaning products. The buckets were buckets. The horrible thing was, in fact, old peanut butter. And there was a gate on one end. I slipped one of the flashlights into my waistband and emptied all the batteries from the rest into my pockets. I grabbed a bottle of glass cleaner because it comforted me to hold something in my hand that had a trigger, such as it was.

I pushed out through the gate. Far above was some massive shape hanging from the ceiling. In the dim light I could make out shutters, windows, and shingles. Spare parts, I figured, for the house aboveground. Around me was only darkness, even with the flashlight. The walls of this room were too far away, or there weren't any walls at all. I crept steadily forward, and soon my light found a squat little something in the corner. It looked like an engine, or part of a lawn mower, and I was pretty sure it was a generator. With any luck it had gas in it, so I searched around for the rip cord and gave it a tug. The thing sort of shuddered and coughed, so I pulled it again. And again. On the fourth try it growled to life, and all over and around me lights began to wink and flicker, and soon I could see it.

It was the Haunted House. Hanging upside down. From the ceiling. I was in a big room, an *enormous* room, a room like half a football field, and there was an entire Haunted House hanging upside down in the middle of it.

It was perfect in every detail: the broken shutters, the bent weather vane, even the fake black cat screeching silently over the front porch. On the ceiling itself was a little

plot of land, fake grass and mud, with gravestones and wiry trees hanging down like stalactites. Or stalagmites. I can never remember which is which.

I sat heavily on the floor, dumbstruck. I wondered how I'd know if I was crazy. Is there a blood test, or can you just pee in a cup or something? Once I was in a bicycle accident, and I lay in the street for a long time afterward. People surrounded me and wouldn't let me stand up until the paramedics arrived. When they did, they asked if I knew who the president was, and what state I lived in, and how much was three times seven. When I answered everything correctly they seemed pleased, so they asked my name and I said "Gratuity," and then they wouldn't let me up until I told them it was "Janet."

Anyway, sitting there, I decided to test myself again. But this time the president wasn't the president anymore, and I didn't have a home, and my name was still my name. I could do the math, sure, but I decided all the same to just lie down for a while. I gazed at the roof of the house like I was flying.

Eventually I had to take my eyes off it, so I looked around the cavernous room. It wasn't really just rectangular. It had wide scoops on opposite ends, like wings. Like a huge half-pipe. And all around were doors marked with bright signs. One door said

FROGWORTH'S HOPPING PAD

TOONTOPIA

ABRAHAM SUPERLINCOLN'S TIME MACHINE

and another said

BIG ROCK CANDY MOUNTAIN

GALAXANDER'S LUNAR LANDER

But I knew I didn't have time for those. What I really wanted was through door number three:

MISTER SCHWA'S GRAMMAZING
VOCABULARCOASTER
SNOW QUEEN'S CASTLE

The second thing; not the first one.

I didn't really want to leave the room without some clue as to why the Haunted House, or *a* haunted house, was dangling from the rafters like that. There had to be a sign somewhere with an explanation. But I had things to do. J.Lo would start to worry. I pulled open the door to the castle slowly and quietly, and left the mystery and the humming generator behind.

If I'd been expecting anything remarkable behind the door, I was wrong. It was only a dark hallway, and I flicked my flashlight back and forth in front of me to guard against any surprises. The corridor curved slightly to the right. I passed a door to the Mister Schwa ride, and the corridor curved back, and I saw a light. Not my light, but something soft and orange down the hall. I switched off the flashlight and saw the outline of another door, maybe fifty feet ahead.

I raised my bottle of glass cleaner and fingered the trigger as I crept forward. There were voices. Laughing. In a weird way you can always tell when a sound is a person's voice, and usually tell that they're speaking English, even when you can't make out anything they're saying. I relaxed a little and reached for the door handle, and suddenly felt something against my shoe. Something that gave a little, like a rubber band, and just as I realized what I'd done, there came a great loud noise of cans and spoons clattering together at the edges of the hallway.

I'm not going to write down what I said at this point.

Then the door swung forward, so I hopped back a little and saw a dark shape come at me, and that's when I sort of accidentally squirted it where its head would be.

"Ow! Ooowwwww!" said the shape. I trained my flashlight on it, and saw it was just a kid. A boy, maybe nine or ten.

"Ooooowwwwwwwwwwww!" he moaned, pawing at his face. I heard a rustle from beyond the door, and he was soon joined by other boys, six, then seven and eight of them. They looked at me like they'd never seen a black girl with a flashlight before.

"I'm sorry. That was an accident," I said. First human I meet in three days and I squirt ammonia in his eyes. "He sca . . . startled me. You know, things like this happen when you just go barging through doors like that—"

"Who the hell are you?" said the biggest kid. He was maybe my age, with a dirty face and ratty blond curls. I'd also learn that he tended to swear a lot. I don't care for that, personally, so I'm going to bleep him out from now on. "Did the Boov send you?" he added.

Two of the boys were guiding the one I'd blinded back into the room. I noticed I wasn't being invited in.

"Did the Boov . . . ? Of course not," I answered. "Why would—"

"She's probably a bleeping spy," said the blond boy. "Probably not even a real girl. She doesn't look right."

"Oh, *I* don't look right. Sure. Do you know you have a peanut stuck to your chin?"

"Shut the bleep up! You don't get to speak!"

"*And* you smell like ice cream."

The boy lunged forward, but he was caught by a smaller boy on his left. I stepped back and aimed the squirt bottle.

"Do that again and I'll clean your face for you," I said.

There was a moment of silence. Most of the boys were looking at Curly like they were waiting for orders. Instead it was the smaller boy holding him back who spoke.

"Let's just go inside where we can all see better."

"No!" said Curly. "No girls allowed!"

"Oh, you gotta be kidding me—"

"I'm not asking her to join," said the boy. "I'm saying we should go inside." Nobody did anything, so he added, "In the light it'll be easier to tell if she's just a Boov in a girl suit."

"Yeah," said Curly. "That's good. Back inside!"

We went in. Curly marched behind me like he was my

guard. The door opened onto a huge room, larger than the last. I had some idea what to expect this time, so I wasn't entirely caught off guard by the castle hanging upside down in the middle. This one was whole. Whole and perfect, untouched by the Boov. I could have stared forever at the dancing light that flickered over each icy brick and frosting tower.

"Hey! No pictures!" Curly shouted. He was still behind me.

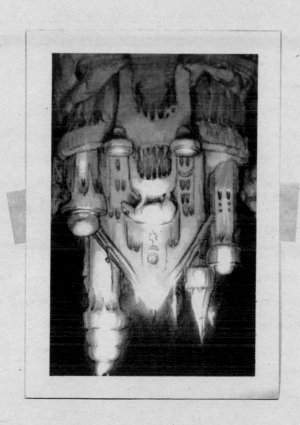

Behind him there was a ring of candles and a little camp stove in the corner of the room, surrounded by boxes and chairs. The boys took up their seats. There wasn't one for me, and I wasn't about to sit on the floor, so I stood.

"Check her back for a zipper," said Curly.

A couple of boys approached me, but a particular expression on my face made them change their minds.

"I saw some graffiti that pointed me here," I said. "So I came. My name's Gratuity. My . . . friends call me Tip."

"Tip!" shouted Curly. He laughed like a donkey, and some of the other boys joined in. "What kind of bleeping name is Tip?"

"The kind *you're* never calling me, you big—"

"I'm Christian," said the boy who'd held Curly back in the hall. He had caramel-color skin and caramel-color hair, like they were both made from the same thing. All the other boys stared at me from their seats. All of them except the one I'd squirted, who was pouring water all over his red face. His eyes looked like cherries.

One by one they gave their names. There was Tanner, Juan, Alberto, Marcos, Jeff, Yosuan, and Cole. I think. They were all between the ages of maybe eight to thirteen. Curly didn't give his name.

"Why are you here?" said Christian. "Why weren't you on the rocketpods like all the others?"

"I decided to drive instead."

"Liar," said Curly.

"Anyway," I said, "weren't the rocketpods supposed to come here? Where is everybody?"

"Arizona," said Christian. "The Boov decided to keep Florida for themselves."

Arizona. I couldn't believe it.

"But . . . they promised it to us. They promised it to us *forever.*"

Curly snorted. I suddenly felt a little foolish. Naive.

"That was before they discovered oranges," said Tanner. "The Boov really like oranges."

"So they loaded everyone back up and took them to Arizona," said Christian.

"They grow oranges in Arizona too," said Yosuan.

"Bleep," said Curly. "Nothing grows in Arizona. It's all desert."

"It's not," Yosuan said quietly. "My grandma lives there."

I thought about J.Lo eating dental floss.

"Waitaminit. Oranges? The Boov actually eat oranges?"

"No . . ." said Yosuan, squinting. "They mostly wear them, I think."

We lapsed into silence again, which Curly broke with a rude noise.

"Okay," I said, "my turn. Which one of you guys is Boob?"

Most of the boys broke up into nervous giggling. Especially the younger ones.

"BOOB is an . . . acronym," said Christian. "It stands for Brotherhood—"

"*Brother*hood!" Curly interrupted. "No girls! And no pictures!"

I gave him a sour look. "The graffiti *I* saw said 'humans.'"

"That's because Marcos bleeped up."

Marcos flinched.

Christian continued as if everyone were still listening. "Brotherhood Organized against Oppressive Boov. It stands for that."

"Shouldn't it be B-O-A-O-B, then?"

"We really wanted it to be BOOB," said Marcos, and all the younger boys giggled again. Christian looked pained.

Christian   CURLY   Boob boys

"Well . . . all right," I said. "So what are you guys doing?"

"Doing?" said one of they boys.

"Yeah. 'Brotherhood Organized against Oppressive Boov,' right? So what are you doing to fight them?"

"*Fight* them?" said Marcos. There were general snorts of disbelief from all the boys. "Have you seen those guns they have?"

"We're . . . we're not letting them have us," someone said. "We're not letting them tell us where to go. That's fighting them."

"And we're eating all this spoiled ice cream and corn dogs, and living at Happy Mouse Kingdom!" said another. "They'd hate that, if they knew."

The boys mostly nodded to each other, and said things like "Yeah, that's showin' 'em," and, "They can't push *us* around." I noticed only Christian looked sort of disappointed. I imagined he and I were thinking the same thing: *Well, so much for the revolution.*

The murmuring died down into uncomfortable silence. A silence as huge and awkward as a castle hanging from the ceiling.

"Okay," I said. "Why are there upside-down buildings underground?"

"Ha! Dumbbleep. Everyone knows that."

Christian looked at Curly. "*You* didn't know it three weeks ago."

"Three weeks? Is that how long you guys have been here?"

"Some of us," said Christian. "Some not as long, some longer. Alberto and I have been here five months."

Five months. Since the time of the invasion.

"Our parents worked here," said Alberto. "So . . . so we knew about the underground . . . and—"

And suddenly, Alberto was crying. He made a fist with his face, and soon loud sobs filled the room.

"Oh, bleep. Here we go. You're such a bleep, Albert."

I didn't know what I'd done. I looked to Christian for help, but he just continued the story.

"Our parents worked here. Alberto's dad and my mom. They have two of every building—every big one, anyway. During the day they clean the one underground, repaint what-ever needs repainting, fix stuff, that sort of thing. Then, in the middle of the night, *fllip!*"

"Flip?" I frowned. "What . . . You're joking. You mean they flip all of the buildings around?"

"Yep. Clean one goes on top, dirty one swings under-ground for cleaning."

"Huh."

Alberto sniffed and wiped his face with the back of his hand. I felt bad for him. He was one of the little kids.

"We came here to hide out when the aliens showed up," said Christian, "because our parents were gone."

"Gone?"

"They disappeared. On Christmas Eve."

Alberto started wailing again. I couldn't believe what I was hearing.

"On Christmas Eve," I repeated.

Christian thought I was challenging him, I guess. "Believe whatever you want, but yes, they disappeared a day before the invasion. I think they must have known too much, and the Boov killed them."

"No-no," I stammered. "I believe you. My mom was taken, too."

"Bleep, you're a liar. Why do you lie so much?" said Curly.

But Christian and Alberto were listening. Everyone was.

"Taken?" said Christian. "Like . . . abducted?"

"Yeah. Not killed. Did your parents say anything about being abducted before then? Weeks before then?"

"No," said Alberto, looking glum.

"Yes," said Christian. "That is, my mom told me about this weird dream she'd had, about being taken by aliens and made to sew pillowcases."

Curly laughed.

"I don't think it was a dream," said Christian. "The aliens she described, they were just like the Boov."

"It wasn't a dream," I said, grinning, happy to have some good news to tell. "It really happened to your mom. Your dad, too," I added, nodding at Alberto. "I'm sure of it. He probably just didn't tell anyone, or he didn't remember. They were only kidnapped so the Boov could learn our languages. My mom spoke two, I think that was why she was chosen. We're Italian."

They all gave me the sort of looks I usually get when I say that.

"My mom's white," I added.

Alberto looked better. "My dad spoke Portuguese! So do I, a little."

"My mom spoke . . . speaks Spanish," said Christian. "And you think they're okay?"

"I have it on good authority that they're safe, and with everyone else."

"Yeah?" said Curly. "*Whose* authority? How does some stupid girl know all this?"

I swallowed. "What . . . difference does that make? The important thing—"

"The important thing is you heard it from a Boov. Because you're a bleeping Boov spy."

I had a feeling telling Curly that he was both right *and* wrong was not going to help my case any.

"For the last time, I'm not a spy! I've been aboveground for the last five months. And I've been traveling. You pick up things." Like fugitive Boov, for example.

Alberto began to sniffle. "My dad may be okay," he said, "but now he's all the way in Arizona! I don't even know where that is!"

Soon he was weeping again, and that was it for me. It was as contagious and sudden as a yawn. I did the last thing I wanted to do in front of the Brotherhood Organized against Oppressive Boov. My face grew hot, and the tears choked out of me like I was sick. My heart was broken, had been for five months, and I couldn't keep it together anymore.

"Oh, look at her," said Curly. "It figures."

I turned my back on the circle of candles. I looked away from the inverted castle and focused on the dark corner of the room, trying to will myself to stop crying. I was trying at that moment to ignore everything that might remind me of the state I was in, figuratively and geographically, so I almost didn't hear.

One of the boys said, "What's that on her back?"

"Zipper," said Curly.

I straightened up, my breath coming in huffs, and tried to see what he was talking about. I couldn't.

"No . . . no it's . . ." someone said. "Is that . . . that isn't . . ."

A few of the boys were drawing near.

"It *is*!" shouted Curly. "It's a *Bee*!"

"A bee?" I whispered.

Everyone was talking now, fast and loud.

"Well, okay," I said, drying my eyes. "Brush it off. I'm not allergic or anything."

Christian had come around to look at me, and I could see it all there in his face, before he said a word.

"It's not that kind of bee."

Oh, I thought. A Bee. I pictured its silver body clinging to my sweater, ready to pop and burn through my skin.

"That proves it! She's a bleeping spy! Why else would she have one of their bees on her?"

They were all advancing on me. Christian stepped between us.

"Now . . . hold on," he said, and I could hear the uncertainty in his voice. "This doesn't . . . necessarily prove anything. Maybe . . . maybe they put the Bee on her to force her down here—"

"I swear! I have no idea why this thing is on my back! I'm not doing anything for the Boov. I haven't even seen a Boov in days!" I said.

So this was arguably the worst possible moment for J.Lo to come running across the room, shouting my name.

"Gratuity! Gratuity!" he said, appearing suddenly from the shadows. "Gratuity! We must to run! We must—Oh. Hello, boy humans."

The collected members of BOOB scattered like pigeons, flapping and knocking over candles and boxes. Alberto started to cry again. Only Christian and Curly remained.

"Bleep," whispered Curly.

"J.Lo! What are you doing here? Why is there a Bee on my back?"

"Oho! You see!" Curly said. "They know each other! I was right!"

"No," I said, "you're not. It's not what it looks like—"

"BOOB boys! Get 'em!" ordered Curly, but there was no one left to order, apart from Christian.

"What is this?" he said.

"J.Lo . . . this Boov," I said. "He's all right. The other Boov hate him. He's like . . . a Boov criminal."

I'm not sure if that was the best choice of words. You had to be there.

"He's hiding from the other Boov?" said Christian.

"Yes!" said J.Lo. "Yes! And they are to coming! They founded our car, and I drove like a superstar, but they will be coming soon!"

"So?" said Curly. "Let's tie him up and leave him here. The Boov will find him and go."

"Don't you—" I began angrily, then checked myself. "Just let us leave," I said, looking at Christian. "I'll make sure they don't find you."

"Us? *Us*?" Curly said. His face was red like a zit waiting to pop. "You'd rather go with a bleeping Boov than stay with your own kind?"

"Well, now that you put it that way, you have made me feel *sooo* welcome—"

"You're a traitor! He stole your mom and still you're a traitor!"

J.Lo cowered behind me. Above us I began to think I could hear noises. Voices. And these weren't human at all.

I grabbed J.Lo's arm. I didn't think anything of it at that moment. Later I'd realize it was the first time I'd touched him. Touched him without trying to hit him, anyway.

"C'mon," I said, and pulled him back in the direction from which he appeared.

Curly was just screaming a laundry list of expletives now.

"No," said J.Lo. "We cannot go from back there. The patrol is behind me."

"If we go any other way they'll follow us through here and find the boys," I said. "Where's the car?"

"Hiding behindto many birds inside toasters."

"The English Puffins ride," said Christian, who was suddenly at our side. "I can show you a quick way upstairs. Follow me."

I smiled, and he gave me sort of a half-smile back. We went to an access ladder and went up, slowly. J.Lo was not great with ladders.

"There's a Bee on my back," I told him.

"A whatnow?"

Then I think he saw what I meant.

"Oh, yes. A bluzzer. A hunting drone. I did to put it there."

"What? Are you trying to kill me?"

"Kill . . . ? Oh, no, do not be ridicumulous. Is not the exploring kind. It told me where you were."

"Like a homing device," whispered Christian.

"Yes, like this homo thing."

I was mad and ashamed at the same time. J.Lo hadn't

trusted me, but I hadn't been trustworthy. I kept quiet as we reached the top of the ladder, which opened into a corridor.

"Take the second left," said Christian. "Then the first right. Go up the first ladder you see."

"Why don't you come with us?" I asked. "You and Alberto. Find your parents."

Christian looked back at me. I couldn't tell what he was thinking. He bit his lip. He looked forward and back.

"No," he said. Then he shook his head. "No. I can't. The . . . Brotherhood, and all."

I thought I understood. If Christian left, Curly would have all the other kids feeding him grapes and rubbing his feet within a week.

"But . . ." he said, "maybe we can still help you out a bit. And if you run into a Marta Gonzales in Arizona . . . tell her Christian is all right. Tell her Alberto is all right; she knows his father."

I promised I would, and we hurried away without even thanking him.

I cut through the halls, nearly dragging J.Lo behind me. It turned out that Boov were not so great at running either, despite all those legs. Around the second corner I heard voices, so I winked off the flashlight. It didn't matter.

"They have seen us!" said J.Lo.

There was a long hall, and a Boov patrol at the end of it. In the middle was the ladder.

"Run fast," I said, and we made for it, hurtling closer and closer to the Boov all the while. There were four of them, and they saw the ladder too. Our only grace was that they couldn't move any faster than J.Lo.

"I can't . . . believe . . ." I huffed, pulling at his wrist, "that we were . . . conquered by you people!"

"Halt!" said one of the Boov. Then he shouted something in Boovish that I'm guessing was also "halt." They might have known we were unarmed, because their own guns weren't drawn. So they were probably surprised when we all reached the ladder at the same time and I squirted the two in front with window cleaner.

"Baaaah!" they shouted, shielding their eyes. "MuNah-ah-ah-ah!"

They stopped dead, blocking the corridor, and their comrades stumbled over them as I pushed J.Lo up the ladder. I followed, with another Boov right behind me. I tried squirting him too, but he swung his wide, garbage-lid mouth open so the ammonia only went down his throat. He lapped it up like fruit punch.

"Do not to feed them!" said J.Lo. "Why are you feeding them?"

We were at the top of the ladder, pushing up through a trapdoor into the blue morning air. The patrol Boov swiped at my ankles, and I was thankful for his tiny frog arms. Still, he'd have me in a moment.

Then I remembered the miniature turkey baster. I pulled it from my pocket, pointed down, and squeezed. A deafening cone of huge, sticky bubbles sprayed out like noisy champagne. It was loud like a jet engine. The Boov were all knocked off the ladder, and J.Lo and I were shot up through the trapdoor like cannonballs. We landed ungracefully a few feet away.

"That . . . that is not what that is for," said J.Lo.

"What?"

"What?"

"Where's the car?"

"What?"

We stood and looked around. Christian had gotten us pretty close to the English Puffins ride. I hoped the car was still there. I hoped Pig was still in the car.

We dashed toward a big ring of toasters with puffins sticking out. The puffins sat in one slot of the toaster, and you sat in the other, and the whole ring spun around while the toaster lever popped you up and down. I'd always hated that ride.

We were nearly there when a statue of Happy Mouse we were passing suddenly didn't have a head or arms anymore, and I realized the Boov were shooting at us.

"Get down!" I shouted. "Hide!"

I pushed J.Lo to the ground behind a snack bar, and wondered if they'd just start blasting everything to pieces.

"What are they doing? What are they doing?" I whispered.

J.Lo peeked around. "They are coming up slow. Trying to surround. They are maybe thinking we are having other things for shooting at them."

I wished it were true. The car was so close. I could see it now, between two puffin heads.

"There is the good news and the not very good news," whispered J.Lo.

"What's the good news?"

"I am believing that they want to take me alive."

"And the bad?"

"I am not believing they want to take you alive."

"Maybe . . ." I whispered, "maybe if we stay real close together, they can't shoot." And then I thought, Why am I whispering? They know where we are.

"Hey!" I shouted. "Heeeeey!"

J.Lo looked at me like I'd finally lost it.

"What . . ." he whispered. "What do . . ."

I screamed my best monster-movie scream. We both peered around the side of the snack bar.

"Why do you do it? Whyfor?"

"Lions," I said. "They can't climb trees, but there's nothing wrong with their ears."

"Ah," said J.Lo, nodding. "Hm. This is some old humans expression?"

138

Then we saw it. A Boov bolted out of an alley with a half-starved lion running behind him.

"Ahh! Big kitten!" said J.Lo.

"Shh! Time to be quiet," I said.

The Boov was shooting wildly behind him, vanishing rooftops and lampposts but not upsetting the lion a bit. They ran behind a snack bar, and three other Boov scurried out, crying like sheep.

J.Lo and I crept out and around the Puffins ride. There was the car, in one piece, and Pig pressed up against the glass.

"I hope he'll be okay," I said as we scrambled into the front seats. I was watching the lion pin a Boov down as the others raced up to help.

"The other patrol Boov will to assist him with the lion," said J.Lo.

I had *meant* the lion, but decided not to say so.

Slushious swiveled around, and I guided it through the park, taking a wide loop back to the entrance.

"We made it," I said. "We got away."

J.Lo was looking backward over the seat. "No," he said. "Not away yet."

I checked the mirror. There were five ships rising up behind us. I threaded the car through cartoon streets, and the ships followed—past Hannibull Lee's Paddleboat, through the cigarette trees around Big Rock Candy Mountain, straight toward the ruined castle of the Snow Queen, which jostled Slushious up and down like a huge speed bump as we passed. Then there was a low grinding noise, like the whole world was clearing its throat, and the ruins swiveled underground while the good castle snapped into place. Three Boov ships scattered while the remaining two smacked into the castle like pinballs—one fell to bits and the other plowed into a carousel.

"Ha!" I shouted as we left the park. "Thanks, BOOB!"

"Three still are chasing," said J.Lo.

They were each small, maybe the size of a city bus, if city buses were shaped like hamburgers. Otherwise, each was different. One had a beard of hoses like the big ships, and a tiny bubble hatch on top. Another had fins and little nubs sticking out every which way. The third had something like fenders with big headlights and a long hose in the back like a tail. And they were all gaining on us.

ᴅᴏᴏᴠɪsʜ ships is a certain preoccu-

figs. 7c-e

"They're faster than we are," I said, steering onto a crumbling turnpike. "Way to build a floating car, J.Lo!"

"Press the button," he said.

"What? What button?"

The little Boov speeders were close now. Something like an enormous plastic claw was unfolding from underneath the ship in front.

"The button. The button withto the snake on it."

"There's no button with a snake—"

"Neversmind," said J.Lo. "I do it."

He pushed in the cigarette lighter, and Slushious took off like a maniac. I was pressed hard into my seat, and Pig rolled screeching into the back. If I'm not mistaken, there was pink flame belching out of the tailpipe at this point.

"What is this?" I shouted, barely able to move my face. "Why didn't you tell me about it before?"

"Is for emergencities. Is not a toy."

We were putting some serious distance between Slushious and the Boov patrol.

"I didn't say it was a toy!"

"The button will either to give thirty seconds of wicked fastness," said J.Lo, "or blow us up."

I stared at him.

"What?"

Just then the car backfired once, twice. Thick blue smoke streamed from our exhaust like tail feathers.

"Aaaah! You Stupid Boov!"

"No, it is okay. It is fine. We are only to running out of the superfuel."

It was true. The car was gradually slowing. Through a grainy haze I could still see the patrol behind us.

"Maybe I can lose them in this smoke," I said, and took the next exit ramp. I whipped Slushious halfway around and pulled beneath the overpass. But it was no good. Two of the three speeders appeared behind us again.

We sailed through the city streets, and here at least we had some edge. The Boov vehicles were bigger and harder to maneuver in close quarters. I could keep them at bay, but I couldn't shake them. And it had been a long time since we'd cloned some gas.

"This is bad," I said. "If you weren't in the car with me I'd be shot dead already."

"No! It is okay!" J.Lo said, hopping in his seat as he watched the speeders. "They are backing off!"

A glance at the mirror told me it was true. But there was something else, something shimmering in the air between us.

"What is that?" I asked. "It's like glitter."

We both figured it out at the same time.

"Bluzzers!" said J.Lo.

"Bees!" I said. And probably the exploding kind, too. They were gaining fast; the swarm of shining specks was very nearly on us.

"What do we do? Is there . . . is there something in your toolbox?"

J.Lo was ashen. "There is nothing," he said.

The Bees were so close they were all I could see in the mirror. Surely one had already touched down on the roof.

"Wait," I said. "Aspirin!"

"Whatnow?"

"Aspirin!" I said again, holding out my palm.

"Is your head to hurting, or—"

"Oh! I mean . . . one of those . . . forget it! Take the wheel!"

I was already in the backseat, with the car fishtailing wildly, before J.Lo did as I asked. He hopped into the driver's seat as I rummaged through his toolbox. Then I found one of the little white things at the bottom.

"Whatfor are you—"

"Keep it steady," I said, and rolled down the back window. The wind batted furiously as I pulled myself half out of the car, facing backward. It was stronger than I expected, and I scratched at the door frame for a better grip while the drove of Bees stared at me with a thousand tiny eyes.

Three of them were already perched on the top of the car, skittering forward, looking for some working part to destroy. The dense mass of followers were not far behind, but I realized I had to wait for the right moment. I had to wait until I could get them all.

"What are you to doing?" said J.Lo, his voice faint and wispy to my ears.

"Keep it steady!"

And then the moment came. There were two, three dozen on the car, with a hundred more about to land, and I threw the aspirin. And the instant it left my hand I knew I'd made a mistake: there was no way I could throw something so small in so great a gale and expect to hit what I wanted. I was aiming for the top of the car, in the center of the swarm, but the pill turned and soared crazily in the air, and just as I thought it was lost, it struck a single Bee with a tiny *tink*.

A fat ball of icy foam erupted outward from that single Bee, expanding its orbit until every one was trapped inside. They hissed and sputtered as their hot little bodies wiggled like live anchovies in a big scoop of the worst ice cream ever. Then the wiggling stopped, and I struck at the ball with my fist. The cold hurt my hand, but the foam unstuck from the roof of the car and hurled itself to the street. I pulled myself back inside.

"Ha-ha!" said J.Lo. "Clever little human!"

I felt good, and dizzy. I crawled back up to the front.

"How are we doing?" I said.

"Hm. Not so good. We are running out of city."

He was right. The roads were getting wider and the buildings smaller. The Boov ships would regain their lost ground soon. I looked backward, into the rising sun, and saw their silhouettes grow larger. I racked my brain to think of a new plan, but I was out of tricks.

"Gratuity," said J.Lo, but I wasn't paying attention. I was watching in disbelief as the Boov seemed to come to an abrupt stop. They seemed to turn and fly away.

"Gratuity . . ."

"They're leaving!" I cheered. "They've had enough!"

I noticed Slushious was slowing down, so I looked at J.Lo, and then I looked where he was looking.

We had passed all the buildings and skyscrapers, and now it was the only thing you noticed: there was an immense purple planetary sphere in the air, like a pimple on the nose of the sky. Just looking at it felt like losing.

"Is that," I said, "is that one of yours?" It didn't look like a fishbowl. It looked like a purple moon.

"No," said J.Lo. "Not one of ours."

Slushious had come to a stop, and J.Lo got out. I followed him to the side of the road. Pig purred and rubbed up against us, but I was barely aware of her. I sat still in the grass, hypnotized by the thing.

"Should . . . should we go?" I said. "Is it close?"

J.Lo shook his head. "Is not close. Is very big, and very far away."

The surface of it seemed to move. It seemed to shudder and writhe. But I thought it might have been a trick of the air. A mirage.

"You probably better tell me about this thing," I said.

"It is a Gorg ship," said J.Lo. "It is the Gorg. They have come now to take Smekland for their own. The Boov will to fight them, but the Boov will lose. And . . . andit . . . it is alls my fault."

His skin was pale and blue.

"This has something to do with the antenna farm?"

J.Lo nodded. "I sent them a signal. I did not to means to. It was for an accident. But I sent them a signal when I was testing the antennas."

"That must have been a strong signal."

"Yes. Yes, too strong. Much too strong. Not pointed correctly. When I did saw where it went, to what part of the sky, I knew the Gorg could catch it. I was to hoping they would not catch it."

"What was in this signal?" I asked.

"Does not matter. The Gorg would to have come no matters what. They would to have come as soon as they were learning that there is a good world here for taking."

The wind whistled by us. I had to stop myself shivering, though it was as hot as bathwater.

"It's so big."

"Mah," J.Lo breathed. "This is the smallest kind."

"But really . . . what *did* you send? There weren't any radio or television stations transmitting anymore."

"No. It was just a little song. I singed a little song to see if the antennas were able to be sending it back to my scooter."

"What kind of song?"

"A kid song. A children's play song."

"How did it go?"

"Hm. It will not to rhyme in humanspeak."

"That's okay."

J.Lo thought for a moment.

"It goes . . . it goes, *Gorg are dumb, dumb like soap, their wives are wider than they should be.*"

"Uh-oh," I said, looking ahead at the big purple ball.

"The funny part," said J.Lo, "is that Gorg do not even *have* wives."

"You should have told me about this. You said the Boov were after you because you made a mistake. This is one hell of a mistake, pardon my language."

"Oh," said J.Lo, "Oh *yes*, I am supposing I should have to told you *all* about it, liketo you were telling me about humans hiding in this Happy Mice themed park? Hm?"

"That's different. Those humans . . . I thought there were people plotting to get rid of the Boov! To kick them off our planet! You wouldn't have understood. You would never have gone along with that."

The sun was higher in the east, and it lit up the big Gorg ship like a heat lamp on a meatball.

"I mean . . . what is it with you people? It's not enough you stole the whole earth and my mom and everything? You had to go and invite Planet Purple and the . . . Purple People, too?"

"Gorg," corrected J.Lo. "And their skins are colored mostly green—"

"It doesn't matter!" I said, standing. "Green or purple . . . it's still the wrong color skin, and they aren't welcome here!"

I breathed heavily and thought.

"Okay, that came out wrong," I said, "but still—"

"The Gorg, they might have anyways learned about this world. They might to have picked up the human televisions—"

"But they hadn't yet, so you thought, 'Hm . . . maybe for I to give my Gorg friends a call, maybe they can to come for my Let's Ruin Everything Jerk Party!'"

"They are not my friends!" J.Lo shouted. His face was

burning pink. "You may not say it! The Gorg are friends of no one! NO ONE!"

"Okay, okay—"

"They are monsters!"

"Okay," I said.

I settled on the grass again, and we sat in silence for a minute. I was kind of dizzy, kind of light-headed, and I had what you might call a vision. Or you might not; that's your thing. But I could see the Boov and humans and J.Lo and me and my mom and everybody all at once, and there were lines connecting us—a constellation. I only got it for a second, like it was a secret.

"I am thinking we are alls in the same car now," said J.Lo. "We should to have no more secretions."

"Secrets."

"Secrets. Yes."

I took a deep breath and nodded.

"And . . ." said J.Lo, "and I might also have gone along with that."

I turned. "With what?"

J.Lo looked at his little feet. "With your plotting humans hiding themed park boys. I am thinking maybe the Boov should not to have come to Smekland. To . . . Earthland."

I kept my mouth shut and listened.

"Before we came, Captain Smek and the HighBoovs told us that the humans needed us. That the humans were just like the animals, and that we could to make them better. Teach to them. We were told the humans were nasty and backwards. It . . . it is what we thought."

"And what do you think now?" I asked.

J.Lo seemed about to speak, but nothing came. He opened his mouth, and closed it, and opened it once more. He clenched his hands and curled his legs up against his body.

"I am thinking I am very sorry, Gratuity," he said.

And I said, "Call me Tip."

So anyway. You all know what happened next, or you think you do. You know what happened with the Gorg. As for what Smekday means to me, this is it: every year as Smekday—as Christmas rolls around again—I remember that day in Florida, and what J.Lo said, and what I decided. How there was nothing to it when it happened. Lightning didn't crash, I did not think, All right then, I'll go to Hell, pardon my language. I just decided to stick by a friend.

Most everyone thinks of Smekday as the day the Boov arrived, and as the day they left, one year later. But the longer they've been gone, the less I care about that. The Boov weren't anything special. They were just people. They were too smart and too stupid to be anything else.

The End

September 6

Miss Gratuity Tucci

c/o Daniel Landry Middle School

Dear Miss Tucci:

It is my great pleasure to inform you that your essay has been selected from more than 15,000 entries to be included in the National Time Capsule. Your unique story and viewpoint made your composition a true standout and the favorite of many judges. Also, you wrote easily ten times more than any of your fellow students, and we believe that should count for something. Enclosed are your savings bond, worth two hundred dollars at maturity, and twenty shares of Taco Stocko, good for a free Taco Taco at any participating Wall Street Taco Exchange.

We hope this experience inspires you to keep writing. You could well be an author one day! Many national newspapers will be printing portions of your winning essay, and I wouldn't be surprised if people are curious about the rest of your story: Did you reunite with your mother? What became of J.Lo? What are your thoughts about the Gorg's defeat at the hands of the heroic Daniel Landry? What is the moral to your story?

I just know one day I'll be buying your biography.

Once again, congratulations!

Bev Doogan

Chairperson

Gratuity Tucci
Daniel Landry Middle School
8th Grade

THE TRUE MEANING OF SMEKDAY
PART 3: Attack of the Clones

That woman from the time capsule committee was right, sort of. I'm not so much "inspired" to write more as . . . compelled, I think you'd say. My brain won't let me stop playing the rest of the story in my head like a movie, and I'm hoping that by writing it all down I can be finished with it.

But I won't be showing it to anyone. I have reasons. Maybe I'll leave instructions that no one can read this journal until the time capsule is uncovered, and I'm already gone, and I won't have to talk about it.

No offense to you.

I'm sure you're all nice people.

Anyway.

* * *

We left Orlando under a cloud. I didn't even check the atlas—
I just drove away from the rising sun, fast, determined to put
some distance between us and the Boov, in case they should
decide to give chase again. We slid through the streets and
highways, following any signs that said "west," setting out like
Lewis and Clark into a wide frontier that had grown wild and
unknown all over again.

We passed a flock of flamingos flying low over the wet
land like gaudy umbrellas carried by the wind. They barely
registered then. Thinking about them now, I realize it was the
first I'd ever known that flamingos flew at all. It didn't suit
them—they looked like sprinting drag queens. But at the time
they were just another part of this new, haunted America,
with its empty cities and huge, sweaty eye in the clouds,
watching over it all.

J.Lo was still a pale blue, curled up in his seat and staring
at some point just behind the dashboard. Pig was happily
dumb to the fact that the world had just ended for the
second time in six months. She brushed back and forth
against J.Lo and me, trying to get a reaction, then eventually
gave up and went to sleep in the back.

I couldn't drive very far. I hadn't had any sleep. I thought
maybe J.Lo would be more alert, and I didn't have anything
against letting him drive anymore, but when I looked I saw
him tipped to the side, fogging up the window with closed
eyes. I made it to some little town called I-don't-know-what

and found a scrap metal yard by the highway. It seemed like the right place for the three of us. I pulled Slushious between two massive piles of discarded city and curled up next to Pig.

I cautiously cracked the window for some air. I thought it would stink like every other dump, but the scrap yard just smelled like pennies. It smelled like the U.S. Mint probably smelled, back when it still made money. Back when pennies were pennies, and not little worthless copper medallions, like prizes at a Lincoln look-alike contest. Back when dollar bills were *not* just wallet-size pictures of Washington.

It was about this time that all the metaphorical bad weather was replaced by the real thing, and the clouds cracked open and rained. I think it was the kind of rain that only Florida gets, the kind that makes you want to start gathering animals in twos, just in case. I looked out the window and saw nothing. The downpour made the world look like a cable channel you hadn't paid for, all static with an occasional flash of something you thought you knew.

Pig was awake now, restless because of the constant rattle against the windows. She sat in my lap, kneading the skin of my leg with her claws. So we watched the storm, watched the wind push the rain around in billowing sheets like the ghosts of old oceans.

I'm sorry. I always get like this when I think about that day. For what it's worth, I fell asleep about now. Later, when I woke up, we were nearly killed in a flood, so that should be exciting.

* * *

I didn't dream at all. I just closed my eyes, and when I opened them a second later, it was night.

I wondered for a moment if I was sick. My stomach lurched and settled over and over, and I thought, It's like I'm on a boat. It's like I'm taking the ferry across the Delaware. And just as I propped myself up enough to see why, the car was hit by half a washing machine.

It had come tumbling down the junk heap and struck one of our fins hard enough to make it fold up like a cheap chair. Slushious bucked and nearly rolled. There was water seeping up through the floor, and water all around us. At least six feet of it. We were floating through a brand-new river, between banks and hills of loose metal. I watched breathlessly as pieces of scrap took wing and circled above like giant bats.

"Oh my God!" I shouted. "Oh my God, I parked us in a scrap yard during a hurricane! J.Lo!"

J.Lo was waking slowly, crawling back from the front seat. "Mlaaa-ak sis?" he murmured. "Whazit?"

Pig was frantic. She tore around the interior of the car, leaping away from the pools of water on the floor, which were everywhere now.

"Hurricane!" I shouted. "Big storm! Everything's flooded and we're floating! And leaking! And . . . I don't get it; it was so clear yesterday!"

"It is the Gorg," said J.Lo, looking out the window. "Their ships, they are too large. They make the weather happen whereverto they go."

He sounded a little too calm for my taste. I tried to impress him with the seriousness of it.

"We're *floating*," I said. "There's water coming into the car, and flying metal everywhere, and we were just hit by a washing machine!"

I was almost pleased when the lightning flashed and some sharp piece of garbage clawed at our roof, as if to illustrate my point.

"Yes," J.Lo agreed. "I have unproperly sealed up the bottom side of our vehicle. I am sorry."

"Yeah. I don't really care about that so much as the scrap metal and floating parts."

"We should to leave."

"Leave?" I said. "Leave the *car*?"

Pig was panting. She had tangled herself up in the strap on my camera, and looked ready to explode into confetti at any moment.

"No," said J.Lo. "Leaveto the metal yard. In the car."

I stared.

"You drive," he said. "I will to remove the water."

Drive? I thought. We can drive?

I climbed into the front seat and took up the controls. Suddenly I couldn't remember how to do anything. I felt it would be a bad time to accidentally cause the hood to burst into flame.

J.Lo was digging through his toolbox. Pig perched like a twitchy sparrow on the top of the passenger seat, the camera dangling from her back legs. She let out one long, raspy meow that lasted until all her breath was spent, then she inhaled and did it again.

Slowly the cobwebs left my mind and I focused on the car. I began to ease it forward, as though we were on dry land, as though we were on a safe empty blacktop that stretched for miles in every direction. And I noticed that Slushious really was moving forward. Pig noticed it too, and took to meowing in short, high bursts like the fire alarm at school.

"We're moving," I said. "The car is swimming."

That wasn't really right. When we started there were bubbles foaming all around Slushious, and then we rose a bit—not above the water, but just about to its surface. Then we began to skim along—not as fast as we would have over land, but fast enough. We left the metal yard behind and passed over what must have been the road. There was a highway overpass, and we just barely fit beneath it, as if it were only a low footbridge over a canal. It reminded me of pictures of Venice.

"Ha! I should sing something in Italian," I said.

"Yes, please," J.Lo answered as he looked over some device he'd found in the toolbox. It looked like two thin tubes connected by a set of tiny bagpipes. I hoped it was what he was looking for. The water in the car had risen up to the gas pedal.

"What, really? Sing something?"

J.Lo blew into the tiny bagpipes. They didn't make any noise, but he seemed satisfied all the same.

"Yes. Please to sing. I know very little of the humans-music."

So I sang the first Italian song that came into my head, which turned out to be "Volare." I'm sure I need not mention at this point that I am a rock star, and it sounded fantastic.

J.Lo rolled down a window. The wind and spray whipped like angry spirits around the car, but he ignored it and snaked one of the tubes over the side. The end of the other tube sank below the rising water inside the car. Then J.Lo blew into each of the bagpipes in turn, and the bag itself began to inflate and deflate, again and again on its own, pumping like a plastic heart in his hands. Water rushed through the tubes and out the car window, and almost immediately I could see the pool drop around my feet.

"Clever little Boov!" I shouted happily. I think J.Lo liked that.

Then something happened. I don't know why Pig did it. I think she was afraid of the water and the wind, and there was a lot more of that outside the car than inside. But a thousand generations of weird cat biology goaded her on, and she pounced from the headrest and straight through the window. She trailed the tangled camera strap behind her, and the camera itself knocked and almost caught the edge of the glass. J.Lo made a grab for it, but it all came free, and Pig and a vintage Polaroid dropped into the floodwaters below.

I drew a sharp breath, but before I could shout or scream, J.Lo had forced the window all the way down and dived in after her.

I was suddenly alone and useless inside the car. The rain battered the roof like a drumroll. I could think of nothing to do. Not one thing. And then J.Lo shot out of the water like a salmon in a nature film and dumped Pig through the window. She was fine.

J.Lo hung there for a moment by his fingers. Then he said simply, "Camera," and dove back under.

I realized what he meant. The camera was free of Pig's legs and still in the water.

"No!" I shouted, much too late. "Forget the camera!"

The only answer I got was a sneeze from Pig. She looked like a miserable wet hairbrush.

The window was still open. "You're not going to jump again," I asked. "Are you?"

"Mrooooowrrr," said Pig.

I went to wrap her in a towel, which made her fidget and growl, but eventually she gave in to it and any other indignity I had planned. I probably could have dressed her up in a sailor suit if I'd wanted.

But all I could think was that J.Lo had been gone an awfully long time. Hadn't he? Thirty seconds, a minute? I started to count under my breath: one alligator, two alligator. When I had sixty alligators I gave in to panic.

"Okay . . . okay . . ." I whispered, looking all around me, looking at the rushing current outside. "Think. Think think think think think. I need a rope!"

I scattered J.Lo's tools around the car, searching for some kind of rope, or something that could be used like a rope. I should have paid more attention to anything that looked like a pencil sharpener made of lemon Jell-O that, when cranked, would spit out superstrong yarn that smelled like ginger ale. I only mention this because J.Lo really did have such a thing. He told me so later. But at the time I was too busy looking for an honest rope, and too distracted to notice that J.Lo had resurfaced and was peering over my shoulder.

"If you areto looking for the pink squishable gapputty," he said suddenly, "it is smooshed in the gloves box. You will have to use brown."

I jumped and grabbed for the toolbox, but it tipped over and everything tumbled out. I stared at J.Lo like he was a ghost. The fact that an alien was at least as weird as a ghost wouldn't occur to me until later.

"What?" I said.

"You will have to use brown."

"Brown. Brown what?"

"Squishable gapputty," he said. "The pink is smooshed into the gloves box."

He was just hanging there, arms folded over the window's edge like he wasn't waist-deep in churning water during a hurricane. I had trouble swallowing. I was so sure he'd drowned.

"Why," I said. "Why is the pink gapputty smooshed in the glove box."

"It was rattling."

"The putty?"

"The gloves box," J.Lo said as he hoisted himself inside the car.

"And just so we can put this behind us," I said, "squishable gapputty *is . . .*"

"Something you smoosh into places for making them stop rattling."

"Right."

"I supposed you were looking for it. It is the only thing missing fromto my toolsbox."

I just fell forward and hugged him. I didn't think about it. I squeezed my arms around him and hugged. His body gave more than I expected, like dough, except for a hard boxy shape that cut into my hip. It was the camera. He'd brought back the camera.

J.Lo patted my head. "If this is about the gapputty, you can still use the brown. Is just as good, just not pink—"

"Shut up," I said, and pulled back to look at him. Then I climbed into the front seat so he wouldn't see me cry.

"We better get to higher ground," I said. "Roll up the window."

I found a half-finished building a half mile away. It was just a skeleton of girders and partial floors, and I could thrust Slushious up through the gaps until we were a few stories above the rising water. Here we waited out the storm. This took two days, and J.Lo and I managed to explain a lot to each other about humans and Boov. He didn't understand, for example, about families. I began to get why he never seemed to think Mom's abduction was as big a deal as I did.

"So . . . the humansmom and the humansdad make the baby all by themself," J.Lo said slowly. "Aaand . . . afters they make the baby they . . . keep it?"

"Yes."

"As like a pet."

"No."

"No?" J.Lo frowned and opened and closed his hands.

"No. Not like a pet. Like a baby. It's their baby," I said, "so they love it and take care of it. The mother and father together. Usually."

"Usually," he repeated. "But not with Tip?"

It was funny to hear someone just ask this question like it was nothing at all. It didn't bother me to talk about my dad, but people always figured it did.

"No, not with me," I said. "My mom raised me, of course, but I never knew my dad, and he never knew me."

"Ah, yes," said J.Lo. "This is the way it is being with the Boov. Nobody knows their offspring, and nobody knows their parents."

"Nobody?"

J.Lo explained. It seemed that, of those seven Boov genders he'd mentioned before, nearly all had some part to play in order to make a baby Boov. When a female had an egg to lay, she did it and just walked away. There were special places to leave them all over the cities. And if a passing boy, or boyboy, or whatever, saw that there was an egg that needed attention, he did what needed to be done and left. Eggs that were ready to turn into Boov were collected by those whose job it was to do so. Somebody else had the job of feeding and raising the babies, and still another Boov taught them. The closest thing the Boov would ever have to a family was the work unit they were assigned to as adults.

"Well, that's one thing we humans do better than you Boov," I said. "Families are better."

J.Lo shook his head as much as an alien with no neck can do that.

"Families are meaning you have to care about some

peoples more than others," he said. "But all peoples are just as good. Alls have a job to do."

I didn't know how to argue with that.

"I haveto seen the human families," he added. "Some of them, the peoples, they stay in a family they do not like."

"Yeah? What's *that* supposed to mean?"

J.Lo flinched. "Did I say wrong? I meanted only that some humans do not have an easy living with their family-mates. The brothers and sisterns, especiably."

"Oh. Yeah. Some families . . . don't always get along like they should," I agreed. "Some people even hate their family sometimes. But they love them, too. They still love them. You Boov . . . do you . . ."

"Do the Boov what?"

I didn't know how to ask what I was asking. So I just asked it.

"Do you have love?"

"Maaa-aa-aa-aa-aa!" J.Lo laughed. "Of course the Boov love. The Boov love *everything*!"

I didn't feel up to arguing about it, but I was pretty sure if you loved everything you didn't *really* love anything.

I changed the subject and asked more about Boov stuff. Eventually J.Lo explained that all Boov could breathe just a little bit underwater—enough to last for a half hour or more. He was shocked to learn that most humans could only last for about thirty seconds.

I complained that he should have told me about this before, and that he'd as good as tricked me into hugging him, but then I forgave him. He was enthusiastically grateful.

I could try to tell you all that he told me, but I doubt I'd remember everything. And I might as well let him tell some of it himself.

J.Lo made this after we left Florida. He was sure his people would have to leave Earth now that the Gorg had arrived, and he wanted us humans to understand who the Boov were. He couldn't write, of course, but he could draw okay. Apparently comic books were, like, a serious art form on Boovworld, not just stories of badly dressed men hitting each other.

A PICTORIAL HISTORY of the BOOVISH RACE
with PICTURES
by J.Lo

Edited & Lettered
by Gratuity Tucci

Millions of years ago, 3:15 P.M.—

God creates life.

The God of Boovworld is not a person,
or a ghost, or animal or such. Our God
is the sea. She covers most of the planet,
still creating and shaping the world.

Some Boov don't believe
the water is God.

They believe that
water is water.

100,000 years ago –

Primitive CaveBoov live in
holes in the ocean floor.

8,000 years ago – Boov leave their caves, invent farming, form clans.
Different clans begin warring with one another.

Whether they are working or fighting, Boov cooperate to get the job done.

7,900 years ago—
Tools invented.

7,800-6,000 years ago— Many other things invented such as

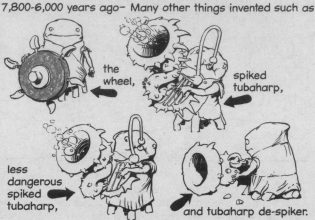

the wheel,

spiked tubaharp,

less dangerous spiked tubaharp,

and tubaharp de-spiker.

5,000 years ago— First Boov ventures onto land on a dare.	By running up the beach,	touching the closest tree,	and running back,	he wins 5 dollars and dies of asphyxiation.

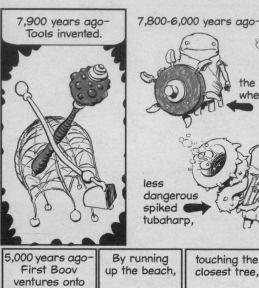

There is no human word for his name, but the Boovish word looks like this:

It is pronounced like the sound of a crying baby riding a duck that is talking with its mouth full.

Sound Of A Crying Baby Riding A Duck That Is Talking With Its Mouth Full becomes an inspiration to the Boovish race.

4,990 years ago—Touch the Tree is the most popular Boov sport, more popular even than Loudly Question the Superintendant or Stickyfish.

4,980 years ago—Boov who play Touch the Tree seem to be less likely to die from asphyxiation than before.

4,970-3000 years ago—

See previous panel.

4,700 years ago—Great schools of learning are formed. Boov study science, create great art. Industry grows, spreading its octopus ink through the waters.

Many Boov continue to play in secret, however.

3,000 years ago—All clans unite under the HighBoov. The HighBoov are our leaders and top priests of the sea. They consecrate Touch the Tree as a sacred act, to be played only by the HighBoov.

2,000 years ago—
Many schools closed by the HighBoov, because **Money Is Needed Elsewhere.**

Boov are told not to worry about learning unimportant things. Boov are told to learn one useful thing that may be done over and over again and give their life meaning. HighBoov devise clever tests to find which Boov should be taught more, and which Boov should not be taught because **Money Is Needed Elsewhere.**

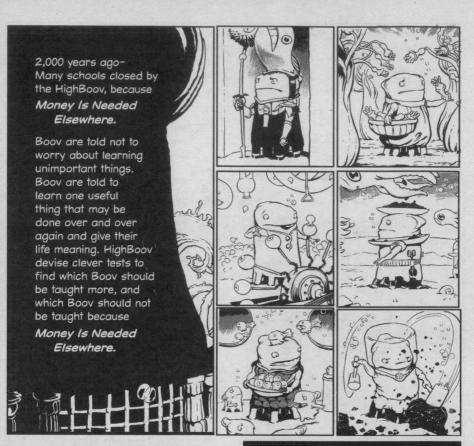

1,150 years ago – Certain Boov who were taught many things announce that industry is polluting the waters of Boovworld.

These scientists predict that the oceans soon will no longer be able to sustain life, unless things are changed.

1,149 years ago – HighBoov declare that these warnings of pollution cannot be **proven,** so therefore nothing should be changed. The scientist Boov who gave these warnings are declared **evil-evil** that they should call our God unclean. These Boov are named the **Forgotten** and sent onto land into exile forever. Some of them die of asphyxiation. Most don't.

1,003 years ago—

God dies of asphyxiation.

1,002 years ago – Many Boov are very sick. The waters no longer hold life. The HighBoov declare that it is our **Grand Destiny** to live instead on the land. All Boov play a game of Touch the Tree from which there is no returning.

Some die of asphyxiation. Most don't.

1,001 years ago— Life on land is hard. The Boov do not know how to live.

The Forgotten find the Boov in great distress, and show them the ways of land.

The Forgotten are different, now.

Their skin is darker gray, and their speech has changed.

They have built a new world for themselves.

1,000.8 years ago— The Forgotten are kindly asked to leave, because **the Forgotten Are Needed Elsewhere.**

500 years ago – Boov society has reached an *amazing pinnacle of greatness.* Much of the sea has begun to live again, but the Boov stay on land.

They live in majestic cities and keep the *long-eared koobish* as livestock.

Where once Boov made things, now things make things.

Boov have fabulous new careers keeping records of what the things do, or have done to them.

47% of Boov are statisticians.

not statisticians

other

statisticians

18% work to determine what color things should be.

400 years ago– Art is replaced by entertainment.

350 years ago– Entertainment is replaced by Talking About Entertainment.

325 years ago – Talking now almost always occurs over vast distances– on phones or by computer. Face-to-face communication is carried out mostly by T-shirt.

300 years ago—
Boov scientists
try to send
first koobish
into space. The
koobish, named
Peeches, gets
loose in the
capsule and
leans against a
big red button
labeled **NO.**

Capsule
explodes before
leaving atmosphere.

296 years ago—
Second attempt.
A restrained koobish
named Poolah makes
it into space.

Space has no air.
Poolah dies of
asphyxiation.

294 years ago—
Third attempt.

A restrained koobish named Haanie
with a breathing mask and air tanks
enters space and hits a capsule
from a neighboring planet
going in the
opposite
direction.

293 years ago—
Scientists stop naming the koobish.

292 years ago—
Anonymous koobish
enters space, circles
Boovworld twice, splashes
down correctly in ocean.
Koobish recovered from
capsule, alive but cross.
She is given nice meal and
parade, during which she
dies of natural causes.

* * *

By the end of the second night, we were trying to learn each other's language. J.Lo already spoke mine pretty good, of course, but he wanted to read and write as well. He even said something along the lines of how he was going to *have* to learn to read and write humanspeak now. I wondered what he meant. It sounded like he was fixing to stay on Earth even after the Boov left. I knew he was afraid to face his people, but I still expected he'd suck it up and go back to them at some point.

As for me, there was no way I could learn to speak Boov. According to J.Lo, I didn't have the anatomy. I said we just needed a sheep and some bubble wrap, but J.Lo had no idea what I was talking about.

He thought I might be able to *understand* Boovish one day, though, and I could probably learn to read and write. I was especially into trying that bubble writing in the air. It was pretty, once you got used to it.

"Okay . . ." I said, steadying the little turkey baster thing, "so . . . if I add a smaller bubble here—"

"No. No," J.Lo said, and I could see he was trying to hide a smile behind his hand. Which must have been a human habit he'd picked up, because Boov smiles are about three feet wide and Boov hands are the size of wontons.

"This bubble must to be lapping over."

"Overlapping."

"Yes. Over-lapping," he said. "The small bubble must be over the lap of the big bubble."

I tried again, but I squeezed too hard.

"Too big! Too big," J.Lo said, and now his wonton hand was forcing back a laugh, which honked out around the edges like he had an invisible trumpet.

"C'mon," I said, "it can't be *that* funny. I'm really trying, here."

"Yes . . . snnrx . . . yesss. I am sorry," he said, hopping up and down. "It is only that you have not written 'Gratuity' now, but instead a rude word for 'elbow.'"

"The Boov have a rude word for 'elbow'?"

"Yes."

"You're a very advanced race."

"You see? I am saying."

"Anyway." I sighed and put the baster down. "YOU have no room to laugh, that's all. I'm not doing any worse with Boovish than you did with English."

"Get off of the car," J.Lo huffed. "I am an English super-star."

"Uh-uh. There's no comparison. 'Gratuity' in written Boovish has seventeen different bubbles that all have to be the right size and in the right place. 'J.Lo' in written English only has three letters, and you *still* spelled it 'M—smiley face— pound sign.'"

Thunder cracked again. It was kind of all bark and no bite

now. It was drizzling so lightly that we were actually sitting on top of the car. I slid off the roof and looked over the edge of the building to the falling floodwaters below. It made me think of someone else who'd found himself on a high place after the rain stopped.

"I *told* you," said J.Lo as he joined me. "Was *not* a 'smiley face.' Was a 'five.'"

"You know," I said, "we have a story in the Bible about a flood. God tells this guy named Noah to build a boat big enough for his family and two of every animal on Earth. Then it rains for forty days and nights."

"Huhn. This is very interesting," said J.Lo. "The Boov have a religion story about a girl who keeps all the animals into a big jar of water for when there is a year of *no* rain."

"Do they make it through the year okay?"

"No. She forgets to punch the airholes and they die of asphyxiation."

"Ah."

Soon it would be dry enough to leave. The water had dropped, leaving a dark bathtub ring on every building in the city. The clouds were even breaking up, and needles of sunlight poked through. It was also perfectly possible to see the Gorg's big purple ship again.

And I wondered what it was like for Noah, thinking the rain had stopped and the worst was over, but no—he still had a family and about a million animals to lead down a mountain.

And he had to find a place to live, and build shelter, and start the whole world over again.

"When I was a little girl," I said, sitting down, "the wallpaper in my room had pictures of the Noah story."

"Pictures of forty nights of raining?"

"Well, no," I said. Now that I thought about it, that wallpaper didn't show any rain at all. Wasn't rain the whole point? "No, it had cute pictures of Noah's ark. His boat. Adorable little zebras and elephants and things. It's a popular story for little kids, I guess because of the animals."

"Little people like the animals," said J.Lo, nodding and folding his hands. "Is true with the Boov as well."

"You know what's weird, though? It's weird that the ark would be such a kids' story, you know? I mean, it's . . . really a story about death. Every person who isn't in Noah's family? They die. Every animal, apart from the two of each on the boat? They die. They all die in the flood. Billions of creatures. It's the worst tragedy ever," I finished, my voice tied off by a knot in my chest. I'd been speaking too fast without breathing, and I sucked down air before speaking again.

"What the *hell*," I said, "pardon my language, was that doing on my wallpaper?"

J.Lo understood me well enough by now not to answer. So I looked off to the west in silence, and saw a thousand miles of hopeless wasteland before we reached Arizona, with only a terrible new purple god to watch over it.

J.Lo's hand was on my shoulder suddenly, and he said, "Rainbow."

I looked up. First at him and then at the sky where he was pointing.

"A doubled rainbow," he said. "These are lucky. I have been missing rainbows. On Boovworld we had them alls the time."

It was a perfect, bright, unbroken rainbow stretching over the western horizon like a door. It was so beautiful it looked fake. Above it was another, fainter one in reverse, and I exhaled and thought, Of course. Of *course* there's a rainbow. 'Bout time. We sat and looked at it for ten minutes. I stared until I couldn't stand sitting still any longer.

I hopped up. "We should go. Don't you think? Don't you think it's safe to go now?"

J.Lo looked at me funny. He probably wondered why I was smiling.

"Yes. I am thinking it is. Safe. Safe for going."

"We have a lot of ground to cover, after all," I said, bounding back to the car. "It'll be at least a few days before we get to Arizona. And once we're there, we have to help everyone get rid of the Gorg. Or the Takers. Whatever you want to call them."

"Get . . . get rid of—?"

"We'll do it," I said, looking J.Lo square in the face. "I think we will. But I'll . . . we'll . . . y'know—need your help, maybe."

"Yes. Okay, then."

The sun was really coming through now, and birds were beginning to test the air. A cool breeze that smelled like pennies brushed my face. We got back in the car, and I hopped it down through the construction, landing again and again on an extra-thick cushion of whatever it was that made Slushious float. Each time we dropped to a lower story, my stomach leaped like I had a rabbit in me. At least once I couldn't stop myself from laughing. And when we reached the surface of the great big wading pool that was Florida, I turned west, speeding into a beautiful day that seemed more and more like a promise.

* * *

J.LO'S **8** Things You Have Always Wanted to Know About the *Gorg* But Were Afraid to Ask the *Gorg* Because the *Gorg* Might Punch You In The Face:

WEREFOR YOU KNOWING IT?

1 Many assume Gorg is the name of a race, or a species. A common mistake! They are known across the galaxy as the **Takers**...

...but the real name of this race is the **Nimrogs**.

NIMROG

And every member of the race is now named **Gorg.**

HELLO! My Name is GORG

I hope this clears everything up.

2 HOW LARGE?

Gorg are about eight feet tall, and weigh one kiloboov. In the Gorg's own units of measurement they are exactly one Gorg tall and weigh roughly a Gorg.

3 The *Gorg* smell like a bouquet of lilacs... sprinkled with cinnamon... and buried under a shoulder-high pile of rancid dogmeat.

4 The earliest Nimrog languages were based on punching. Much of this ancient language has been rediscovered and studied. At right and below is the conjugation of the Old Nimrogish verb "to punch."

"I PUNCH"

"YOU PUNCH"

"WE PUNCH"

"HE, SHE, IT PUNCHES"

As Nimrog culture developed they formed new languages out of poking and light slapping.

5 For a long time Nimrogs were only a danger to other Nimrogs. They fought one another in a three-hundred-year-old civil war that is believed to have started over a parking space.

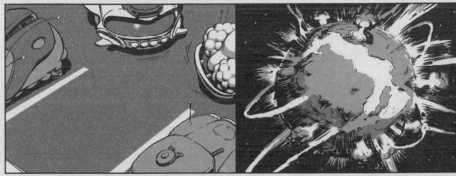

6 When the Nimrogs first began to reach out to other worlds, it was often to take, and sometimes to trade. When the wars ended at home the Nimrogs, now all Gorg, took to policing other planets. They would attack worlds that they decided had bad governments, in order to free the people living there. But many noticed that they were really only invading planets known to have good restaurants.

WHERE WILL THE GORG LIVE?

■ GORG
□ WATER

WEREFOR YOU KNOWING IT?

If you took every Gorg in the galaxy, and stacked them one on top of the other, the Gorg would kill you.

7 All Gorg are left-handed.

8 All Gorg enjoy musical theater.

"I'm sorry, but it's *still* pulling to the left," I said as I drove Slushious through a really nowhere part of Texas. J.Lo had made a new fin out of the side of a green Dumpster, but it wasn't adjusted right.

"Yes. I am knowing now what is wrong. Pull it over for fix— MAA!" he said suddenly. "Seventeen!"

He was pointing out the window at another armadillo. He couldn't get enough of them.

"What is it with you and those things?" I asked.

"Ah. They look like something we had on Boovworld."

"Not those koobish things you mentioned?"

"No," said J.Lo. "The long-eared koobish is taller. Withto a short nose. And dark curledy hair."

"Is there a short-eared koobish, then?"

"Mmmyes . . ." said J.Lo. "But it is technically not really a koobish. Is more alike a kind of singing pumpkin."

We had conversations like this all the time, where I just eventually gave up.

I pulled off the road and down a ramp that emptied right next to a MicrocosMart parking lot. So I drove up to the store entrance, which was barricaded by a big security gate. And that was interesting, because I thought it might mean there was still some stuff inside.

"Twenty minutes," said J.Lo as he opened his toolbox. This could have meant anything. J.Lo was either one of those people with no real concept of time, or else he actually didn't know how long a minute was. I crouched down to have a look at the lock on the gate.

It was like a bike lock. It needed a cylindrical key, and couldn't be picked with a hairpin.

I turned back to J.Lo and shouted, "Can you toss me the purple thing?"

"Which one?"

"Um . . . shoot. You know, the purple thing. With the things?"

J.Lo reached into his toolbox and threw me what I wanted.

"Thanks."

"Do not even mention it."

I pressed the narrow end of the purple thing against the keyhole and pushed one of the things. A black fluid oozed into the hole, filling every nook. After a few seconds it had hardened, and I turned the new key and pulled up the gate.

"I'm going inside," I said.

J.Lo didn't look up. "See if they have shaving cream," he said.

"What flavor?"

"Mountain Freshness."

I entered the store and saw I was right: there was still a lot of merchandise on the shelves. I could have filled the car with all kinds of stuff. Instead I just filled a basket with the things we really needed—food, water, a toothbrush for J.Lo so he wouldn't keep using mine, a new toothbrush for me for roughly the same reason, and so forth.

This time twenty minutes must have meant about a minute and a half, because I ran into J.Lo in the stationery section. He was carrying armfuls of junk we didn't need.

"What is all this?" I said. "Is that a hockey stick? What are we going to do with a hockey stick?"

"I do not know," said J.Lo. "I *like* it."

"It's because you're a boy," I said. "Boys always want to carry sticks around. It's like a sickness with you. What about all this?"

I was looking at a heap of paper, ink pens, pencils, and a sparkly pencil sharpener shaped like a frog's head.

"Is for drawing. I have not drawed in a long time."

I could see this was a big deal to him. "Fine. But not all this other stuff."

"You have stuffs."

"I have stuff we really need," I said. "Look, I know I kinda just grabbed everything I could get my hands on before, but that was different."

"Whyfor?"

"That was before I decided we were going to get rid of the Gorg . . . before I knew that people would be returning to their homes, hoping their stuff was still there. Now it's stealing. We can only take what we really need."

"Ooh," said J.Lo. "We need this." He was holding up a

baseball cap with a little battery-powered fan hanging down from the bill.

"That wouldn't even fit on your head."

J.Lo frowned at it.

"It goes on your head?"

"C'mon," I said. "We should get going."

"But we will be needing the tiny fan head for the Arizona hotness. Your car has not any air conditions."

"It doesn't have *air-conditioning*," I said, "because you drank all the Freon."

J.Lo set the hat down. "We should gets going."

We stepped back outside, blinking in the sunshine, and I locked the security gate.

"You know," I said as we got back into Slushious, "you could always just clone some more Freon."

We drove up the ramp to the highway.

"Neh," said J.Lo with a wave. "It never tastes as good when I make it. MAA! Eighteen!"

"That's the same one."

"Oh."

It was nighttime when we made the decision to change course.

We were riding off into the sunset. You really can do that in the west. The sunsets do something there that they don't do in Pennsylvania. The sun holds on a little tighter to the day, and has to be dragged down screaming, with a kind of angry beauty that makes the sky burn away into pinks and oranges and violets. It's unrealistic. You see the day flame out through a car windshield like you were watching it on TV, with thick trails of clouds like party streamers, and blazing light, and you can't help but think that that's really a bit much, isn't it? Let's not over*do* it. Then the next night it all happens again, but brighter.

So on this night the sun went down, fighting as usual, and J.Lo started to make sort of obvious yawning noises, and I was ignoring him because The Trip Was Taking Too Long. Texas was all there had ever been and all there ever would be, and I was getting panicky. I've since heard about deep-sea scuba divers going nuts just thinking about all of the water above them and below them and all around, so that some have been known to suddenly freak out, rip their tanks off their backs, and kick hard for the surface. I was going through a similar sort of thing, where I had to fight the urge to halt the car, leap out the door, and make a run for it.

I mean, who ever thought a state that big was a good idea? It's just arrogant.

So I was trying to get as far across as possible before we had to stop for the night. Then the car suddenly shook, and I thought the sun was going down again, as a glowing ball soared over us and toward the horizon, *fast*. Then there was another one, and I saw it was trailing hoses. Boovish ships. The big kind, like huge fishbowls of light. There was a third and fourth, tearing toward the Gorg. This was hard to see, because at this time of night the Gorg ship was only visible as a great disk of blackness where it blocked out the stars.

I looked over at J.Lo. He was alert, no more fake yawns and heavy eyes.

"They are probably to shooting at them," he said.

I looked back at the horizon. "The Gorg, you mean? They're shooting?"

"The Boov," he answered. "They are probably to shooting at the Gorg. We will not be ables to see."

I realized what he meant. The Boov guns didn't make any light, and the Gorg ship was too dark to see any damage. But then I saw a flash of light in the big circle of darkness.

"Ha! There," I said. "Your guys got 'em there! You could see the—"

"No," said J.Lo.

Then a Boov ship, barely visible in the distance, burst like a flashbulb. It exploded too close to another ship, and that one bled light as it sank as slow as a soap bubble toward the earth. You couldn't hear the Gorg fire their guns from here, but the destruction of each Boov ship was loud like a firework in your skull. Suddenly the Boovish weapons, which had always seemed so sneaky and sinister, seemed almost like a gentle way to kill.

"J.Lo . . . I . . ."

There was another flash from the Gorg, and two seconds later a third ship went down. The fourth turned fast and headed back toward us, but it wasn't any use. Another flash, and the glass bowl was full of fire that crawled down each hoseleg like they were cigarettes.

I had come to a stop without meaning to.

"I would like to keep driving," said J.Lo.

Before I could answer, there was another flash in the darkness.

"That's weird," I said. "They fired again, but there aren't—"

The blast punched hard into the ground, about fifty yards from Slushious, and pushed up a tidal wave of dirt and weeds that rained down as we rolled from the shock. Pig screeched and tumbled around the cabin. A moment later we were right-side up again, with a broken back window and a missing fin. The new one, of course.

"AAAAAAAA!" J.Lo shouted. "DriveDriveDriveDriveDrive!"

I turned off the road and into the desert. Slushious started off slowly, too slowly, but then we got a push as another Gorg barrage exploded behind us.

"They . . . they aren't *really* shooting at us, right?" I said. I couldn't believe it.

"Oh, no," said J.Lo, "they are probably just playing a little jokeYES THEY ARE SHOOTING AT US!"

The Gorg backed J.Lo up by way of destroying a small mountain just to our left. I swerved and hit the gas.

"But . . . from there? They're shooting at us from, like, Mexico?"

A convenience store ahead of us erupted in a mushroom cloud of flame and old magazines. J.Lo gestured at it impatiently.

"Okay! Okay!" I shouted. "They're shooting at us! I just thought maybe it was a coincidence."

"Oh, yes. You are always having to be right about everything. If *Gratuity* says it is a coincidence—"

Another explosion sent Slushious into a tailspin and spared me from the rest of J.Lo's point.

"Superfuel?" I asked, feeling sick.

"Alls gone! Nothing even to clone."

"What do I do?"

"Just keep to driving! They will lose us soon." There was another blast, but farther away. "We are wicked lucky to be small and hard to hit. The Gorg probably only were noticing us because the Boov flied so close."

The blasts had stopped. But I kept driving farther into the desert, herding a pack of terrified coyotes ahead of me. I looked back to check on Pig, who was cleaning herself spitefully on a floor mat. Then I looked at J.Lo.

"I'm sorry," I said. It was such a useless thing to say.

"Yes," said J.Lo. "We should not always try to fight them in this way. It has not ever worked."

"We couldn't see the Gorg ship. Maybe you Boov did a lot of damage."

J.Lo didn't answer.

"We'll figure out something new," I said. "Maybe your people and my people will figure out some new way together."

J.Lo smiled a little, quickly, then faced forward again. "We haveto drive more north. We are having to put more space between us and the Nimrogs."

"Right," I said. "What?"

"We haveto drive more—"

"There are Nimrogs now, too?" I asked. "Who are they?"

J.Lo fiddled with the tape player to tilt his seat back. "All Gorg are Nimrogs. All Nimrogs are now Gorg, also, but they did not always used to be."

"I can't even imagine what we're talking about."

"We are talking about the Nimrog race. Tip says she is going to get rid of them."

"Yeah," I breathed. I suddenly felt like I'd promised to lift a horse over my head. "But . . . what is Gorg . . . like, a nickname?"

"Oh, no. Gorg is their real name. Gratuity is Tip's real name," he said, then he made a noise like a drowning yodeler—"OOOlahluhlaaharlHEEdoo is J.Lo's real name. Taker is their nickname. They have many other nicknames; they are given them alls the time. Some people call them poomps, pardon my languages."

I tried to stay calm. "So all the Nimrogs . . . all of them . . . are named Gorg?"

"Yes."

"All of them?"

"Alls of them, yes."

"How . . . how many are there?" I asked.

"How many Nimrogs?"

"How many Gorg."

"They are the same thing."

"Then why did you ask?"

"There are many, manys Nimrogs. As many as they are wanting. They can always make more."

"I swear I will crash the car into a coyote if you don't start making sense."

"Ah," said J.Lo. "Hm. Ahhh . . . long ago, before perhaps Tip was born . . . How many years are you?"

"Eleven and a half."

J.Lo wheezed and sat upright. "Eleven! You have only eleven years? When I was eleven I was barely out of my inflatable training clothes."

"Back to the Nimrogs," I said.

"Yes. The Nimrogs had once many names. Like the Boov. Like the humans. But the Nimrogs, these are so awful they can not to even get along with themselfs. They fight each other—over land, over ideas. When alls the land belongs to one group of Nimrogs who think the same ideas, they find reasons for fighting one another. The right-handers fight the left-handers. Then the left-handers who enjoy musical theater fight at the left-handers who do not enjoy musical theater. And sos on. One day only two Nimrogs remain, named Aarfux and Gorg. Aarfux falls for the old your-shoelace-is-untied trick, and then there is only Gorg."

"Gorg," I repeated. "There was only one Nimrog named Gorg."

"By this time, yes. Beforethen there were many Nimrogs named Gorg. Gorg was a popular boy name, like Ethel."

I was aching to mention that Ethel was neither popular nor a boy's name, but I felt we were really getting some-where.

"But then . . . did the Gorg . . . did the Nimrogs always . . ." I trailed off. "How did Gorg make more Gorg?"

"He cloned. With teleclone machines, likewith I make the gasoline."

"But you said that was impossible."

"Impossible for the Boov," sighed J.Lo. "The Nimrogs found a way. They took the Boovish telecloners and changed them up."

"How did they get Boovish telecloners?"

"We . . . gave them."

"J.Lo!"

"I know, I know."

J.Lo explained that it was good strategy at the time. A lot of the early Nimrog wars were over resources like fuel. It was common for the Nimrogs on the losing side of battle to destroy their food and fuel and whatever so it wouldn't fall into enemy hands. The Nimrogs eliminated everything good on their planet this way. So different groups started raiding other planets, stealing what they could. The Boov thought teleclone machines could stop all that—if the Nimrogs could clone what they needed, they wouldn't need to leave home. So the Nimrogs got the machines by promising to stay in their own neighborhood. It worked for a while, but somehow they managed to start cloning and teleporting complicated things. No one knows how they did it.

"At firsts they cloned and teleported only dead things, like food. No one Nimrog wanted to be the first to try. But when Gorg was left onto the planet by himself, he had not anything to lose," said J.Lo. "Gorg became the worst kind of enemy. He had outlived all other Nimrogs. He was the most tough and strong. He could not get sick, and would not ever tire. And he had only to set one teleclone booth onto your planet, and soon there could there be a thousand Gorg, or a million. They could have Gorg everywheres. They could even cover their ships with them."

"Wait," I said. "You lost me."

"Yes?"

"Cover their ship—?" I said, then gagged. I remembered the way the big Gorg ball seemed to move on the surface. Its skin seemed to crawl, I thought, just like mine is crawling now.

"You don't mean they . . ."

"Yes," said J.Lo. "The shipskin is made of Gorg. Mixed-up Gorg, like from a blender. Is not even that hard—not hard like Boovish metals or plastics—but it heals. They can keep onto making more and more skin for replacing the old—"

J.Lo stopped talking when he saw the look on my face. I wanted to escape from the tight little car and run for it, now more than ever, but there would still be a whole black ocean of stars all around, pressing close, closing in.

"That is the grossest thing ever!" I shouted at the clear desert morning.

I'd gone to sleep thinking about a ship covered in skin and woken up the next morning thinking about a ship covered in skin. In between I'd dreamed of being captured by

Gorg, who all looked like Curly from Happy Mouse Kingdom. They demanded to know what made Slushious float, so I popped the hood, and the engine had changed to guts and organs, pumping and growling from hunger. I've had better nights.

"The grossest thing!" I said again. "Look at it. Look at it back there. It's closer than yesterday, isn't it."

J.Lo, who was driving, glanced at the rearview mirror.

"Yes. Closer, I am thinking."

We'd found our way through the desert brush to another wide, western highway. Down a six-lane road with a concrete divider big enough to have its own gift shop, we passed plaster box buildings and signs for chain restaurants. On the side of an antique mall, which I suppose was either a mall that sold antiques or else a really old mall, was a quote spray-painted in slashing letters:

> This is the way the world ends
> This is the way the world ends
> This is the way the world ends
> Not with a bang but a whimper.
> > T. S. Eliot

It made me feel strange.

"What happens when the Gorg get closer?" I asked. "What are they going to do?"

J.Lo sighed. "When they arriveto Smekla—to Earthland,

they will take some of the young and strong as for slaves,
and some of the less young and strong for furniture.

"*Then* their Gorgship will tear itselfs open a mouth,

and it will eat the world, and those peoples still on it.

"It willto teleport enormongous bites of Earthland away to Gorgworld as if eating an apple."

I looked again at the Gorg ship. It was definitely
closer. But the Boov seemed to have done some damage—
there were long red scars and a scattering of something
like bits of toilet paper stuck with blood all over its surface. In
the near distance I could also see schools of Boov ships
kicking through the air like shining octopi.

"The Boov willto hold them offs as long as is possible.
Could be weeks, could be months."

"Make the next right," I said.

"Yes."

We passed out of the town and into the great wide

nothing again. I wasn't even sure what state we were in, until a sign passed that read ROSWELL 50 MI.

"Huh. That's funny," I said.

"Funnies strange or funnies ha-ha?"

"A little of both. That sign just said we're gonna pass through Roswell."

"Yes?" said J.Lo, watching the road. "This is a city?"

"I guess so. It's just that it's famous for being where a UFO supposedly crashed like . . . sixty years ago or some-thing."

"What is 'you if oh'?"

It was crazy that he didn't know this. "It stands for 'Unidentified Flying Object,'" I said. "A flying saucer. An alien spaceship."

J.Lo hit the brakes. I was dumped off my seat and hit my head on the dash.

"Ow!"

"Seat belts," said J.Lo.

"What was that for?"

"We have to stop in the Roswell! We canto see the spaceship!"

I winced. "Yeah . . . except . . . I don't really think there ever was a spacesh—"

"You said! Tip saidto it crashed-landed!"

"No. No, it's . . . there's no proof. It's just something people say, but there's no proof. Like with Bigfoot, or Nessie."

"Bigfoot? Nessie?"

I sighed. Then I explained about Bigfoot, and about the blurry photos. And I told him about the Loch Ness Monster in Scotland, and about the blurry photos of that. Then I had to explain where Scotland was, and he asked what was a loch, and I didn't know so I made something up.

Finally he sat still and nodded his head. "So no Bigfoot. No Nessie."

"Probably not," I said. J.Lo sounded sad. It was sort of sad, come to think of it. Sad to admit that there wasn't really any-thing so mysterious and great. And then I remembered for the eight hundredth time that I was talking to a space alien. I was trying to explain to a space alien that there were no such things as monsters.

"If something that big lived in a lake in Scotland," I said, "I think we'd have found it by now."

"Yes. It would haveto be very big to be a lochniss monster."

"Yeah."

"Bigger even than the snakewhale."

"Yeah," I said. "Bigger than the what now?"

"The snakewhale," he said. "That lives in waters near Scot'sland. I am not knowing the right name for it."

"Well," I said, "I guess I don't either. I don't know much about Scotland."

J.Lo began to drive again.

"One of the Boov ships," he explained, "it wasto collecting interesting Earthland animals, for like a zoo. The Boov had elephants, and the armadillo, and many bugs and fish. Many other things.

"Say," he said with a grin, "like your Noah's arkboat."

"Yeah. Sort of. And this snakewhale was one of the fish?"

"Yes. I am sorry I do not know the reals word. I only remember it was captured near your Scot'sland. Very pretty. Sixty feets long, if you are counting the neck."

I looked out at the road for a moment, mouthing the words *Sixty feet long. Counting the neck.*

"Can you draw it?" I asked.

J.Lo stopped the car, and I fished out his paper and pencils. And he drew the snakewhale:

I stared at it for the longest time. I stared so long I must have hurt J.Lo's feelings.

"It is . . . not very good," he said. "I made the flippers too small."

"No," I said. "'Sfantastic. I bet it looks just like her."

Maybe there really was a spaceship, I thought. Way back then.

"Could one of your Boov ships have visited Earth so long ago?" I asked.

"I am doubting it. Earthland is not in a very nice neighborhood. Maybies it was the Habadoo. Say, do you wants to hear a funny joke about the Habadoo? It seems that a Boov, a KoshzPoshz, and a Habadoo all are walking inside a mahahmbaday. And the Boov sa—no. Wait. I am forgetting to say the KoshzPoshz is carrying a purp. So the Boov—no. The KoshzPoshz says—"

I wasn't really listening. I was thinking about the whole UFO craze. It felt ridiculous, now that we'd been invaded twice, to think about all the Top Secret alien visitors we'd supposedly had all these years. It was all crop circles and mystery, when the truth turned out to be as obvious as a giant purple ball you could see from five states away.

". . . So then the Habadoo, he says: 'That's not your purp, that's my poomp!'" J.Lo hiccuped with laughter.

"Uh-huh," I said.

"You are not a fan of ethnical jokes, ah? Look, is

okay if I tells it, I am one sixteenth Habadoo—"

"Y'know, I don't want you to get your hopes up too much about seeing a crashed spaceship. I was just thinking about all those old UFO stories, and they all agree that the army or NASA or someone hid the spaceship someplace called Area 51. I don't know where that is."

"N'aasa?"

"Yeah. NASA."

"In Boovish, 'n'aasa' means soft and beige."

"That's not what it means here. It's a name," I explained. "It stands for something else."

"The name . . . is standing?"

I thought for a moment.

"It's a name that's made up of other words and . . . stands for them," I said. "UFO's the same way. Or TV or . . . or J.Lo."

"What."

"What, what?"

"You did to say my name," said J.Lo, "but then afters my name you did not say anything—"

"No," I said, "that's not what I meant. I was saying that J.Lo's like NASA."

"Do not."

"Do not what?"

"J.Los do not like the NASA," he said. "We do not even know the NASA—"

"Okay. No. Time out. I mean that NASA stands for

something, just like J.Lo stands for Jennifer Lopez."

"I do?"

"Yes."

J.Lo frowned. "I suppose I might do if he asked me."

"NASA," I said, "stands for . . . National American Space
. . . Association. Or National Air and Space . . . something. I
don't remember."

"I stand for Jennifer LOH-pez," J.Lo whispered.

"Or Never Answer Stupid Aliens," I said. "Maybe it stands
for that."

"Aaah." J.Lo nodded. "You are meaning the NASA is an
acronym."

I stared at him for a moment, then frowned and kicked
the dash.

"Yes."

"And it is being a kind of . . . space club?"

"Yeah. It was part of the government. They built satellites
and space shuttles and things."

"And the soft beige space club hided the ship?"

"Maybe. Nobody knows. The government says that none
of it's true. There are people—*were* people—around here who
claimed to see UFOs all the time, but the government always
said they were just weather balloons. The UFOs, I mean."

"They are to hiding something!" shouted J.Lo.

"Jeez," I said. "All right."

* * *

J.Lo was still driving when we hit the highway sign and skidded over the shoulder. I was rooting around in the back for Pig's food. But as Slushious hurtled forward, I turned to squint into the green reflected light from the road sign, which had impaled itself into something really important-looking on the car hood, and watched as we snapped the barbed wire, terrified the antelope, fishtailed past the all-too-accurate WRONG WAY sign, and barreled toward a fiberglass shed.

"Hit the brakes!" I shrieked.

"No working!" said J.Lo, pumping the pedal. "Sign pokery in theyl ALARM!" His English got really bad when he was under stress. He swerved around the shed, and used his free hand to pound the dashboard again and again in the same spot, as if something good would come of it.

"Activate!" he shouted at the dash. "Deploy!"

He wasn't watching the road, or rather the alpaca farm, so I stretched forward to slap his hand away from the tuner and grab it myself. I steered us through the animals and into what appeared to be someone's homemade motorcross course. We ducked and dove through gullies, and launched over hills and ramps tall enough to keep Pig airborne most of the time and ensure that I bit my tongue at least twice.

"Whah ah thoo twying to do?!" I asked as J.Lo kept punching the dash.

"Yes, please!" J.Lo answered. "Feeds them to me as I drive!"

"No . . . whath are hyoo twying to do?"

"Ah! Trying to *make! Safety! Devices! Work!*" he said, punching after each word. "Work! Work! Work!"

We were through the obstacle course and drifting toward what I would later learn was an arroyo, but could easily pass for a big ditch. But brakes or no brakes, we were running out of momentum, and I sighed with relief when we finally came to a stop right at the arroyo's edge.

"Yes," said J.Lo. "Good. But still I am wondering—"

There was a noise like *boof*, and a limp parachute farted out Slushious's backside.

"Aha. But that is still not explaining what happened to the—"

Eighteen enormous pink beach balls sprouted out of Slushious in every direction and bounced us end over end into the arroyo.

J.Lo smiled weakly as the cloud of dust and jackrabbits settled, and the beach balls began to squeal and deflate. I squinted at the highway sign that was still lodged in front of our windshield. NOW ENTERING ROSWELL.

"Ha. Well," I said, "the next time someone claims no aliens ever crashed here, I'll know what to tell him."

"Is not my fault!" said J.Lo. "There was a boy human onto a bicycle!"

"A boy hu—a kid?"

"Onto a bicycle! Bicyclisting! I swerved to miss, and missed missing the green sign instead."

"Are you sure? Maybe you were just . . . what's the word . . . hallucinating."

"I am assured."

"Look, J.Lo, once back in Florida I thought I saw a bunch of goats in little cars. I was just tired—"

Then, in the distance, I heard a shout—maybe the word "Hurry," but definitely a kid's voice. J.Lo's and my eyes met.

"Ohmygosh," I said. "We have to go."

"But . . . Slushiouscar cannot move until the Safetypillows unflate! And we have no brakes—"

There were more voices, a group of people, a many-legged multiheaded thing coming to get us.

"Go!" I whispered. "Hide in those trees!"

J.Lo squealed something in Boovish and looked every which way, grabbed a bedsheet from the backseat of the car and forced a door open, then pushed his way through the hissing beach balls and ran, half shrouded like a billowing ghost, with Pig chasing after.

I hesitated. Should I stay or go? The voices were close, right on top of us. Suddenly I was beating back the beach balls and pushing a door open, too. I ran halfway to J.Lo's hiding place when I remembered his toolbox. If the weird car didn't give him away, the weird tools certainly would. So I raced back, grabbed the box, and stumbled through the low shrubs and stones to the little copse of trees where I'd seen Pig and J.Lo disappear.

I rustled through the leaves and stinging branches to find J.Lo small and huddled, clutching the bedsheet around his face like a shivering old woman. Pig squatted between a few of his legs.

"I didn't know what to do," I whispered. "Like, should I talk to them? Try to explain about the—"

"Sh!" said J.Lo.

A group of people were shuffling down into the arroyo. They circled Slushious but kept their distance, like it was a strange dog. The Safetypillows were flat and waggling now like pink tongues, until they slipped with a *Thwip!* into the car's cracks and gaps, and were gone.

Everyone jumped—the kids, the women, the men—and took a step back. Slushious was quiet now, looking as innocent as a car can when it's floating six inches off the ground.

"Hello?" one of the men called out.

"Shhh!" said another.

"What?"

"What if the driver isn't human? What if this is an alien car?"

"Kat, this is a Chevy Sprint."

"So what if it is?"

"It *is* hovering. . . ."

"Shut up, you guys!"

I counted two men, two women, two little boys, and a baby girl. The boys were peering into Slushious and calling dibs on our food.

"It tried to hit me," said one of the boys. "But I did . . . I did a jump on my bike and I jumped over the car, and the car missed me and it crashed. *BKOOOSH!*"

"You weren't supposed to be riding your bike this far out in the *first place*," said the woman named Kat, and the boy scowled.

"Dibs on the bug spray!" said the other boy.

"Nuh-uh!"

"Yes-huh!"

"I called it first!"

"Did not!"

J.Lo leaned toward me. "But *I* called it first," he whispered. "You heard me do, back in Mississippies."

"Shh," I said.

The adults were fanning out, trying to understand what they were dealing with. It was only a matter of time before they found us. I looked at J.Lo's sheet, and remembered that I was holding his toolbox.

"Is there anything in here that'd be good for cutting cloth?" I asked.

J.Lo quietly rummaged through the toolbox and produced something that looked like a fat ballpoint pen.

"Squeeze the handle and draw the cut," he said.

"Good. Put your helmet up."

"Whatnow?"

"Put your helmet up. I have an idea."

"I do not want my helmet up. It gets hot."

"Please."

J.Lo said a word in Boovish I couldn't make out. Something like "Claap," but with a popping sound in the middle. The clear bowl snapped up from all sides and met in the middle, above his head. There was a little circular vent in the front. I pulled the sheet all the way over him.

"Ah, aha," whispered J.Lo. "Good. With the sheets as this, we will not be able to see the mens. Here is my question: can not they still see us?"

As he spoke I trimmed the excess sheet where it lay in the dirt. Then I cut a little circle where I thought J.Lo's eye might be.

"Oh, hello," he said.

I lined the hole up with his eye, then cut another.

"Aha," said J.Lo, then he made another Boovish noise. The glass of his helmet turned a dark blue. "Better?"

"Yeah. Really good. Now follow my lead."

Then I walked out from the trees, bold as anything.

The boys were still looking at the car. Some of the adults had formed a little huddle to decide their next move. Others searched the bushes. None of them were looking our way. I cleared my throat.

"Hi!" I said.

"Gaa!" said the closest man, and fell backward on the seat of his big khaki shorts.

"Where did *you* come from?" he asked.

"Pennsylvania," I answered.

Everyone gaped. A stout woman wearing a T-shirt that read, "Don't blame me, I voted for Spock" stepped forward.

"Well, hi there. I'm Vicki. Vicki Lightbody," she said, offering her hand. "You don't have to call me Mrs. Lightbody, you can call me Vicki."

"I'm Gr . . . Grace," I said. I didn't feel like having that conversation. "This is my little brother . . . JayJay."

J.Lo had been sort of half hiding behind me, but now he poked out his sheet-covered head and made like he was going to shake Vicki Lightbody's hand, too. I pushed him back.

"Hey, Halloween's not for a few months, kid," said Kat.

"Yeah . . ." I said, "but when the aliens invaded he got real scared and he put his ghost costume on, and now he refuses to take it off. Mom says he has a condition."

"Yes," said J.Lo. "I am conditioned."

I could have slapped the both of us. "Plus, he talks with a funny voice," I added. "It's part of the condition."

"Is not funny," J.Lo whispered, but I kicked at him with my heel.

Vicki looked at us with a sad, oh-you-poor-things sort of look. It stinks to have people look at you like that, but it was the effect I was going for. Kat wasn't so sympathetic.

"I'll take it off him," she said, and strode forward.

"No!" said J.Lo.

"No!" I said. "Don't do it. If anyone tries, he starts screaming and . . . wets himself and stuff."

That stopped Kat cold. She stepped back again.

"Well, he sounds like a Boov."

Vicki clucked her tongue. "That's a terrible thing to—That's not true, JayJay. You don't sound anything like a Boov."

"Sounds *exactly* like a Boov."

"Shut up, Kat."

Vicki Lightbody gave her a look, a look that said the subject was closed, and Kat backed down; but not without stealing little glances at J.Lo from time to time. I casually stepped between them.

"Where are your parents?" asked one of the men.

"It's just me—just us and our mom," I said. "And hopefully she's in Arizona. That's where we're going."

"But why—"

"We got separated because of the aliens," I continued. "I thought I could make it to Arizona on my own."

"That's a lot to handle for two children all alone," said Vicki Lightbody.

I'm not a big fan of the word "child." I don't know any kid who likes it. But somehow we all grow up to be adults who say it all the time. It's an insult when they use it to describe another adult, but they still turn around and use it to describe us. Like we're not going to notice. Mostly adults only talk about "children" when they're trying to make us seem precious and defenseless anyway.

"It's a lot for *anybody* to handle alone," I said. "But . . . luckily, we met this Boov in Pennsylvania who . . . wasn't all mean and stupid like the rest of them. He fixed up our car so the trip would be easier. It might have taken a little longer without him."

Nobody said anything for a few breaths. The rustling leaves sounded like faint applause.

"Well," said Vicki, "one of the guys will drive your car back, and we'll all see about some dinner."

"Why . . . why don't we just leave the car here," I said. I couldn't mention the brakes—we were going to have to fix that problem on our own, and do it without letting these people know how handy my so-called little brother was with Boovish machines.

"It has a sign sticking out of it," said a man. He tried to pull it out but snapped his hand back with a yelp and a spray of blue sparks.

"Yeah, it always has that," I said. "Should we go?"

Vicki Lightbody had a baby daughter named Andromeda. They mostly lived alone. I say "mostly," because everyone else apparently came and went through Vicki's apartment as they pleased, as though it were the only place in Roswell with a shower.

Vicki busied herself in her kitchenette while Andromeda

the Lightbodies

sat in her high chair and banged a spoon against the tray.

J.Lo and I shifted our feet, not knowing where to stand.

"You said I was not mean and stupids," J. Lo whispered.

"I know. Shut up."

"You *like* me."

"Shut *up.*"

I saw Vicki watching us.

"So . . . you all decided to stay in Roswell?" I asked.

"It's my home," Vicki answered. "I've lived here for forever. And it's a pretty important place, don't you know. It's smack in the intersection of two powerful ley lines. That's why so many spacecraft crash here."

J.Lo and I glanced at each other.

"And the other people . . ." I said, "they're your family?"

"Oh, no. No. They're just visitors that got stuck here when the Boov closed the roads. They were in town for the big UFO festival we have every summer."

Kat and one of the men entered the apartment and said they were using her bathroom because "David" was "stinking up the one in the museum." J.Lo went to get a better look at Andromeda. I thought about what Vicki said.

"So . . . this UFO festival was when?"

"Last month, just like it always is. Right before the Boov announced Moving Day, as it turned out."

"So you still had your UFO festival? I mean, the Boov had already been here for five months."

"Ha!" said the man. "You catch on fast, kid."

I didn't know what he meant.

"What better time to hold the U-Fest-O than after the invasion?" asked Vicki. "It's a meeting of the greatest minds in paranormal research from all over the world! We know more about the Boov than anybody."

"Like about the Boov crashes in '47 and '63," said Kat as she emerged from the bathroom. "And all the hundreds of sightings, and how the Boov want to impregnate us women to save their dying race."

The man snorted. I mouthed "You do?" at J.Lo, but he quickly shook his head.

"Don't forget the crash in '85," said Vicki. "That's what alerted us to the link between the aliens and the Agarthans.

The Agarthans are an ancient race of people who live inside the earth, Grace."

I'd forgotten my name was Grace, so Kat spoke before I did.

"I didn't 'forget' the crash of '85," she said. "You know how I feel about it. The evidence points to a government thought-control dirigible, not to—"

"The *evidence*," said Vicki, "to anyone who isn't too blind to see it, is that the indwells and outwells of energy from the earth's hollow core create—"

"Whoa, hey. I know. I know what you're saying, but you fail to—"

They went back and forth about it. Andromeda shrieked and started hitting her spoon against J.Lo's round ghost head. The man knelt down beside me.

"You believe any of this, kid?"

I got the impression he didn't.

"I don't know," I said. "I believe in aliens now."

"Who doesn't?"

Kat noticed us talking.

"Don't you go poisoning her young mind, Trey," she said. "You people want proof about the alien conspiracy? Have you tried looking south recently?"

"I've never *said* there weren't any aliens!" Trey said. "I only said they haven't been visiting, abducting, and impregnating us since 1947! And I still say it! If you claimed that elephants have been visiting Roswell for sixty-five years, and then the next day the circus came to town, that wouldn't prove anything, now would it!"

Vicki approached while the two shouted.

"Grace, could you be a dear an' go across the street to the museum and tell the rest that dinner is ready?"

"Sure," I said. "Come on, JayJay."

"So," I said to J.Lo as we crossed the street, "if you're gonna impregnate me, I think we should get married first."

"That lady is crazy," said J.Lo. "You know already howto the humans and Boov babies are made differently. I may as well impreganate the car."

We were approaching the International UFO Museum. It looked like an old movie theater.

"Speaking of Slushious," I said, "what are we going to do about that? We'll have to sneak away to fix it."

"I am afraid the problem might be being bigger than this. That roads sign has stuck into the Snark's Adjustable Manifold."

"Important?"

"*Ff.* Is your heart important? Should you be okay with only three livers?"

"But you can fix it."

"I do not know. It was a part from my scooter. If I cannot fix it, there is no other."

We'd have to go back for Pig and J.Lo's tools, but otherwise we could leave the car if we had to. We could borrow another—Roswell was full of cars. Even now I could just barely see a turquoise pickup truck driving past a saucer-shaped burger restaurant at the end of a row of streetlamps painted to have alien eyes.

The important thing was getting to Arizona. But the truth was, I wanted to do it in MY car. Slushious. We wouldn't be *borrowing* another car, I thought as I pushed open the door of the museum. We'd be stealing.

We walked into the lobby, to have all our senses assaulted at once: rumpled threadbare sleeping bags like snakeskins all over the floor, empty bags of potato chips and pork rinds, a model flying saucer, the smell of chocolate and feet, a diorama of the 1947 crash site labeled "Foo Fighter," an almost untastable taste of eggs in the air, scraps of plastic wrap and paper, a dead rubber alien on a gurney overseen by a human mannequin in surgical scrubs, a paperback book called *Life, the Universe, and Everything*, and enough pairs of underwear for thirty guys. I mean, really, it was a lot of under-wear, like these guys were just wearing each pair once and then cracking open a pack of new ones.

"I wonder where the rest are," I said.

J.Lo had his face pressed up against the alien autopsy exhibit.

"What is this?" he asked.

"That's a fake dead alien. The fake doctor is going to cut it up."

"Not very neighborlike."

"Do you recognize the alien? Is it a real kind of people?"

"Hm. No. Looks unlike any race I know. Lookses a little like a M'Plaah. They are a sort of octopus for milking."

"Right. I was just going to say the same thingWHERE *IS* everyone? HELLO?"

"Hello?" came a faint reply.

"Where are you?"

"On the roof . . . the stairs are by the restrooms," said someone.

We found the bathrooms, which were labeled "Aliens" and "Femaliens."

"Finally," I said to J.Lo. "Here's a bathroom you're allowed to use."

"I do not have to go."

We opened a STAFF ONLY door and climbed the stairs to the roof. A man with the worst beard in America and the two little boys were up there with about ten telescopes of different sizes and shapes. The man hunched over a short fat telescope pointed south while the boys ran around.

"What's all this?" I asked, to which one of the boys shouted "Boob!" Then they both cracked up and shouted "boob" some more.

"Hey!" the man said. "The new kids! Come look at this!"

He had a thick, soft face that just flowed downhill into a thick, soft neck. A pencil-thin beard and mustache traced a line between the two, like an imaginary border on a map. There should have been a mountain range of jawbone to separate head from neck, but there wasn't, so he'd done what he could.

"Look at what?" I said. "The big purple ball? We've seen it."

"You haven't seen it this close," said beard-guy. "Look in here."

I knew what I was going to see, and I didn't want to see it. But J.Lo and I walked over anyway, and I squinted into the eyepiece.

"Isn't that weird?" asked Beardo. "Doesn't it look almost alive?"

With the telescope you could see the texture of the Gorg skin—its pores, blemishes, scabs, and freckles.

"Yeah," I said. "Almost alive."

"My turn," said J.Lo. "You are hogging."

But I didn't give J.Lo his turn, because I saw something weird in the corner of the view. A spot on the skin of the ship was swelling.

"What's that thing it's doing?" I asked. "You know, where the skin starts to bubble up like that?"

"I don't know what you're talking about," said Beardo. "Let me have a look—"

"It is my turn. I am the next."

"How do I move it," I asked, while pushing the scope with my hand.

"Whoa. You don't do it like that," said Beardo, and he was right, of course. The view veered way, way too far to the right.

"Get it back, quick," I said.

"You're bossy," said one of the boys.

"Hold on," said Beardo, looking at a notebook. "Where was it before . . . um . . . right ascension 17 hours, 29 minutes, 16.4 seconds . . . declination negative 40, 47, and one second."

The view went blurry, then I could see the swollen bit again. There was a whitish spot in its center, like a pimple.

"Move it up and to the right a little," I said.

The sight came back into focus just in time. The fat shuddering balloon of skin suddenly doubled in size and spat the white bit out like it was popping a zit.

"Whoa!" I shouted, and backed away from the telescope. I scanned the sky to see if I could spot where the white part went.

J.Lo tried to lean into the viewfinder, but Beardo beat him to it.

"I see it," said Beardo. "The bubble's deflating. There's a hole in the center."

Just then I spotted two bright shapes over the mountains and grabbed J.Lo's shoulder.

"Look!"

Far off, two Boovish ships were racing toward each other from different directions. When they met, their hoselegs fumbled around in the air between them. Whatever they were doing, they didn't do it for long—the Gorg ship fired, missed, fired again, and popped one of the Boov ships like it was a glass balloon. The other ship limped away and was brought down with another blast.

Everyone on the roof was hushed for a moment, even the boys. Not for long, though.

"That was awesome!" said the loud one.

"Totally awesome," said the other loud one. "The big ship was all, *BSHOOM!* An' the little ship, one of the little ships—"

"It went, like, *KSHHH!*"

"I'm telling it! *Dad*!"

J.Lo looked miserable. You wouldn't think you could tell that when a person's wearing a ghost suit, but you can.

"That's not the first time we've seen the ball destroy Boov ships," said Beardo airily. "They've done it a couple times."

Of course, it wasn't the first time J.Lo and I had seen it either, but it seemed like too big a coincidence that it had happened right after I saw something launch out of the Gorg's moon. And the Boov ships hadn't been charging the Gorg ship; they'd only charged toward each other. Each other, or toward something else in the sky that was too small to see. . . .

"Ricki say time for dinner," said J.Lo.

"*Vicki,*" I hissed.

"Bicki."

One of the boys heard us and shouted, "This meeting of BOOB is—"

"It's my turn to say it—"

"—offishialy over!"

"Dad!"

"Just a minute, kiddo," said Beardo.

"Waitaminute," I said. "BOOB?"

"It's the name of our club," said boy number two.

"Are you guys from Florida or something?"

"No," said Beardo. "Why?"

"Nothing."

Both boys shouted over each other.

"It stands for—"

"Backyard—"

"Shut up!"

"Backyard telescope Ob . . . Observation of—"

"Of Occupation by Boov!"

"Farthead!"

We descended the stairs.

"I don't know why I ask," I said, "but shouldn't your acronym be like, BTOOB or something?"

"BOOB sounds better," they said.

Boys. Honestly.

Dinner was sen*sational*. I'm not kidding. You don't realize what a casserole can do until you've spent two weeks eating from what, in honor of one of those UFO exhibits, I'm going to call the Four Foo Groups.*

"More hot dish?" asked Vicki.

"Yes. This is amazing."

"Your brother doesn't seem to think so."

"Oh, don't worry about JayJay. He's one of those kids who never eats anything. We think he's solar-powered," I said, knowing that J.Lo had eaten all the little decorative soaps out of Vicki's bathroom when he was supposed to be washing up.

"Well, I hope so," said Beardo. "'Cause you kids might be here a while."

I put my fork down. "What do you mean?"

"Well, that car of yours looks to be in pretty bad shape. And we could never let you just drive off on your own, anyway."

I swallowed hard and felt a big wad of casserole stick in my throat. "I've gotten this far on my own. I'll be fine. We'll be fine."

"Oh, my," said Vicki. "Such spunk. You must've been a handful for your mom."

The casserole made it the rest of the way down, but it burned my nose and made my eyes water. I thought about Mom.

"All right. So . . . what if someone did drive us the rest of the way? Why wait?"

Vicki and maybe a couple others chuckled.

"None of us has a car, Grace," said Beardo.

---

*Salt, Fizz, Animal-shaped, and Blue

"So we borrow one. The town is full of them."

There was outright laughter now.

"And how do you suppose we start this mystery car?" asked Vicki.

"We've already been looking for a car or truck we could use," said Kat. "You'd be surprised how many people took their keys with them when Roswell was evacuated. You can help us search, though. Eventually we'll find keys that fit *something.*"

"We could hotwire a car," I said. "Don't you just cross some wires or something?"

There were blank stares all around the table. Beardo coughed.

"Grace, we're paranormal researchers—"

"Which means they don't know anything useful," said Trey.

"Which *means* . . . that we don't know about that kind of cop show stuff. Why don't *you* tell us how to hotwire a car, huh, Trey? Break it down for us."

I listened as they argued, my head in my hands. I'd already forgotten that things like missing keys could cause problems. J.Lo probably had perfume that could hotwire a car by smell, or some kind of car-starting hat or something.

Speaking of J.Lo, I barely noticed when he said, "Truck."

"What?" I mumbled.

"The bluey truck," he said. "From beforeto."

"Hey, yeah! We saw a turquoise truck earlier, driving

through the streets. Which one of you was that?"

There was silence. Only Trey was smiling, which I was beginning to understand didn't mean anything good. I'm not saying I believed all, or any, of the things these people had been saying about the Massive Alien Conspiracy, but I thought Trey could maybe disagree without being a jerk about it.

"Are you going to tell her?" asked Trey. "I'll happily do it if you won't—"

"You saw Chief Shouting Bear," said Beardo. "He's a . . . he's just an eccentric old junkman that lives around these parts. He's kind of a town legend."

"Ha—yeah. The Legend of the Crazy Indian," said Vicki. Then she looked sideways at J.Lo and me and added, "No offense."

"For what?" I asked. "We're not Indians. Or crazy."

"I am one sixteenth Habadoo," said J.Lo.

"Tell them the best part," said Trey. "Tell them Chief Shouting Bear's the guy who found the flying saucer that crashed in 1947. Tell them he has it in his basement."

Beardo sighed. "The Chief . . . claims he has the spacecraft. He really was here in Roswell back then—he was in the air force or something during World War Two."

"There was no air force in World War Two," said Trey. "The air force was founded in 1947, and he got kicked out of the military *for believing in UFOs!*"

"So have any of you seen it?" I asked. "The spaceship?"

"All of us," said Kat. "It's sort of a rite of passage. You

come to Roswell, eventually you end up in Shouting Bear's basement looking at that piece of crap."

"I want to see the ship," said J.Lo.

"Don't bother, kid."

"We'd recognize the '47 saucer if we saw it," said Vicki, and everyone but Trey started nodding. "The ufology community knows what that ship looked like. We've known for years."

"Decades."

If anyone spoke next, it was drowned out by loud, dry booms like dud fireworks that seemed to turn the whole night inside out. We raced to the window to see the Gorg and the Boov fighting again—maybe fighting over some small white object in the plum sky.

That night I told Vicki that we planned to sleep in the UFO museum. "Y'know, because the other kids are there." Even though at this point I would sooner have slept next to seasick howler monkeys than Beardo's two boys.

"I thought you two could bunk in the living room," Vicki said, holding pillows and looking hurt.

"Maybe tomorrow night? Come on, JayJay," I said, finding J.Lo's hand under the sheet and pulling him out of the apartment.

"I am not feeling so well," said J.Lo as we went downstairs. "I think those littles soaps were not the eating kind."

"You have more food in the car. We have to be quick now, in case she looks out the window."

We walked toward the museum until the last possible moment. Then I checked Vicki's windows behind us, and we rushed down an alley and wound our way back out to the main road a few blocks away.

"I want to visit the shouty bear man," said J.Lo. "He sounds nice. Also I want to see his ship."

"Me too," I said. "Right after we get Slushious fixed. You know, a few weeks ago I would have said that spaceships couldn't look like big meatballs. A year ago I wouldn't have thought they'd be all glass and hoses. Maybe the Chief's ship just doesn't look like people expect. Maybe you'll recognize where it came from."

"The peoples do not think it is authentical."

"Yeah, well, they're nice people, but those guys could get licked on the lips by a Lhasa apso and they'd still claim it was the Abominable Snowman."

"Yes. I do not know what this means."

We neared the arroyo. I was out of breath but happy to be doing something constructive after sitting around all day. As we grew close, I could see Pig meowing silently to us through the passenger window. I let her out and gave her a scratch behind the ears.

"Sorry, Pig. We're here for the rest of the night now."

J.Lo tossed off his ghost costume and got immediately to

work. He squirted some liquid over his hands, quickly congealed into gloves, then poured me a pair, too. Together we wrenched the road sign out of the hood.

"Hm," said J.Lo.

"What?"

"Nothings. To work! Pass to me the flocked bootpunch."

"Can you describe it?"

"Pink. Fur. Twisty parts."

"That's like, three things in here."

"It will be quivering a little."

"Aha. Here."

Two hours passed, and I had to admit I wasn't good for anything except handing J.Lo tools that had been described really well beforehand. I'd been playing with Pig for a bit and was beginning to drift off when I realized that J.Lo was just sitting there, staring.

"What is it?" I asked.

"I cannot fix it. Slushious requires a new Snark's. A new bipaa'ackular humbutt would not hurt anything, either."

I nodded. "That's it, then. We have to steal a car. It's not our fault. Maybe we can hotwire a police car—you know, something that doesn't belong to just one person."

J.Lo packed up his tools.

"Anyway," I went on, "we should do it and leave soon. I think Vicki wants to adopt us. And I don't like the suspicious way Kat keeps looking at you."

"Is Kat the one having the glasses and dark hairs?"

"No, Kat is a woman."

"Hm."

There was a rumble that I first thought was thunder, but then it came again, loud as anything, and the night sky lit up orange over the northern hills.

"That was close," I said.

Boov ships passed overhead and shone through the trees like flashlights through cobwebs. I ducked without thinking, then watched them race toward the fire and noisy sky.

"Let's go," I said. "I want to find out what's going on."

"I already do know what it is going on," said J.Lo.

"Tell me."

J.Lo Explains What it is Going On

"The Gorgship makes the bubblespot liketo you saw and

shoots forth the teleclone booth FOOMP!

"As the booth falls to the planet, it is then activated,

and Gorg jetpackers teleport through POP! and POP!

"Afterswhich they grab the booth and lower it unto the ground."

"So the Boov ships always shoot off toward the booth," I said.

"And destruct it beforeto it reaches ground," said J.Lo. "Or shortly afterthen. And the Gorg ship destructs the Boov ship. Is all very efficient. Except, eventually the Gorg make success in setling up a telecloner, and then it is all over. Gorg spill out over planets like ants onto gum balls. With their angriness and barking guns they force the Boov to evacuate—then the Gorg ship eats the world."

"Well," I said, climbing into Slushious, "let's just have a look. Maybe we can learn something."

"Is not safe."

"Because of the Gorg?"

"Becaused by the faulty Snark's Manifold."

"We won't need brakes if I'm careful," I said. "It's not like there'll be traffic. Get in."

"Is not only the brakes—"

"Grab Pig, too," I said. "C'mon."

"We could *explore*!" said J.Lo with panicky eyes.

I looked at him for a moment, trying to read his face.

"Right," I said. "We'll just have a look around."

A second passed, then J.Lo and Pig got in. J.Lo buckled himself and gripped the safety belt with tight blue fingers.

"I will stick on you," he sighed.

* * *

As we drove, the sky grew lighter and brighter, and smelled

like fried hair. The boom of galactic war was deafening. Up ahead, a bright but damaged Boov ship staggered through the air, keeping low as the Gorg ship drew hundred-mile lines of fire in the sky.

"Slushious is handling a little weird," I said. The car shuddered and listed right and left like there was ice on the road, putting aside for the moment that it was summer, and we weren't near a road, and we wouldn't have been touching it if we were.

"Yes," J.Lo said through clenched teeth. "That is the danger of exploring."

"I guess," I said. I thought he was being awfully philo-sophical all of a sudden.

We crested a hill and looked down into a wide pit where once there had been some kind of mining operation. On the ground were the remains of a second Boov ship and, near that, the Gorg teleclone booth. And the scene around the booth was, frankly, just awfully gross. Gorg were streaming out of the booth and, just as quickly, being shot to pieces by the struggling Boov ship. It was my first look at the Gorg, but I wasn't able to form much of an impression. They had the booth backed up against a steep cliff wall, and hordes of them clung to it in an attempt to protect it from the Boov's weapon. In the darkness and sickening swaying light, they just looked like a knot of bodies, and parts of bodies, and I'm already thinking about it a lot harder than I ever wanted to.

Meanwhile, from somewhere in Mexico, the Gorg's huge, fiery blasts took aim at the glowing Boov ship, which used the ravine for cover and bobbed around in a way that must have been making a couple dozen Boov crewmen airsick.

"What is that glowing gas, anyway?" I said. "The stuff inside the Boov ships."

"Is the brains," said J.Lo. "The main computer."

"The computer is gas?"

"It is tiny molecules. Human computers are electric switches—off on, off on. Many switches. How these turn off and on tells the computer whats to do. Boov computers are the same, but are electric gas. Each tiny molecule is the switch. Billionses of switches. Trillionses."

Suddenly the Gorg ship lowered its aim and began punching huge holes in the landscape, opening a line of fire toward the Boov. Slushious, which was already shaking enough, rocked from waves of force and sprays of rock and earth. Pig let out a deep whine like a slow fire engine.

"Um, I think we'd better move," I said, and coasted down the hill to a safer distance.

A string of Gorg suddenly appeared above the lip of the pit like huge lightning bugs, with their green jetpacks. They shot at the Boov, and the Gorg ship shot at the Boov, but the Boov dove toward the booth down below.

"Brave Boovish boys," said J.Lo in hushed tones. "And girls and boygirls and girlboys and boyboys and boyboygirls and boyboyboyboys. They are soon to lose, but they will make one last try."

Just then the Boov ship rocketed out of the gorge, followed by cannon fire, and ten or twelve Gorg jetpackers in hot pursuit.

It was almost quiet, except for the rumbling of the car.

"I am wondering," said J.Lo. "Did we do it? Did the Boov steal away the teleclone booth?"

"Steal?" I asked. "Not destroy?"

"We shouldto go look. Hurry! There would not be much time!"

I urged Slushious forward, toward the ravine, though the shuddering and knocking of the engine only grew worse.

"The greatest hope of the Boov has been to one day capture a Gorg telecloner," said J.Lo. "This. way the Boov could discover howfor they made teleporting and cloning work on persons and complexicated things. The Boov could have then their own endless armies."

"Why do you think your guys captured one this time?"

"I do not think, not really, but there was no loud noise from the ground hole. Usuallies, when the Gorg realize they cannot set up their booth, they explore it into a millions pieces!"

"They . . . *explode* it?" I asked.

"Ah yes. *Explode*. I am always doing that."

We pulled up to the ravine.

"Waitaminute. Have you meant 'explode' *every* time you said 'explore' tonight?"

"Lookit!" said J.Lo. "Down in the hole!"

"Slushious might *explode*?"

"At any moments, yes. But look!"

Despite myself, I looked where J.Lo was pointing. First I saw the piles of Gorg parts all around. But then I realized what wasn't there—the booth.

"The Boov got the booth," I said.

"No," said J.Lo. "Up there!"

Driving up the steep road on the other side of the mine was the turquoise truck. And in the truck bed was the booth.

"Hey. *Hey!*" I shouted. "He doesn't get that; *we* get that!"

"I am not thinking he can hear—"

I floored it and drove around the edge of the pit.

"J.Lo, are we going to explode?"

"Maybies. The Snark's Adjustable Manifold is very instable. But Tip said she wanted to drive anyways."

"Well, I got this crazy idea we were going to be *exploring*, not *exploding*," I said. Then I glanced at J.Lo's face.

"You came with me. Even though you thought the car might explode."

A flash appeared to the northeast. The Gorg had finally brought down the second Boovish ship. J.Lo pressed his face against the passenger window.

"He's out of the ravine," I said. "Chief Shouting Bear. I bet

Slushious can catch him if we don't blow up first. What are you looking for?"

"They are coming back. Gorg jetpackers. I see sevens."

"Oboy. What . . . what can we do?"

J.Lo had a real hopeful sort of look on his face. Like he needed to borrow money.

"The Boov have never before captured a Gorg teleclone booth. It is the most important thing," he said. "The most important thing is to not give it back."

I sighed and shut my eyes and nodded my head. My mind raced, searching for a good idea.

"Allll right. Here we go."

I cranked the steering knob way to the end of the a.m. dial and spurred Slushious on toward the approaching jet-packers. Their taillights traced alien symbols in the air as they drew closer. I liked thinking that they really were as small as they looked and would smack our windshield like the pests they were. But they kept getting closer and larger. They saw us and dropped lower in the sky, and I finally got a decent look at the things. It was just as well that I hadn't before or I never would have let myself get so close to one, much less seven. When they were within a hundred feet they aimed rifles the size of streetlamps at us.

"Whatfor will you do?" asked J.Lo.

"They're in our way," I said. "I'm going to honk at them."

I mashed my palm into the horn as hard as I could. Just

like it had two weeks ago in Pennsylvania, the hood flew open and belched orange fire into the sky. The Gorg scattered, and I turned hard to the right and hit the gas.

"I don't suppose that got rid of any of them," I shouted, as our windshield was blindfolded by the clanking car hood and I had to drive with my head out the window.

"No. But they needed some seconds forto their eyes to readjust. And for this they did not see the boothtruck. They are following on us."

I glanced up at the center of the hood. You could see the Snark's Adjustable Manifold there, hissing and spitting blue fireworks against the window glass.

"That thing looks ready to pop," I said. I could feel it buzzing through the steering wheel and in the seat of my pants.

"Yes. Drive unto the arroyo."

"Are you sure?" I asked, my eyes snapping back and forth between the Gorg in my side mirror and the dark desert ahead. "I was thinking—"

"I have a idea."

I pressed on toward the highway and checked the mirror just in time to be blinded by the flash of the Gorg rifles. They pockmarked the ground all around and sheared off our antennas, and I weaved Slushious right and left and behind flagpoles and fence posts.

"J.Lo, I really think we should—"

"Please onto the arroyo," he said as he searched his tool-box and produced what looked like a pencil sharpener made of lemon Jell-O that, when cranked, would spit out super-strong yarn that smelled like ginger ale. "Trust on me."

I retraced our path from the day before, through the hilly obstacle course that shook every last thing out of J.Lo's toolbox but made us a hard target. Gorg fire sheared the tops off of dunes and filled the night with pulverized dirt. In the meantime I chewed myself up inside trying to decide whether I should see J.Lo's plan through or do what I *really* thought was best. I was furious that he'd put me in this position—we both knew I was the smart one.

"Almost to the arroyo," he said. He'd tied one end of the superyarn around his middle, the other end around the passenger seat. "Turn into it."

The Gorg were gaining. They were faster and more nimble. They'd love it if we went into the arroyo with all its rocks and low branches and high logs. Plus, I could barely see.

"I hope humans and Boov go to the same heaven," I said as we skimmed down the hill. "I might want to say a few things to you later about this plan of yours."

I gave us an extra cushion of air under the car and squinted into the rushing wind and stinging bugs. We barely missed boulders and fallen trees, and barely hit shrubs and thin branches that came from nowhere and whipped against the bumper, or hood, or my face. The Gorg were down in the trench, too, and blasting a red smoldering path through the brush.

"What are you doing?" I shouted to J.Lo, though it was pretty obvious he was climbing out the side window and onto the windshield. He shouted something back that was lost to the roaring wind.

Just then, a Gorg blast came awfully close to the car, and J.Lo lost his grip. He tumbled sideways and down the side of Slushious until his yarn lifeline went taut.

"Hwhoa," I heard him say.

It was hard enough to navigate through the wash with a small army of flying death on your tail without worrying about J.Lo getting smacked against some tree trunk. I was beginning to take us up out of the arroyo when his face appeared in the window again.

"No!" he said. "Only oneother minute!"

He pulled himself hand over hand back up the yarn and onto the windshield again. The he peered backward over the roof of the car and reached for the Snark's Manifold, which I was shocked to see was glowing hot pink.

The Gorg drew closer. J.Lo looked back over his shoulder at the Manifold, then squinted at the Gorg again.

"What," I shrieked, *"in GOD'S name are you—"*

J.Lo ripped the sparking Snark's from its place in the hood and threw it over the back of the car, trailing blue lightning in its wake. I watched it catch in a tangle of thorny branches right in front of the swarm of Gorg, then *Flash! Bam!* and the cabin of the car went bright with blue-white light, and the big clap of force somersaulted Slushious over and again on its fat pink Safetypillows.

We shuddered to a stop.

"Wroooo," said Pig.

"Yeah. Me too," I answered. "J.Lo?"

I could see one of his hands wiggling.

"I am fine."

He was fine, pressed firmly between two cushions on the hood.

"That was a good plan, J.Lo."

"I am quietly proud," he said through the high whine of the shrinking pillows.

Slushious couldn't be driven after we lost the Snark's Adjustable Manifold, but it still floated, so it wasn't too difficult to push once the Safetypillows disappeared again. We moved it as far as we could from the arroyo, in case any Gorg came poking around. We pushed around the edge of the city until about five or six in the morning, when the air was waking and open- ing its big blue eyes. The birds were singing, and I felt weirdly happy, considering we were talking about all the things that didn't exist anymore, now that the Boov and Gorg had arrived. We hid Slushious in a car wash, between the part with the huge spinning brushes and the part like a big pasta maker.

"There used to be a ton of TV channels, maybe hundreds. Now there's just the Emergency Broadcast System."

"Hm."

"And there's no World Series this year. Probably no baseball teams at all, because there are no states. And . . . no countries anymore, either. Not really."

"Mm," said J.Lo. "I am not knowing if these countries were evers such a good idea in the first place."

He frowned. "Which place is this first place, anyways?" he asked, looking at the atlas. "Is it Delaware?"

"Maybe you're right," I said. "About countries, I mean."

"Yes. And I am thinking, if the baseball was being played before, it is still being to."

"Maybe."

"And televisions will return. Earthland never had so much to beginto."

"Are you kidding? There were so many channels that they had one just for old cartoons. And about five just for new cartoons. And a music video channel that didn't even play music videos."

"Fhf. Boovworld had once five million channels beforeto the Purging."

"The what?"

"The Purging."

"Purging."

"Yes. In the Purging, all channels but one were eliminatited, to prevents the death of society."

"Oh. Yeah. People are always going on about how TV is going to ruin Earth, too."

"Is well proven. Let us say, after televisions are invented, that there is only then a few channels. Three or four. We will call them A, G, Semicolon, and Pointy."

"How about we call them A, B, C . . . and ABC."

"Whatevers. Let us now think of these channels as like four cups filled with eggs. Cup A holds inside News eggs, and Sport eggs, and Variety Show eggs. Cup B has News and Animated Story eggs and Situationally Comedic eggs. So on. More big cups are added because peoples want More Choices."

"Uh-huh."

"Soon it is noticed that between the cups there is room for *smaller* cups.

"These cannot hold much. Maybies there is one with only News eggs all the time. Maybies one with only Funny. But maybies Funny is your favorite sort of egg, so you like this cup.

"Then even smaller cups are made for inbetween the small cups and even smaller between those. The more cups, the more new gaps to fill. Every kind of show is invented. Shows like *Pillowbusters!* And *What Are People Willing to Put in Their Mouths?* Or *The Week in Balancing*, or *Watch Out, Baby Animals! Cavalcade, Big Celebrity Poomps, Guy on a Table* . . . lots of shows."

"So what was the problem?" I asked.

"It went out of the control," said J.Lo. "Shows had to be recorded whilst even more shows were watched. Not enough time for seeing everything a Boov wanted to see, so some had to quit their jobs, or hires someone to watch for them."

"Um . . ."

"Televisional scientists theorized a point into the future when each and everys Boov has his own show, and this show only shows him watching shows. So HighBoov decree: no more television but what the HighBoov say. And the HighBoov mostly say cooking shows."

"Uh-huh. I'm really tired, J.Lo."

"Yes. I also."

I curled up next to Pig in the back of Slushious.

I awoke in the afternoon to find a note from J.Lo saying he'd gone ahead to Vicki's to eat soap. Actually, it just said "JLO(BiKi5OP," but I thought that was pretty good. I fed Pig and walked back through town.

I entered Vicki's apartment, ready to launch immediately into explaining where we'd been all night. But no one was there. Not even J.Lo. I went downstairs and squinted down the hot street. Trey appeared on a corner.

"Hey! Grace, right?" he said. "We've all been looking for you."

"Sorry," I answered. "We realized we had to go check on our cat, and then we were tired so we just slept in the car, and have you seen J.Lo?"

"Who—the actress?"

"I mean JayJay."

"Not today."

I sighed and shaded my eyes from the hot July sun that made everything look flat and washed-out.

"Maybe he was abducted by aliens." Trey laughed.

I didn't think it was a very funny joke, all things considered, but I let it go.

"You don't believe in any of the stuff they do," I said, meaning the other Roswellians. "Do you?"

"No reason to. There are perfectly rational explanations for everything."

"Like weather balloons?"

"Scientific balloons," he said. "Sure. You know that NASA has a ballooning facility just a couple hours from here? They send up these enormous silver balloons all the time. I've seen them launch one. But the UFO nuts never tell you about that, do they?"

I was reminded of something else they probably wouldn't tell me.

"Do you know where Chief Shouting Bear lives?" I asked.

"Gonna go see the flying saucer, huh?"

"Just for fun."

He told me how to get to the right road, and how to follow it out of town to the big scrap yard that surrounded the Chief's house.

"Go," said Trey. "Look for yourself, that's what I say. Don't take these jokers' word for anything. You're not one of them, I can tell. You're like a young me."

"Yeah," I said, "but I'm working on it."

"What?"

"Thanks. If you see JayJay, send him back to Vicki's, okay? Oh, wait—look."

I almost said, "There he is," but stopped myself when I realized I was not looking at a Boov in a ghost suit—I was looking at a Boov.

"Whoa," said Trey.

This Boov wasn't even wearing the right color uniform. It was white with green and pink trim. He, it, looked back and forth, right and left. It saw us, but barely paid us any mind. Then there were more Boov following behind, wearing all kinds of colors. Many were armed, especially the ones in green, and Trey stepped backward toward a shop window. I approached the group.

"What's going on?" I said. "Why are you here?"

"Whyfor are *you* here?" shouted a Boov in green, and he

raised his weapon. But the one in white told him something in Boovish, and he put it away again.

"You are supposed to have gone to the Human Preserve," said the Boov in white.

"I know. I'm trying. What's going on?"

I saw now that there were more than a hundred Boov, all moving quickly through Roswell on foot. None of them looked happy.

"The Gorg, they established a . . . an outpost south of here," said the Boov. Then it looked at me for the first time. "The Gorg are the newcomers, in the big rounded ship."

"I know. I mean, I heard."

"Some of our number were onto a warship, fighting forwith

248

the Gorg. Some of we were just living in New Smeksico. We are moving away fromto the Gorg. So should you, also."

"Are they coming?"

"They might do. And they will not show unto humans the same respect you were shown by the Boov."

"Respect?" shouted Trey. *"Respect?"*

"Shh!" I said to Trey, and waved him off.

"Say," said the Boov, stopping next to me, "you do not happens to have any cats, do you?"

My heart skipped.

"What?" I said. "No. Why du . . . Why?"

The Boov shrugged.

"The Gorg, they love cats. They are wanting all the cats for themselfs."

"Why? Do they . . . do you mean for pets, or for food, or . . . ?"

"Who can understands the Gorg?" asked the Boov in white. "I only thought if we had some cats, we could trade them for not killing us."

The Boov then joined the rest, and the last of them passed by. Trey and I watched them leave.

"Hey," said Trey, when they were out of earshot, "you have a cat, right?"

"I gotta go find J.Lo," I muttered.

"You mean JayJay," Trey called after me.

I ran a figure eight around a couple of city blocks, then a couple more, but no J.Lo. Then I saw a little white ghost in front of Vicki's building just as I was going back.

"Where *were* you?" I asked.

"The U if O museum. For using the Boovs' room."

"I was *looking* for you."

"I am sorry. I could not to stay near Bicki. She tried to feed to me something called pasta, which seemed to be mostly noodles."

"Yeah. What are you holding?"

J.Lo was cradling a bundle with his sheet.

"When I left, Bicki gave me granolas bars and cans of Goke. Tip can eat the bars, and I can eat the cans!"

"Good. C'mon. Trey told me where the Chief lives, and we're in a hurry."

I ate the granola as we walked. J.Lo pulled up his sheet and bit into a soda can, causing cola to shoosh out the sides of his mouth and through his nose.

"Mm. Spicy," he said.

It was a long walk. We cut across the wide streets of town until it became more trees than buildings and more scrub than trees. Before I could see the junkyard, I heard barking. It was steady and regular, more like a clock made to sound like a dog than an actual dog. But then we saw it: a big gray Great Dane, sitting comfortably, folded up like a deck chair.

"So much for the element of surprise," I said as the big pony of a dog trotted over and stuck its nose everywhere.

Behind the dog was a high wooden fence covered in faded, peeling signs. Signs like from a circus, or carnival.

SEE! THE WONDER OF TWO WORLDS! said one.

GAZE! UPON THE ASTRONAUTIC AERODISK THAT ASTONISHED THE ARMY!

IT MADE THE OSS SAY "OH, 'S WONDERFUL!"

That sort of thing.

The fence was too tall to see any of the junk inside. Standing this close I could just see the top of a distant water tower, dry and rusty with a gaping hole in its side.

"That's where the UFO stopped," said a low voice.

I looked down to see a thin, dark man, like a strip of jerky—the Chief. His head was covered by a faded red cap with flaps and a strap that hung down past his ears. It looked like something a pilot might have worn long ago. He otherwise wore the same clothes as anybody else—no buckskin or beads or anything. I'm probably an idiot for even mentioning that.

the Chief

"The UFO . . . crashed into the water tower?" I asked. Despite all the signs, he hadn't said it like a carnival barker. He'd just said it like it was fact, and one he'd gotten used to a long time ago.

"You two the new arrivals? Got here yesterday afternoon?"

"Yeah," I answered. "Did the others tell you about us?"

"Nah. Just saw you around."

I wondered if he'd seen us around the mine the night before.

"You drive here all by yourselves?"

"Yeah."

"Hrmm. If you're here to see the saucer, can we make it quick?" he said. "Got work to do. C'mon, Lincoln."

I figured he was addressing the dog, because the big lanky thing stopped sniffing around J.Lo's sheet and galloped back up to the fence, casting a long contrail of dog spit behind him.

"What kind of work?" I asked. J.Lo and I followed Lincoln to the gate.

"Top secret. All right. Here we go."

Past the gate was a big yard dotted with piles of unwanted everything: halves of cars, burned-out motorcycles, rusted kitchen appliances, and what I think was an entire airplane nose cone full of hubcaps. There were bales of sheet aluminum tied together with wire, baby strollers piled high

inside a Stonehenge of bathtubs, and a jukebox with
sunflowers growing out of it. We were walking toward a small
house in the center of it all, every inch of which was covered
by pennies, and shingled with scraps of dull brass. The Chief
launched into what sounded like a prepared speech that he
wasn't keen on giving.

"Behold, the wonders of the discarded world, what
treasuresliewithintherustedrefuse blah blah, the grime
that time forgot, seetheancient circle o'tubs that the Druids
called Bathhenge, beholdthepile of doll parts that reputable
blah blahs from the University of blah believe hides Egypt's
shortest pyramid, mysteriouslytransportedtothehighplains
of Roswell in the year blah-blah-and-six A.D. But that
is not what you have come to see, isitnowmyfriends?"

"Um—"

"No!" he answered, unlocking a pair of basement doors.
"Youcametoseethefantasticcraft that crashedherefrom-
pointsunknown, lo thesedecadespast."

We went down concrete steps to the edge of a big dark
room, and the Chief turned to face us with his hand near a
row of switches on the wall.

"I give you . . . pause for dramatic effect . . . the *flying
saucer* cue music cue smoke machine cue lights."

As he flipped the switch, music began to play, and a
machine somewhere rumbled and hissed thick fog into the
room, and flickering green and blue lights outlined a dim

shape about as wide as a kiddie pool and twice as tall. The fog was mysterious. The lights were mysterious. The music was "A-Tisket, A-Tasket."

"Sorry," said Chief Shouting Bear. "I put on some Ella Fitzgerald after everyone left town. Used to be 'Thus Spake Zarathustra.' Very stirring. Hold on."

He turned off the music.

"The flying saucer!" he said again, and threw a final switch.

The main lights winked on, revealing the absolute worst UFO in the universe. I mean, this was elementary school-play kind of stuff. It was misshapen but mostly saucer-shaped, made out of paper-maché, and covered in tinfoil. It stood atop three legs made from PVC pipe and old satellite dishes. In the side was the round door from a front-loading washing machine, and it still said *Speed Queen* along the rim. Topping the whole thing was a TV aerial.

"Can I take a picture?" I asked.

"Knock yourself out."

"Go up to the yard and look for that telecloner," I whispered to J.Lo. "I'll keep him busy down here."

"Can you just . . . go around the corner into the room," I said to Chief Shouting Bear, "so I can get a clear shot? Thanks."

With the Chief out of sight, J.Lo scrambled up the steps and was knocked over by the Great Dane. I fumbled around with my camera until he recovered. Then the camera flashed

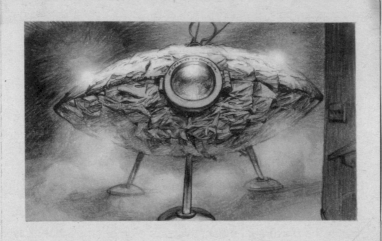

and a picture snapped out the front.

"Old Polaroid," said the Chief. "Don't see those anymore."

"Yeah. Uh, thanks for showing us the UFO. I can't wait to tell everyone I've seen it. Y'know, the famous Roswell UFO. And all."

He gave me a funny look. "An' you don't find anything unusual about this thing?" he said, waving toward the saucer. "You don't question its authenticity?"

"Um . . . I dunno. I like to, you know . . . keep an open mind. Why? Don't *you* think it's real?"

"I have things to do, girl. Where did that little spook kid go?"

"He's my brother."

"Fine. Where'd he go?"

"I'm sure he's around."

Chief Shouting Bear pushed past me and climbed outside.

"This isn't a playground. Hey, Spook! Time for you an' your sister to go."

On the opposite side of the junkyard, J.Lo walked around, inspecting different pieces of scrap, and keeping a wary eye on the Great Dane. It stayed one step behind him, sniffing at his ghost costume—like they were reenacting a Scooby-Doo cartoon.

"Lincoln sure likes your brother," the Chief said. Or the way he smells like fish, I thought.

"I don't think the feeling's mutual," I said.

"Lincoln's harmless. Unless you're allergic to dog spit."

"Why do you live in a junkyard?"

"I trade it and sell it," the Chief said. "Or I used to."

"Oh. Is there . . . a lot of demand for junk?"

"More than you'd guess."

I thought about mentioning that we'd nearly been killed in a junkyard in Florida, but I wasn't sure if it would sound friendly or not.

We were interrupted as J.Lo ran toward us, waving his hands under the costume, Lincoln loping behind him. With his arms in the air he was hoisting the sheet up a few inches, and you could make out Boov feet if you knew what you were looking at. I stood and blocked the Chief's view as I caught all thirty pounds of J.Lo right in the gut.

We fell in a heap, and Lincoln straddled us and put his wet nose in my eye.

"Hoof," I said. "What is it? If this is about the dog—hey! No licking, Lincoln. If this is about the dog, you are totally overre—Knock it *off*, Lincoln!"

It wasn't about the dog. J.Lo got to his feet and snapped his little sheet-covered hand over mine, pulling me up.

"I think he wants me to see something," I said as J.Lo yanked me to a shady corner of the yard.

"What? What is it? Did you find it?" I said when we were out of earshot. Lincoln turned circles around us until J.Lo stopped right in front of a weird metal cage the size of an elevator. Some of the bars were blackened and warped at the bottom, but right away I could tell this wasn't human junk—the metal didn't look right, and there was some Boovish-looking machinery piped into the back. And at each intersection of the metal bars, the cage had a tiny plastic nozzle, like a rosebud. Other parts had been removed, it seemed, and were arranged on a towel nearby.

"Is the telecloner!" J.Lo hissed.

Just then I heard the dirt crunch behind us, and turned to see the Chief.

"Your brother's a smart kid," he said. "Could tell this thing doesn't belong here."

"Yeah . . ." I said. "What, uh, what is it?"

"Not sure. Have some theories. Suppose I can tell ya it belonged to the aliens, though. The new ones. Heard some explosions last night, drove out there, stole this thing while

the aliens were fightin' each other."

J.Lo was hopping all around the telecloner, inspecting it from every angle. Each time he stopped looking at a spot, Lincoln would approach and lick it for good measure.

"So," I said. "Do you usually drive *toward* explosions?"

"I'm a junkman," the Chief answered. "Explosions are like dinner bells to us."

"And you just picked this thing up yourself?"

"It's lighter than it looks."

I nodded. So far, every alien thing I'd held was lighter than it looked.

"So . . ." I said, "what do you want for it?"

"Want for it?"

"Sure. You sell and trade junk, right? How much for it?"

"It's not for sale, kid."

I couldn't accept that. Here we'd found something the Boov had been trying to get their hands on for decades. The Chief didn't even know what it was. But J.Lo could probably figure out how it worked and make more.

"There must be something you want," I said.

"Nope."

Should I just tell him? I thought. Should I tell him my brother's a Boov and he can figure out how to use it? Or would that make things worse?

J.Lo pantomimed a steering wheel under his sheet. I sighed when I realized what he meant, and that he was right.

"Our car," I said. "I'll give you our car. A Boov helped us build it. It floats."

The Chief eyed me suspiciously.

"Your car has Boov parts? For real?"

Suddenly the air was cut by what sounded like a huge, shrill bird.

"Grace! JayJay! Grace! Are you in there?"

Vicki Lightbody was stalking the outside of the junkyard fence, looking for the way in.

The Chief groaned. "Friend of yours?"

I shrugged. "She's been feeding us."

Vicki stuck her round, moony face through the gate, and Kat followed behind.

"There you two are!" she called out. "I just knew I needed to check up on you. Here, take these water bottles."

I resented anyone suggesting we needed to be "checked up on." On the other hand, I noticed for the first time that it was getting dark, and that my throat was cracked from thirst. I drank, and J.Lo poured half of his bottle over his head and slipped the rest under his sheet to drink.

"Mm. Um, this is Vicki and Kat," I said. "I guess you both know the Chief?"

"DON'T STEAL MY LAND, JERKS!" shouted the Chief, and I must have jumped three feet. "YOU PALEFACED DEVILS!"

I looked at him, wide-eyed. Where had that come from?

"Well, I just think everyone in our little community knows Chief Shouting Bear by now," Vicki said. Her voice had changed from birdsong to something more like the sound of windshield wipers on dry glass. Otherwise, neither she nor Kat seemed too surprised.

"Ma'am," the Chief replied.

"We should all be heading home," said Vicki. "Doncha think?"

"Why don't you bring that car of yours back tomorrow," the Chief said to me. "I'd like to have a look at it."

"Well," I said, "it's kind of broken. But we could push it. Yeah. We'll come."

"Actually, I think you kids were going to stay with me all day tomorrow," said Vicki.

"We were? Since when?"

"LET 'EM COME, INDIAN GIVER! I WON'T KEEP 'EM ALL DAY."

"It's dangerous for young children to be playing around all this rusty junk," chirped Vicki. "They'll get lockjaw."

"It'll do 'em good," said Chief. "Rusty junk is all that's gonna be left of this planet soon. HAWOOOO WOO WOO WOO!"

Lincoln sat down at the Chief's feet and howled with him.

"JERKS."

Vicki Lightbody clucked her tongue.

"You could do with a more positive outlook," she said with an angelic smile. "When life gives you lemons, you make lemonade is what I say."

Chief Shouting Bear told Mrs. Lightbody what he thought life had given him. There was a tiny break in her otherwise shining face, like a crack in an Easter egg.

"Well, I don't know what to make with *that*," she said.

"Look, it's no problem. We'll come back for a few hours in the morning," I told the Chief. "See you."

Chief Shouting Bear nodded.

* * *

Once we were outside the gate, Kat let out a whistle.

"Man, I don't know how you kids can stand him. Doesn't all the yelling get on your nerves after a while?"

"He's a poor man," said Vicki. "A poor, sick man."

"Actually," I said, "he didn't yell at all until you guys showed up. Not really. Maybe he only yells at grown-ups."

Vicki sniffed.

"Well, you are not going back there tomorrow. We cannot have two children spending time alone with a crazy man, and Trey never should have told you the way."

I looked at J.Lo. He leaned over and whispered an escape plan that ended with Vicki Lightbody inside a ball of superyarn and cold foam. I hoped it wouldn't have to come to that, but it was a good plan.

We went home with Vicki that evening and ate her food, and slept in her living room, and politely declined her invitation to build a fort out of the sofa cushions. Actually, to be totally accurate, J.Lo was all over the sofa cushion–fort idea and was drawing up plans and talking about this kind of insulation versus that kind of insulation and asking if New Mexico had a history of earthquakes before I shot him the look that'd come to mean *I can't explain right now, but you need to stop discussing central heating and start talking about Power Ninjas or something before everyone realizes there couldn't possibly be a ten-year-old kid under that sheet, you dumb alien.*

Luckily, it was just us plus Vicki and Andromeda in the apartment, and Vicki was way too excited about finally getting what she wanted, to notice what she actually had: not two grateful and happy children, but a space alien and a suffocating eleven-year-old girl who was beginning to feel she could run the rest of the way to Arizona if she had a good breakfast first.

"Wakey wakey!" sang Vicki the next morning. "Eggs and bakey!" She giggled at her rhyme, then frowned.

"What is that noise? Is that the smoke detector?" she asked, and hustled off to check. J.Lo leaned toward me and listened.

"Hm. It is you," he said.

I took a breath and the sound stopped.

"Sorry," I said, and rubbed my palms against my eyes. "I guess I was accidentally screaming a little bit with my mouth closed. I just want to get on the road again. And I'm worried about Pig."

Then I told J.Lo about the big group of Boov the previous day, and the Gorg's cat fancy. J.Lo gasped and clapped his hands over his mouth, then looked thoughtful.

"I have never hearded of the Gorg liking animals which are not superlarge and dangerful with teeth or kicking strong feet or sitting upon you BAM! with heavy bottoms."

"Maybe they like how cats taste. Maybe they just think they're cute, I dunno."

"Maybies. It is often spoken that the Gorg are fussy eaters."

264

By the end of breakfast I thought I had Vicki figured, so I told her I had to go feed my cat and play with her and change her litter, because having a pet was a Big Responsibility and I wanted to be a Good Cat Owner.

If Vicki had smiled any wider, the top of her head would have fallen off. She said what good kids we were, and promised we'd leave as soon as she changed clothes and fixed her hair. I gotta admit, I ate up the praise as much as the breakfast. I hadn't been anybody's good kid in a while.

I followed her into the bedroom.

"Great," I said. "And afterward, we're going to visit Chief Shouting Bear, because I promised him I would and I think it's important to keep promises, because . . . because a person who doesn't . . ."

Vicki's sunny expression clouded over and turned dark. Eyebrows swooped like vultures.

"After we check up on your cat," she thundered, "you two will come with me for an educational tour of Historic Roswell. We're going to see the *old courthouse*."

Italics can only do so much, so I'll clarify that she said "old courthouse" like it was the number one scariest thing in the world.

"Come on, J—JayJay," I said, nearly botching the name for the hundredth time.

"You two march right back in . . . get back here!" Vicki shouted. "I don't have my shoes on!"

She followed us to the top of the stairs.

"What about keeping your promise to go sightseeing with Andromeda and me?!"

"What are you talking about?" I said on my way down the stairs. "We never agreed to anything like that."

"Hold on," Vicki shouted. "You just . . . hold on . . . I . . ."

Vicki turned abruptly and rushed back into her apartment. I watched her leave.

"Wow. What crawled up her butt?"

J.Lo looked.

"It could be any manner of things, judging by the size."

We stepped out into the oven-baked air and walked a couple blocks.

"You know," I said, "I think Mrs. Lightbody might be a little nuts."

"Little nuts?"

"Yeah. You know—crazy."

"Ah. Yes. I thought this also whento she tried to feed me the pasta with noodles. Do you know she covered it with a tomato sauce? That cannot be right."

I saw a huge pear out of the corner of my eye and recognized it as Vicki Lightbody, dressed in a green blouse and matching stirrup pants that made a zippering sound as she walked.

"Oh, jeez. Here she comes. Walk faster."

She had her shoes on now, and a diaper bag slung over

one shoulder. In the opposite arm she cradled Andromeda, who was wearing both her Legolas onesie *and* her Keebler booties. Which seemed wrong, you know—mixing two different kinds of elves like that. So now I *knew* Vicki was crazy.

"Wait for us!" she sang. "Our first stop is a *very* powerful magnetic convergence point where two ley lines cross under an Arby's. This is where the Agarthan race makes—"

"We're going to the car," I said. "We're going to see my cat, remember? You were okay with that part."

"I can not throw the cold foam pellet," whispered J.Lo to me. "You are not supposed to get babies in it."

"That's okay."

Vicki followed us to the car wash, explaining all the way that dogs make better pets than cats, and how when she was a little girl she listened to her parents, and that using ginger ale instead of cold water when making Jell-O gives it a little kick, and did we think they tried to pack too much into the fourth season of *Babylon 5*? She didn't.

I used to live in a city, so I had a lot of practice ignoring people, but Vicki Lightbody was pushing me to my limit. J.Lo and I greeted Pig and let her out for a bit while we pushed Slushious through the wipers at the exit of the car wash. We pushed right into Vicki.

"We won't be needing your little car, you sillies."

Andromeda wasn't in Vicki's arms anymore. It wasn't hard

to follow the crying to the spot near a hedge where the baby lay on her back. Pig was sniffing at her head.

"I think you kids don't understand what's happening," said Vicki. "We can't all go around doing our own thing and . . . and changing everything! Children do not drive cars. They do not visit old Indians in junkyards. How can things go back to normal when everyone keeps *changing everything*?"

I decided that was one of those rhetorical questions. I scooped Pig up again and put her safely back in the car. I had a feeling we might have to make a break for it at any moment.

"All my life . . . all my life I've waited for the aliens to come, and now they're here!" she said. *"Now they're here!"*

She was more right than she knew. As she spoke, two crablike monsters the size of gas grills scuttled down a distant avenue. Then one of them turned away and headed straight for us.

"It wasn't supposed to be like this," Vicki creaked. "*My* aliens don't push people around and cause families to break up, make people move and desert their wives and daughters! *My* aliens are nicer."

The creature paused right behind her. It was some awful mixture of meat and machine, and I wasn't at all surprised when J.Lo whispered that it was a robot sent by the Gorg. It was green and purple all over, with a back end that formed a round cage. And in the cage were two stray cats, shivering in the heat.

It was a small yowl from one of these cats that made

Vicki Lightbody turn around, and when she saw the crab robot, she gave a squeak and rushed over to clutch Andromeda to her chest.

A scooped-out section at the front of the robot crackled to life and projected a moving image of what I guessed was the head of a Gorg. The reception was terrible.

"A MESSAGE FROM THE ASSISTANT REGIONAL DEVASTATOR GORG THREE-GORGS!" the head said in a tinny roar. "A MESSAGE FROM THE ASSISTANT REGIONAL DEVASTATOR GORG THREE-GORGS! A MESSAGE

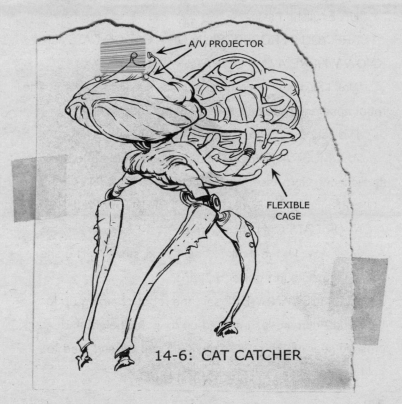

A/V PROJECTOR

FLEXIBLE CAGE

14-6: CAT CATCHER

FROM THE ASSIS—MESSAGE BEGINS. HUMANS! YOU
ARE HEARING THIS MESSAGE BECAUSE A CAT OR
CATS WAS RECENTLY DETECTED IN YOUR AREA! ARE
YOU IN POSSESSION OF A CAT OR CATS, OR KNOW
WHERE A CAT OR CATS CAN BE FOUND?"

I looked quickly at J.Lo, then at Mrs. Lightbody. She was
staring back at me and . . . smiling? I held my breath.

"YOUR REPLY WAS NOT UNDERSTOOD. TO CON-
TINUE IN ENGLISH SAY **ENGLISH**! *GU POZGIZLU IZ
NIMROG, FEL—*"

"Uh, English!" I said.

"ARE YOU IN POSSESSION OF A CAT OR CATS, OR
KNOW WHERE A CAT OR CATS—"

"No!" I said, and hoped Pig had the sense to stay low. The
robot apparently couldn't detect her inside the car.

J.Lo said no, too. Vicki didn't say anything.

"ALL MUST ANSWER!" said the robot, and turned
its flickering Gorg face toward Vicki. "ARE YOU IN
POSSESSION OF A CAT OR CATS, OR KNOW WHERE
A CAT OR CATS CAN BE FOUND?"

"Well, now, let me think . . ." said Vicki, smirking like she
was eating cake in front of orphans.

"ALL MUST ANSWER!" said the robot, charging up to
Vicki and Andromeda. It craned up to its full height and
pressed near the baby. Vicki gave a sharp cry and tried to
hold her out of its reach.

"POSSIBLE CAT!" screeched the robot. "INVESTIGATING!"

"It's not a cat!" I said. "It's a human! A human infant!"

The cat hunter eased away and relaxed its posture again.

"CORRECT. MESSAGE CONTINUES. ALL CATS MUST BE SURRENDERED TO A GORG OR GORG REPRESENTATIVE BY SUNDOWN TONIGHT! ANY HUMAN FOUND TO BE HARBORING A CAT AFTER THIS TIME WILL BE DISASSEMBLED! HIS CLOSEST NEIGHBORS WILL BE SEVERELY PUNCHED! MESSAGE STOPS."

With that, the crab scurried away, its joints and feet making chewing and ticking noises across the pavement. I felt like I had an all-over sunburn.

"Thanks," I told Vicki. "For not . . ."

She didn't really look at me when she answered. She would have been looking at my hat if I had been wearing one.

"You'd better let your cat go," she said flatly, "or turn it over before tonight. You can't fight things."

She turned to leave.

"Maybe I'll pop in and check up on you later," she added, and zipped off home.

"Let's go," I said.

We jogged alongside Slushious for a while, pushing it as fast as we could manage. Then we jumped in and rode until it ran out of momentum, and we had to jog again.

"What does she keep having to 'check'?" I said. "You'd

think we needed watering or something."

We coasted along in silence for a minute. A big ball of burgundy ponytails and black braids rolled across the road ahead of us.

"Look," I said halfheartedly. "Another one of those tumble-weeds made out of old hair weaves."

"Tumbleweave," said J.Lo.

I frowned at the rearview mirror as we slowed. "Were people this crazy before you guys invaded?"

"I was not around beforeto us guys invaded."

"It was a rhetorical question."

"Ah. Then the answer is yes."

We opened our doors and propelled the car forward again. More cat hunters moved through the town, down at the ends of streets where the air shimmered.

"J.Lo?"

"Yes."

"I'm not trying to be bossy all the time. It just comes out that way. You know?"

"Yes."

"Maybe that's what makes me crazy. Always having to have it my way. Maybe that's what makes both me *and* Vicki crazy."

"Chief Shouty Bear is perhaps crazy," said J.Lo after we'd hopped inside again.

"Yeah," I said. "Or he wants people to think so."

The tall fence appeared in our windshield, and Lincoln the Great Dane sprang from it and turned circles around the car as we pulled up. The Chief's place was on a small hill, just a bump, really, but it made it difficult to keep Slushious in one place.

"Here," said the Chief as he emerged from the yard and propped open big double doors. Then he grabbed our front bumper and helped us move the car inside.

J.Lo and I were panting, and we sat down against Slushious in a thin slip of shade. The Chief disappeared into the house and came back with water.

"Thanks," I said.

"Should've offered yesterday. Not hospitable of me."

I gulped down the water.

"Well . . . not to be rude, but you don't really have a reputation for hospitality around here. I mean, I guess it's a part of your . . . of who you—"

He stood staring down at me for a moment, his face dark with the sun behind his straw hair.

"The shouting, you mean."

"Right," I said. "What's the deal with that?"

"Hobby," said the Chief. "I'm retired."

"You didn't raise your voice once when it was just the three of us. Well, you did a bit during your whole carnival spiel. Which could use some work, if you ask me."

He huffed.

"But then Vicki and Kat show up and you're all, 'GO AWAY, TREATY-BREAKER! DON'T . . . UM . . . DON'T—"

"I never said 'treaty-breaker.'"

"Yeah, well, that was the basic theme, anyway."

"I only usually shout at the white people," he said. "Tradition. I've got no beef with you."

"I'm *half* white," I said, folding my arms.

"Hrrm. Which half?"

I blinked. "Uh . . . dunno. Let's say it's from the waist down."

Chief Shouting Bear nodded. "Deal. I only hate your legs."

We looked at each other for a moment, during which I could hear him breathe like an old house.

"I'm Gratuity," I said. "People call me Tip. And that's Pig in the car."

"Frank," he answered, and offered his hand. I shook it.

"Oh," I said. "I thought . . . I heard . . ."

"You heard my name was Chief Shouting Bear," he said. "It doesn't matter. You can call me whatever you want, Stupidlegs."

"Deal."

J.Lo approached and tapped the Chief's elbow.

"Hey, Spook," said the Chief. J.Lo handed him a small card I'd helped him write. With the way the Roswell BOOBs looked at him every time he opened his mouth, we agreed he shouldn't push his luck with the Chief.

"My name is JayJay," read the Chief in a monotone. "I am

ten years old. I have taken a vow of silence and wear this costume in solidarity with our Boovish cousins in their fight against the wicked Gorg."

The Chief gave the card back. "Nothing wrong with that," he said. "Hell, I wore a feather headdress for a while in the sixties."

I popped the hood on Slushious, careful not to make all the tires fall off, while the Chief closed and latched the gates again.

"You say a Boov modified this for you?" he asked as he stepped up.

"Yeah. In Pennsylvania."

"An' it's broken."

"Right. Still floats, but doesn't drive anymore."

"An' it was broken yesterday, when you tried to sell it to me?"

"Um . . . yeah."

"Hrm."

He poked at hoses and unfastened gaskets. I sincerely hoped he wasn't doing anything dangerous, because J.Lo was suddenly nowhere to be seen. I expected he'd slipped off to examine the teleclone booth again.

"Should be something here," the Chief said, pointing to the housing for the Snark's Adjustable Manifold. "That's how come it won't drive."

I blinked. That *was* how come it didn't drive, but how could he know that? Of course, there was sort of a gaping hole in the middle of the hood. It wouldn't take a rocketpod scientist to see Slushious was missing something.

"Hey, you're pretty good," I said. "We had to get rid of that part after it started exploding too much. How'd you guess?"

"Could tell you," said the Chief, "but then I'd have to start shouting again."

I frowned.

"That's a weird thing to say."

"You're telling me."

I'd thought Lincoln was off somewhere with J.Lo, but suddenly he was at our sides, barking his head off. The Chief had his head buried under the hood, but he looked back over his shoulder.

"Lincoln—what's wrong with you?" he said, and spat. "Doesn't usually bark much."

"Chief," I said, my voice thin.

Gorg jetpackers buzzed over Roswell like flies at a picnic. And one of them had broken away from the rest to head right for the junkyard.

Chief Shouting Bear saw him too, and sped immediately toward the house.

"Gotta move the booth," he said. "You hide under the car."

"Chief!"

He skidded to a halt and looked back.

"They're hunting cats," I breathed.

A moment passed, and he rushed back. Pig didn't want to

leave the car with Lincoln near, so I had to pull her out with a floor mat still attached to her feet. The Chief scooped her up and ran off again.

"Under the car!" he ordered.

He didn't have to tell me a third time. I dropped to my hands and knees and slid under Slushious, choking on dust.

It was very quiet. I only noticed the birds had been singing when they abruptly stopped.

I don't know what I'd expected it to feel like, with Slushious floating over me. I don't think I'd expected anything at all. But it was cold, like standing in front of a refrigerator.

Somewhere behind me I heard exactly the sound of a Gorg wearing a jetpack land in the yard.

I tried not to breathe. I tried not to think about the way my lungs felt scratchy with New Mexico dirt. Then it was suddenly bright. Slushious was shoved aside, and I squinted up at the ugliest face in the universe.

J.Lo disagrees with me about this. He says the title of Most Ugliest goes to the Goozmen of the Crab Nebula, which are apparently just blobs of carbon. But I could see how a blob of carbon might look nice with soft lighting. What stood over me was a Gorg, and he looked like a half ton of anger in bicycle shorts.

He was a dull olive green, with bloodred splotches around his head and shoulders. Here and there he had thick purplish plates growing out of his skin like giant fingernails. If crea-

tures really evolve to suit their surroundings, then the
Nimrogs surely were a race of backstabbers, the way their
backsides were covered in armor and horns.

I didn't know if I should stay down or get up, but then
he helped me decide by nearly yanking my arm out at the
shoulder. I found my feet but avoided looking him in the
eyes.

"HUMAN!" Gorg barked. When he spoke, his frowning
mouth gaped like a fish. "WHERE IS THE STOLEN BOOTH!"

Oh, I thought. My eyes began to water. The stink coming
off him could perm your hair.

"Um . . . what now?"

"ARE YOU LOUD BEAR CHIEFTAIN?!" said Gorg,
cracking his knuckles. They made a sound so low you could
feel it in your bones.

"Who?"

"CHIEFTAIN LOUD BEAR MAN!"

Gorg paced around me, scanning the piles of junk and
scrap. He seemed especially taken with Bathhenge. I didn't
know where the Chief was hiding Pig and the booth, but I
didn't think he'd had enough time.

"I, uh, I don't know who you're talking about," I said. "You
must have the wrong place."

He trod forward on thick legs and bent over me. I did
my best to look calm on the outside, but my insides were
dancing and throwing off sparks like a fork in a microwave.

"IT IS NOT THE WRONG PLACE. *YOU* ARE THE WRONG PLACE!"

"Um."

"I WAS TOLD TO FIND THE SHOUTING ANIMAL MAN IN HIS GARBAGE COOP!"

"I'm sorry, but—*I'm sorry!*" I yelped and skipped backward as Gorg advanced on me. "You were given bad information. Probably some human's fault."

"I AM PRINCIPAL ANGER COORDINATOR ASSOCIATE-OF-THE-MONTH GORG FOUR GORG! HUMANS WILL GIVE ME BAD INFORMATION **AT THEIR PERIL!**"

He didn't look like a principal. He looked like something Hercules ought to be wrestling on the side of a vase.

Gorg bent further and raised a fist over my head. He's bluffing, I thought. It's just to scare me into changing my story. To make me blurt something out. I straightened up as tall as I could and breathed through my mouth. I looked him right in the eye. And when I couldn't bear that, I looked him right in the nose.

You have a ridiculous nose, I thought, tears running down my face. Look at it. It's like an oak leaf made out of steak.

And suddenly it was as if I had mental powers. Gorg's nose twitched. It twitched again. He scrunched his whole face, and his nose closed up like a Venus flytrap.

Then his torso snapped back and forward again, and he made the weirdest, wettest noise I ever heard. It must have been a sneeze, but it sounded like an elephant being forced through a drinking straw.

"WHERE IS IT?" Gorg howled, looking at my feet.

I looked too, confused. If he meant the booth, I sure wasn't standing on it.

"Where is what?"

"ANSWER ME, BOY! THE GORG ARE NOT TO BE TRIFLED WITH!"

I scowled. "I'm a girl."

He leaned in close, looking me over, breathing on my hair. Something like molasses ran from his bat face.

"YOU ALL LOOK THE SAME."

"Ha! You're one to talk."

"YES, WE ARE!" he bellowed. "THE GORG ARE GREAT ONES FOR TALKING! TALKING AND **POUNDING**!"

"Hey!" came a shout from the house, and I exhaled. Later I'd wish the Chief had stayed hidden, but at the time all I felt was relief. If my thoughts could have formed words they'd have said, *Please, treat me like a child. Come save me.*

"Leave her be!" shouted Chief Shouting Bear, striding toward us. "Y'wanna deal with someone, you deal with—"

Gorg's great trunk of an arm swung fast and wide, and struck the Chief in the head. He was felled with one blow.

I'm sorry for that word "felled." I only looked it up just now. I had to have just the right one to do this justice. Mark Twain said the difference between the right word and the almost right word is like the difference between lightning and the lightning bug, and people think he was good, right? Didn't write any decent girl characters, as far as I can tell, but otherwise fine.

The Gorg *felled* Chief Shouting Bear. The Chief's legs shot up from under him, and he came down hard on his back with a sound louder than I thought a human body could make. Then he lay there. There was a red X on his forehead, getting larger, and it was the only thing that moved.

"DO NOT BE IMPUDENT, BOY. THE GORG CAN DO TERRIBLE THINGS TO YOU."

I had been thinking of something clever to say, but now that part of my brain was static. It was all I could do to keep my eyes open.

Gorg squinted some more at me, then nodded, satisfied. He turned on his heel and thundered off like an angry building. He turned Slushious over and scattered the piles of scrap metal. He threw washing machines like huge dice and cracked each bathtub with a blow from his fist. Large sections of the outer fence fell under a volley of tires and engine blocks. Then he knocked a wall of the Chief's house in with a rusted-out town car and took the rest of it apart, piece by piece. When there was no longer any house standing, I wondered what had become of J.Lo and Pig. And Lincoln. And the booth. Gorg tore the basement door off its hinges and squeezed down the stairs. Angry noises roared up from below until he emerged a minute later. Finally, with everything in ruins, Gorg looked around to where I sat pressing the Chief's hat to his head. Then he grunted and went back into the sky, where he belonged.

Seconds stretched out like little lifetimes as I crouched there on my legs and willed the Chief to wake up and be fine. Suddenly J.Lo was at my side, holding Pig.

"Run get his bedsheets, or a towel," I said. J.Lo dropped Pig and ran off. Pig went and hid inside Slushious when Lincoln returned from wherever he'd been hiding and licked the Chief's head.

"No, Lincoln . . . don't . . ."

J.Lo arrived trailing a white bedsheet. I bunched it up and pressed hard onto the head wound. Right away the sheet blossomed like a red carnation.

"I don't know what to do," I said. "I think we need to take him into town."

We tied Lincoln to something heavy and managed to get Slushious right-side up with nothing more remarkable than a tire jack. The car was in sad shape now. The left side fin was crushed again, and the roof was crumpled like a paper sack. But it still floated, and it was the only way we were going to get one hundred and fifty pounds of unconscious Indian to the UFO museum.

We spread out the bedsheet and slipped it under the

Chief's body. It was only then that I noticed the two circular cuts in the fabric.

"This is your ghost costume. You're not wearing your ghost costume."

"No. I will get outfrom Slushious befores we arrive. I will hide."

We needed a ramp to get the Chief into the hatchback. Luckily, we were surrounded by a little of everything. J.Lo stacked sections of white PVC pipe up an old refrigerator door, and we rolled the Chief in.

We got a good start, coasting down the shallow hill with the setting sun behind us. I kept checking the movement of the Chief's chest in the mirror. Then I looked at J.Lo.

"Where were you? Could you see everything?" I asked.

"Only did I hear," said J.Lo. "I hid. I feared the Gorg might smell me. They haves very good noses."

"Not this one," I murmured. "He had a cold."

"Get out of town."

"He did. He had a cold."

"He could no have had this. The Gorg do not get sick."

"He sneezed."

"Tip was probably very scared. Imagined it."

"I did *not*—"

I paused when I noticed we were nearing one of those mechanical cat hunters.

"Get Pig down. Hold her there. Shoot, we should have left her at the scrap yard."

"No Gorg around," said J.Lo. "A few cat robots, but no Gorg."

"Suits me."

"I also. But if the Gorg have put onto the land a working telecloner, they could be everyplace. Why not for?"

"Maybe Gorg don't like being around Gorg any more than we do. C'mon, we need to run some more."

Another ten minutes and we were close to Vicki's apartment and the UFO museum.

"You better get out here," I said. "Take your toolbox and go see if you can find some food and water, and a police car or something we can borrow. Please," I added.

J.Lo ran off, and I started shouting.

"Hey! Anybody! Help! *Heeeelp!*"

The combined members of BOOB, Roswell Chapter, came running out of the museum.

"Oh, man," said Trey when he saw the Chief. "What happened?"

"He tried to stop a Gorg from hurting me," I said.

"What's a Gorg? Are those the new aliens?"

"You saw one up close?" squealed one of the boys.

"It tried to hurt you? Cool!"

"Boys, quiet," said Beardo.

"Hey, Chief," said Kat as she and Trey eased him out of the car.

"Hey," said the Chief.

"He's awake?" I shouted, and ran to the Chief's side.

"Hey, Stupidlegs."

He was slurring his speech a little.

"Has he been drinking?" asked Vicki, who'd just come across the street. I gave her a dirty look but it bounced right off her. I was so mad I could have spit acid.

"No, Vicki," Beardo said. "He got hit by one of the big aliens."

"Don't you look at me like that. I was just asking is all. Indians drink—I saw a special about it."

Chief Shouting Bear was carried into the UFO museum and over to the alien autopsy exhibit. The fake dead alien was pushed aside and the Chief was placed on the gurney. The adults leaned over him while the boys, already bored, moved into the lobby to play some kind of slapping game they'd invented.

"God, he probably has a concussion," said Trey. "You shouldn't even have moved him."

"Well, I couldn't call an ambulance, could I?" I said. "How did the Gorg know where to find him, anyway? They knew his name and everything."

No one answered, but all eyes turned to Vicki Lightbody. She picked at a hangnail and didn't meet our gaze, but I understood. She mumbled something about checking on Andromeda, and left the museum.

I sighed. "Can anyone help him?"

"Just need a bag of ice," said the Chief. "Got any ice?"

"I don't know, Chief," said Kat. "I don't think anyone has ice."

"Go outside," he said. "Get some snow."

Everyone exchanged worried looks.

"And whiskey," the Chief added. "Ask one of the pilots."

"Can anybody help him?" I asked again.

"I can," said Trey. "My ex-girlfriend was a nursing student."

"That doesn't really count, Trey."

"Can any of you do better?" he snapped. "I used to quiz her before tests, and before the big exam. I'm practically a nurse myself."

The Chief looked up at my face.

"Always said you were the prettiest nurse," he creaked. "Don't care what the other boys think."

I wiped at my wet eyes with the heel of my hand.

"Don't tell anyone I said," he added. "Gota girl back home."

"Chief," said Kat, and the Chief blinked his eyes a couple times. He looked around at the other faces.

"Chief," said Kat, "do you know what year it is?"

He didn't answer.

"What's the President's name," Beardo said. "The last one."

"Roosevelt," said the Chief. Beardo frowned.

"Roosevelt was the last *real* president," the Chief said. "Every one since has been a jackass."

When it became clear that Trey really did know what he was

doing, I relaxed a little. Beardo and I walked out to the street.

"We all have to get out of Roswell as soon as possible," he said. "It's getting dangerous. Those . . . Gorg? . . . were flying around all afternoon, shooting at cats. You'd better keep a close eye on yours."

"What, were they eating them?" I asked. "I thought they *liked* cats."

"I think they just like shooting them. I mean, after those guns erase them, there's nothing to eat."

"Erase them?"

"Yeah," said Beardo, looking up at the stars. "You've seen how those guns work, right? No noise, but they make stuff disappear? Kat thinks they emit antimatter particles. I don't know."

"But those erasing guns are the kind the Boov use," I said. "Gorg like loud noises and explosions and stuff."

Beardo looked at me hard for a moment. "Where's JayJay?"

"Still at the Chief's place. I'm going to go back for him now."

"You know," said Beardo, "Kat is convinced your brother's a Boov under that sheet. She hasn't figured out what you are yet."

I paused too long before answering.

"That's ridiculous. Why would my brother be a Boov? It's impossible. That Kat should have her head—"

"I don't care," said Beardo. "Just go get your brother and stay close to me after that. Kat's pretty worked up about it."

That was that. J.Lo and I had to leave right away.

"What's your name?" I said. "I never asked."

"David."

"Okay," I said, and took off toward Slushious.

I opened the door and pushed the car around until it was pointed at the Chief's house again. I noticed that Pig wasn't inside the car anymore. Had I left a window open? No—they were cracked but not open. Maybe she'd slipped out in all the confusion surrounding the Chief. Maybe J.Lo had her.

"J.Lo!" I hissed.

The headlights hadn't worked for a couple days, but the parking lights still did. I flashed them on and off and on, and that's when I saw someone in the dull orange glow.

It was Vicki Lightbody, and she was holding Pig.

"Oh. You found her," I said, trying to be civil. But then I got a good look at her, hunched over Pig like a blond goblin, hands tight around the scruff of her neck. You could see in her eyes she was having a full-on crazy.

"I found your little J.Lo all right," said Mrs. Lightbody. "And we're all lucky I did! She's a cat! You still have a cat!"

Sometimes you really want to say "Duh," but you can't. It's a part of growing up, I guess.

"Why don't you let me take her," I said. "I'm sorry she got out—"

"Oh, no. No one's taking little J.Lo except the aliens. Do you know what could have happened to us if they knew we were harboring a cat after sundown? Do you? I don't think you do."

Pig began to yowl. Mrs. Lightbody was hurting her. I looked in every direction, hoping to see David, maybe, terrified I'd see lights in the sky or hear the whir of one of those cat hunters.

"This is just what I'd expect from little *Grace*. I know all about you. You've fooled the others, maybe, but *Iseeright throughyou*."

What she didn't see was J.Lo creeping up behind her. He'd found a new sheet, and was in ghost costume again. I was trying to think how I might signal him to crouch behind Mrs. Lightbody while I gave her a push. I'd seen it done once in a Marx Brothers movie and had always wanted to try it out. But my mind went blank when J.Lo pulled off his sheet and retracted his helmet. He had no costume, and all Vicki Lightbody had to do was turn around.

He said, "Excuse me." She turned around.

I was only a little pleased to hear her shriek at the sight of a Boov so close. But I couldn't imagine what he thought he was doing.

"Good evening," said J.Lo. "I am Chief Animals Control Officer Cher. I understands you have a cat for us."

Vicki was frozen in place. Pig made a sound like an electric toothbrush.

"How . . . how did you know to come?" Vicki asked.

"Powerful telescopes."

"Oh. Uh-huh." Mrs. Lightbody nodded.

"Put now the cat in the bag, please," J.Lo said, holding his sheet out in front of him. Mrs. Lightbody did as she was told.

"It was this girl that was keeping it," she said. "*I* was going to bring it to you!"

Pig scrambled around a bit, but went limp as J.Lo drew the sheet tight.

"We know. You have our thanks. For your good service you will receive prizes. Flowers! And an expensive hat."

"Oh! Well, that's very . . . very . . . wasn't it the other aliens who wanted the cats?"

"Mmmmyes. The Boov are . . . doing little favors for them. So they will stop shooting us. Now move along! Everyones back to their homes!"

Mrs. Lightbody gave me a smug look and hustled off.

J.Lo got in the car and let the cat out of the bag, so to speak.

"Fuh," he said, looking at his sheet. "Covered in cat's hair."

J.Lo had really kept busy while I'd been in the UFO Museum. Apart from supplies and a new ghost costume, he'd found us a police car. Sort of.

"It's not a police car," I said.

"It is," said J.Lo. "Looknow. Lights for flashing."

"That's true."

"Writing on the sides."

"Yeah, but the writing? It says 'BullShake Party Patrol.'"

"Yes. Whatnow?"

BullShake was one of those energy drinks. Do you still have them in the future? They came in these tall, thin cans and were supposed to make you feel vital and hyper so you'd have the drive and focus to save lives, or run that extra mile, or solve that unsolvable math problem or whatever.

"Looks just alike a police car," said J.Lo.

"Except it's smaller. And police cars aren't usually red. And don't normally have six-foot-long cans of energy shake on their roofs."

"Can we not take it?" asked J.Lo.

We took it. We towed Slushious back up to the junkyard, which looked sad and flat, apart from the big busted water tower standing a couple hundred feet away. J.Lo got right to modifying the Party Patrol car so it would be easier to drive and see over the dashboard.

"Waitaminute," I said. "Let's just get the teleclone booth and make sure it'll fit in this car before we waste too much time on it."

We untied Lincoln and let him run around, and J.Lo took me to the center of the naked wooden floor that used to be the Chief's house. He hunched over, searching all around his and my feet.

"You know," I said, "after that Gorg sneezed, he was all looking around my feet, too."

"The Gorg did not sneeze."

"He did. And then he shouted *'Where is it?'* and looked at my feet. Is there something I don't know about teleclone booths, like how they shrink real small when they're not being used or something?"

"I am not looking forto the booth. I am looking to the hole. Ahanow!"

He put his fingers to a spot on one of the floorboards and pried it up. A large square door lifted clean out of the floor.

"Oh, cool," I said. I defy you to say anything less stupid when you discover a secret trapdoor for the first time.

J.Lo found a switch on the wall. Bare lightbulbs winked on, giving a dull glow to the space below.

"This is where you hid?" I asked as we toed our way down a metal ladder bolted to the side of . . . well, to the side of an enormous pipe. A huge concrete water pipe that bottomed out about thirty feet below.

"Yes. And to where we hids the teleclone booth. Arounding the corner."

We reached bottom and I saw we were standing at the intersection of two huge pipes that made an upside-down T.

One direction, leading toward town, was invisibly dark. But in the opposite direction the lights stretched out a long way. The pipe was all dry and full of stuff. The teleclone booth was here, and a stack of metal lock boxes, and a bunch of regular cardboard boxes filled with antiques. There were big round army helmets and old newspapers. There was a Bible in German and a pewter plaque with the Declaration of Independence on it.

"And look," said J.Lo. "Talkie-walkies." They must have been Chief's from the war. They were the Incredible Hulk of walkie-talkies: really big and green, about the size and weight of a half gallon of milk, with a long antenna and a mouthpiece like a telephone.

There was a poster in Chinese on the side of the pipe next to a signed picture of Betty Grable, and a kind of embarrassing pinup painting of a girl getting her skirt lifted up by a pelican.

J.Lo kneeled by the teleclone cage and started loosening connections.

"I can make it into pieces," he said. "Then will it be more easier to move."

"Okay, good," I said. "Why do you think the Chief lit this half of the tunnel, all the way down? He's got all his stuff piled right here."

J.Lo was muttering to himself in Boovish. "Five minutes!" he told me, never looking up from the booth.

I walked down the length of the tunnel away from him, until I came to an elbow and a ladder leading back up. I suddenly had a weird feeling I'd never left Florida, and the ladder would open onto the Broadway of Happy Mouse Kingdom all over again.

I started up the ladder, and the pipe soon got narrower and darker around me. But above me, way high above me, there was a little square of moonlight.

"Someday soon," I told myself, "Mom's gonna ask what I did all this time on my own, and I'm gonna say, 'Climbed ladders.'"

I had that feeling of déjà vu again when I realized I'd been climbing too long—that I'd passed the ground and kept going. I must be in the water tower, I thought. I must be getting close to the tank. The pipe brightened, and I looked up at wire mesh stretched over a hatch above me. Moonlight filtered in, I supposed from the big hole in the side of the tank where the Chief claimed his paper-maché saucer had crashed. I pushed up the hatch and poked my head through to get a look at things.

"Oh," I said. "You have *got* to be kidding me."

"No pushing!" said J.Lo. "I am no so good with ladders."

"Really? You think?"

"You could have just to told me what. Instead of all this climbing."

"Almost there," I said.

J.Lo popped up his helmet and used it to push against

the mesh hatch in the floor of the water tank as he climbed. The helmet snapped back.

"Koobish!"

He scrambled up into the big cylindrical room and rushed over to the larger of the two animals.

"Naaaa-aa-aa-a-a-aa-aaah!" said the koobish.

"Maa'apla nah!" said J.Lo.

"I thought they might be koobish," I said. "They look just like one of your drawings."

They were four-legged, with wiry hair in tight little curls. Their feet were round and made *pock-pock* noises when they walked. The smaller koobish came up to J.Lo, and he took a bite out of its ear.

"Hey!" I said. "What was that?"

"Is okay," said J.Lo, beaming. "They do not feel pain. They are fine so long as you do not eats the head."

"Huh."

"Try a littles bite of tail. Is crunchy."

"No."

Instead I pet the small one as it whinnied happily. The Chief had made it nice for them. The tower was lined with water troughs and filled with hay, and there was even a little potted tree under the big hole in the tank where the UFO had come in.

Oh, yeah, I thought.

"J.Lo?"

"Yes?"

"What if a spaceship really did crash into this thing in 1947? A Boovish ship."

"YES! Of coursenow! The ship that crashed onto Roswell must have to been the Haanie Mission!"

"Haanie's capsule was supposed to have exploreded 294 years ago. I mean exploded.

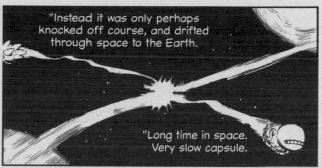

"Instead it was only perhaps knocked off course, and drifted through space to the Earth.

"Long time in space. Very slow capsule.

"Koobish reproduce alls by themself.

"Baby koobish start as pimples that grow and fall off.

"If then they fall into water, they are a new koobish.

VOOP!

"If not, they dries up in the open air.

"Haanie must have been growing such a pimple when her capsule launched. When it detached, there was no water for making it grow, but there was no air to make it shrivel.

"The capsule kept baby fresh, like koobish-in-a-can.

KOOBISH

"Then the   capsule   crashes into water,

and Fa-da! New koobish!"

"But . . ." I said, "that means . . . that the Chief really does have a spaceship."

We held each other's gaze for a second.

I was already heading down the ladder again when J.Lo ran to the hatch. Then he ran back a moment, took another bite of koobish, and started down the ladder above me.

"Will the koobish be okay?" I asked, my voice echoing. "We can't bring them with us to Arizona."

"They shoulds be fine. They have plenty water to make an hundred babies, and the Chief put out enough chlorine for to last them a year. An Earth year."

I'm faster on ladders, so by the time I got outside I was way ahead of J.Lo. The entrance to the Chief's basement was just a gaping hole now, with the splintered remains of doors barely attached by crumpled hinges. I hurried down the steps and groped around for the light switch.

Only about half the lights came on. No "A-Tisket, A-Tasket." The Gorg had trashed everything. He'd even thrown the UFO against a wall, and it lay there on its end, paper-maché crunched against the rough concrete.

"I don't get it," I whispered. The saucer looked just as bad as it had two days ago. Worse. "There's no way that thing's real."

J.Lo arrived, panting. "Did you to . . . is it . . . Tip should to . . . have waited . . . so much . . . running . . ."

"You don't think he would've . . ." I said, and trailed off. There was something funny about the whole scene.

"Yes? . . . What."

I stepped over and tore some of the cracked paper-maché off the fake spaceship. Inside was a real one.

* * *

"How's it coming?" I asked. We needed to leave while it was still dark, and I was feeling tired and antsy.

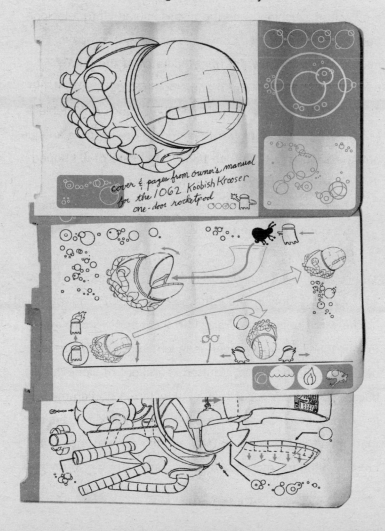

cover & pages from owner's manual for the 1062 Koobish Krooser one-door rocketpod

"Superfine," said J.Lo. "This Chief Shouty Bear, he is some smart fellow. Do you know he drained out and cleaned the Snark's Adjustable Manifold his self? And fixed the humbutt, I do not know how he did that, let me tell you. These things would have taken hours for doing. Howfor is the BullShake?"

The big can of BullShake Energy Drink was strapped to the back of Slushious, and the disassembled Gorg teleclone booth was inside. And J.Lo was completing the repairs. He made Slushious a new fin from the hatch of the three-hundred-year-old rocketpod and smoothed out the roof. He swapped out some parts, including the Snark's Adjustable Manifold. It was a bit bigger than our old one, and an antique, but apparently the Chief had taken good care of it. I hoped the BOOBs were taking good care of the Chief.

J.Lo put down his tools and raised his oil-stained face. "Alls done!" he cheered.

J.Lo had to drive. I was dead tired. I put out a bunch of food and water for Lincoln and left a note for BOOB and the Chief on the windshield of the Party Patrol car and we tore away from Roswell, trying to cover as much ground as possible before any Gorg noticed. I drifted in and out of sleep in the backseat, my body a question mark with Pig dotting my feet. It was nice in the backseat, feeling like a little kid again, so that when I awoke an hour later and the car was stopped, I half expected my mom to lift me up and carry me to my bed.

There was a soft glow of lights in the back windshield. I propped myself up and stared out. Then I stumbled through the car door and joined J.Lo, standing by the rear bumper.

We were higher up, looking down and about eighty miles southeast at where Roswell used to be. Maybe you future people have rebuilt it—that would be nice. The big Gorg sphere was closer than before, and was the color of a fresh bruise in the moonlight. And Roswell was glowing in the dark.

"What are they . . . why are they doing it?" I asked.

J.Lo glanced at the big metal can on our car, then back at the town. It was all the answer I needed. The Gorg hadn't found their teleclone booth; they were burning everything for a hundred miles so nobody else would have it, either.

"They got out, don't you think? Chief and David and everybody? Lincoln?"

Cannon fire set the horizon ablaze, and impossibly huge Gorg giants stamped it out again. I would have thought I'd dreamed it all, if not for the pictures.

"We betters get going," said J.Lo.

We drove in shifts, caught some sleep, and steered north more than ever, because it looked like the Gorg were on the move. It was hard to tell with a ship that large and that far away, but it seemed like they were aiming right for us. We could have made it to the Arizona border in a few more hours if we hadn't been distracting each other with stupid little arguments. Don't get me wrong; I like J.Lo fine. I've made that bed. But I'm not sure there's a person in the world I could be with twenty-four hours a day for three weeks without getting a little snippy. If I ever meet such a person, I'm marrying them. We were probably somewhere around Four Corners when we actually had a fight over whether water was wet. I guess I knew I was wrong, but there was no stopping me when I got going.

It was weird country. Really barren, with these loops and piles of rock that looked like poured frosting. But I knew we were nearing the Arizona border when I started seeing little threads of smoke in the air. They were from campfires, I thought. They were from people.

"You better put on your costume," I said. "And I don't think you're going to be able to talk to people with that voice of yours. That Kat woman was on to you."

J.Lo cleared his throats. "WHAT IF I TALK LIKE THIS."

I jumped. He sounded just like someone on TV.

"OUR PARTING CONTESTANTS WILL RECEIVE THE FOLLOWING CONSOLATION PRIZES."

"That's amazing," I said. "Now do a little kid voice."

"THIS IS THE ONLY VOICE I CAN DO."

"Oh. I don't think that's gonna help, then."

"Just as well," said J.Lo. "It makes my teeths hurt."

He pulled the sheet back on. We'd made him some arms now as well, with white sleeves and mittens.

"Booo," said J.Lo the ghost. "Boowoooooo!"

"Okay," I replied, smiling. "Thank you."

WELCOME
TO THE UNITED STATES
OF ARIZONA

said a big sign, and I let out a sigh. According to the sign, Arizona is known for cotton and copper. The state bird is the cactus wren, and the state canyon is the Grand Canyon. Way to go, Arizona.

A few minutes more and I could see tents and little houses dotting the land. And people—more humans than I'd seen in one place for three weeks. Hundreds of people, and they were all staring at us.

"Why is everyone staring?" I said. Then I answered myself in my head: Why *wouldn't* they be staring?

I tried to look sixteen, which is really hard to do if you're not concentrating, and lowered Slushious closer to the ground, the back tires just skimming over the asphalt. But there were still the extra fins and the hoses and BullShake can and the ghost in the passenger seat to contend with, so people stared. J.Lo stared right back.

"Ah! Looksee? The Boov are helping."

It was obvious where he was pointing. There was something like a transparent soccer ball filled with shampoo near the main road. People with buckets and coolers crowded around it, but they'd stopped whatever they were doing to watch us pass.

"It is a telecloner," said J.Lo. "The peoples can use it to make water, and to make food."

"Food? I thought the telecloners couldn't do that. The Boov ones, I mean."

I wished I hadn't added that bit about the Boov. I hadn't meant anything by it, but I thought I heard an edge in J.Lo's voice afterward.

"Is not *complicated*," he said. "The telecloners can make a healthy milk shake. Has everything you need."

"That's nice of them," I said. "Nice of the Boov." And the crazy thing was, I really meant it. The Boov had invaded our planet, erased our monuments, taken our homes, and dumped us in a state they didn't want, and I was already so used to the whole idea that it seemed like a sweet gesture that they hadn't left us to starve in the dark.

I coasted Slushious down a hill past what used to be a Buy-Mor but now seemed to be home to a bunch of people. They gawked and pointed at our floating car, so I started shouting "Magic trick!" out the window as we passed. It didn't mean anything, but it got about half of them to nod and go back to what they'd been doing.

It wasn't ten minutes before we were stopped. I saw blue and red lights flashing behind me, and heard a siren, but you couldn't imagine a sweeter sound. It was just a siren—nothing weird about it, nothing new. It was an ordinary cop car, carrying two ordinary probably-scared-half-out-of-their-minds cops.

I pulled over. The squad car slowed and parked some distance behind me. A man cop got out and crouched behind the open door, training his gun on Slushious. A woman cop got out the driver's side and crept slowly up on us like she expected the car to change into a robot. After a minute of this she leaned over and looked in my window.

I thought the police officer was supposed to take the lead in these kinds of situations, but this woman just stared at us. I smiled back sweetly.

"Hi."

The policewoman frowned at my "hi." I think her instincts kicked in.

"Do you know why I stopped you today, ma'am?" she said.

"Because I'm only eleven and my car is floating?"

The officer stared for another moment, and coughed.

"Yes," she said.

"Sounds like you'd better take me down to the station, then," I replied.

I figured I wasn't going to find Mom by driving all over Arizona shouting her name out the window, so I knew I'd end up going to the authorities anyway, if there were any. At the station I explained about my mom's abduction, and the mysterious Boov who rebuilt our car, and how my brother JayJay would throw up for ten minutes if anyone tried to touch or talk to him. I got a lot of practice telling this story, as I had to repeat it to no less than fifty people over the next few days. Soon I had a police escort down to Flagstaff, where a lot of former government types were trying to collect information and help people reunite with friends and family. It was funny that there were so many people trying to find one another when we were all crowded into one state like this. But I guess unless you were all on the same rocketpod, you had no way of knowing if your loved ones were living in Mohawk or Happy Jack or Tuba City. I swear I'm not making these names up.

The Bureau of Missing Persons of the United State of America was in a university building. I was introduced to a thin man in a little suit named Mitch. Two more men in identical suits stood behind him with their hands behind their backs.

"Name," said Mitch. I was staring at the pine trees and snow-speckled mountains through a window and wondering why I'd thought Arizona was all cactus and sand dunes. It took me a few seconds to recognize that he was asking me a question.

"Oh, um. Gratuity Tucci."

He glared at me over his clipboard. "I don't have time for jokes?" he said. "I have a lot of people to see? What is your name."

"Gratuity. G-r-a—"

"That is not a name."

I frowned. "Isn't that sort of between me and my mom?"

"Uh-huh? And is this your mom?" he said, motioning at the policewoman who had pulled us over and was now in the corner trying to keep J.Lo entertained without speaking or making any sudden moves.

"Wow," I said. "You are good. Here I am, looking for my mom, and you find her before I even leave the building."

"I have a lot of people to see?" Mitch said again. "For the time being I am going to put you down as Gratuity."

"It'll have to do."

"Last name."

"Tucci."

"Middle initial."

"I don't have one."

Mitch looked at me like I didn't have a middle name on purpose.

"What is the name of the person or persons you wish to find."

"Lucy Tucci," I said. "My mom."

"How old is she."

"Uh, thirty."

"And what is the nature of your relationship with Lucy Tucci."

"Ummm, pretty good," I said. "I mean, we fight sometimes—"

"No," said Mitch. "No. "Who is she to you. What is your connection."

"She's my mom. I'm her daughter."

Mitch scribbled on his clipboard. I suddenly remembered a promise I'd made.

"Oh! And can you also find, uh . . . Marta! Marta Gonzales. And when you do tell her Christian and Alberto are safe and living under Happy Mouse Kingdom."

You could actually see a little part of Mitch die inside. He hugged his clipboard against his stomach.

"There is no form for that," he said.

"Well," I said, "could you—"

"If there's no form, I don't see how we could possibly . . . Michaels? See if there's a form for that?"

"Yessir," said one of the men in suits behind him before hustling away. Up to now I'd assumed they were just back there to catch Mitch if he fell over.

The policewoman walked up and said, "Your brother is eating pencils."

"He'll do that," I answered.

"You know," she said, "you should put your mom's name on the Lost List."

"Oh, dear," said Mitch. "You may as well tell her to throw darts at a map."

"What's the Lost List?" I asked.

It seemed that Americans were not waiting for the Bureau of Missing Persons to find everyone for them. Some people had taken to carrying lists of names around. Everyone had ten names, and when they got a new one it was added to the top and a name was crossed off the bottom. As they went about their day they might call out, "John Hancock looking for

Susan B. Anthony," or "Buddy Holly looking for Ritchie Valens."
If you heard them and you knew a Susan B. Anthony or a
Ritchie Valens, you'd stop and tell them what you could.

"A lot of people have been reunited that way," said the
woman.

"Do what you like?" sniffed Mitch. "Okay? But the Bureau
is the simplest, fastest way of finding missing persons I know
about. Now here's your ticket," he said, handing me a blue slip
of paper.

It read, CASE FILE #9003041-CHARLIE BRAVO in black ballpoint, and under that, LUCY TUCCI, MOTHER OF CLAIMANT. On the
reverse was a coupon for a car wash.

"Thanks," I muttered.

"Hold on to that," he said. "You won't be able to claim your
mother if you lose it. Check back with us in ten to fourteen
business days."

They learned to really hate me at the Bureau of Missing
Persons. I did not check back in ten to fourteen business
days. I checked back the next day, and the day after that, and
the day after that. All the while J.Lo and I lived in Slushious,
just outside of town. They wanted to find us something better,
but I resisted. We moved around a lot so we wouldn't be too
easy to sneak up on (J.Lo had to get out of his costume once
in a while), and we used the showers and bathrooms on the
university campus. I registered Mom with the Lost List people.

They had a sort of office in the back room of an empty pet store. There weren't many working phone lines yet, but they had a shortwave radio. This was different from a regular radio in two ways I could tell. First, you could talk into a shortwave. If someone else was listening to your frequency, they could hear you, and the other Lost List offices in other cities always listened to the right frequency. Second, people who use shortwave radios *really like* shortwave radios. I had to listen to this pale guy named Phil talk about his for forty minutes.

J.Lo and Pig and I got on okay. We were out of food, but there was plenty of milk shake. J.Lo was right about that. Most communities near cities had teleclone machines for water and food, but people were trying to farm anyway, because the milk shakes tasted like whipped cardboard.

In the evenings, J.Lo worked on the teleclone booth. I kept coming back to the charred and broken corner of the cage.

"Is it missing something important here?" I asked finally. "Is the damage bad?"

"I do not believes so. Probably only lost a couple of nozzles. Still workable. Hold the flashlight still, please."

"Are you sure? I mean, if we ever try this thing, I don't want to teleport out the other side missing a foot or something."

"You will have on both feet. The damage, it is lucky, actually. It disenabled the receiver."

"That's good?"

"That is good. With no receiver, no mores Gorg could be

made, or teleported. With no receiver, the Gorgship could no send the self-destruct command. Hm."

"So if the Boov hadn't damaged the booth just right, the Chief never would have been able to steal it in the first place. And you can fix it?"

"Sh," whispered J.Lo. "Concentrating."

He looked over every inch of the cage, the machinery, the bits he'd disassembled and set aside. He put the whole thing together in a matter of minutes, then took it apart again.

"I cannot understands," he said finally. "It is just as a Boov telecloner. It is alls the same."

"There must be *something* different."

J.Lo didn't respond. He crouched by a nozzle and frowned at it.

"I bet they all got out of Roswell," I said. "The guys had that car. And they'd have the Chief's truck, too."

J.Lo whacked the nozzle with a stick.

"Plus the Party Patrol car," I added. "Did you leave the key in it?"

"Hm?"

"That key you made for the Party car. Did you leave it in the ignition?"

"Ah. Yes."

"So they could have used that too," I said. "If they wanted."

Nearby, two crickets were talking back and forth, again and again, same question every time:

Are you there?

Yes. Are you there?

Yes. Are you there?

Yes. Are—

J.Lo smacked himself in the eyes. *"It is alls the same!"*

"Shhh!"

He pored over the booth, brushing his fingertips across the nozzles, mumbling to himself. The crickets picked up where they'd left off.

"Well, you said it still has to be connected to a computer, right?"

"Yes," said J.Lo. "By signal. But this makes no difference."

"But . . ." I said, "couldn't a computer keep track—"

"No," said J.Lo. "No no no. Is too complicated. No Boov has ever built a computer so powerful as to keep on track all of the participles of a person."

"Not even one of your gas-cloud computers?"

"Not even. To be safe enough, this computer would have to being thousands of times larger than a Boov ship. Than even the *largest* Boov ship. If it even could be done. Who would build such a thing? Where would a person keep it?"

"It would really be that big?"

J.Lo chuffed. "It would have to be alike a small moon!"

We each stared at the other without speaking. Even the crickets stopped chirping. Then we both turned at once and looked at the small purple moon hanging over Mexico.

"You don't think . . ." I said.

"No," said J.Lo, but he sounded less certain. "The electric brain would have to take up the most of the ship. No space for alls the Gorg and supplies."

"How many Gorg and supplies do you need when you can just clone more?"

"Hm."

J. Lo Explains How He Thinks the Gorg Did It, by J. Lo

"Nimrogs most likelies sent up a satellite, with telescoping teleclone nozzles.

"Nozzles cloned up a thick ball of Nimrog skin around the satellite,

and new cloners were placed onto the surface.

INNER LAYERS WOULD BE CLEARED AWAY.

"This would all have been repeated, until the ball was a magnormously-sized skin balloon, a wiggly-fleshy beach ball as big as—"

"Got it, J.Lo. Thanks."

"I am only saying. Wicked large.

"The satellite cloner in the center would then begin pumping electrical computer gas to fill the sphere. More computing participles than was in one place before.
The smartest computer ever, now!"

"Smart enough to clone people?"

"Possiblies. Pass to me the rubber cement, I am hungry."

"I can't believe you drew that."

"This is good," I said. "If you're right, then you can fix the receiver and build more teleclone booths, and we can use them, too. Humans will be able to use the Gorg's own computers against them."

"Possibily."

"We're gonna have to tell someone. Soon. Maybe someone at the Bureau of Missing Persons. I was planning on maybe dropping by there tomorrow to see if they found my mom anyway."

We did go to the bureau the next morning, but the offices were empty except for the suit man named Michaels.

"Oh, it's you," he said without any hint of surprise in his voice. "We haven't found your mom yet."

"Yeah, well, not to be rude," I said with a wave of my arm, "but it doesn't look like you guys are trying very hard."

"Tch. It's just because of the meeting."

"What meeting?"

Michaels grinned. "I thought everyone knew. The meeting with the Boov representatives on the quad. It's going on right now."

"What are the Boov meeting with us for?" I wondered aloud. We were walking to the center of campus to check it out.

"Maybies we should tell these Boov about our telecloner," said J.Lo.

I wasn't crazy about that idea. I couldn't blame J.Lo for still wanting to think the best about his own people, but I thought the Boov might just arrest J.Lo, use this new information to beat the Gorg, and go on treating us humans like the rejects they thought we were.

There was a big crowd of people on the quad—a thousand at least, facing a plywood stage. And on the stage stood five Boov. One of them had fancier clothes than the rest. He was speaking to the crowd.

J.Lo gasped.

"Smek!" he whispered. "It is Captain Smek himself!"

"They are a horrible sort," Smek was saying, "and will not show the Noble Savages of Smekland the respectfulness that you have enjoyed fromto the Boov. The Gorg are known

acrosst the galaxy as the Takers, and they canto only take and take and take!"

The Boov guarding Smek snapped their fingers again and again. It's what the Boov do to applaud.

J.Lo was shaking and pushing up against me. I kept a hand on his shoulder and steered us to the back of the audience. "We knows of the meeting between to the Gorg and Smekland leaders yesterday," said Smek. "The Gorg have probabilies made for you some fancy promises. Do not be believing them! They lie! They will enslave your race, just as to they have done so many others! They will destruct our world!"

There was a lot of grumbling in the audience. Smek was not a popular guy around this part of the Milky Way, for obvious reasons.

"In closing," said Captain Smek, "the Boov are beseeching you: do not give up to the Gorg our world because of petty grudgings! Fight with us—"

A guardBoov whispered something to Smek.

"Fight *alongside* us," Smek said, "for a brighter, shiny Smekland!"

The guardBoovs snapped their fingers again.

Smek took a breath. *"Repito. Señoras y Caballeros del Estado Unido de América—"*

"Fat lot of good this'll do," I whispered to J.Lo. But I would be wrong about that. Some people would end up joining the Boov to fight the Gorg. Not that it made any difference.

Folks were already leaving, talking among themselves, mostly about how they didn't believe a word of it. A few gave J.Lo weird looks, but there was plenty of reason for that without suspecting he was a Boov. It might seem crazy that we passed him off as easy as we did, but I think people mostly see what they expect to see. You could look at us and suppose we were a girl and her alien friend wearing a Halloween costume in August, or you could see two kids being kids. Which would *you* see, honestly?

"Don't look at him," one mother even said when she noticed her daughter was staring at J.Lo. "He's just trying to get attention."

When I finally noticed Smek again, he was repeating the final, resounding line of his speech:

"—para una Tierra luminosa de Smek!"

Then came the finger snapping again. By now some of the little kids in the front were doing it too. A few adults booed, but most everyone who had stayed was silent.

Captain Smek stepped down from his stool and left the podium, and a little man took his place.

"Oh, look," I said to J.Lo. "It's Mitch from the bureau."

He was holding up his hands and shaking his head at the people who still jeered at Smek, and trying to hold the dwindling crowd. Smek and his bunch looked like embarrassed children as they hustled away from the quad.

"People? People?" he was saying. "Can we show a little

hospitality? Captain Smek took the time to explain his case, and that took some courage, and now I think we should give him a hand. No? Is everyone leaving? Just a couple of announcements? Tucson Airport District leader Dan Landry will be speaking tonight about his recent conference with the Gorg? That's in Prochnow Auditorium at eight . . . also . . . People? Also, there are new test dates scheduled for doctors to get recertified? These are posted on the big tree next to the . . . thing . . . you know the one. Until we can prove who is a real doctor and who isn't, people, remember: use good judgment. Just because he has his own scalpel doesn't mean he should take your appendix out."

Nearly everyone was gone now. J.Lo and I made our way up to the stage.

"One last announcement? People? No? Don't come crying to the bureau when you don't know where to get your milk shake vouchers. Oh, hello, Gratuity."

His voice was still being amplified, so he pushed the microphone aside and sat down on the edge of the stage.

"Your mom will be found soon. Have some patience?"

"I talked to Michaels already," I said. "We just came to hear the speaker."

"You should make up your own mind, of course? But I do *not* think we should be listening to these Boov. They are on their way out. Our leaders? They're making great headway with the Gorg. *Great* headway. Dan Landry especially. You should go to his talk tonight."

"Yeah, maybe," I said. "See you tomorrow, Mitch."

"Oh!" said Mitch. "I nearly forgot. Someone's looking for you? A Native American gentleman at the hospital, I believe."

"Chief!" I shouted as we ran into his room.

Well, no. That's not entirely right. "Chief!" I shouted, after J.Lo and I drove to the hospital, fought our way past a crowd at the door and through a maze of people in chairs and on stretchers and gurneys with IV tubes running from bags on hat racks, got the Chief's room number from a woman at a desk, were informed by a nurse or somebody that we couldn't see a patient unless we were family, politely shouted at that nurse or whatever that *Aren't we all kind of family now when you really think about it, stupid?*, then slipped past while he was distracted by a dog in a wheelchair, and ran into the Chief's room. There.

Anyway.

The Chief shared the room with a sleeping patient on the other side of a curtain.

"Mr. Hinkel," said the Chief, jerking his head toward the sleeping man. "He thinks Indians like me ought to live somewhere else. Likes to tell me about it a lot."

I didn't really want to talk about Mr. Hinkel.

"Well, maybe they'll let him go soon."

"Doubt it," said the Chief. "Got beat up pretty good by

someone who thinks gay people like *him* ought to live somewhere else. Good to see you, Stupidlegs, Boov."

I smiled, then what he'd said sunk in.

"Kat told you?"

"No," said J.Lo. "I told him. By my having my sheet fall off while helping him hide the telecloner. I forgot to say."

I winced.

"Are you . . . okay with that, Chief? Are you gonna tell?"

The Chief shrugged. "When you're Indian, you have people tellin' you your whole life 'bout the people who took your land. Can't hate all of 'em, or you'd spend your whole life shouting at everyone."

"Of course," I said, "that's pretty much what you did anyway. But that was all an act, wasn't it? If you act crazy, you can tell people flat out that you have a UFO, and no one will believe you."

The Chief grinned. He had good teeth for a ninety-three-year-old.

"An' if you hide that UFO inside some piece of crap you made yourself—" said the Chief.

"—then anyone who still thinks you have the real deal will feel like an idiot for coming to see it, right?"

"Worked for sixty-six years. Till you two found my animals, I'm guessing."

"Koobish," said J.Lo. "They are called koobish."

"You still called JayJay?"

322

"No. I am J.Lo."

"No way I'm calling you that."

"You canto keep calling me Spook."

"Deal."

I couldn't wait any longer. The suspense was eating me alive.

"Chief," I said, "did everyone get out of Roswell? Before . . ."

"Yep. Can thank those UFO jerks for that. They were up on the roof looking through their telescopes, saw the Gorg comin' from miles off. Some escaped in the car you left behind, though they puzzled over the plastic key a bit. I packed up Lincoln and the . . . koobish in my truck, an' me an' that fella Trey got out just in time."

"Trey went with you?"

"I . . . couldn't do any driving yet. Too dizzy. We left the koobish by the Rio Grande. Trey's watching Lincoln till I stop . . . till I get out of here."

He coughed a bit. I don't mean anything ominous by that—in movies and stories, people only ever cough to foreshadow them getting really sick or dying or something. The truth was that the Chief had coughed a lot since I'd met him. All the time, even before the Gorg hit him. But I noticed it now.

"Are you going to be well?" asked J.Lo.

"Hold on now, it's my turn," the Chief said. "Tell me about that Gorg cage thing. Is it safe?"

J.Lo explained what the teleclone booth was, and why it

was so important, and how we had it hidden but nearly ready to use.

"I thought we should tell someone in charge about it," I said. "But this government guy we know is all about trusting the Gorg and making deals, and I'm afraid he'd give it back to the Gorg. I don't know who to trust."

"Just keep it safe till I get out of here, then we'll work together. Learned a lotta stuff in the army that'll be helpful if I can remember half of it."

"Okay, but . . . Chief, I haven't seen my mom since Christmas. If I find out where she is I'm going there."

"I also," said J.Lo.

The Chief nodded his head and closed his eyes. It was time to go.

A second long week in Flagstaff passed. We visited the Chief, stood in line at the Boovish telecloner for water and milk shakes, did odd jobs for people in exchange for real food and supplies, and read together. I read aloud to J.Lo from *Huckleberry Finn*, which he liked, and *War of the Worlds*, which he found to be too one-sided. We started our own junkyard, and J.Lo tried to work out a way to make more teleclone booths out of human technology, or soup up the milk shake cloners so that they could handle bigger things.

I learned a lot more from the Chief.

"So after World War Two you were sent to New Mexico?"

I asked him on one of my visits. I was alone this time, checking out his new digs at the old folks' home they'd moved him to when they needed his bed at the hospital. He hated it.

"To a training ground in Fort Sumner. Didn't like it there—lot of bad history for my people. You know I grew up near here? On the res."

"Yeah, you said. So you're . . . Navajo, then?" I'd been learning a bit about the area.

"Prefer the name Diné, but yes."

"So after Fort Sumner . . ."

"I asked to be transferred to the air base in Roswell. Bought some land when I heard a rumor the city wanted to build a water tower on it. So they'd have t'pay me rent."

"Aha. But skip to the UFO crash."

"Hrm. How much you know already?"

"I know something crashed near Roswell, in 1947. And that people had seen weird things in the sky before that. Lights. They definitely found some bits and pieces of wreckage, but the government said it was a scientific balloon, and the ufologists say it was a spaceship and that there were alien bodies besides."

"Good. So, the thing of it is, there really was a scientific balloon."

"Wait." I frowned. "What?"

"The Boov pod hit it on its way down. Lucky shot. Destroyed the balloon and its payload."

"So the wreckage . . ."

"Was debris from the balloon. Then the koobish pod hits the ground, ricochets another eighty miles, finally stops after crashing into the water tower they'd built in my backyard. Wasn't damaged much. The pod, I mean, not the tower. The tower was totalled, and the city abandoned it—they never much liked our arrangement anyway. Somethin' about paying an Indian for land that rubs white folk the wrong way."

I gave the Chief a look.

"Don' mind me," he said. "Old habits. So—when the government says the crash was a balloon, it's 'cause they mean it. Didn't know about the spaceship. And they get real tight-lipped about it 'cause it's a top-secret balloon, meant to keep an eye on the Russians. Meanwhile, I'm tryin' to tell my superiors that I have a flying disk and an alien in my basement, but everyone acts like I've gone nuts. Post-combat fatigue, I think they called it at the time."

"Did they ever figure it out?" I asked.

"Eventually, a bit. They looked at all the evidence from the crash and saw things didn't add up. So they came calling, lookin' to see if I'd been tellin' the truth after all. But by then I'd finally had it with the army. Had a lot of other grievances. So I played the crazy Indian bit to the hilt, had the pod hidden inside my little stage prop, an' acted like I was all too happy to show it to 'em. They yelled at me for wasting their time, yelled at each other a bit, never came back.

"I spent the last sixty-some years trying to figure that spaceship out," he said. "Got it up in the air once."

"You didn't."

"Yep. Programmed it to take me up to about five thousand feet, make a loop, an' come back down in my own yard. Well, twenty miles from my own yard, as it turned out. *That* was a long walk."

"You programmed it? How?"

"Punch cards. That's what we had in the fifties, instead of CD-ROMs. Paper with holes in it."

"J.Lo says you took good care of it."

The Chief seemed to study me for a second.

"Rumor is, the Boov will be surrendering soon," he said. "And leaving."

"Yeah, I know," I said. I looked out the window as if I'd be able to see all the Boovish ships crowding around the Arizona border, or the Gorg closing in. "J.Lo knows, too."

"When's he goin' back to his people?"

"I don't know that he . . . that he's decided anything. We haven't talked about it."

"Hrm."

"I should probably get back," I said.

When I neared our camp I saw J.Lo backed up against the car in his ghost costume, facing some guy on a dirt bike. Pig was hissing from a window. I broke into a run. Was this guy threatening him? Did he know J.Lo was a Boov?

J.Lo saw me approach.

"Finally! I have been trying to tell this person I do *not speak his language*," said J.Lo, turning momentarily to the man, "but he will not to leave me alone."

The man wheeled around.

"Latest edition!" he shouted. *The Nose Celebrity Weekly!* Which Two-Timing Skunk Gets Dunked for Hot Hollywood Hunk? Which Leading Lady's Rankled After Getting Tanked and Ankled? Only the Nose Knows!"

At first I thought he was mentally ill, so I was going to give him a little something. Then I noticed his canvas bag full of newspapers. That was new.

"Spielberg Wheels and Deals Over New Spiels as Studio Execs Fix to Nix Pix! Special insert this week: revised map of the United State of America!"

I didn't have a clue what the rest was about, but I wanted the map.

"How much?" I asked.

"A buck ten," he said. "But for you? Because I like your face? A dollar."

"What do you mean a—you mean a *dollar* dollar? As in real money?"

"I don't got time for haikus, kid. You got the dollar or don't ya?"

"Everyone around here just trades stuff," I said. "Money isn't worth anything."

328

"It'll be worth something someday. You want this paper or not?"

I asked him to wait as I rummaged through the car and found a dollar in change. I hadn't saved any paper money. Later J.Lo and I sat down in the shade and looked over *The Nose Celebrity Weekly*.

"What does it say?" asked J.Lo.

"I don't believe it," I said, flipping through the pages. "It really is a paper about TV and movie stars. These people don't even do anything anymore."

FILM STARS CONTINUE TO WAIT FOR SOMEONE TO MAKE MOVIE

NEW HOLLYWOOD (FORMERLY SCOTTSDALE)—American actors fill their days with activities such as smiling and waving at cars as they anticipate the eventual restart of the film industry.

"Before the invasion I was working on a buddy comedy about a talking dog that fights crime," said heartthrob Evan Vale to *The Nose*, outside the Lexus dealership he calls home. "If *Good Cop, Bad Dog* never gets finished, it'll be like the aliens have won."

Good Cop, Bad Dog Executive Producer Marty Allen said filming would resume soon. "As soon as we can get Tom [Stone] back in the director's chair, we're good to go."

Director Tom Stone is currently a potato farmer in Holbrook and could not be reached for comment.

RECORDING ARTISTS TO PERFORM
AT "LIVE ALIEN 6"

SEDONA—America's musical artists, seventy percent of whom live in the northern Arizona town of Sedona, will once again hold a benefit concert to raise awareness of the alien invasion.

The concert, called "Live Alien 6," will feature more artists than the previous five "Live Alien" shows, and for the first time will have a working sound system and be open to the public.

Pop sensation Mandi, who is expected to sing her new single "This Land Is My Land, This Land Ain't Smekland," will host the event.

Other confirmed performers include Bruce Springsteen, DJ Max Dare, The New Draculas, Madonna, Displacer Beast, and Big Furry.

It went on and on like this. But I was more interested in the map.

I don't know if I've ever bought that whole America-as-Melting-Pot thing, but now that the whole melting pot had been dumped in Arizona's lap, I thought we might all mingle a little more. No.

The city of Payson was now something like ninety-nine

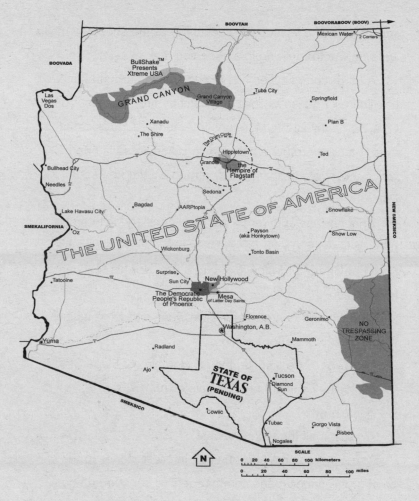

The United State of America

BOOVTAH

BOOVORABOOV (BOOV)

BOOVADA

Mexican Water

2 Corners

Las Vegas Dos

BullShake™ Presents Xtreme USA

GRAND CANYON

Grand Canyon Village

Tuba City

Springfield

Xanadu

Plan B

The Shire

The Drum Circle

Hippletown

Ted

Bullhead City

Granola

the Hempire of Flagstaff

Needles

Sedona

Lake Havasu City

Bagdad

AARPtopia

Snowflake

SMEKALIFORNIA

Oz

Payson (aka Honkytown)

Show Low

Wickenburg

Tonto Basin

Surprise

Tatooine

Sun City

New Hollywood

The Democratic People's Republic of Phoenix

Mesa of Latter Day Saints

Florence

Geronimo

NO TRESPASSING ZONE

Washington, A.B.

Mammoth

Yuma

Radland

Ajo

STATE OF TEXAS (PENDING)

Tucson

Diamond Sun

Cowlic

Tubac

Gorgo Vista

Bisbee

Nogales

SMEKSICO

NEW SMEKSICO

SCALE

0 20 40 60 80 100 kilometers

0 20 40 60 80 100 miles

N

percent white. There were really large numbers of senior citizens in places like Green Valley, Sun City, and Prescott. Prescott had been renamed AARPtopia, for some reason. Environmentalist and hippie types were living around Flagstaff. The incense should have tipped me off. There was a section of Tucson called Mallville, where a big group of the sort of girls who wished they could live at the shopping mall were now actually living in a shopping mall.

A lot of communities had already moved around because of wildfires. I guess Arizona just catches fire from time to time. So nearly all the Mormons in America had relocated from the northern border to a town called Mesa, around which they were building a very strong wall to keep out Phoenix.

Phoenix was apparently this shaky military dictatorship ruled by a warlord who called himself Beloved Leader the Angel of Death Sir Magnífico Excellente. Not his real name, I think.

J.Lo wanted to know where we were, and what it said next to my finger after I pointed.

"We live . . ." he said, "in the . . . Hempire of Flags Staff?"

"Actually, we might be in Hippietown."

"Hippietown."

"Explains all the naked people."

There were some short human-interest stories in the back of the paper. It seemed that getting conquered and shipped to a new home where no one's really in charge doesn't bring out the best in most people. A surprising number of arguments were being settled with the kind of challenges you used to see only on reality shows. Proving you were the owner of a truck by eating the most cockroaches, for example. And since cockroaches vary in size a lot from place to place, let me just say that Arizona cockroaches are big enough to help you move.

Anyway.

Here are a few other things I learned the first couple weeks in Arizona:

—Most folks will steal if they can get away with it.
—Most people want to break other people's things and roll cars over, but won't unless their planets are invaded by aliens, or their basketball team wins the finals.
—About one in a hundred people resent having to wear clothes all the time.
—Alien invasions make people stick flags on *everything*. Not just American flags, either. The Jolly Roger made a real comeback around this time.

"Enough reading," I said. "We have an appointment at the BMP."

* * *

It was hot enough outside to make asphalt soft. That's not a figure of speech. You could walk across one of the campus parking lots and feel your shoes sink like they were in dough. J.Lo said it was the sort of hot that made you want to gather animals in twos and keep them in a huge jar of water with holes poked in the lid. He had to keep his ghost costume wet all the time so his skin wouldn't dry out. He happened to be dumping a bucket of water over his head, in fact, when we reached the steps of the Bureau of Missing Persons.

I was just about to partake of my daily exercise of visiting the BMP and shouting "Where's my mom?!" and listening to Mitch tell me how I "need to show a little patience?!" while J.Lo walked around the office eating things. We were halfway up the steps when I heard Phil from the Lost List behind me.

"Gratuity! Gratuity!" he shouted. And even though we stopped and turned around, he kept shouting it anyway. When he reached us he was out of breath, and for good reason. Guys like Phil are not built for running. They are built for sitting in front of radios and for growing curly red Abe Lincoln beards that make their bald heads look wrong-side-up if you squint.

"Why . . ." Phil panted, ". . . are you squinting?"

"No reason. What's wrong?" I asked. And then it hit me.

"Did you find my mom?"

Phil nodded. He nodded hard, like he was trying to shake a bug off his scalp. After that he had to sit down for a bit with his head between his knees.

"She's near Tucson," he said, after a minute. "Living in a casino. She's so excited, she's been looking for you for weeks."

I hugged J.Lo and even hugged Phil. He smelled milky. Then we went inside the bureau to tell them to call off their search.

"I think you must be mistaken?" said Mitch, looking unsteady. His aides stood behind him as usual, and I wondered if they might finally have something to do.

"Nope," said Phil. "We're sure. She's living in the Papago lands south of Tucson, in the Diamond Sun Casino."

Mitch blustered. "Tucson? Tucson. I'm sorry, but we checked that area thoroughly? I checked it myself. I told Williams to check it myself."

The hope in me flickered a little. I didn't have much faith in Mitch, but what if he was right? I couldn't get my hopes up.

Mitch hadn't stopped talking. "Why, we even have some of our most reliable census figures from that area. Michaels! What portion of the new Tucson population have we on record?"

Michaels looked at his own clipboard.

"Forty-two percent, sir."

"Forty . . . forty-two percent! Well, that's really very good!" said Mitch. "You have to admit? That's quite good so soon after Moving Day?"

It did seem pretty good.

"No," said Michaels, "I'm sorry. That's not a four, that's one of those 'less than' signs. Less than two percent. I thought it was a four."

Mitch exhaled. Phil and I exchanged looks. J.Lo sat in the corner licking the glue off a Post-it.

"Michaels," said Mitch, "bring me the file on Lucy Tucci?"

Michaels hesitated. "There's bound to be more than one," he said.

"She's thirty," I offered. "Dark hair. Daughter named Gratuity."

"Black," said Mitch.

I coughed. "Black?"

"I'm sorry," said Mitch. "Do you prefer African American?"

"Uh, no, I prefer you call her white, actually, because that's what she is."

"The file says she's black."

"Are you really arguing with me about this?"

Mitch looked tired. "I wrote down 'black,'" he said.

"I didn't tell you to write that," I answered, and then I could see the whole thing. "Have you been telling everyone to look for a black woman this whole time?"

He had. The bureau had been sending out what they thought was Mom's description, while the Lost List had been asking for a Lucy Tucci with a daughter named Gratuity.

Mitch tried to brush past it, and turned to Phil. "Where did you say she was?"

"Word is she's living with a group in some place called the Diamond Sun Casino."

"Diamond Sun . . ." said Mitch as he trailed his finger down a list of place names. I could tell he was trying hard to seem official, but his list was written on the back of a RavioliOs label. "Diamond . . . Diamond . . . here! Here it is. Diamond Sun Casino. Well, it's in Daniel Landry's district! Lucky you."

"Daniel Landry?" I said. "Is that the guy who gave the talk I didn't go to?"

"Sure. He's the overseer there."

"Overseer."

Mitch nodded. "Mmm-hmm. You know, like the governor. Or mayor. I don't know what he likes to be called. The leader of Ajo insists everyone call him King Awesome."

"So every place has some kind of leader?" I asked. It had all happened so fast.

"Sure. Most of them are former state governors, or senators, or whatever. The president runs a little town called Rye."

"Just a little town?"

"Yes . . ." said Mitch. "He's not very popular anymore, because of the invasion. People assume it was his fault somehow. But we have to have leaders. We have to have government."

"I guess," I said.

"Daniel Landry's district is far south of here," he said, "on some former Indian land."

"Indian land? Like a reservation?"

"That's right."

"Is this Dan guy an Indian?"

"I don't think so, no. I'm pretty sure he's white. He wasn't a governor or anything before, but he's really rich, so I imagine he's a good leader."

"Uh-huh. But he's white," I said. "The Indians elected a white guy?"

"Well . . . I don't know. I imagine all the other people

elected him. It's mostly white folks living on the reservation now."

I frowned. "And the Indians are okay with this?"

"What do you mean?"

"Well . . . it was a *reservation*," I said. "It was land we promised to the Native Americans. Forever."

Mitch looked at me like I was speaking in tongues. "But . . . we *needed* it," he said.

I ran to a wall map. I didn't care. I couldn't leave fast enough.

"Sooo," I said, "I take this road . . . seventeen? And then change to ten in Phoenix?"

"Mmmm. I don't think you want to go through there. Phoenix is a bit . . . rough."

"Rough?"

"Lawless," Mitch said, "with violence and looting and so on. The government there gets overthrown every few days."

"Fine. We'll go around. We'll go through the desert, I don't care," I chirped. "Thanks, Phil! Thanks, Mitch! J.Lo! We're going!"

"Coming!" said J.Lo, grabbing a bottle of Wite-Out for the road.

"J.Lo?" said Mitch. "Wait! You can't go by yourself!"

Or at least that's what I think he said. We were so gone.

* * *

"Am I happy to have that sheet off," said J.Lo for the third time. "Yes I am."

"You might want to try to get used to it," I said. "I think you're gonna have to wear it for a while."

He was making me nervous. Anyone could see us on the road. And Mitch had been right about Phoenix.

Even on the outskirts I could tell it was trouble. Gunfire sounded off like popcorn. Tires screeched in the distance. Someone somewhere was listening to Foghat really loud. I was raised to believe that cities like this one got visits from angels with flaming swords, so I was glad to be avoiding it.

There wasn't much south of Phoenix. There was a town called Casa Grande that looked to be mostly outlet stores and tents. Somewhere around Dirt Farm, Arizona, we could see ostriches wandering around the sides of the highway.

"Mah! Big bird!" shouted J.Lo.

"We are *not stopping*," I said. "I don't care if there are ostriches, I don't care if I don't understand *why* there are ostriches. Someone can explain it to me later, we are *not stopping*."

We were near Tucson now, and my heart was buzzing in my chest. Two glowing Boov ships whizzed overhead, and somewhere in the desert to the west came a very loud and bright explosion. All this seemed totally appropriate to me—I was excited beyond words and my insides felt like that part in the *1812 Overture* when all the cannons go off.

But this is what I also thought as I watched the waves of trash crash over the cracked and broken road: that for the rest of us, Arizona would always be one of our places now. It would be on the list of things we own in our heads. Don't we all have this list? It's like, everything that secretly belongs to us—a favorite color, or springtime, or a house we don't live in anymore. We all gained Arizona by coming here, but for the people who already lived here, we could only take something away. I expected to return home to Pennsylvania one day as if I'd only stepped out for a fire drill. It would still be mine. But we'd turned Arizona into a motel room. It was our unmade bed.

"Look out!" J.Lo screeched.

I swerved just in time to avoid a line of Gorg on foot, carrying rifles. One of them barked something in his own language, and thumped his chest.

"SEG FOY S'XAFFEF, LU F'GUBIQ YAZWI!"

"What was that all about?" I whispered.

"He said, 'Get some glasses, you stupid monkey.'"

"No, I mean, why so many Gorg around? In our own state. They're everywhere."

"Four miles to go," said J.Lo, noting a sign. He knew his numbers now, at least, and his directions. "Lots of fighting outo the southwest. The last huzzah for the Boov."

"You think so?"

"I know this is so. Is almost over now."

I was barely listening. I was only talking to distract myself. I felt a chill as I suddenly saw a billboard for the Diamond Sun Casino, next exit, right two miles.

"What did that say?" asked J.Lo.

I took a breath.

The outside of the Diamond Sun Casino could not have looked more ordinary. Okay, it was pink, but I thought these kinds of places were supposed to be glitzy, and this one squatted down the road like a big cake box. And there was a white wedding cake next to it—a huge tent, really, that glowed faintly inside. The gaudy sign by the road was unlit. But there was one light down below, waving back and forth under the chin of a round-eyed girl. I pulled up alongside her.

"Are you Gratuity?" she asked. "You are, aren't you?"

I tried to answer but she was well on to other subjects.

"Is this your car? Does it float? Did *you drive yourself*? How old are you? Is that a ghost?"

I saw my opening and pounced.

"Can you take me to my mom?"

The girl frowned. "Mimom?"

"My. Mom," I said.

"Oh, yeah, but they said not until after the meeting. The big meeting in the poker tent. Your mom's kind of leading it."

That couldn't be right.

"Did you say my mom is—"

"Not till after the meeting. But you can go in if you want.

Do you need someone to drive your car up for you?"

I was already on my way, pulling around a lot of other cars to the tent.

"I think someone made a mistake," I said to J.Lo.

"Whyfor?"

"It must be a different Lucy Tucci. Mine wouldn't be leading a meeting. She . . . just wouldn't."

J.Lo was silent.

"I can't believe it," I said, and I felt a sting in my eyes. "We've been trying so *hard*. Things are . . . God! Things are supposed to work out when you . . . when you've been . . ."

"I am thinking we should go insides," said J.Lo "I am thinking we should see what is and what isn't."

I bit my lip and nodded as Slushious shuddered to a halt.

At the entrance to the tent were two men with guns. Big, black guns like from action movies. One man had the wrong size neck for his head and was dressed completely in green army camouflage. If I'd been in a less jumpy mood I might've suggested he not stand in front of a glowing white tent in the desert if he was trying so hard not to be seen, but it never felt like the right moment. The other guy wore a black T-shirt that said "Bad Dog." But they both smiled a little when we approached.

"Hey, you two," said Camo Guy. "Is your mom or dad inside?"

There it was. That was the question, right? I tried to answer but I absolutely couldn't. It was like I forgot how. Too many seconds passed.

"YES," said J.Lo, in his announcer voice. "OUR MOMMY IS INSIDE OF THE GIANT SHEET. THANK YOU."

I came back to my senses. "Can we go in," I asked. "Please?"

The men exchanged looks.

"Hey, I know this is going to sound stupid," Camo said to J.Lo, "but we should probably have you take your costume off. Just to check."

After I hurriedly explained about JayJay and his condition with the barking and peeing on people's legs, they stepped back. But that wasn't really what got us inside.

"Please," I said. "I've been trying to find my mom. Her name is Lucy Tucci."

Both men were suddenly all smiles.

"She's your mom?" said Bad Dog. "Aw, she's wonderful. She helped us get the water turned on in our trailer park three days early."

"She's got Dan Landry's ear, that's for sure," said Camo.

It took me a moment to realize this was just a figure of speech.

"I heard you were on your way," Camo added. "I thought there was only one of you."

"Nope," I mumbled. "Two." But who could say, really? The

Lucy Tucci inside *this* tent might have six kids, for all I knew. She could have twelve and weigh three hundred pounds and be Chinese.

"Tell her 'Hi' from Bob Knowles," Camo said. "And Peter Goldthwait!" said Bad Dog. Then the men lifted the tent flap for us, and we slipped inside.

"Next time," hissed J.Lo, "I would like to decide what is my condition, thank you."

The tent was strung with white Christmas lights and packed with people, all facing a stage on one end. And on the stage stood a redheaded man in a wifebeater with a Viking tattooed on his chest. People were booing him.

"I don't know who that is leading the meeting," I sighed, "but he doesn't even *look* like my mother."

"Shut up!" the redhead was saying. "I have the stage! All I'm saying is, now that we've all had to leave our real homes, we got a chance to get America right! There can be a place for the Saxon Americans, and a place for the coloreds, and a place for—shut up!"

The booing was getting louder, and thank goodness. I tried to look the audience over, but I'm short for my age, and the Christmas lights gave only a dull amber glow that made it hard to see.

I grabbed J.Lo's arm and led him through the crowd toward the stage. It was slow going, and we got a lot of dirty looks. I scanned the faces and almost thought I saw

Mom a couple times, but each time I was wrong.

For a while it seemed perfectly quiet. All I could hear was my own heart echoing in my ears. I guess the last two minutes of the redhead's speech just turned into a stampede of swear words, so it's just as well.

Then suddenly I found her.

Redhead left the podium and stepped down, and my mom took his place. She was holding up her hands and nodding at the people who still jeered him, and she glowed like an absolute candle in the stage lights.

"I know, I know," she was saying. "You have every right. Just like he has the right, right? You don't have to like what he says, but letting him say it makes us Americans, and treating people the way we'd like to be treated makes us human, doesn't it? That's how I was raised, anyway."

I watched in awe as the boos stopped and people even started nodding their heads, shouting, "That's right," if you can believe it.

"Now, I think we should take this chance to talk about everything we've heard from our speakers tonight. Does anyone want to take the podium?" Mom said as her eyes swept the room. "Let's see some hands," she said, and hands went up. "Who wants to—good, a lot of us. Um . . . why don't we star—"

Then her face shined right on me, and the word she'd been saying was cut short. She was beaming, and everyone turned to look at me. Some of the people in the crowd must have understood who I was, because they were beaming, too.

She looked so beautiful. And I was mad that my eyes were wet, because I wanted to see her perfectly, to remember little things. I tried to say "Hi," but all I could get out was the *H* in a hot breath. Mom covered her nose and mouth with her hands, but you could see she was smiling.

"I . . . I still have your Christmas stocking," she said.

I started pushing my way through the people, and I think they tried to move aside, but there wasn't much of an aside to move to. Mom was coming down the stairs, and we met in front of the stage.

So what do you want to know? Do you want to know that she squeezed me and lifted me up so that only my toes

touched the ground, and that I hugged her back? Do you want to know if I felt her wet eyelashes against my cheek, and if she stood back and held my face in her hands and laughed? And I laughed? You want to know how it felt?

None of your business.

* * *

The meeting let out a little early, as you might expect. People were so happy for Mom. They all applauded. When we left the tent, Mom held my hand, so J.Lo sidled up and took her other hand in his mitten.

"Oh, uh, hi," Mom said. "Have you gotten away from your—"

"Hold his hand," I whispered, smiling at everyone we passed, "until we get home. Please. I'll explain everything, but it's really important."

"'Kay . . ." said Mom.

"Hey, who are these two?" asked a dark, curly-headed man with glasses.

"Hi, Joachim," said Mom. "This is my daughter, Gratuity—"

"And her son and my brother, JayJay," I finished.

"That's a real cute ghost costume," Joachim said, and while he turned his attention to J.Lo, Mom gave me this look like she was trying to see through my head.

"Doesn't talk much, does he?" asked Joachim.

"He's . . . shy," said Mom. "And so the costume."

"He'll grow out of it. They all do. 'Night, now!"

Mom and I said our good nights.

"That was good," I said as we continued home. "'He's shy.' Much better than what I was going.to say."

We went into the pink cake-box building. It used to be the casino itself, and was mostly one big room full of slot machines and fake plants. Except now the slot machines were pushed together and stacked on one another to make walls. Other walls were made of folding tables or hanging sheets or just scrap wood and tin. It was dim. Only some of the overhead lights were working. When my eyes adjusted I could see that the carpet had a pattern of playing cards and poker chips.

There were more people in the casino who wanted to say hello, and introductions were made. Mom called J.Lo JoJo instead of JayJay once, but otherwise it went fine.

Eventually we made it to our new home—another room made from stacked tables and slot machines. Our door was a door, but it was just leaned up against a space in the wall.

"We're . . . going to get real hinges soon," Mom said as we stepped inside. "So . . . what do you think, Turtlebear?"

I thought it was great. Loads bigger than the car I'd been living in. There were two mattresses on the floor, and stacks of books next to an emergency exit. There was an old chrome dinette set with two chairs, and a tiny fridge underneath that wasn't plugged into anything. There was a kitchen counter made from part of a restaurant buffet, sneezeguard and all. Under the guard were two clean metal buffet trays to serve as sinks. And in the middle of everything was my mom. And next to her a space alien in a sheet.

"You're gonna want to sit down," I told her.

"Is this about your friend?" said Mom, keeping an eye on J.Lo.

"I'll tell you as soon as you're sitting."

She sat, and I stood at her shoulder. J.Lo stepped right in front of us.

"Okay," I told him. "Go ahead."

* * *

"He's been a big, big help! I owe him! We sort of owe each other. When I tried to drive our car here, it broke and he fixed it! Oh! We should probably go get the car and put it somewhere safe. And Pig is still inside it!"

"P-Pig . . . Boov . . ." said Mom. "Wait. Pig? You have Pig?"

The way she said "Pig," she might as well have said "rabies."

"Yeah," I said. "Pig. She's fine. J.Lo here saved her life once."

J.Lo's head puffed up a little, but Mom didn't even look at him.

"Oh, baby, I'll be so glad to see Pig, but . . ."

"I know. The Gorg, right?"

"You know?"

"I know."

We retrieved Slushious late that night when everyone was asleep, and parked it beside the fire exit next to our apartment. Mom was concerned someone might try to steal it, but I told her if any thief figured out how to drive Slushious away, he deserved to have it. Mom picked Pig up and kissed her purring face, and rubbed her nose in Pig's tummy, and sneezed, and petted Pig's head as she spoke.

"It's common knowledge the Gorg love hunting cats. With those guns that make things vanish," said Mom.

J.Lo clapped his hands to his mouth.

"Boov guns?" he asked. I hadn't told him.

Mom looked at him sideways. Until now, you could tell she was trying not to look at him at all.

"I don't know," she said. "Don't Gorg have those guns, too?"

"No no. The Gorg, they like the guns for making noise and pain. For scariness. They reject the Boov guns."

"Well," said Mom, looking back at me, "they got their hands on some Boov guns for cat hunting. I dunno. And now they've made it illegal to have any cats in Arizona. They said so when I met with them."

"Whoa," I said. "You met with the Gorg? When? Why?"

"About a week ago. Daniel Landry set it up. He's kind of a local leader, but he has the whole state behind him now. All kinds of big shots came—congressmen, the president . . . I sat right next to Chelsea Clinton."

I didn't know who that was, but Mom seemed sort of proud so I let it go.

"Daniel asked me to come and take notes for him," she said. "Here, I'll get them."

With Pig in one hand, she grabbed a notepad from a stack of books with the other. The books were odd—Mom never read anything besides magazines before.

"Let's see. The Gorg said they'd shortly be sending the Boov away . . . It would just be them and us . . . That we should not try to resist them . . . That we could stay safe if we met the Gorg's demands."

"Demands?"

"Yeah . . . They would let us have Arizona, Nevada, *and* Utah—that was a big deal, Daniel getting us Utah—but if they found us anywhere else, they'd shoot us. And if we were found plotting against them, they'd shoot us. And we can't use any air vehicles. Or they'll shoot us. And also no cats."

"I heard about the cat rule in New Mexico," I said. "It's so . . . random."

"I know. But the Gorg said they wanted all the cats, that they loved to keep them as pets and also to shoot them, and that they would kill any human who still had a cat after last July 31st."

"What was July 31st?"

Mom's face fell. "The Gorg sent around these awful robots with cages in back. People everywhere turned over their cats. It . . . was awful. I saw the cages flying by, filled with them, piled on top of each other . . ."

She trailed off and hugged Pig to her chest. Pig let out a yowl.

"Shhh! Shh shh. No, baby," Mom whispered. "No noise. Poor Pigbaby, you can never make noise again."

Getting to bed that night was awkward. I realized Mom had set up the second mattress for me, but that didn't leave any place for J.Lo. When Mom had heard that someone named JayJay was coming with me, she'd assumed he was an adult who'd given me a ride to Arizona, an adult who would have his own family or friends to stay with. I'd been sharing close quarters with J.Lo for so long, I didn't think anything of sharing the new mattress with him. But Mom quickly said, "Here, Turtlebear, why don't you sleep with me," and J.Lo got it all to himself. She even made kissing noises at Pig, and I think she went to bed disappointed that Pig curled up in J.Lo's legs anyway.

"He's okay," I whispered when it was dark. "Kind of a pain sometimes, but he has a good heart. Or whatever it is they have—"

"He can't stay," Mom whispered back. "It's bad enough we have a cat. We're putting the whole casino in danger."

"So . . . what, are we going to just . . . We can't turn him over to the aliens. He's not a pet."

"We can talk about it tomorrow."

"But—"

"Tomorrow, Turtlebear."

But tomorrow came, and Mom left at noon. "Jury duty," she said. Two families were arguing over who got to live in an ice-cream truck, and Mom was one of the people deciding the outcome.

"Stay here," she said. "I won't be long. When I come home I'll knock the secret knock."

We'd always had a secret knock. It was "I'm a Little Teapot."

"Don't let anyone in," she added. "And don't go anywhere."

"We will not," said J.Lo. Mom glanced at him quickly, then left.

We stared at each other.

"Your mom is nice," said J.Lo. "Very tall."

"She'll get used to you," I said. "She just needs some time."

"We all need this time. Our home is very new."

I took his point. It was strange, living in the casino. It didn't have any windows, so the ceiling and walls were full of little holes where people had drilled to let in the sunlight. But that let in bugs, too, so the holes were covered in cloth or wire mesh. All these tiny shafts of sunlight gave only a dim haze to the building. What little electricity the casino got went to keeping the fans running. And it was still hot.

A knock at the door made us both jump. It wasn't the secret knock.

"Um . . . yeah?" I answered, waving J.Lo behind the refrigerator.

"It's Katherine Hoegaarden, honey," said a voice. "We met last night? Is your mom around?"

I'd met a lot of people the night before. I had no idea who this woman was.

"She had to go help with some ice cream–truck thing," I said, giving Pig to J.Lo to hold. "She'll be back later."

"Well, I'm bringing her some books she asked for. Then I thought I could show you two around."

"Uhhh, yeah? Except she said not to let anyone in. Or go anywhere. While she's gone."

"She won't mind me, hon. Your mom and I are good friends."

I could feel her pushing gently on the door.

J.Lo whispered, "What do we do?"

"Umm . . . we can run Pig out to Slushious real quick. And we can cover Slushious with a bedsheet so no one can see in."

"Oh, this is your answers for everything," said J.Lo. "Throw a sheet over it."

Pig meowed suddenly. We froze.

"Honey?" said Mrs. Hoegaarden. "Was that a cat?"

"Okay," I said to J.Lo. "Get your costume on and follow me."

With one swift motion, we slipped through the door and blocked it. I took the books and tossed them inside, startling Pig enough to ensure she wouldn't go near the door again for at least the rest of the day.

"Oh. Hello, there," said Mrs. Hoegaarden.

"Hi," I answered. "We're ready to go."

"I thought I heard a cat."

"No. You heard JayJay. He meows."

Mrs. Hoegaarden gave J.Lo a look. J.Lo sighed a tiny Boov sigh and meowed quietly.

"Well, I'll be. He sounds just like a *real* cat."

He did. So that was lucky.

"Yeah," I said, "he's been doing it ever since he heard about the cat massacre. In solidarity with our fallen cat cousins. He'll probably do it again, any second. Just listen."

J.Lo turned his ghost face and glared at me a moment. Then he meowed as we followed Katherine Hoegaarden through the casino.

"I'm not surprised your mom is off doing something or other," said Mrs. Hoegaarden. "She always is."

"Some men I met talked about her like . . . she was some kind of local hero," I said, wondering if that was the right word.

"Oh, my! Well, I suppose. Why not? She's just been such a big help to everybody, you know. I'll bet she's met everyone in the Airport District. That's where we live, honey, the Airport District."

"Yeah."

When we walked outside, the morning sun was like fire in your eyes. We blinked and squinted into it for a few moments before moving on. In the daylight I could see that the pink building was surrounded by small tents and shacks and pickup trucks. It was like a tailgate party that never ended.

"If you need a hand, you go ask Lucy Tucci, that's what they say. She reminds me of me—that's how people thought of me back home in Richmond. 'Just ask Honey Hoegaarden,' they'd say. People call me Honey, honey. But I imagine your mom'll slow down now. She'd almost have to—she's dug ditches, and taken food out to the old folks and shut-ins, and helped set up a clothing swap and sewing circle for the moms, and of course she just seems to be Dan Landry's favorite. Always taking notes for him and telling him what the people need."

"She wasn't so . . . active back home," I said.

"Well, I think Mr. Landry's rubbing off on her a little."

"Gross."

"Oh! Ha! My goodness, that's not what I meant. I just meant she's taking after him a bit. And she just had to stay busy while the Lost List people looked for you. She'd have gone mad with worry, otherwise. Now, here's our cloner. You two know how to work one of these things?"

We let Mrs. Hoegaarden explain to us how to work a tele-cloner, and then she showed us around the showers and bathrooms. Then one of her kids needed her, and she hustled off.

"You two know your way back?" she called over her shoulder.

"We're fine," I said. "Thanks!"

"I meow now?" hissed J.Lo when she was gone. "What comes next? Do I juggle fire?"

"Look, I'm sorry, but it's good this happened. Mrs. Hoegaarden will probably tell people you meow, and we'll spread the word, too, and soon if anybody hears Pig they'll just think it's you."

"Yes!" droned J.Lo, throwing his hands up. "A foolsproof plan! Thank Mother Ocean that you do not use your genius for evil."

"All right, I get it."

"I wants to go to the pink box home and work onto the teleclone receiver. I have ideas."

"Okay," I said. "Maybe I should try to meet more people. We still don't know who we're gonna tell about it. We can't trust anyone."

"Can't trust anyone?" said a voice. "That's an awfully grim thing to say for such a young girl."

It could have been a superhero's voice. Then J.Lo and I turned around to see my mom standing next to Clark Kent.

She was smiling kind of wider than usual. "Turtlebear," she said. "Uh, JayJay, this is Daniel Landry. He's the governor of the Airport District."

"Oh, right. Hi," I said, and shook his hand. J.Lo meowed.

"It's nice to finally meet you," Landry said, and his eyes flicked around at passersby, the way people do when they're looking to see who's looking at them.

"We were meeting with some new settlers down by the airport," Mom said as she swept her hair back behind her ear with her fingers. "Mexican families. Daniel—Mr. Landry— needed me to translate."

"You don't speak Spanish," I said.

"I get by," she said. "Kind of. It's a lot like Italian."

"Between your bad Spanish and my bad English," said Landry, "we're a perfect pair!"

They both laughed, Mom a little too loudly, and she smoothed her hair back again, though none of it had become mussed. I managed a chuckle and a slight shrug at J.Lo when he looked at me.

"So what can I do for the kids of the Airport District?" Landry asked, like he was on TV. "We're looking to build some sports parks and playgrounds in the area. And there's the big fireworks show tonight."

"Actually," I said, glad to be asked, "I was wondering what people were doing to get rid of the Gorg. We can help."

Mom looked startled, but Landry laughed a big belly laugh.

"Oh, you are too much, Miss Tucci," he said.

I didn't like this "Miss Tucci" stuff. "That's my mom's name," I said. "Call me . . ."

I trailed off, like my brain and my mouth couldn't get their orders straight.

"Call me Gratuity," I finished, blinking.

"Well, Gratuity, I hear you're very brave," said Landry. Mom smiled and brushed her hair back, and I thought, It's not gonna get any more behind that ear, Mom.

"I heard you drove out here all by yourself, and got chased by Boov and shot at by Gorg," Landry went on. "That sounds like enough adventure for one girl for a whole lifetime. Right now I think the best way you can fight the aliens is to stay healthy and study. Read all you can, 'cause we're going to have the schools open soon."

I sighed.

"Okay," I mumbled. *Good plan. The Gorg will be devastated if I learn algebra.*

"Besides," said Landry, "the Boov were the bigger problem, and they're leaving on Labor Day."

I felt J.Lo twitch. He'd been right. It was almost over for the Boov, and I still didn't know if he planned to stay or go. I glanced at him, and in my head I thought, Don't go. All of a sudden. I didn't know where it came from.

"Actually," Landry continued, his voice losing some of its tenor, "they don't really want us to call it Labor Day. It's now called Excellent Day. For the time being. I suggested Gorganization Day, but they're not real big on puns."

J.Lo was wringing his mittened hands and hopping up and down. I knew he wanted to tell me something but couldn't.

"We're all going to gather at the airport, everyone in the district, and the Gorg are going to give an address and I think hand out food. It'll be fun!" Landry insisted with a big TV smile. "Mark your calendars, September second! Okay, very good. You two stay out of trouble, now!"

Mom still had some work to discuss with Landry, so J.Lo and I headed back to the casino alone.

"This is super bad, right?" I said.

"Yes! This is it. The Boov will leave, and the Gorg will get alls the humans to come together. There are probablies many meeting places alls over Arizona. Then the Gorg will take peoples for slaves and furniture, and kill the rest."

I shuddered. "Just like that?"

"Just like. Just like for they did to the Voort."

"Who're they?"

"A young race, like to the humans. A race that had no made contact with other planets beforeto. They also had a not so Excellent Day, and now they are a peoples no longer."

We walked along in silence. Inside the Diamond Sun we found our little apartment again, and J.Lo immediately started reassembling the teleclone booth. I set Pig in my lap and stroked her while I thought.

"That's it," I said finally. "We have to tell someone about our telecloner, and soon."

"Tipmom will be told, yes?"

"I . . . don't know. I want to, of course, but she seems really into this Dan Landry. And he seems kind of into the Gorg. No. I'm going to go to him first. If I can convince him that the Gorg are bad news, he'll be a good guy to know. The whole state is talking about him."

Mom knocked "I'm a Little Teapot" and came inside.

"I thought I said stay here," she said to me. "Is this how it's still gonna be? I'm trying a lot harder here, Turtlebear."

"It couldn't be helped, I said. "I swear. This Hoegaarden woman was going to push her way in. She would've seen Pig. We have to get a lock. And hinges."

"Well . . . I'm going to say something to Mrs. Hoegaarden. She should have talked to me first. But when Mr. Landry and I found you, you were alone."

"J.Lo was with me," I said. "He's a grown-up. He's thirty-six."

"And a half," said J.Lo.

"He does not take care of you. I do. If anything, I take care of him, too—this morning I had to stop him drinking the water out of a car battery."

"Is good that way. Tangy."

I elbowed J.Lo.

"It's just that . . ." said Mom, "I don't think you should be outside too much with . . . him." She waved her arm at the Boov.

"J.Lo," he answered.

"Yes. Him. What is that he's building?"

"It's a kind of Boov shower. Look, J.Lo will be fine," I said. He's fooled all kinds of people."

"But now I want to make more littles cards to explain whyfor I wear the ghostsuit and do not talk. To give to peoples. I want you to help me to write it down."

"Okay."

Mom watched silently as J.Lo hopped off his chair and

looked for a piece of paper. She leaned over and held my arm.

"We just need to be careful," she said. "We need to be so careful."

"We will."

"No. I know. But listen . . ."

Her breath was warm against my face and smelled like cherry lip balm. I waited for her to speak. Her eyes had a kind of knowing look I hadn't remembered.

"We can not get separated again. We can't. These Takers can take anything they want but you. Anything but you."

I nodded. And I was suddenly aware of J.Lo, standing rigid beside me. He'd brought pencils and paper.

"Ahem. I will also be careful," he said. "I am promising, because I do not want Tip to lose Tipmom again, on account I know all about families, and know that LucyTucci made Tip and took care of her and did not just lay her egg and leave it in the streets for others."

Mom gazed into my face like she was in a trance. I smiled a little.

"And Tip has also in my opinions been very brave, having only eleven years but wanting to findto her Mom so much she had to drive and get shot upon and also beat me up once. Which could not be helped."

I turned to J.Lo.

"Have you been practicing this?"

"A littles bit," he said.

With what looked like titanic effort, Mom turned her face from mine and looked J.Lo dead in the eye for maybe the first time since his sheet came off. They just watched each other for a bit. I heard someone say once that when two people look into each other's eyes for longer than five seconds, they're about to either fight or kiss. I didn't really want to see either. Then Mom spoke.

"It's good she wasn't alone. I'm . . . glad she had someone with her while we were apart," she said, and J.Lo's face went a little orange. "I understand you're going to be staying with us for a while."

"Yes, please."

Mom rose and nodded as she straightened the kitchen.

"La nostra casa è la vostra casa," she said.

"I wants to come," said J.Lo. "Tipmom gave both us permission."

It had been a few days since we'd met Dan Landry, and I knew from Mom that he'd be in his office down by the airport all day.

"I know," I said. "I'm sorry. But Landry's office is in a hotel by the airport, and people say that area is crawling with Gorg. We wouldn't want them to sniff you out."

"Ah," he said. "Yes. It is fine. You know, I was wanting to wash my sheet anyways. Someone got cat hair and milk shake alls over it."

So I drove to the airport, thinking of how he looked after he said that, thinking about how he really just nodded and lay down on the bed. He was spending more and more time in bed.

Up ahead, past a gas station, I saw the high-rise hotel where Landry watched over his district. I parked in the lot next to a big saguaro cactus. I was still getting used to cacti. They made the rocks and brush of the desert look like the bottom of some fierce ocean. I walked under a big awning hanging over the entrance to the hotel, dodging a lot of people that were coming and going. As I opened the glass door to the lobby, it reflected a hulking green shape bending over my car.

That wasn't another cactus, I thought as I turned to look, knowing what I'd see. A Gorg walked around Slushious, peering in, keeping one scabby hand around a shoulder strap attached to either a large rifle or a small chimney.

"Um," I said, stepping slowly back toward the car. Gorg didn't move, but his bloodshot eyes snapped up and trained on my face. I could almost feel crosshairs there.

"A Boov made it for me," I said. "Back in Pennsylvania. Really far away."

Gorg drew himself up to his full height. His body uncurled like a centipede's, and it made me think of the caterpillar from *Alice in Wonderland*, though not in a way that made my heart pound any less.

"WHO ARE YOU," Gorg said, as if he'd read the same book.

"Um . . . Gratuity," I said. "I guess . . . I guess I don't really need to ask *your—*"

"THE GORG KNOW THIS VEHICLE," he said. "THE GORG ATTEMPTED TO DESTROY THIS VEHICLE."

"Oh . . . yeah. Hey, uh, was that you? Small world."

Gorg approached, a mountain of muscle and beetle skin on legs. I could see other humans standing around the edge of the parking lot, watching. In the distance were three more Gorg walking in line with their rifles held in front of them like flagpoles. Then I could see nothing but Gorg stomach as he stopped in front of me, very close. I've heard a lot of foreigners don't have the same ideas about personal space that Americans do, and I guess it's true.

"DO NOT FLY THIS VEHICLE HIGHER THAN THREE GORG, OR YOU WILL BE FIRED UPON AGAIN," Gorg said.

I guess he meant about twenty-five feet. "Oh, don't . . . don't worry," I said. "It can't even go that high. It only . . . it only goes maybe one and a half Gorg high. At most."

"VERY GOOD." Gorg nodded. He wasn't really shouting. I think his voice just had a natural loudness because of his big head. Then he turned to leave, and I heard a familiar sound: the lawn-mower-over-whoopie-cushions sound of a Gorg sneezing. His head snapped back and his eyes, growing ever redder, stared at me hard.

"WHERE . . ." he said, then, "DO YOU . . ."

I tried my hardest to meet his gaze. These Gorg always seemed to get really angry after sneezing, and it had a way of making me feel guilty even when I'd done nothing wrong.

His face was crimson like a cherry, and stuff ran from his eyes and nose. But I thought as I looked at him that he couldn't be the same Gorg I'd met before. His face was different. Wrinklier, anyway.

"YOU. YOU ARE HUMAN YOUNG. A . . . CHILD."

". . . Yeah," I said, wondering if this would make him more or less likely to kill me.

"THE NIMROGS HAD CHILDS ONCE."

I didn't know what to say, so I said nothing. Gorg stifled another sneeze with his fist.

"GO ABOUT YOUR BUSINESS," he said, and walked off wiping his nose.

As he left, all the nearby humans looked in different directions and marched quickly away, trying not to draw attention. This Gorg encounter had gone much better than the last, I thought. Maybe you just had to get used to them.

I entered the hotel and had to give my name to a security-type guy in the lobby and explain why I was there, and then he said I couldn't see Landry, and we had a really interesting and loud conversation about that, and then he asked if I was related to a Lucy Tucci, and when I said I was he let me go on up. And I decided that at the first opportunity I was going to make up some "Lucy's Kid" T-shirts and wear them every-where. I climbed nine flights of stairs and felt like a sap when I realized the elevators were working, and then I found the door I was looking for. It was dark wood with a brass knob and Daniel P. Landry, District Governor in gold letters. It also had one of those do not disturb things hanging on the handle, but I knocked anyway.

No answer.

I knocked again, this time to the beat of an old Gene Krupa drum solo. The door flew open.

Landry's face was as angry as a dried cranberry. But as he looked down and saw who I was, it softened quickly into more of a peach, all pink and fuzzy. If that's not forcing the fruit metaphor.

"Gratuity Tucci! As I live and breathe! How are you? Come in, come in. How's your mom?"

Inside was the largest hotel room I'd ever been in. Granted, that's not saying much—Mom and I always stayed in the sorts of places that posted the price right on a sign facing the interstate. But this room was easily big enough to play racquetball in.

"Hi, Mr. Landry—"

"Dan."

"Hi, Dan," I said, trying to make it sound natural. "If I'm bothering you, it won't take long."

"No! No bother," he said. "Anything for Lucy's daughter."

And I thought about my T-shirt idea again as I looked around the room.

If there had been a bed, it was gone now. On the deep green carpet stood plush chairs and a dark wood desk upon which Landry could have reanimated Frankenstein *and* still had room for his pens and golf calendar. But what really got me were the bookshelves. Landry had a library of big, hardback books. Heavy, serious books you could knock somebody out with if you swung hard enough.

"Ah, a book lover, are you?" he said, and paced in front of the shelves. "Before you are some of the greatest works of literature. Tolstoy. Pynchon. Ellison. Hemingway. Many are first editions. I've read every one. Each and every one. I read them, and I put them up there. You know my secret? I'm a

Dan Landry

speed-reader. Officially. They have a test you can take, my certificate is over there."

I looked at the certificate.

"You see this one?" he asked, pulling a book down from the shelf. "*The Grapes of Wrath.* Pretty thick, right? I read it in one sitting."

I began thinking that this was a guy who displayed his books the way another guy might display his animal trophies. Each wall of bookshelves was more like a wall of mounted heads, and the important part was not really the animal so much as how it was killed. "Here is the head of a Siberian tiger," he might be saying. "One of the world's most deadly beasts! The animal weighed six hundred pounds, but I downed it with one shot after two days of tracking."

"Here, now, is *Ulysses* by James Joyce. Considered by some to be the most challenging book in the English language. It weighs in at 816 pages, and I read it in a day and a half!"

"Very nice," I said. I could hear his nose whistle when he breathed.

"Well," Landry said, and then there was silence, apart from the shaky monotone of the air conditioner. I suddenly thought I should have showed more interest in his hobby, so I put on a smile. But it felt weird, so I put it away again.

"How can I help you, Gratuity? You didn't come to hear me drone on about my books."

"No, no. They're great." I cleared my throat. "Anyway, Dan—"

"Mr. Landry. You were right the first time."

"Oh. Mr. Landry, have you heard of any kind of resistance group against the Gorg?"

Landry folded his arms.

"You know, your mom told me you were getting all worked up about this."

"She said that?"

"Gratuity, you need to trust in your leaders. I know you kids might not think that's 'cool,' but the Gorg have a lot to offer us."

"Nothing that wasn't ours already," I muttered.

"On the contrary. They are driving away the Boov, first of all—the Boov, who thought one state was enough for an entire country. The Gorg are giving back the whole Southwest, and we're very close to getting California as well. Did you know that?"

"But—"

"And there's more than that. They have a big surprise waiting for us on Excellent Day, during the Nothing to Worry About Festival. I can't talk too much about it yet."

Darn right they'll have a surprise for us, I thought.

"It doesn't bother you that they're asking us all to meet in one spot like that?" I said. "It doesn't seem dangerous?"

"Have a little faith, Gratuity," Landry said, his smile fading. "I've met with them. I understand them better than possibly anyone on Earth. They are a little rough around the edges, yes, but—"

"But I know them, too. I know a lot of stuff about the Gorg that nobody else knows. A Boov in Florida told me things," I said, and it was sort of true. "Like that they're all clones of each other."

"Yes, I know."

"Oh. Well . . . their ship? It's also covered in Gorg skin, if you can believe that."

"I can believe it," said Landry, "because I knew it already."

I frowned. "You did?"

Landry walked around to the other side of his desk and sat down. He looked like he was telling the truth. He wasn't surprised at all.

"There are people resisting the Gorg. People fighting with the Boov, and humans working together against all the aliens. Yes. And they're good Americans and brave citizens. But the best thing for everyone right now is to play along. Be good and obedient to the Gorg. They'll all leave soon anyway."

"Really? They said so? When are they leaving?"

He was up and pacing again, looking everywhere but at me. From time to time he'd stop and touch something, a paperweight or little statue.

"Of *course* they didn't say so," he said. "You're being naive. But I know so."

"How?"

"Their whole plan, their whole operation . . . it won't work. It's untenable. It's like a galactic Ponzi scheme."

I didn't understand a word he was saying. "A Fonzie scheme?"

"Ponzi. Ponzi scheme," he said, staring up at the ceiling. "Named for . . . for . . . someone named Ponzi. It's the same as a pyramid scheme."

I will admit that I was picturing Egypt at this point.

"And so . . ." I said.

"Their whole society is based on paying and feeding old Gorg by making new Gorg and conquering worlds. They have to keep making more and more, sending them out in every direction. They're stretched too thin. Sooner or later they'll have too many Gorg and not enough resources, and the whole operation will implode."

I frowned. "*Im*plode?"

"It's the opposite of explode."

"Wouldn't the opposite of exploding be a good thing?"

"The point is," he said, "if we bide our time and do what they ask, then fewer people get hurt. Eventually the Gorg will leave, or at least have to pull back their operation. And *that's* when we fight, if ever."

I stood up.

"I'm just saying . . . what if there was a way to fight them now—"

"I have to get back to work," said Landry. "You can let yourself out."

I sighed and walked away from the desk in a daze.

"Hmm. Maybe you can't," Landry said. "That's the broom closet. The door you came in is over there."

I turned and sped from the office, mortified.

When I got back home I told J.Lo everything that had been said. Except the part about the broom closet. He didn't like what he heard.

"This . . . this Ann Landers fellow—"

"Landry," I said. *"Dan* Landry."

"This Dan Landry has the whole thing wrong. The Gorg have not 'stretched thin.' They will not run out of the resources; they have telecloning. They cannot run out."

"Yeah . . ." I said, "but then why do they invade other planets? Why do they spend so much time taking other people's stuff away if they can just make their own?"

"Fff. Because *they are jerks!*" said J.Lo, throwing his arms in the air. "They are *poomps! Kacknackers!*"

He called them all kinds of other Boovish words I'd have to bleep if I translated.

"I agree," I said. "I totally agree. I'm just suggesting that maybe we don't know everything about them after all. You said they can't get sick, but I've seen two of them sneeze. Or the same one sneeze twice."

"It could not have been a sneeze."

"Their noses were running. Something was making them sick. Are you saying Gorg just make stuff come out of their noses for fun?"

"Yes!" said J.Lo, pacing. "For fun! Why not? Who wouldn't want something coming out from his nose?"

He was as bad as I was—he'd say anything when he got this upset. I cleaned my fingernails and waited for him to calm down. He finally stopped and stared at the wall. He took a breath.

"Maybe . . . maybe it was a comfort . . . a comfort to think of the Gorg as unstoppable. It is not so bad to be beaten when you are believing the enemy is an army of perfect monsters."

"I dunno," I said. "I think maybe something has changed. You guys would have noticed these symptoms before. This last Gorg looked like he cried motor oil."

J.Lo started pacing again. Somewhere in the casino, music was playing.

"You know," I said, "back when Slushious's tape deck actually played tapes, Mom and I would copy our music so we could listen to it in the car."

J.Lo said nothing, but he stopped pacing.

"The copies we made never sounded as good as the original. And if we had to copy a copy? It got even worse. So, what if the Gorg never perfected complex cloning? What if they've been making clones of clones of clones, and getting weaker every time?"

Mom came home just then.

"Hi, Turtlebear, J.Lo."

"Mom," I said, "you met with some Gorg, right? Before J.Lo and I got here?"

"Yeah, a few."

"Did any of them sneeze?"

"Sneeze? Not that I noticed."

"You would have noticed," I said.

"Then no."

"Did they wipe their noses, or get teary eyes or anything?"

"No," she said. "Nothing like that."

"You're sure?"

"I was right next to them the whole time."

"That Landry guy said the Gorg were going to have a big surprise for us."

"You talked to Daniel?"

"Yeah. He said there would be this surprise at the, uh . . . festival. I forget what it's called."

"The Nothing to Worry About Festival," said Mom. "Isn't that nice? No worries . . ."

"This surprise is gonna be bad news, Mom. I swear. Just ask J.Lo."

"Yes. Ask me."

"Turtlebear . . ." Mom said, sounding exasperated. "Look,

don't tell anyone else, because it's really supposed to be a
surprise, but the Gorg are bringing us the cure for cancer."

"What?" I said.

"What?" said J.Lo.

"I know! Isn't it amazing? They really want to earn our
trust."

I crossed my arms.

"Sounds like they already *have* our trust," I said.

J.Lo gasped. When I looked to see why, he had one hand
to his mouth and the other pointing at me.

"You . . ." he squealed, wagging his finger, ". . . your *hand*!"

I raised my hand to my face, turning it over and back
again.

"What? What's wrong with it?"

"You are bearing the mark! The mark that has been
fore*told!* You are The One . . . The One who will bring peace
onto the *galaxy*!"

"What, this? This is taco sauce," I said, wiping it clean.

J.Lo stared at my palm for a moment, then turned back to
the wall.

"Never mind," he said.

There came a knock at the door, just two short raps, very
functional. We scrambled around for a few seconds. Soon the
Boov was in the ghost suit and Pig was in the car, which
would be a good lyric for a bluegrass song, now that I think
of it. I went to answer the door. J.Lo had rigged up some

strange hinges and a lock, and I slid the bolt back and peered through the crack.

"It's the Chief!" I shouted. His red cap was in his hand and his peppery hair was combed. He looked better.

"Hey, Chief," I said. "Come on in."

"Much obliged, Stupidlegs."

Mom frowned at this, but took his hat all the same. She looked confused as J.Lo removed his costume and I retrieved Pig.

"I'm sorry," she said, "who—?"

I hadn't mentioned the Chief. It seemed whenever Mom heard any details about our trip she'd go pale and start crossing herself, so there was a lot I hadn't mentioned.

"His real name is Frank," I said. "He's a junkman."

Mom winced. "That's not very nice."

"Oh, no. I meant—"

"I used to trade and sell junk," the Chief said.

I rattled off a bit of the Chief's history. Without specifically mentioning the teleclone booth, I still managed to work in the part where the Chief got walloped by a Gorg.

"My God," Mom breathed, and crossed herself. She looked shaken. "Thank you for protecting my daughter."

"Don't mention it." He sniffed the air. "You have real food."

"Just a little," Mom said. "We're still having milk shakes, mostly. But I have some potatoes and onions, and it's no trouble cloning olive oil. Will you stay?"

"Be honored," he said, then caught sight of the telecloner. "How's my booth?"

"Your Boovish shower booth?" I said quickly. "It's fine."

The Chief stared at me.

"Good to know," he said, and sat down with a chorus of pops and creaks at our dinette.

After dinner J.Lo helped Mom wash up, and I walked with the Chief out to his truck.

"Got some friends and cousins comin' down from the res," he said. "Should be here in a couple days. And I'm gonna leave tomorrow morning to round up some more. Friends of friends, and air force types. People we can trust."

"Do you know some of the Papago Indians around here?" I asked.

"Tohono O'Odham," said the Chief. "The Tohono O'Odham Nation. Papago is derogatory. Means 'bean eaters.' And yeah, I know a few. What's the story 'bout the 'Boovish shower'?"

"Oh, yeah. My mom's been working with that Dan Landry guy, and he seems pretty pro-Gorg. So I'm worried maybe Mom is, too."

"Heard a lot about him. Seems like a snake."

"I think she likes him," I said. "I guess he's nice looking, in a cornflakes kind of way. He probably likes her, too. He sure wants her around a lot. I mean, we're a hundred miles from the Mexican border and she's *still* the best Spanish speaker he can find?"

"Be careful of him. He's got some skeletons in his closet."

"No," I said, "just brooms."

"Huh?"

"He has a broom closet attached to his office. I almost walked into it."

"That's weird."

I caught some movement out of the corner of my eye.

"Hey, Lincoln!" I shouted, and ran up to where he strained against his leash, nearly pulling the truck in two. I patted him down, and he made sure my face was good and slimy.

"Do you two need a place to stay?" I asked.

"You don't have the space. We're fine sleeping in the camper bed. You could store a couple boxes for me, though, so we got a little more room."

I walked back to the casino with two boxes of the Chief's war souvenirs to put in Slushious. He'd promised to be back in two or three days.

The next morning, word started to spread: the Nothing to Worry About Festival had been rescheduled. Excellent Day was no longer Labor Day. Excellent Day was tomorrow.

"That can't be true," said Mom. "Why would they do that?"

I ran outside to look for the Chief's truck, but he'd already left. As I walked back I saw a great swarm of Boov ships to the east. They flew slowly, close together, not on the attack. They were going to formally surrender to the Gorg.

Six times that morning I saw J.Lo stare at our old cell phone.

"Chief's gone," I said as I reentered our place.

"Old people get up really early," said Mom. "He probably left hours ago. Don't worry . . . this place is always full of rumors."

But by early afternoon the Gorg's crab robots were clacking around, delivering the news.

"DUE TO UNFORESEEN EXCELLENCE," Gorg faces announced through the robots' jittery screens, "THE EXCELLENT DAY FESTIVITIES WILL BE HELD TOMORROW MORNING AT SUNRISE. HUMANS OF THE AIRPORT DISTRICT WILL MEET ON THE AIRPORT TARMAC TO WATCH THE BOOV RETREAT. ATTENDANCE IS MANDATORY! **MANDATORY**! MESSAGE ENDS."

"This is ridiculous!" said Mom. "It must be a mistake. I'm going to talk to Daniel. Don't go anywhere this time. For real."

She ran out of our apartment still holding one shoe.

Without a word J.Lo went back to the dishes he'd been washing. I stood and rested a hand against the dinette. Then I thought maybe I should sit, but I got up again a second later and stared at my shoes. Stalling.

There were ten different kinds of playing cards in the pattern of the carpet. There were hundreds of cards, of course, but they were the same ten, over and over. Sixteen poker chips, eight red and eight blue.

"The Hoegaardens have dice on their carpet," I said.

"Ah," said J.Lo. "Yes?"

"Yeah. Pairs of dice all over. All the pairs add up to seven."

"I see."

"They live where the craps tables used to be," I added. "Pardon my language."

We fell into a silence again. J.Lo's hands sloshed around in the water.

"We really have to talk," I said. "Don't you think? We have to?"

J.Lo grabbed a bowl and dunked it in the sink.

"If you are wanting to. What should we talk about?"

I'd been holding my breath without realizing, and the last of it came out in a puff. "You know . . ."

"Ahh. About the Boov. About me leaving Earth."

"You never really said what your plans were."

"I would be as a criminal to the Boov," he said, scrubbing the bowl. "The greatest bungler ever. I brought to our doorsteps the Gorg."

"Would they . . . kill you?"

"No. The Boov are not having capitalized punishment any longer. I would be made a prisoner. Or given a very bad job."

"Like what?"

"Legtaster, maybe. Or Bearer of Droppings. It would be bad, but not so very. These jobs have a certain quiet dignity."

"Uh-huh."

We stared at each other for a moment, then J.Lo rinsed the bowl and picked up a plate.

"Sooo . . . should I leave, then?" he asked. "Go back to the Boov?"

"I can't tell you what to do. It's up to you. Right?"

J.Lo looked into the sink and nodded a little nod. It was like I could see him deciding. It was like watching a slowly falling balloon that would burst if nobody caught it.

"But," I said, "but if you . . . It would be harder around here if you left, of course. More chores for everyone else. That's all I'm saying."

"True."

"It would be hard to explain to everyone why JayJay wasn't around anymore. If you left. But you need to do what's best for you."

"Yes."

"I'm only saying it would be harder. And you could give us a lot of help getting rid of the Gorg, knowing what you know."

J.Lo paused with his hands in the water. I suddenly felt like I was standing very strangely, so I shifted my weight to the other leg, but it didn't feel any better. The house was hot. I could feel it in my face.

"It seems," said J.Lo, "it seems it would be the best if I stayed. There are things here to do. I can be a help to my family."

He looked like he was going to say something else, then

nodded and picked up some spoons. He dipped them in the water. I stood by him at the counter and dried as he washed.

"So it's just like the milk shake cloners," said Mom, looking at the booth. "But for people."

She'd come home angry, unable to see Landry or even get near his building, for all the Gorg patrols around. So J.Lo and I told her about the telecloner, knowing that we couldn't reach the Chief and we were almost out of time.

"It's not just cloning, though," I said. "It's teleporting, too."

"I don't know that word."

"A person or thing," said J.Lo, "can be sent from one booth into another. To another booth on the Earth, or inside the Gorg ship. Maybies evento booths on other planets."

"Like e-mailing a person," said Mom.

"Yes."

"I'm glad you told me. But we need to get other people in on this."

I nodded.

"Mr. Hoegaarden was a police officer," said Mom. "He knows some good people. Here. Take these books back to Mrs. Hoegaarden and see if anyone's home."

I took the books and walked across the casino, cutting through the kitchen to the Hoegaarden's area. It was a smaller section than the slots floor where we lived, with only two apartments and a single wobbling ceiling fan that looked like it was trying to unstick itself and fly away. It was hard to tell one apartment from another, but they'd written their name on the back of a keno ticket and pinned it to their door. I knocked.

My knock was maybe the third loudest noise I've ever heard. That doesn't sound as impressive as I'd like, but it had been quite a year for loud noises.

Mrs. Hoegaarden threw open the door.

"I didn't do it," I said. "I swear."

I really hadn't. The noise had actually come from out in the main hall. The air still rang with it.

We raced to the corner and peeked around to see a Gorg lift a change machine over his head.

Frightened people were pressed up against the walls, as far from Gorg as they could be. Just past him I saw the door he'd come through—it was a metal taco shell now, and dangling off one hinge.

"HUMAN PERSONS!" Gorg spat. "WHERE IS THE ONE CALLED GRATUITUCCI!"

Oh, God, I thought. Why is it always me?

"Um," said Joachim, "who?"

"GRATUITUCCI! GRATUCCITY! **OR SOMETHING SIMILAR!**" said Gorg, and threw the machine to the floor. It spilled its silver guts out onto the carpet.

Our neighbors were silent. But they must have understood who Gorg was talking about. Mrs. Hoegaarden sure did.

"Oh, dear," she said. "Listen: take this hall, go in the first door, through the office, through the door on the other side, and you'll be in the hallway with the restrooms and the exit to the loading dock. Hurry!"

I did as she said and ran through the casino. I could still hear Gorg's booming voice.

"I WAS TOLD TO GO TO THE LARGE OFFENSIVELY COLORED BUILDING. THE BUILDING WHERE HUMANS WHO ARE BAD AT MATH GIVE AWAY THEIR MONEY! THIS IS THAT PLACE! BRING ME GRATUITUCCI!"

I slipped through the last door and out to the blinding air, stumbled down off the loading dock, and sprinted around to the emergency exit where Slushious was parked. J.Lo was already there in his costume, tying the telecloner to the top of the car.

"I have Pig," he whispered. "We should drive away—Gorg might smell me."

"Okay. Where's my mom?"

J.Lo looked at me, then back at the casino.

I'd left her again.

"We have to help her."

"We have to hide away the telecloner!" gasped J.Lo. "He will search out here!"

I swiveled around and noticed the big white poker tent lying rumpled and deflated on the ground.

"Looks like he already searched there. C'mon."

We drove up to the edge of the tent, and I lifted the surprisingly heavy canvas while J.Lo drove Slushious underneath. I was already running back to the emergency exit before J.Lo even crawled out from under the tent. I got close enough to see that the door had been torn off its hinges.

"No," I whispered. "No no no."

I ducked into our apartment and saw it had been trashed. The sinks were overturned and leafs of scorched books fluttered through the air. But Mom was gone. There was no sign of her.

I bolted through our apartment door, to see a crowd of people staring out the front of the casino.

"Gratuity!" said Joachim as I approached. "Hold on—"

I ignored him and forced my way through the crowd, just in time to see two Gorg strapping jetpacks to their backs. One of them had my mom thrown over his shoulder.

"QU LU EHED SEG FIP'W AR NI'IZS IHEX?" said the Gorg holding Mom as he slapped the other Gorg across the face.

"FUD," said the other, poking and then punching the first Gorg in the arm. *"NAG IG'F TAD'Q GU VEF'G FGAB, LU W'ZO?"*

"Your mom . . . she said she was you," explained Joachim.

Then something amazing happened. The Gorg holding Mom made a noise.

"Was that a sneeze?" someone asked.

J.Lo arrived just in time to see the other Gorg sneeze, too. Then both of them were in fits, sneezing back and forth as they fiddled with their jetpacks.

Mom raised her head and looked right at me. Then the rockets ignited, and all three of them disappeared into the darkening sky.

I was breathing hard. Everyone around started trying to console me and put their hands on my shoulder, but I only wanted them to go away.

"Say," J.Lo whispered, "they sneeze near to any person who has spent a lot of time around a Boov. Did you notice? But . . . the Boov never did make them sick before."

"No, the Boov never did," I agreed.

And suddenly I had a plan after all.

"Oh, are they gonna get it," I said as we soared across the desert. "I will destroy them. You can't kidnap my mom and expect me not to destroy you. I would have destroyed the Boov, but you gave her back just in time."

"Thank goodness," said J.Lo. "Explain, please, again about the cats."

"The Gorg are allergic to cats! Seriously allergic! You saw how they were around Mom."

"But Tipmom is not a cat."

"We have cat hair *all over us*. Trust me. When you own a

cat it's unavoidable. And why else would the Gorg go to so much trouble to get rid of all of them? And Mom—Mom said she sat right next to some Gorg before we arrived, and they didn't sneeze at all. But after we brought Pig into the casino? Boom!"

"Boom!" shouted J.Lo. "Boom!"

"Thank God we didn't lose Pig that night. Thank God we kept her safe."

"But whereto are we going?"

"Somewhere secret," I said as I steered Slushious through camps of scattered tents. "Somewhere we can hatch our plan."

"This is exciting," said J.Lo. "We are sneaky agent men, like Bond James Bond."

"I don't know where you pick this stuff up."

All traces of the city were far behind us when we neared a rustic sign that read "Old Tucson Studios."

"Oh, perfect," I said.

I pulled Slushious into the center of a Wild West ghost town in the middle of the mountains. There were authentic-looking saloons and general stores and a Spanish church lining the dusty street.

"This should do," I said.

"Now we can teleport to the Gorg bases or their ship," said J.Lo, "and find Tipmom and bring her home!"

"We're going to do a lot more than that," I said.

"Yes? What are we going to do?"

I grinned and said, "Feedback loop."

"Feedback loop?"

"Feedback loop."

I stood in the middle of the street, with J.Lo eyeing me nervously. If I'd had a six-shooter I could have looked just like Clint Eastwood, but the only thing I was staring down was a teleclone booth. Plus, I was wearing a World War II army helmet, so the image was shot.

The helmet was way too big for me, but my hair kept it in place. I had a handful of aspirin—the cold-expanding foam kind—for emergencies. The Gorg telecloner had cloned them from the last remaining pill in J.Lo's toolbox. It worked. The aspirin were complex things no Boov cloner could make, but we'd made them.

In the last twenty minutes, J.Lo had put the machine back together and inspected it over and over. I'd stroked Pig and looked through the Chief's boxes.

"I have a signal," J.Lo had said finally, next to the softly humming machine. "We are connected to the Gorg computer."

So we'd tested it by making aspirin, and now I was standing in front of it, wondering how I got here.

"There are signals from many other teleclone booths. Gorg bases. Twelve bases in Arizona, more elsewheres."

"I guess we should just try the closest one."

"I should go," J.Lo said. "I should be the one to test it. It is my fault if it fails."

"If it fails," I said, "you're the only one who can possibly fix it. So *I* have to go."

In my other hand was a pebble. If I managed to teleport anywhere without getting turned into milk shake I would send it back so J.Lo would know to follow with Pig.

"Okay . . . okay," I said, shaking out my hands. "Okay." I was breathing hard and fast, probably hyperventilating. I was suddenly thinking that maybe I would just faint. Then I wouldn't have to teleport. Nobody could expect you to teleport after you fainted, it was like an unwritten rule, it was fairly common knowledge that you were never asked to teleport after—

"Okay," I said. "Okay. Anything else you can tell me?"

"Hm. Well, it would be betters if you were chewing gum, your ears will probably pop—"

"AHHH!" I shouted, then ran for the cage, and crossed my fingers, and jumped.

There was a flash of light in my skull.

There was a loud snap.

My ears popped.

It was utterly dark. I couldn't see anything. I couldn't even feel my own body. And I thought, Great—I died right when I was in the middle of something.

I couldn't feel my body because the teleportation makes you numb for a bit, but I wouldn't know this until I started tingling all over a few seconds later, like I was carbonated. First I stretched my jaw to clear my ears, because I heard voices.

One of them was familiar. It had that TV announcer sound, but it was more of an off-camera, demanding-more-doughnuts-in-his-dressing-room sort of voice.

I remembered I had a flashlight, so I drew it out of my pocket and nervously switched it on against my hand. Through the red glow of my fingers I could see a curtain drawn in front of me. I edged around it. I was in a very small room. Past the curtain there was a mop and bucket. There was a dustpan. And there was a familiar dark wood door with a brass knob, confirming what I'd only just guessed.

I was in Daniel Landry's broom closet.

Five minutes later I jumped back through the telecloner and saw the flash and heard the snap and landed, ears popping, back in the ghost town. I expected J.Lo to be right in front of me, and panicked when he wasn't there.

"Oh, boy. Oh, boy—J.Lo! J.LO!" I turned. "How does this thing shut off . . . how does it—"

J.Lo's head poked out the car window.

"We have to shut this down!" I shouted. "How does it turn off?"

"You are alive!" J.Lo sang.

"Focus, J.Lo! How do I shut it down?"

"What? Oh. Green thing!"

There was, thankfully, only one green thing, shaped like a racquetball on a golf tee. I grabbed at it, wondering if I was meant to squeeze or pull or push or what, but it instantly gave a gassy noise and deflated as the booth stopped humming. I sat back and breathed, my head no longer filled with visions of Gorg armies pouring into the moonlit street after me. Pig brushed against my legs. Then I noticed J.Lo at my shoulder.

"Where was the *pebble*?!" he shouted. *"What about the pebble?"*

I hadn't thrown it back to tell him the booth worked. I'd been too busy eavesdropping, and I said so.

"I thought Tip was dead! Or in troubles! And I could do nothing! *Nothing!*"

"Why were you in the car?" I asked.

"I was about to leave. I was to try driving to find you."

"Thanks."

"But the booth, it worked? Why did you turn it off?"

"There were Gorg on the way. I thought they might teleport here."

"Then they saw you?"

"No," I said. "Listen. I got there, and it was all dark, and I could hear voices, right? And that's when I knew I was in Dan Landry's broom closet."

"No!"

"Yes!"

"Get out of town."

"It's true!" I said. "And Landry was shouting at someone, shouting, 'We had a deal!' and 'They were only questions, I wasn't accusing you of anything!'"

"What questions?" asked J.Lo.

"Well, wait a second. It gets worse. Then a Gorg voice answers—"

J.Lo gasped.

"—then a Gorg voice answers, 'THE FESTIVAL WILL PROCEED AT SUNRISE. THE HUMANS WILL BE COUNTED AND SORTED.'

"And Landry says, 'She was just a kid. Kids get upset. Now you've kidnapped her?' So the Gorg admits they screwed up and got Mom instead, but they still want me 'cause I fit the description of a girl who *stole* something from them."

J.Lo muttered something in Boovish.

"But here's the kicker," I said. "The Gorg says, 'WE WILL HONOR OUR PROMISE. YOU WILL HAVE YOUR POWER. WE WILL SEE YOU BECOME LEADER OF YOUR PLANET.' And then some other Gorg chuckle, and he says, 'WE WILL RELEASE THE MOTHER OF GRATUITUCCI AFTER THE FESTIVAL.' And now the other Gorg are laughing, you know, because there isn't going to *be* any 'after the festival.' That's when I came back through the booth."

J.Lo shook his head. "He was just wanting to be leader.

He wanted to be the king of Earth and call it Danland."

"Yeah. Maybe. Except, what about all that stuff he said to me about the Gorg leaving soon? What if he really believed that? Maybe he really thought by cooperating he could keep more people alive until the Gorg left on their own."

"Or maybe he is just a poomp, pardon my language."

"Maybe. Anyway, that wasn't a Gorg base. But right before I teleported back, it sounded like the Gorg were going to use the broom closet to leave, and I was afraid they'd get here right behind me."

"We will try another one, then," said J.Lo.

"The next closest booth?"

"Hm. I am thinking, why not the strongest, instead of the closest. The strongest signal. This would more likelies be an important base."

J.Lo tuned the booth, and we gathered our stuff. We each had enough aspirin to cover Mount Everest. J.Lo put up his helmet, and I still had mine. I had a backpack full of cat treats and my camera, and J.Lo had his toolbox, as usual.

"And looksee," said J.Lo. "The talkie-walkies. I have fixed them up with power cells. "Now we can talk *and* walk. J.Lo to Tip, J.Lo to—"

He was holding them no more than ten inches apart, so his gravely, squawking message got echoed back and forth and made the Worst Noise In The World. And I've heard Gorg sneeze.

I tried to put the walkie-talkie in my cargo pants. It made

me feel like I had a peg leg, so I put it in my bag instead. The four-foot-long antenna stuck up through a gap in the zipper and bobbed as I moved.

"I can't *believe* people used to run around with these while getting shot at," I said, because I didn't know what I'd be doing a half hour later.

J.Lo stared at the antenna. "You look cool."

"I look like an RC car."

"Yes. I do not know what that is."

We gathered up Pig and stood before the teleclone booth. J.Lo fired it up again.

"Can we all go at once?" I asked. "Will we get mixed up?"

"I am sure we can alls go at once. Pretty sure."

Nobody moved.

"Might be a lot of Gorg on the other side," I said.

"Yes," J.Lo said, and gave Pig a pat.

"I have enjoyed being your brother," he added.

"It's been nice having one."

We walked into the booth—

—and out the other side. I was numb again, and Pig made a low noise. But it was bright enough here, and there were no Gorg in sight. There was nothing in sight but white tile and two rows of urinals. We were in a boys' bathroom.

"Out of the booth," said J.Lo. "I should shut it off. Gorg might come."

As if in agreement, thudding footsteps echoed toward us. Around the corner of this hall of urinals came a Gorg with a rifle like an outboard motor with a car muffler sticking out of it.

"*LU! F'GAB!* GET AWAY FROM THAT!" Gorg bellowed.

We stepped forward and to the sides, crowding the urinals. Pig squirmed and hissed in my arms. J.Lo threw an aspirin, and then another, but the cold foam didn't slow Gorg down much. He batted chunks of snow away and raised his rifle. Then he noticed Pig for the first time.

"RRRR. THAT IS . . ." he said, at a loss for words. "SURRENDER THE ANIMAL!"

He pointed his gun at my head.

"SURRENDER THE ANIMAL!"

"Okay," I said faintly. "Sorry, Pig."

And I threw her right at his stomach.

Pig screeched and dug her claws into Gorg as a cloud of hair rose off her back. Gorg looked down in horror and loosened one hand from his rifle to knock her away. I threw an aspirin at it, and kicked Gorg in the shin, which stubbed the hell out of my toes, pardon my language. It didn't do a thing to the shin. But with his hand covered in foam, Gorg couldn't hurt Pig, and she leaped away and hid behind the teleclone booth.

What happened next was the absolutely worst allergic reaction I'd ever seen. Gorg's stomach turned red and formed fat bubbling hives like tomato soup. It spread up to his neck and head, and he went into spasms of gasping and sneezing. I think he even tried to fire his rifle, but his fat red fingers couldn't work the trigger. I circled around him.

"Get the booth ready!" I said, and waited for J.Lo to give me the thumbs up. Then I shoved Gorg as hard as I could, which wasn't very hard, but an unlucky sneeze on Gorg's part helped me force him into the cage, and *pop!* went the weasel.

"Where did you send him?" I asked.

"Whydaho, I think," said J.Lo.

"Idaho."

"Yes. This place," he said, turning the booth off again. He consulted some kind of computer terminal on the side of this telecloner. On the top of it was a mass of rubbery-looking goop, and J.Lo poked and mashed it like he was working with clay. Shapes and symbols appeared in the air above the stuff, telling him what he wanted to know. I coaxed Pig out of hiding and gave her some treats.

"I will never do that again," I told her. "Most likely."

"This computer says there are other teleclone booths very close—within a squared mile, maybe. If I keep to looking, it might tell me where did they put Tipmom," J.Lo said.

"Good. You do that, and keep Pig safe. I'm going to see where we are."

"Be careful. Call on the talkie-walkie if you are in·danger."

I crept around the corner and found another hall of sinks and stalls, and the exit door. And next to that, a smaller exit door, like one was for adults and the other for kids. The small door was labeled "Mice" and the other one "Men," and there's only one place I know of that does that. It's The Nicest Place on Earth.

"No way," I whispered, stepping outside.

I saw the Vocabularcoaster and Rumpelstiltskin's Spinning Wheel. Above were the twin tracks of the Duorail and the tops of thick-bearded palm trees. Right in front of me was the Castle of the Snow Queen.

I realized I was out in the open, so I slinked over to a line of shops and crouched in a doorway. At least it was nighttime.

"We're in Happy Mouse Kingdom," I said into the walkie-talkie. "We're back in Orlando. Over."

Shhhch "No way," said J.Lo's voice, as shrill and crackly as a drive-through menu. "Over."

"It's true! That big signal you found is Happy Mouse Kingdom. I'm looking at the castle right now. Over."

Chh "This makes sense, actually. The Boov liked Florida. So then the Gorg push them out from Florida and set up base camp, to be poomps."

And yet there were no Gorg to speak of—not around the castle, not down by the newsstand or by Chairman Moo's Calfeteria. I ducked into the Calfeteria, wondering where you would keep a prisoner in a theme park. I didn't even know what I should be looking for. Cages? Giant nets? Jars with holes poked in the lids?

It was then, far down Broadway, that I heard noises. I peeked around the edge of the Milk Bar and saw four Gorg exit another restroom, this time a ladies' room, and walk my way. Another teleclone booth, I thought. Or maybe Gorg always go to the bathroom in groups.

I backed up and crawled behind the bar. The floors here were covered with sticky, black rubber mats that were rotten with the stink of spilled milk and feet.

The Gorg voices drew closer. They spoke to each other in their own language, which they punctuated with pokes and jabs at each other's shoulders and ribs. I reached up and stopped the ticking of my walkie-talkie antenna against the dairy case.

They weren't even going to notice me. There was no reason to, unless they came behind the bar looking for spoiled milk. But then a question that had been bubbling in the back of my mind suddenly came to the surface. Why would a group of Gorg teleport into that restroom down there, only to walk all the way up here?

Because they tried the booth J.Lo shut off and it didn't work, stupid. Now they're going to go find out why.

When they passed and were only feet from our restroom, I grabbed an empty milk bottle and hurled it across the street. It crashed and spread glass all over the floor of one of those stores that sells electric nose hair trimmers and solar-powered vacuum cleaners. The noise or the motion or both set off two Dancin' Santas and a robot dog. The Gorg turned around and went to investigate where all that barking and *Feliz Navidad* was coming from.

I held the antenna still and sneaked back toward the men's room, only to hear a screech come from my backpack like a tiny train wreck. The walkie-talkie. I froze, then scurried into a gift shop—one filled with the kind of gifts people only buy on vacation. Hiding behind a rack of Happy Mice wearing T-shirts that read "Official Souvenir," I ripped the walkie-talkie out of my bag.

"What?" I hissed.

Shhhhkk "I did it!" the speaker shrieked.

"Not so loud," I whispered, and peeked around the edge of the rack. "Did what?"

Chuuk "Tipmom! I found Tipmom! She is here!"

"Is she okay?"

Shckuk "I do not know."

"Well, ask her," I said, and tried to make myself small as I heard approaching footsteps.

Chhhrk "No no. She is in the computer! The Gorg did teleport her, but not alls the way. She is stored into the computer as datas!"

I groped around in my backpack and pulled out the camera.

"Ohmygosh. Can you get her out?"

Shhhsh "Yes! I will bring her here, safe as sounds!"

"Hold on."

I slipped the walkie-talkie back into my bag and looked up from the floor at the circle of Gorg leaning over me.

"Hi," I said. "Cheese."

The camera in my hand flashed, and all four Gorg recoiled slightly as I threw about sixty aspirin straight up in the air like a referee. Half the Gorg recovered enough to try following me as I dove out between the others' legs, then the falling aspirin burst on their backs, and I was lucky to catch the edge of the quickly expanding planet of snow that engulfed the store. The cold foam punched me like a big boxing glove into the street. A glance over my shoulder showed a snowball the size of a hot air balloon and getting larger, with bits and pieces of Gorg and cartoon mouse poking out here and there. But the snowball was already coming apart, and I dashed down the street, past J.Lo's restroom, and fished the walkie-talkie out by its antenna again.

"Hello? J.Lo?"

Chhhk "Where did you go? What is happening?"

"Nothing. Stopped to take a picture. Is Mom there?"

Chuk "No—you said to—"

I missed the rest as I heard a rumble of feet and ran toward a familiar-looking trapdoor in the street. Guns went off behind me and tore the top off a churro stand. I wrenched open the door and threw myself down a ladder.

Shch "What was that?"

"Just a thing. Don't bring Mom back until the explosions stop, okay?"

Chch "Yes."

Fire rained down the ladder behind me.

"Good! As soon as you're through, begin Operation: Catastrophe!"

The Gorg struggled to follow me down the hatch, but they were too big.

Chk "I thought we'd decided to call it Operation: Piggyback."

"Can't talk about it right now. Busy."

I was sprinting down the dark hall as the Gorg fired,

their flaming ammo slamming into the pavement above. I couldn't see it, but they were making the hole bigger.

Shhhk "You nevers want to talk about my ideas. *When is it J.Lo's time?*"

The hallway met up with another that I was sure would take me under the Snow Queen's Castle. From there I could get to the English Puffins ride and surface again, just like J.Lo and I had before.

"I never agreed to Operation: Piggyback," I said into the mouthpiece. "It's stupid."

Chh "You only do not understands it. You see, it has the word 'back,' like as 'feedback loop.' And it has the word 'Pig' as in 'Pig.'"

Ahead was the orange outline of a door.

"If you have to explain the name," I shouted to J.Lo, "then it's not a good name! And *please* tell me you're making cats while we're talking about this!"

Chhh "Of course. Listen—I have learned something interesting from the computer."

Just then I felt a tug against my ankle, and heard the clanking of cans and spoons.

"I am such an idiot," I sighed.

Ssssk "Are you there?"

"Just a minute, J.Lo."

The door didn't burst open this time. I didn't squirt a little kid with window cleaner. Instead I pushed the door open myself and peeked in. Twenty feet off stood the BOOB boys, half a castle hanging upside down behind them. They were aiming guns and looked terrified.

"Hold your fire!" said Curly.

I relaxed a little and rushed toward them.

"We all have to get out of here," I said. "The Gorg—"

There was a noise like *Bwak bwak,* and I felt a stinging in my chest.

"Bleep, Alberto," Curly groaned. "I said 'hold your fire.'"

"He didn't mean to," said Christian. "Look—his hands are shaking."

I looked down at my shirt and saw a wet red stain where I'd been hit.

"What . . . what did you do?" I said.

"Relax," said Curly. "They're only paint guns."

"Oh," I said, feeling dumb. Then I heard noises in the hall behind me.

"What the bleep is going on up there?"

"We gotta go," I said. "The Gorg will be here in a second."

This caused pandemonium. From the shouting it was obvious they weren't even certain who the Gorg were, but it hardly mattered.

"Everyone shut up!" Curly shouted.

"What do we do?" said Yosuan.

The boys looked at Curly. Curly looked at Christian.

"The back way," Christian said. "Single file. Go!"

We rushed through a far door. Christian was the last one out, and he shut off the lights and pulled two levers that started the castle turning.

"Paint guns?" I asked.

"It slows the big aliens down if you shoot them in the eyes," Christian said. "You gave us the idea."

I probably blushed. An orchestra of banging and roaring could be heard behind us. The Gorg were making their way through the spinning castle room.

"We need a teleclone booth," I said as we entered a space hung with an upside-down candy mountain and bindle sticks.

"A what?"

"Oh . . . uh . . . it's this cage-booth thing."

"Oh, those. There's one in the Motorama bathroom. Make this left, guys!"

"HALT, MONKEYS!" shouted a Gorg behind us, and comets came shooting after.

Ssch "Tip?"

I drew the walkie-talkie out of my bag again.

"Okay, quickly," I said to J.Lo while passing an upside-down model of the solar system. "What did you learn from the computer?"

CHHshh "You were right! The Gorg did not perfect the complex cloning! There are mistakes!"

"Mistakes?" I said.

Up a ramping hallway, Christian told the other boys to dump all their paintballs behind us. I wouldn't understand why until I heard the Gorg slip and fall on them a minute later.

Shh "Yes! Whento you clone—no Pig, no biting—when you clone the complicated things, there are flaws. Errors. And if you clone a clone, it only gets worse. A clone of a clone of a clone, much worse."

We reached the base of a ladder and the smallest boys started up first. And let me tell you, being chased by thousand-pound aliens with guns did not improve their climbing any.

Chh "All of the Gorg are now clones of clones, or clones of clones of clones. Some are even clones of clones of clones of clones! This is why they can get sick! And they cannot clone food too much, or it turns into poison!"

For a moment it seemed like Christian and I were going to have a contest to see who could be last to go up the ladder, until finally I just grabbed him by the arm and shoved him up.

"J.Lo?"

Chh "Yes."

"I'm coming back. What was that last part you said?"

Chhhk "Cloning food turns it—down, Pig!—to poison."

I began to climb, sweating and wheezing, and at that point I really should have put the walkie-talkie down.

"Wait," I said. "We've been . . . eating nothing but milk shake for six months, and it's . . . it's poison?"

Chukk "No no. Simple—stop that, kitten—simple sloppy cloning works fine. Evens teleporting works fine. But complicated cloning, not so good *I said stop, kitten!*"

That was it. That was why the Gorg pillaged planets for food. That was why they didn't just overrun them with clones.

Of course, *my* planet still had more Gorg than was healthy. Two of them turned the corner and began to fire, and I was still on the ladder. I threw the walkie-talkie up through the hatch and scrambled up as fire burned all around me. I wasn't even hit but I still cried out in pain. My left leg was charred and bleeding. My shoulder felt wet and hot against my shirt as the boys pulled me through the trapdoor. I kicked it shut and threw asprin until it was buried under snow.

Now I heard meowing. A lot of meowing. A cat chorus. It was getting light out, and I turned to see hundreds of cats milling around, sniffing each other. And every one of them was Pig. Hundreds of heads turned. Two thousand eyes watched me.

"Hi, Pigs," I said.

"Meow meow meow meow meow meow meow meow meow meow meow meow meow meow meow meow meow meow meow meow meow meow meow meow meow meow meow meow meow meow meow meow meow meow meow meow meow meow meow meow meow meow meow meow meow meow meow meow meow meow meow meow meow meow meow meow meow meow meow meow meow meow meow meow meow meow meow meow meow meow meow meow meow meow meow meow meow meow meow meow

meow meow meow meow meow meow meow meow meow

meow meow meow meow meow meow meow meow meow

meow meow meow meow meow meow meow meow meow

meow meow meow meow meow meow meow meow meow

meow meow meow meow meow meow meow meow meow

meow meow meow meow meow meow meow meow meow

meow meow meow meow meow meow meow meow meow

meow meow meow meow meow meow meow meow meow

meow meow meow meow meow meow meow meow meow

meow meow meow meow meow meow meow meow meow

meow meow meow meow meow meow meow meow meow

meow meow meow meow meow meow meow meow meow

meow meow meow meow meow meow meow meow meow

meow meow meow meow meow meow meow meow meow

meow meow meow meow meow meow meow meow meow

meow meow meow meow meow meow meow meow meow

meow meow meow meow meow meow meow meow meow

meow meow meow meow meow meow meow meow meow

meow meow meow meow meow meow meow meow meow

meow meow meow meow meow meow meow meow meow

meow meow meow meow meow meow meow meow meow

meow meow meow meow meow meow meow meow meow

meow meow meow meow meow meow meow meow meow

meow meow meow meow meow meow meow meow meow

meow meow meow meow meow meow meow meow meow

meow meow meow meow meow meow meow meow meow

meow meow meow meow meow meow meow meow meow
meow meow meow meow meow meow meow meow meow
meow meow meow meow meow meow meow meow meow
meow meow meow meow meow meow meow meow meow
meow meow meow meow meow meow meow meow meow
meow meow meow meow meow meow meow meow meow
meow meow meow meow meow meow meow meow meow
meow meow meow meow meow meow meow meow meow
meow meow meow meow meow meow meow meow meow
meow meow meow meow meow meow meow meow meow
meow meow meow meow meow meow meow meow meow
meow meow meow meow meow meow meow meow meow
meow meow meow meow meow meow meow meow meow
meow meow meow meow meow meow meow meow meow
meow meow meow meow meow meow meow meow meow
meow meow meow meow meow meow meow meow meow
meow meow meow meow mcow meow meow meow meow
meow meow meow meow meow meow meow meow meow
meow meow meow meow meow meow meow meow meow
meow meow meow meow meow meow meow meow meow
meow meow meow meow meow meow meow meow meow
meow meow meow meow meow meow meow meow meow
meow meow meow meow meow meow meow meow meow
meow meow meow meow meow meow meow meow meow
meow meow meow meow meow meow meow meow meow
meow meow meow meow meow meow meow meow meow

meow meow meow meow meow meow meow meow meow

meow meow meow meow meow meow meow meow meow

meow meow meow meow meow meow meow meow meow

meow meow meow meow meow meow meow meow meow

meow meow meow meow meow meow meow meow meow

meow meow meow meow meow meow meow meow meow

meow meow meow meow meow meow meow meow meow

meow meow meow meow meow meow meow meow meow

meow meow meow meow meow meow meow meow meow

meow meow meow meow meow meow meow meow meow

meow meow meow meow meow meow meow meow meow

meow meow meow meow meow meow meow meow meow

meow meow meow meow meow meow meow meow meow

meow meow meow meow meow meow meow meow meow

meow meow meow meow meow meow meow meow meow

meow meow meow meow meow meow meow meow meow

meow meow meow meow meow meow meow meow meow

meow meow meow meow meow meow meow meow meow

meow meow meow meow meow meow meow meow meow

meow meow meow meow meow meow meow meow meow

meow meow meow meow meow meow meow meow meow

meow meow meow meow meow meow meow meow meow

meow meow meow meow meow meow meow meow meow

meow meow meow meow meow meow meow meow meow

meow meow meow meow meow meow meow meow meow

meow meow meow meow meow meow meow meow meow
meow meow meow meow meow meow meow meow meow
meow meow meow meow meow meow meow meow meow
meow meow meow meow meow meow meow meow meow
meow meow meow meow meow meow meow meow meow
meow meow meow meow meow meow meow meow meow
meow meow meow meow meow meow meow meow meow
meow meow meow meow meow meow meow meow meow
meow meow meow meow meow meow meow meow meow
meow meow meow meow meow meow meow meow meow
meow meow meow meow meow meow meow meow meow
meow meow meow meow meow meow meow meow meow
meow meow meow meow meow meow meow meow meow
meow meow meow meow meow meow meow meow meow
meow meow meow meow meow meow meow meow meow
meow meow meow meow meow meow meow meow meow
meow meow meow meow meow meow meow meow meow
meow meow meow meow meow meow meow meow meow
meow meow meow meow meow meow meow meow meow
meow meow meow meow meow meow meow meow meow
meow meow meow meow meow meow meow meow meow
meow meow meow meow meow meow meow meow meow
meow meow meow meow meow meow meow meow meow
meow meow meow meow meow meow meow meow meow
meow meow meow meow meow meow meow meow meow

meow meow meow meow meow meow meow meow meow meow meow meow meow meow meow meow meow meow meow meow meow meow," said the Pigs.

A thousand cats, and they were all underfoot.

Pigs

They purred like a swarm of really big bees. Or really small motorcycles.

I slogged through them, trying to make my way to the boys.

"What . . ." said Christian. After a second he said it again.

"Bleep," said Curly.

"I'll explain later," I answered. "Maybe. Where's that booth?"

We ran into Motorama, which was this gleaming white motorized vision of the future. Conveyor belts that bring you toast in bed. Robots that brush your teeth. Mostly the future was all about never having to move your arms. But I suppose you time-capsule people know that already. How's it working out?

The Gorg were beating their way through the foam as we approached the automated bathroom. There were Pigs streaming out of it, but I expected that. If things were going according to plan, there were Pigs spreading all across the earth, great herds making miniature stampeding noises from each and every booth the Gorg had had the nerve to put on my planet.

"J.Lo!" I shouted into the mouthpiece. "We're at a telecloner on the other side of the park! Can you bring us to you?"

Sch "Hold on," J.Lo answered. "Did your booth justnow stop cloning Pigs?"

"No."

Kkc "How for now?"

"Yes! That's it! That's the booth!"

The booth's hum died down and stopped, and a *wheeeeee* noise came in its place.

Shh "Alls ready."

"You," I said to one of the young boys. "In the booth."

He couldn't know what was going to happen, so he did as I asked. There was a spark and a crackle, and he was gone.

"Who's next," I said. "Go."

"Bleep! What'd you do to Tanner!" said Curly.

"Go find out," I answered, and I pushed him into the booth. When he disappeared, too, the other boys began to back away from me.

"Do what she says," said Christian, and then he teleported by example.

I was the last through the booth. It was a crowded bathroom on the other side, with about fifty cats and eight boys and Mom, all with the same look on their faces. I hugged Mom. The Pig production started up again behind us.

J.Lo was sitting on one of the urinals with his legs pulled up, snacking.

Chchk "You look terrible."

"You don't have to use the walkie-talkie anymore, J.Lo. What are you eating?"

"Cake," he said, and plucked another toilet deodorizer from the neighboring urinal.

"We should shut the booths off at some point," I said. "With any luck, the Gorg will want to use them to leave."

"YES," came a voice behind me. "PLEASE. LET US LEAVE."

The thing that spoke was almost unrecognizable as a Gorg. There were others behind him, and they were all fat inflated raspberries with limbs. Their guns dangled uselessly from their swollen fingers. They all bobbed their heads from sneezing.

The boys were flipping out. I asked Christian and Curly to take them out to the street, and they edged away, backs against the toilets.

"WE CANNOT BEAR IT," said a Gorg in the middle as his eyelids puffed up like microwave hot dogs. "PLEASE.

"LET US GO. WE ARE BEATEN. EARTH IS NOT FOR THE GORG."

His words echoed off the tile.

"EARTH BELONGS **TO THE CAT.**"

"Stop half the booths," I said to J.Lo. "After a few minutes, start them up again and stop the other half."

J.Lo squeezed and prodded the booth controls, and the flow of Pigs stopped. I grabbed some treats out of my backpack.

"Treat?" I sang. "Pigs! Treat?"

I pushed through the crowd, tossing treats as I went. The Pigs followed me outside, and a long line of Gorg rushed immediately for the booth. There was a crackle of pops, and they were gone.

When the cat food ran out, Mom and J.Lo joined me on the street. The Gorg must have stopped the Snow Queen's Castle turning when it was good-side up, and Mom stared at it with moist eyes.

"See?" she said. "See what I mean? Always perfect."

"Yeah," I said, and squeezed her.

"The Gorg are not going to like it onto their ship so much," said J.Lo. "Look."

You could see the huge Gorg ship in the early morning sky, but there was something wrong with it. It was growing darker, and redder. When I realized what I was seeing, I could make out volcanoes of red rash erupt on the surface, and the whole globe seemed to shudder and ooze. More than usual.

"There are ten thousand cloners on the ship . . . No . . . down, Pigs," said J.Lo. "Cloners for to make its skin. I sent a handful of Pig hair to every one."

"The ship has hay fever." I laughed.

Around us the boys were mostly petting cats. Alberto was even talking about adopting one, and he and Cole argued which Pig was best.

Suddenly I had a sinking feeling.

Where was Pig?

It was a ridiculous question, of course. We were surrounded by them. But I didn't want the copies. I wanted *Pig*.

Behind me, with no more treats to occupy them, some five hundred cats turned their attention to J.Lo. They slinked around his legs and licked his feet. They put their claws into his suit and bit his knees.

"Maa-a-a! Look, they all—no, kittens! No! Good kittens!"

I stood apart from them and watched as the ship began to move.

"Tip! No, no, kittens! Tip? Tipmom? Helpnow! TIIIP!"

Then I felt something brush against my leg, and looked down. A cat, purring, rubbed the side of her head against my shin. She was the only one.

"There you are," I said, and picked her up. "I thought I'd lost you."

All eleven of us plus Pig teleported back to Old Tucson and piled like clowns into the car. Mom and J.Lo had to share the front seat, and Mom was so happy she even kissed him on the top of his head and wiped her mouth with her hand. We drove back to the casino, to find the Chief sitting atop his truck with Lincoln, looking out over the southern horizon at the big red ball that was slowly sailing away.

"Ha!" I heard him shout. "That's what you get, jerks."

* * *

People returned to their homes and shot their guns up in the air in celebration. Word spread quickly: the Gorg had been defeated by Dan Landry.

They were preparing to slaughter and enslave the human race when Landry, in keeping with an ancient Gorg tradition about which the details were a little fuzzy, challenged the Gorg leader to a duel of strength and wits. He emerged victorious, and banished the Gorg from Earth, and their departing ship could actually be seen to turn red with

Artist's rendition of the Great Contest of the Ancient Gorg Challenge Event, as described by Daniel Landry (pictured).

embarrassment and shame. Well, you know the details. You've probably read his book.

Anyway,

That's it. I saved the world. J.Lo helped.

We can't take all the credit. For months after the Gorg left, stories poured in from around the world about humans fighting back. I can't get into all of them here, but lets just say the Gorg were *not* prepared for the Chinese. Ditto the Israelis and Palestinians, who managed to work together, for a change. And I hear they didn't even set foot in Australia. And word even got around about a group of Lost Boys living under Happy Mouse Kingdom who made life miserable for a local Gorg encampment. And we couldn't have done it without the Chief.

Frank José, the Chief, died this past spring. He was ninety-four. He said it was his time, but I wish his time and mine had overlapped more. We donated some of his war things to a museum, and gave away everything else. Except Lincoln. Lincoln we kept.

The Boov were in a much weaker position than before, and they owed us humans for getting rid of the Gorg, even if they weren't sure how we did it. They helped people all over the world relocate, signed a lot of treaties, and left Earth for good on Smekday, one year after they'd arrived. Word is they're thinking of trying one of Saturn's moons, but it's a bit of a fixer-upper.

Mom and J.Lo and Pig and Lincoln and I moved back home, but then we moved again. We all agreed to be very slow and careful about revealing J.Lo to the world, and slow and careful was not going to work in a big city. GM bought our patent for the floating car, so money wasn't a problem, and we bought a nice house near a lake.

So far we've only introduced J.Lo to close friends and family, but it's gone well. Every now and then I catch him looking at the sky, and I figure I know what he's thinking. But then he might notice me and say he's considering building an escalator to the moon, just for day trips, so I don't know what to think.

One day he discovered that his name wasn't as common as he thought, so he decided to change it. For a while he went by Spoon Possums, and then he was Dr. Henry Jacob Weinstein, and for a couple of days he was The Notorious B.B. Shaq Chewy before changing back to J.Lo, which I'd never stopped calling him anyway.

And speaking of famous people who get married too much:

Right now you're probably wondering why I never told anyone about what J.Lo and I did. Maybe you even think I'm lying. A person would have to be crazy not to want the fame, and the spotlight. Well, maybe I am. I've earned my crazy. But let me tell you something about the famous Dan Landry.

He hasn't had a moment's peace since the Gorg left. Not one. His every movement has been reported, his every word recorded, his every stumble and blockhead idea captured on film forever. He has, in fact, in the past year alone, been married twice (pop star, anchorwoman), divorced three times (clerical error), and suffered one *very* public nervous breakdown (Chinese restaurant, wrestling). At the moment, I understand, he's recovering from "exhaustion" at a hospital in California.

If that's not enough to convince you that keeping quiet was the right thing to do, then think about this: *I saved the world.* I saved the whole human race. For the rest of my life, even if I live to be a hundred and ten, I will never again do anything as fantastic and important as what I did when I was eleven. I could win an Oscar and fix the ozone layer. I could cure all known diseases and I'll *still* feel like my Uncle Roy, who used to be a star quarterback but now just sells hot tubs. I'm going to have to figure out how to live with this, and I sure don't need everyone I meet bringing it up all the time.

So.

You asked what the moral to my story was. I'm not sure real stories *have* morals. Or maybe they have so many it's impossible to choose. But here's one: what goes around comes around. And as far as pets go, a cat is a nice thing to have.

chlorinated water from residents' pools. US Fish and Wildlife officials state that measures will have to be taken to control the New Mexican koobish population as early as next spring.

113-Year-Old Dies At Time Capsule Unveiling

WASHINGTON, D.C.— Local senior Gratuity Tucci, who as a young girl contributed an essay to the National Time Capsule Project, died of a heart attack at the capsule unveiling during a Washington ceremony this morning.

Tucci's essay, entitled "The True Meaning of Smekday," was only one of many items in the unearthed time capsule, including a lock of Daniel Landry's hair and a recording of DJ Max Dare's single "Hit the Road, Smek (Moove, Boov! Mix)."

Tucci has been asked to comment on rumors of an extended version of her essay that documents her life through the end of the Gorg occupation.

"I don't know what you're talking about," Tucci said on Saturday. "And you can leave that capsule in the ground, as far as I'm concerned. I was supposed to be dead before now."

Participants at the capsule unveiling report that Tucci collapsed, muttered something unintelligible, then added, "Pardon my language." These were her last words. She was rushed to St. Landry's Hospital, where she was pronounced dead at 10:23 a.m.

Gratuity Tucci is survived by her husband, two children, five grandchildren, eight great-grandchildren, and a Boov.

Us, Summer 2015

J.LO in: "Smektastic Voyage"